THE DOORSTEP CHILD

From a tender age little Evie spent her early years left outside on the step. With a drunk for a father and a neglectful mother, all little Evie has ever craved is a safe home and a normal existence. Her young eyes had seen so much but this never tainted her spirit. If it wasn't for her best friend Gary, she might never have made it to her sixteenth birthday. She meets Ken, a sweet brown-eyed boy, not much older than she is. Perhaps her fortunes have changed? But no sooner does she give over her heart, she is betrayed, not for the first time in her young life...

THE DOORSTEP CHILD

THE DOORSTEP CHILD

by

Annie Murray

Magna Large Print Books
Long Preston, North Yorkshire,
BD23 4ND, England.

British Library Cataloguing in Publication Data.

A catalogue record of this book is
available from the British Library

ISBN   978-0-7505-4553-2

First published in Great Britain in 2017 by Macmillan,
an imprint of Pan Macmillan

Published in Large Print 2018 by arrangement with
Macmillan Publishers International Ltd.

Magna Large Print is an imprint of Library Magna Books Ltd.

Printed and bound in Great Britain by
T.J. (International) Ltd., Cornwall, PL28 8RW

For Katy xx

I

One

August 1953

'Let me in!'

Evie's hands slapped against the cracked green paint of the front door until they stung. 'I wanna come in! Rita! Shirl! Let me in!'

She heard spiteful giggles from behind the front door – her older sisters, united as usual against her.

Defeated, Evie stopped and leaned to rest the top of her head against the rotten planks.

'Go on, ask us nicely. You gotta say "please", Evie.' This was Rita, the elder of her sisters, her voice wheedling and spiteful. '"Pretty please."'

Evie sank down on the step, her back to the door. The usual bleak sense of aloneness swept through her. Shut out. Always on the outside. No one ever wanted her – not Mom, Dad ... certainly not her sisters. However hard she tried.

It was no use crying because no comfort would be offered. She rubbed her smarting hands which were coated with dirt from the door, before tugging at the hem of her grubby frock. The skirt was too short to cover her plump knees. In a month she would be turning ten years old and she had grown fast this summer, her clothes not keeping up. The bodice was skintight, pressing in on her when she breathed, hurting the sore bruises on her

13

chest. She hadn't managed to move quick enough yesterday when Mom was in a temper.

Fearfully she glanced along the street. Mom would be coming back soon. But for now, all was quiet.

Vaguely, she wiped her hands down her frock, then inserted the first two fingers of her right hand into her mouth and drifted into one of her dreamy states, shutting off her mind from Rita and Shirley's taunting voices. She sank into the moment she was living now, not thinking of anything else.

Her gaze met the mucky blue-brick pavements, smoke-blackened terraces and factories of Inkerman Street, in this neighbourhood of Ladywood, Birmingham, where they had only been living for a couple of weeks. In many ways it was no different from where they had lived before in Aston. There were the same soot-encrusted terraces and back-to-back houses; the same smoking chimneys and bomb pecks littered with weeds and rubble; the same filthy puddles, dried to mud now in the warmth; the same sort of cobbled streets, dozens of kids playing on them and the houses along them teeming with occupants.

But still, everything felt strange. They were living in a front house, opening onto the street, instead of onto a yard, the way they had been before. Every morning now, she had to stagger all the way round and down the entry, the family's morning wee bucket yanking on her arm, to the yard lavs to slop out. It was always her job. But here she did not see any of the familiar faces she had known all her life.

The night they left their back house and yard,

they never went to bed. Their father, Ray Sutton, sober for once, cuffed at them, cursing any sound they made – 'Don't wake them cowing nosey parkers.' They loaded their few sticks into a van and fled both the yard and the rent man, to this crumbling house at the corner of a yard entry where another house met it back-to-back. It was in worse repair than the one they'd left, on the yard off Alma Street, Aston.

When she let herself think of it, Evie ached with missing the neighbours who had been kind to her. Mrs Booker – Rachel to her friends – and her daughter Melly, who was a couple of years older than Evie. There was old Mrs Poulter, who wore black and had blue eyes that seemed to look deep into you, and Mo and his pretty wife Dolly – Mr and Mrs Morrison. They had given her what her family almost never did – kindness and comfort. And now there was no one. Or so she thought.

'Won't they let you in, bab?'

She hadn't seen them coming. For a second the kindly voice seemed to come from a golden-haired, smiling face which had drawn level with her, mouth open, a pink tongue lolling in the muggy warmth. The face of a big, hairy dog. Evie's heart fluttered at the sight. It was so friendly, so furry and soft!

Evie pulled her fingers out of her mouth and looked at the dog's owner – a middle-aged lady in a print frock and flat brown shoes, her frizzy grey-brown hair clipped back on one side with a kirby grip. She was scraggily thin, with a wart on the left side of her nose and a lopsided smile. And she looked homely and kind.

15

'That's not very nice, is it?' she added. 'Leaving you out on the step?'

Evie did recognize the lady. She lived in the house on the other side of the entry. She and her husband, called Mr and Mrs Waring, had knocked on the door the day after they moved in to introduce themselves. But Evie had seen Mrs Waring's expression after the 'welcome' she got from Mom – arms clenched aggressively across her chest, 'What d'*yow* want then?' – and didn't think she'd be seeing her again. Since then she had only caught sight of her and the dog in the distance.

'Can I stroke 'im?' Evie said longingly.

'Course you can, bab.' The lady smiled at her, revealing gaps in her teeth. People did smile at her, and often told her she was pretty, with her sweet waves of blonde hair and plump cheeks. 'Our Whisky likes a bit of attention. 'Er's a good old girl – a lady dog, bab, not a boy. There you go, Whisky, say hello to the little girl.'

Evie plunged her hand into the dog's warm fur. It felt so silky and lovely. Whisky turned her head and panted amiably at her and Evie fell to her knees and threw her arms round the dog, pushing her face into her comforting coat.

'Eh, go easy. You don't want her to snap,' Mrs Waring said.

The dog didn't seem to mind. She was a soft old thing. Despite Evie's enthusiastic affection she just shifted on her feet a bit and carried on panting.

'Tell you what, bab,' Mrs Waring said. 'D'you want to come in and see our birds?'

Evie nodded and got to her feet. They walked the short distance past the entry to Mrs Waring's

16

house and all the time Evie kept her hand on the dog's back. Oh, if she could only have a dog like Whisky, a true friend, there all the time.

Soon she was inside a neat downstairs room. Despite the rotten state of all the houses, it was simply furnished and reassuring; the range was polished, there was an embroidered cloth on the table and everything was in its place. On the sideboard to the left was a cage with two budgies perched inside. One was green, one blue.

'That's Billy and Bobby,' Mrs Waring told her as Evie pushed her nose right up against the thin bars of the cage. There was a sour smell and she felt the air move against her face as they fluttered their wings in panic at her sudden appearance.

'We've got a cat called Charlie somewhere,' Mrs Waring said with a chuckle. 'They don't like Charlie.'

Evie stared, mesmerized, into the cage. This house felt blissful. She wanted to stay forever.

As she was looking, a voice sounded at the door. 'Cooee! Mavis?'

'That you, Con?' Mrs Waring called.

'Just thought I'd pop in,' the voice continued. 'I'm on my way back from getting Bill's bit of liver... Oh, who's that?'

'It's one of the new ones at number twenty-nine,' Mrs Waring said. She lowered her voice to say something Evie couldn't hear. But at the end she heard her say, '...poor little mite. Such a pretty little thing. I can't understand it... But seeing that mother of hers, she's...' Her voice sank again and Evie only caught snatches. '...so quarrelsome ... Mrs Charles, of course ... *coloureds* ... seems

17

decent enough ... no call for it...'

When she turned round, Mrs Waring and the other lady, who was short and plump, were both looking at her.

'Can I stroke the dog again?' she asked in a whisper.

'Course you can, bab,' Mrs Waring said.

She saw the ladies look at each other but she took no notice, cuddled up against Whisky's hot coat and rhythmic breathing, a loving haven away from everything.

'Where've *you* been, pig face?'

As soon as Evie stepped back in the house, Shirley jumped on her, forcing her against the wall, an arm each side of her. Shirley, the younger of Evie's two sisters, was nearly twelve. Rita was getting on for fourteen. Both younger sisters lived in fear and dread of Rita. Sometimes, when Rita was not around and Shirley was bored, she was nice to Evie. Mostly, though, she tried to keep on the right side of Rita.

'Come on, out with it.' She moved her face threateningly close to Evie's. Her breath smelt of bad teeth.

'Nowhere.' Evie wriggled and ducked, trying to get out of Shirley's grasp. There was no one else in this, the only downstairs room. Mom must still be out. Feet came thumping down the stairs accompanied by Rita's voice:

'Is that 'er back?'

'Yeah,' Shirley said, with triumph. 'I got 'er.'

Shirley had a bit more flesh on her than Rita, who was scrawny as a plucked fowl. Shirley favoured their father with his handsome looks. As she had grown, her hair had gone darker. Like him, she was brown-eyed, big boned and sultry looking. She was wearing a coffee-coloured frock down to her knees and scuffed black lace-up shoes, the soles shored up with cardboard inside.

Evie stood very still, her heart pounding. Her sisters were never nice to her but it wasn't often she got trapped with them like this. They were stuck for something to do. The long, empty school holidays left hours free for bullying. Especially now, because they didn't know anyone else in this new neighbourhood.

In seconds, Evie's animal senses took over. Jolted out of her dreamlike refuge, she was fully alert. Hopeless as it seemed, she tried the only trick she could think of. It might work with Shirley, who was slow-witted like Mom.

She gave a sharp look over Shirley's shoulder as if she had seen something and bawled with urgent force, 'Shirl, quick! Watch it!'

Shirley's head whipped round. As Rita reached the bottom step, Evie ducked under Shirley's arm and was out of the door again, tearing along the street. She ducked into an entry, waiting for the drumming footsteps to follow her. But there was nothing. Her sisters were too idle to run. No Rita with her scheming face; no Shirley with her sharp, scratching nails. It had worked. For now.

Her frock was so tight it made panting an effort. Standing in the entry's dank shade, her blood was beginning to steady until she realized, with a shock that made her heart bang hard again, that she was not alone. There was someone further along in the gloom, crouched in a cringing posture against the wall, arms wrapped round bony knees and peering up at her as if expecting the worst.

Two

For a moment they stared at each other. Whoever it was squatting down there, hugging those skinny legs, seemed poised on a knife-edge, ready to leap up and run for it.

In the gloom she made out eyes, wary as an animal's, watching her from behind a pair of wonky wire spectacles with thick lenses. White shinbones ended in enormous boots which made the legs look even thinner. Evie wasn't sure at first whether the child – who she guessed to be a bit younger than herself – was a boy or a girl. Round the pinched face hung a matt of chaotic, mucky brown hair.

At last, with an air of getting it over with, the gawky creature looked up at her and said, 'I s'pose you're gunna lamp me an' all?'

Evie began to relax. There seemed no need to be frightened. This person did not appear to be out to get her. But she folded her arms across her, just in case.

'No,' she said. 'Why d'yer think I am? Why're you sat down there?'

He – she could hear from his gruffness that he was a boy – got slowly to his feet, wiping his fore-arm across his nose with a squelchy sniff. Evie thought he looked as if he had been crying, which surprised her. She never bothered with crying anymore. It never got you anywhere. He was wearing shorts so scant that they showed off a daft amount of his grubby legs. At the top was a baggy shirt, filthy and held together at the front by one remaining button.

'This 'un's a double knack,' he said, jerking his head at the yard behind him. 'If they come down 'ere, I can gerraway.' The yard, unlike most, had two entrances, one to get in by and one to escape through – a double knack.

'Who's chasing yer?' she asked, intrigued to find someone else running away.

The boy shrugged and looked down, seeming ashamed. 'Them. Out there.'

She wasn't sure who he meant. There were crowds of children who played out in the street. So far she didn't know any of them and she didn't remember seeing the boy before. There was a silence, before he looked up at her.

'Who're you running away from then?'

'My sisters.'

'Lamp yer, do they?' he said with a sense of gloomy inevitability.

She nodded. Yes, they hit her. Scratched, poked, did Chinese burns, tricked, ganged up on her... And Mom and Dad lashed out – especially when the drink was in, which was often. She shrugged.

'I ain't seen you before,' he observed. 'Which one's your 'ouse? In the yard?'

'Number twenty-nine, Inkerman Street,' she repeated mechanically.

Voices began at the end of the entry, lads shouting. The boy let out a whimper and stiffened like a cat that's seen a fierce dog. He squinted along the entry towards the road and without another word, spun round and tore off towards the yard behind. She heard the clump of his *Mail* boots as he dashed away.

'Evie ran off,' Rita shouted later, in the direction of their mother who was by the gas stove in the scullery. Mom had managed to get back into the house without falling out with anyone, it seemed, which was a miracle in itself.

Smugly, Rita added, 'She defied me. I told her to stop 'ere.'

Rita was supposed to be in charge when Mom was out and she queened it over them. The only skinny one of the females in the family, she had a white, mean face with narrow eyes, a sharp nose and lank brown hair. She spent a lot of time looking in the cracked glass over the scullery sink. If there was one thing that drove her to a distraction of jealousy, it was anyone saying how pretty Evie was – which she was, with her rounded, peachy looks and Cupid's bow lips. She had all the best of their mother, who had once been naturally blonde and curvaceous but who was now thickened and achieved blondeness out of a bottle.

Their mom, Irene Sutton, was stirring a stew. When she bothered to cook at all, stew was the only thing she knew except eggs. She would keep a pot on the stove, throwing things into it day after day until whatever scraps of bony meat had started it off were long gone and it turned to a mush of carrot and turnip in a distant memory of gravy. But now a real, brown stew smell filled the room, hinting at the actual presence of beef. It was Friday night: meat bought on the strap, on the promise of today's pay packet.

The pay packet she was waiting for this very moment.

The Sutton family were making a new start. The house, like all the other jerry-built, bomb-damaged, infested buildings in the area, was fated for eventual demolition. It was a rotting wreck – ceilings sagging, the rooms damp, mildewed and alive with silverfish and roaches, the remaining stair treads perilous. But one piece of luck was that the previous occupant, an elderly widow called Mrs Garnet, had died. Her son had found very little in the house that he wanted and most of her chattels remained, providing the Suttons with more furniture than they had possessed in a long time. In Aston, the few chairs they owned had been so worm-ridden that Ray, their father, had gradually fed them into the fire and they ended up sitting on a stool and orange boxes.

There had not been much upstairs when they arrived in the new house: a couple of bedsteads, one with the mattress in a most unspeakable state. They had to take it out, burn it on one of the bomb pecks and get another. But the other, which Rita and Shirley slept on, was all right and the downstairs living room seemed positively crowded to Evie. Inside the front door was a sideboard, the wood sticky with soot and grease, but also containing some crocks yellowed with age and a sheaf of old Mrs Garnet's papers which were even more so. The table – a surprisingly new utility thing –

23

occupied half the room, near the range. Along the front wall, at right angles to the range, was a wooden settle. Its leather upholstery might once have been red and the leather was so old that it had melted into the wood frame. There were also three wooden chairs round the table – an unheard of number of places to sit down! Not that Evie ever expected to sit on one if anyone else was about. She had never in her life slept in a bed that was not a makeshift thing on the floor, or sat on a chair for long without being turfed off it.

Three weeks ago Ray had been sacked from the Kynoch Works in Witton, after his weekend drinking bouts had spread into the week. He had not been in the forces during the war, but on munitions at Kynoch's. There had been plenty of work for him to earn the means to pour as much down his throat as he wanted and still just make the rent. And he had been younger then, before – as he saw it – life and the womenfolk had taken their toll.

Until Kynoch's kicked him out, Ray had never been handed his cards in his life before. It was a shock. For now, he was trying to pull himself together. Ray, just turned forty years old, had been a man of gleamingly handsome looks, now largely scuppered by drink. His coal-black hair was thinner, his cheeks, dark with thrusting stubble, were now flaccid, the chin less well defined, his belly like an overhanging cliff. But he could still scrub up when vanity or lusts of the flesh required it, slick his hair back, brush down his one decent jacket and flash his money around as if it was in bottomless supply.

Unemployment meant the rent man knocking

and no money for the boozer. After their moon-light flit he had got himself taken on for a heavy job at Docker's, the paint factory, hauling sacks of fossil gum from trucks and hefting them over the side of the steaming vats, emptying in the contents for melting into varnish. He came home worn out and oil-smeared and coughing – but with a wage packet. This, bar the rent, he felt entitled to spend entirely on himself. Their mother had to wrestle money for food out of him.

'I dunno why they had to go and change every-thing,' Irene moaned to Rita from time to time. Rita was about to turn fourteen, but the school leaving age had been raised to fifteen. 'Wasting yower time in that cowing place when you could be earning yower keep.'

'Why don't you go out to work, Mom?' Shirley once asked.

Irene rounded on her, furious. 'I ain't going out to be a dray-horse – that's yer father's job.'

Asking Mom questions was always risky. Her childhood in Netherton, in the Black Country, was a blank mystery to them. But an innocent query like, 'Why ain't we got a Nanna and a Granddad?' would be met with a crash of Mom's fleshy hand round the head and, 'Shut yer cake'ole and stop mithering me!' She specialized in getting you in the ear and leaving your head ringing.

Now, in the steam-filled room, the walls run-ning with damp, Rita waited for her mother to take her side over her dig at Evie, but she didn't even turn round. 'Shurrit, Reet,' was all she said, moodily. 'Get these spuds done.'

Evie saw Rita scowl and look daggers at her.

25

'Why do I have to do it?' she whined. 'Why can't Shirl? Or Evie? Make her do it!' She turned towards Evie who was sitting on the splintery bottom step of the stairs, keeping out of the way. She looked down at the floor, the lino so thin you could see every floorboard through it.

'Dain't yow 'ear me? I said shurrit!' Irene bawled. 'Now gerrover 'ere!'

Rita got up with an exaggerated flounce of her bony body. Her cotton dress, pale pink and made for a full-grown woman, hung on her, puckered into folds round the waist by the belt. Barefoot, she winced as she trod on something on the floor. Evie thought she looked like one of the scrawny starlings that flapped in the road.

She kept her head down, trying to avoid notice. Even though she looked miles away most of the time, Evie's whole being was constantly on alert for trouble, as if the hairs on her neck were permanently standing up. It was second nature to her to such an extent that she didn't notice it. Rita would want revenge. Rita had a long memory for even the slightest of grudges. Luckily she was also as lazy as a sozzled cat. If she kept out of Rita's way this week, Evie calculated, then school would start and they'd all be away from each other and it would soon get so that Rita couldn't be bothered...

''Er went out without telling,' Shirley added, making a face at Evie across the room. She was sprawled voluptuously along the settle, twitching one leg up and down being her most obvious activity. Baiting Evie was her way of sucking up to Rita.

'I said *shurrit!* Stop yer mithering!' Their mother turned, brandishing a metal spoon. 'And where's that cowing father of yours?'

Irene had bleached her hair that afternoon, tied it with rags and curlers. It was set in waves round her fleshy face and under her apron she was wearing an electric blue silky dress, fresh from Rag Alley in town. She had big eyes, enormous curves, full lips, coated at this moment in scarlet lipstick. She was fearsome, loud, childish and intimidating. You never knew which way her temper would go and usually, if she was in a rage with Ray, it was the rest of them who copped it. Ray would be coming home soon and this was her way of trying to keep her wayward husband at her side. It was Friday night, there was food in the house – not yet paid for but the money was coming – Ray was in work and it was time to celebrate this new start with her man.

But the factory bulls had boomed out long ago, signalling the end of a shift, and there was still no sign of him, nor of the famous wage packet he had promised to bring straight home.

She kept going to the door to look out, wiping her hands on her pinner. Evie could feel, by the second, Mom's mood growing more explosive. All of them could. The three girls scarcely dared move. Rita shoved Shirley up and sank down on the settle beside her. The sisters exchanged looks. They even met eyes with Evie, across the room on the stairs, their feuds forgotten – for the moment.

Sooner or later, Mom would blow. They knew it was coming. The room was thick with tension like the ominous rumbles of a thunderstorm.

Three

It was not until a sultry darkness had fallen that they heard the unsteady approach of boots and a voice singing, in a slurred tone of seduction, 'How I love the kisses of Dolores...'

Evie's stomach clenched with dread. Her sisters sat side by side now, looking scared. Dad sang this song often when he was tanked up, a song guaranteed to be a red rag to their bull mother.

None of them had had a bite to eat. Evie's stomach was growling with hunger, but now that was forgotten. Mom was like dough swelling in a bowl. She kept pacing the room. Hearing his voice, she strode to the door just as their father appeared at it. She stepped back as he lurched towards her and he had to prop himself against the door frame.

'Where the cowing 'ell 've yow been, yow bastard?' she yelled at the top of her voice, not caring who heard these affectionate overtures.

The girls sat very still. Evie hugged her knees as Mom launched into a diatribe about how he said he'd be home and where was the money and how was she supposed to feed them all without a brass farthing in the house, all at a volume that must have regaled the whole street.

'Oh shurrit, yer cowing...' Ray stumbled into the room, searching his befuddled brain for a telling insult but drawing a blank and resorting

28

to, 'cow...' He sank onto a chair and belched extravagantly.

Evie watched. This was the moment that would decide things. Mom was drawing breath to begin on him again. If Dad turned on the charm and said something to make things better, there might be tears and sulks but it would settle down. But if he said... Or if Mom said...

'Where've yow *been*, Ray?' Irene bawled again, hands on hips, legs positioned wide apart, feet spilling out of her badly fitting white shoes with pointed toes and high heels that made her ankles rock. Her voice had risen high now, and she was poised between rage and tears. 'I know where yow've been all this time and I ay gunna put up with it! Yow've bin with *her* – with that bitch on heat and her brat!'

Her. The woman who had birthed their father a son just before Evie was born. Nance, the woman who haunted all their lives with her boy called Raymond after his father. Who Dad swore he never saw and Mom never ever believed him, even though Nance was over in Aston. And if he wasn't with Nance, then it was some other floozy...

'Oh, just shut yer cake'ole, yer stupid cow,' Ray mumbled. 'Where's my cowing tea then, eh? What's a man got to do to get some grub round 'ere?'

They all wanted their tea but the girls knew better than to say so. All of them tried to remain invisible.

'Oh, so yow want yower tea now, do yer?' Irene bent towards him. 'Come swanning in after yer've been God knows where, like a dog leaving his piss

29

on every lamp post...'

And then he said it. Evie could see Dad was going to do it by the look on his face. By the way he stared up at his wife, bleary but brazen, the way he curled his lips back. Evie gripped her knees with her hands as the words spilled.

'No point in poking a barren cow like you, is there?'

With a roar, Irene ran to get the poker but her husband, with surprising agility, leapt out of his chair and grabbed hold of her.

'Don't you hit me, yer mardy bitch! It's only the truth, ain't it? Yer as dry as an ash heap!'

'I'll hit yow if I cowing want to!' She was writhing in his grasp, teetering on the thin heels. She paused and kicked them off, bending to pick one up and lash out at him with the heel. 'Yer a bastard, Ray Sutton. A–' He grabbed her arm and, with his other fist, managed to land a punch against her shoulder. Irene let out a pig-shriek of pain.

There was suddenly no space in the room and they were only getting warmed up. Evie saw Rita and Shirley sidle off the settle, round the side of the room and away from their brawling parents, and head for the stairs. The three of them crept up to the room they shared – Rita and Shirley slept in the bed, Evie on an old mattress on the floor. In the almost darkness, the yells and curses ramping up downstairs, Evie sank down onto the lumpy old thing. A pungent whiff of wee reached her nostrils. She sometimes wet the bed still.

'I'm that hungry I could eat a dead horse,' Shirley moaned.

'Well, you ain't getting any so you might as well shurrit,' Rita snapped. She flung herself down on the bed with a clatter of bedsprings. 'We ain't even got a candle.' A second later she jumped up again and came at Evie, slapping her hard across the face. 'This is all your cowing fault, you little worm. Why did she ever have to have you, eh? Mom can't even have any more babies now, thanks to you. Why couldn't you've been a boy?'

Evie curled up on the mattress, a hand held to her burning cheek. She stuck her fingers in her mouth. They'd be all the tea she was getting tonight. It was no good saying anything. She didn't even remember the time when Mom had to go to hospital and have some operation which meant she couldn't have babies anymore and now she'd never have a boy like the one Nance had given Dad. She would not even have known about all this if their father had not kept throwing it in their mother's face.

'Go and live with the bitch then!' they had heard Mom shriek at him for years and years. 'If 'er's so cowing marvellous, go on, bugger off!' But he never did and Nance had evidently found another bloke years ago but it didn't stop Mom thinking Dad was always off visiting her and, if not her, someone else. 'Nance' seemed to have come to mean any other 'floozy' Dad might be playing about with, whether real or only in her mind.

Downstairs things were getting going. They had not had one of these big fights since they had been in this new house.

'I knew it was too good to last,' Rita moaned.

31

'And we've got chairs and cups...'

As if in answer, a terrible smashing sound came from downstairs, along with a bull-like yell from their father, and Mom screeching as if he was scalping her.

Evie sucked her fingers and thought about Whisky the dog, about cuddling up to her with her warm, soft fur and, despite it all, she managed to fall asleep.

Someone was shoving her roughly awake.

'Gerrup! Reet, Shirl, Evie ... come on, shift!'

They all groaned, sleepy and bewildered. Evie could sense, rather than see, her mother's bulky form standing over them. The house had gone quiet.

'Get moving, all of you. I ain't stopping 'ere a minute longer with that...' A string of vile appellations fell from her mouth. 'Get yer shoes on. We're going to Vi's.'

'Oh Mom,' Rita groaned. 'That's miles...'

'Shurrit,' Irene snapped. 'Get moving. Yer father's on the floor. There ain't gunna be anything 'ere for 'im when he wakes up and it'll cowing well serve 'im right.'

Even to Evie, Mom sounded – as she often did – like a petulant little girl.

'But Mom...' Rita attempted. 'We'll only have to come back...'

Evie heard a swift movement followed by another slap.

'Do as I ******g well tell yer. Gorrit?'

Evie had not even taken her pumps off. She got to her feet, feeling muzzy, but her heart was hammering with the shock of being woken so suddenly and she felt a bit sick.

'Get yerselves downstairs now,' Mom was saying. 'And don't wake 'im up.'

Certainly none of them wanted to do that. They crept down to find their father flat out along the settle, one leg sprawled on the ground, head back, snoring like a pig.

'Look at that,' Mum said in disgust.

Under the weak light of the bulb they could see her dishevelled state. The carefully curled hair now hung in clumps and her face was puffy and covered in red marks and cuts. Her eyes seemed sunken into their sockets. She had replaced the white high-heeled shoes with her everyday old brown flats, wide as barges. She looked in every way smaller.

They crept silently out into the night streets. While they lived in Aston, Mom had dragged them over to Auntie Vi's a number of times, only before it had been in the middle of a fight, with Dad raging and Mom frightened of him. This time was different. Evie could see that she wanted him to think they had left him. Evie, young as she was, also knew this was never going to happen. All her life, her mom and dad had threatened to leave in turns, as if 'I'm leaving yer! I'm gunna go and live with her!' and 'We won't be 'ere when you get home!' were the choruses of a song that was sung so often the words had gone stale.

Vi, their father's sister-in-law, lived in Lozells. It had felt a long way from Aston, and from Lady-wood it was even further. The three girls set out behind their mother, Silent, resigned, still half

33

asleep. It was quiet, the pubs long turned out. The day's heat had faded but luckily it was not cold and the night air smelt of hot buildings and factory smoke and stuff rotting in the heat. Evie walked just behind Rita and Shirley. Their mother plodded ahead of them. Evie had no idea how long it would take to get there, or where they were. She didn't think about any of it. Her legs were tired. She heard the desolate whistle of a locomotive in the distance. A rat scuttled along the gutter and vanished into a drain and her arms came up in goose pimples of revulsion.

Everything felt like a dream, lit by the dim street lights. Mom moved at a steady pace ahead of them. After a time, when they had walked on and on in the malodorous air, never seeming to get anywhere, Evie could hear her mother crying.

She woke on the floor in Vi's downstairs room, a scratchy rug laid over her. Even before she opened her eyes she knew she was at Vi's because everything stank of cigarettes. Mom and Dad smoked, but not with the same dedication as Vi. Opening her eyes, she saw, by the thin bar of light coming through the curtains, that Rita and Shirley lay asleep to her left. She looked across at the picture of a hillside covered in purple heather which she always saw when she woke up at Vi's house. Auntie Vi was Scottish and she met Uncle Horace, Dad's elder brother, when she came down in the war to work in munitions.

She could hear voices from the back kitchen, Mom complaining to Vi. Sometimes she tried complaining to Horace, but that was no good.

Horace always grunted and said, 'Oh, take no notice.'

Evie got up to go to the brick privy in the yard at the back. When she pushed open the door of the back room, her mother was right there facing her and shot her a look of loathing.

'Are you all right, hen?' Auntie Vi said, in a quick break from inhaling smoke. She was a big, eagle-like woman with hunched shoulders, a mop of greying hair down her back and yellow-tinged skin. The first finger of her right hand was mustard coloured. She was wearing a pale green dressing gown. Vi was kind to them, though she was always saying to Mom, 'There's no anything more I can do, Irene, you know that. If he was my own brother, it might be different...'

Evie knew no answer was required. As she headed to the back door Evie heard Vi say, 'You can't just keep blaming that poor wean for the way he is, Irene. It's no right. What's done's done and you need to try and keep your temper.'

Evie did her business out in the cool morning. Sitting in the cobwebby privy she could just hear the little noises made by Horace's pigeons in their coop. She always thought Horace looked a bit like a pigeon himself, with his beady, startled-looking eyes and slight stoop. He didn't look at all like her father. And he always smelt of boiled onions and smoke.

She went back in and lay down beside the others again, glad they were asleep, glad, for a while, to be in Vi's house which, though a tiny terrace, was still bigger than theirs, and felt safer. And Rita and Shirley pretended to be nice to her when they were there.

She closed her eyes. They would all have to walk home again, as usual. And nothing would be any different. But for now, the grey blanket felt cosy and smelt of cigarettes and refuge.

Four

'Oh, it's you again is it?' Mrs Waring said the next morning, finding Evie waiting by her front step. 'I tell yer, Con, I think this one's set to move in with us.'

Evie looked up at Mrs Waring, who was standing at her front door in her pinner, addressing these words over her shoulder to someone behind. Mrs Waring's narrow feet in brown lace-up shoes were planted side by side on the step, to which she applied elbow grease and red cardinal polish every morning. Not like theirs at number twenty-nine, which looked as if it had been a stranger to soap and a brush for a very long time. A smell of liver and gravy emanated from inside the house, as well as something sweet. Saliva rose in Evie's mouth.

That morning they had left Vi's early. They glimpsed the cut on the walk back, a mist still hanging over the narrowboats and joeys. It seemed to take forever to trudge all the way back to Lady-wood. They saw shopkeepers flinging up their blinds for Saturday's trade. Their father must have taken himself off up to bed after they left and even now he was still nowhere to be seen, sleeping it off at two in the afternoon. The rest of them were all tired and irritable, but without the energy for a fight. Mom was sulking and none of them dared ask for the dinner that was still waiting to be eaten from last night. Vi had given them each a bit of toast, but Evie's stomach was gurgling.

'What is it this time, bab?' There was an edge of irritation to Mrs Waring's voice, but she was a kindly lady and it didn't last. 'You come to see our Whisky again?'

Evie caught sight of the dog approaching from inside with her amiable face and feather duster tail. She nodded, looking up pleadingly. She longed for comfort, like a hunger. She had to cuddle the dog, *had* to.

'Oh, all right then. Dickie!' Mrs Waring turned to her husband who was buried in the paper at the table. The other lady, Con, was there too, big and pink-faced. There were white cups on the white cloth. Evie thought she had never seen so much white. 'It's that little wench from the other side of the entry again, come to see the dog.'

'Oh ar?' Mr Waring looked up, laying the paper down. He was a small, dark-haired, chirpy man with an upright bearing and a friendly way about him. His sleeves were rolled up to show muscular forearms fuzzed with black hair. Evie thought he looked quite pleased to see her. He chuckled. 'The dog? There was me thinking you'd come to see me, little wench!'

'Aah,' Con said, in a husky voice as Evie made a bee-line for Whisky. 'That's nice. You like the doggy, don't yer, bab?'

Evie said nothing. Conversation was not something she was used to. She felt Whisky's hot, tickly breath on her hand and her lips twitched into a smile. She knelt and flung her arms round the dog who struggled in her grasp, but good-naturedly.

'Poor little thing,' she heard Mrs Waring say. 'That mother... You should have heard her yesterday – it's enough to make you curl up. I mean, I'm not sure about all these coloureds, but...'

'That Charles bloke's decent enough,' Mr Waring put in. 'He was in the RAF. Fought for this country – credit where credit's due...'

The Charles family lived across the road – a couple with two sons. They didn't see a lot of Mr Charles, who was a bus driver. Mrs Charles, a tall, slender lady, very smart, nearly always in a neat black hat, passed back and forth to do her shopping. Despite the fact that she was a quiet, dignified woman, Irene could not leave her alone. She would wait on the step. Instead of shouting, as normal, she muttered things about 'dirty' families and 'blackie' hands. Mrs Charles might have been deaf and blind for all the notice she took.

'I mean, there's no call for that,' Mrs Waring was saying. 'That's plain nastiness, that is. The woman's only going about her business. In the end I said to *her*' – she made a disparaging tilt of her head towards the Suttons' house – 'you want to clean up your own mess before you start finding fault with other people. Oh! You should have heard the language I got back from *that* one...'

'D'yer like animals, do yer?' Mr Waring leaned towards Evie, a cigarette in his hand, resting his arms on his thighs.

Evie gave a nod, brushing her cheek against the

soft fur of the dog's neck as she stroked and stroked her. Whisky was the loveliest thing she had ever seen.

'Tell yer what, bab, d'you want to come and see my girls? She'd like that, wouldn't she, Mave?' he said to his wife.

'Oh, I s'pect so,' Mrs Waring said, sitting down beside Con and pouring tea. The two women were rolling their eyes and giving each other little smiles.

'Go and see the hens with Dickie, bab,' Con urged her. 'You'll like them. They might lay you an egg for your tea.'

'Him and his birds.' Mrs Waring rolled her eyes, stirring her tea.

Evie got up reluctantly. She just wanted to stay with Whisky, who had sat down and patiently allowed herself to be petted.

''Ere, you can have one of these to take with you,' Mrs Waring said. She went to the scullery and brought back a little golden domed thing. 'It's a fairy cake.'

Evie took it, round-eyed, and bit into its softness, saliva rushing into her mouth. The cake was warm and sweet.

'You gunna say "ta" then?' Mrs Waring said.

'Ta,' Evie managed, through her mouthful.

As she went out she heard Con say, 'Well, she don't look half starved.'

'No,' Mrs Waring said. 'But I can't see that one getting a square meal on the table very often.'

'Come on.' Mr Waring cajoled her outside.

Evie followed him along the entry at the side of the house. To the right, it led off into the familiar

39

yard behind number twenty-nine. Evie was getting to recognize their neighbours in the yard now, through all her visits lugging the slop bucket. But to the left, there was a wall with a gate in it which she had never seen opened. Her eyes widened in surprise when he unlatched it and led her inside. Their backyard was all bricks: dirty red-brick houses and the blue-brick-paved yard. There was a lamp, a tap, two lavatories and the brew house, a small outbuilding shared by all six houses, two at the front and four on the yard. The brew house was where Mom went when it was her turn to heat water in the copper for her washing. But behind Mr and Mrs Waring's house and the other houses beyond, there were strips of garden. It felt like another world.

'Come on in, shut the gate,' Mr Waring urged her.

Evie did as she was bidden, then looked around her. It was different here from in the yard behind their houses. These two-up, two-down terraces had strips of garden behind. There was an outside lav and a brew house close to the back of the house. The rest of the long, thin garden, apart from the path down the side, was Mr Waring's vegetable patch. Evie followed Mr Waring, the stripes of faded green braces down each side of his back over his shirt. He walked halfway along before stopping for a moment, hands on hips, leaning forward to look.

'Well, I'm blowed. I've never known that before. Summat's been in 'ere, having the last of my onions. I had a whole row of spring onions there and now look.'

40

Evie looked but did not know what she was looking for. Grown-ups seemed to talk in riddles most of the time. All she could see was a tangle of wizened plants. Mr Waring shook his head and moved on.

There were rickety old fences dividing up most of the gardens, but at the bottom of the Warings' was a building with a concrete slab for a roof, which stood in the lane behind, its wall flush with the edge of the garden. She followed Mr Waring's dapper, bandy-legged figure along the path. She could see part of the round bald patch in his black hair, like a half moon.

The coop, a big wood and wire construction, was built up against the wall of the concrete building. Next to it, in the back corner of the garden, a small gate opened onto the lane. When they reached the coop, she could hear little *puck-puck* noises and she saw four white hens inside who looked up at her in alarm. Mr Waring checked round it carefully, bending to press the wire at the bottom into the ground. To one side there was a covered part, next to the pen where the hens were pecking around.

'I have to keep 'em nice and safe – don't want any flaming cats getting in. Good little layers, these girls are. They can go into here at night.' He pointed at the covered-in part. 'Nice and snug.' He talked about the birds as if they were children.

He didn't seem to know what else to say, and neither did Evie. The hens were not warm and soft to cuddle like Whisky. They were rather ugly, with their pinky eyes and funny wobbly combs on their heads.

They were just about to turn back to the house when a sound startled them. There was a bang at the back gate followed by a scuffling noise, as if someone had flung themselves at it. Hands appeared at the top and after a few seconds' scrabbling, a face appeared. A face with a scruffy mop of hair and thick bottle-bottom specs. The face looked aghast at seeing anyone there on the other side and vanished again immediately.

'Oi!' Mr Waring pulled back the bolt and flung the gate open. They could both hear the footsteps tearing away along the entry. 'Little bugger! What's 'e playing at?' He slammed the gate shut.

Back in the house he said to his wife, 'There was one of them kids trying to jump the gate. One of them scruffy little apeths from over the road – I bet it was him had my onions!'

'What apeths?' Con had gone and Mrs Waring was sitting in the one comfortable chair with her feet up, reading something, and seemed unwilling to be disturbed.

'You know, feller whose wife passed on.'

'Oh, Cathleen Knight's boys.' Mrs Waring looked up, her face sad. 'Poor little devils. Don't stand a chance. Stan Knight didn't have a clue when Cathleen was alive and he's got even less of one now.'

'He was by the air-raid shelter,' Mr Waring said, sitting down at the table and lifting the paper again. 'Jumping up on the gate, bold as brass. Little sod.' They both seemed to have forgotten Evie was there, so she knelt down with Whisky again, on the mat by the old range, in a bliss of warm fur.

'Well, you know the kids play there,' Mrs Waring said, settling back again. 'I don't know what'll become of those poor Knight boys, though, I really don't.'

Evie listened, taking all this in. She had not known about the air-raid shelter round in the back lane before. But she did know that the face she saw was that of the boy she had met in the entry, who she had seen since in the street among a gaggle of lads. The boy who, like her, always seemed to be running away.

Five

Later, Evie stood on the front step of number twenty-nine, listening.

Mrs Waring had packed her off eventually: 'Go on home now, bab, or your mother'll wonder where you've got to.' Evie knew that Mom would not do any such thing but she dragged herself away from Whisky, whispering in the dog's ear, 'It's all right, I'll come back. I'm only going next door.'

She took the soft feel of Whisky's coat away with her like a charm. Outside number twenty-nine she put her guard on again, the one she wore at home without even realizing. The door was open in the balmy late afternoon and she heard her father's voice, then her mother's loud laugh. Dad said she laughed like a foghorn. Shirley said something, then Dad and Mom laughed again.

43

Encouraged, Evie stepped inside.

They were at the table, Mom in her best blue frock again, her hair curled at the ends. Dad looked relaxed, cheeks stubbly, shirt open at the neck. He was lolling back with one of old Mrs Garnet's china cups in his hand, half full of a dark liquid which you could be sure wasn't tea. Rita and Shirley were on the settle and there was an enamel jug on the table. Evie could smell the ale on the air. But she could also smell food and the table was littered with plates smeared with brown gravy. They had evidently eaten last night's stew without her.

Irene saw her come in. 'Oh, 'ello, babby,' she said with the complacency of someone whose stomach is full. 'Where've yer bin?'

Evie stood with her hands behind her back. There was no sign of any food for her. But for once, all the family were looking at her. Mom's warm tone made the sun come out in her heart. Immediately she would have done anything for her mother, anything that would please her.

'I went to see the dog,' she said.

Mom laughed again, her body wobbling. Evie wasn't quite sure it was a nice laugh. 'The dog? What dog?' She pushed herself up in the chair. 'You don't wanna go near them filthy whammels. Pass us the jug, Shirl.'

She didn't really want to know and Evie knew it was better not to tell her anything. It might come back in a nasty way later. But she thought her rare and shining moment of attention was over and did not want it to end, so she burst out, ''Er's called Whisky.'

'Ooh, I'll 'ave a drop of that,' her father said. Mom laughed loudly. She was in one of those moods where she'd laugh at anything Dad said because she, too, craved attention and the drink was in and life was good. 'C'm'ere, babby.' Dad also sat up a bit and beckoned to Evie, scraping his chair back. 'Come and see yer old dad.'

'Evie's too big for that,' Rita said in a sour voice.

'Nah, she ain't. Come on, pretty wench, come and see yer old dad.'

Evie went to him and Dad pulled her onto his lap. He hadn't done that in a long time. She snuggled up against him, feeling part of things for once. Feeling favoured by the warmth of an embrace, the rub of his stubble against her cheek. Rita made a face at her from across the table.

'Eh, our Reet, no call for that,' Dad said. His beer-and-fag breath filled Evie's nostrils. She was pressed against his warm chest, his arms round her. 'Not when we're 'aving a nice afternoon – ain't we, eh, all my wenches?'

Irene filled her cup again and sat back. 'Course we are, Ray,' she said. 'In our new house.' She looked round. 'I'd say we've landed on our feet 'ere. Better than that last 'ole we were in.'

Dad wasn't listening to her. 'You're getting big now,' he observed into Evie's ear. 'Sit up a bit, wench, I can hardly breathe! Look at you!' He ran a rough hand down her arm, then clamped his hand over her thigh until it pinched. Evie winced. 'Turning into a ripe one, you are.'

Evie saw her mother's face turn thunderous. Mom was enraged by any attention or compliment from Dad that wasn't sent in her direction. She leapt from her chair and Evie hardly knew what was happening until a slap stung her face and made her ear ring.

'Stop playing up to yer dad like that! Go on, get off of 'im, yow dirty little trollop! Don't encourage her, Ray. Our Reet's right – 'er's too big for all that! Giving 'er ideas!'

Confused, Evie slid to the floor again, seeing Rita and Shirley smirking at her.

'What're you on about, yer soft cow?' Ray protested muzzily.

'C'm'ere, kid,' Irene said, expansive, wheedling all of a sudden, as she sank into her chair again.

Wary, longing, Evie went to her, looking up into her mother's face, the fleshy, pitted skin, clogged at this moment with powder, the full lips with a remnant of red on them, big eyes and bright, blonde hair. Her mother who occupied most of the world, filled the sky like a moody and unpredictable sun that Evie desperately wanted to shine on her at all times.

'Run and fetch me my cardi from upstairs,' Mom ordered her. 'Sun's going down.'

Evie hurried to do as she requested. By the time she came down, Mom was filling her cup again, tilting the jug to get the last drops.

'Shirl, go down the outdoor and get us another jug,' Mom ordered.

'Oh Mom,' Shirley groaned. 'Why do I 'ave to? Can't Evie go?'

'I'll go,' Evie said, desperate to curry favour, to regain her momentary place basking in light.

'You can clear up the cowing table, Shirl,' their

46

mother said.

'Go on then, our kid.' Dad reached into his pocket and pressed coppers into her hand. 'You can earn yerself a ha'penny for going, how's that, eh?'

Glowing, Evie ran along the street to get the jug filled at the outdoor of one of the pubs where you could buy straight from the street. Mom and Dad were being nice to her. She was happy. She didn't think about anything else.

When she got back, Rita had got out a dog-eared pack of cards. Dad plonked a ha'penny into her palm and Evie stowed it in her knicker leg. She sat at the table with Rita and Shirley. Mom and Dad drank and laughed at nothing much and everyone was in such a good mood that Rita and Shirley even let her play Rummy with them. It was the best night Evie could remember in a long time – at least, for as long as it lasted.

By the time darkness had fallen, all of them were hungry again, especially Evie, and the drink was taking its effect.

'What's for my cowing tea?' Dad asked, in the face of there being no obvious sign of any food manifesting itself.

'Don't need tea,' Mom retorted. 'You've 'ad yower cowing dinner. Yow've got yower ale.'

'What d'yer mean, don't need tea? You're a bloody lousy wife, you are.'

'Don't yow cowing talk to me like that!' Mom was on her high horse immediately. 'How'm I s'posed to feed all yow cowing lot when yow've spent most of yower wages by Sat'dy night?'

'I'm the one who earns the cowing wages! I'm

the man of the house and if I say I want a dinner, I want a dinner – NOW!'

And off they went, hammer and tongs again. The girls looked at each other. No tea for them. Again.

Sunday morning was like so many other Sunday mornings at home: the foul-tempered dregs of the Saturday night before. Church bells rang round the city, people walked out in hats and coats and Sunday best dresses and jackets, including Mr and Mrs Charles, who walked along the street with their younger son, all in their smartest clothes, backs straight as ramrods. No one went to church from Evie's house and it stank of the bucket, in the general direction of which Dad had peed liberally before crashing into bed. Their house did not contribute to the inviting smells of Sunday joints roasting along the street.

Mom and Dad slept until almost midday. Mom was in a mean temper once she woke. She sat downstairs drinking tea and smoking and there was no food. Evie sat on the front step, her mouth watering at the meat smells on the air, her stomach rumbling. She had taken a few pinches of sugar off the saucer on the table without Mom noticing but she didn't dare go back for more. She still had her ha'penny, but all the shops were shut.

There were kids all over the street, ropes turning, hoops and carts, but she didn't feel like playing. She had become aware, over the time they lived there, of a house just along the street to her left, where there were always boys going in and out. There seemed to be a lot of them, mostly skinny and white as ghosts, and she couldn't tell them apart.

She looked along at Mrs Waring's house. She was bound to be cooking. Mrs Waring was that kind of person, with cakes and proper food. Evie slid off her step and, looking behind her to see that no one had noticed, sidled along to the Warings'.

She felt silly standing there by the step so she tapped on the door.

'You can't come in now,' Mrs Waring told her. 'I'm just putting our dinner on the table.' She looked down at Evie with her usual mixture of irritation and pity. 'Ain't you 'aving your dinner then?'

Evie shook her head.

'Tell you what. Wait there a second.' Mrs Waring returned with a saucer. On it were two of the most beautifully golden roast potatoes Evie had ever seen. Saliva swilled into her mouth. 'They've got a bit of salt on them, bab. You can sit there and eat them. Give me back the saucer.'

'Ta!' Evie said. She grabbed the saucer and ran along the entry. She wasn't going to eat them sitting on Mrs Waring's step in full view. She didn't want anyone else seeing this prize, least of all her sisters.

She squatted down in the entry, her back against the wall, smelling the hot, crisp potatoes. For a few minutes she ate, lost in a world of oily, salty potato taste and the feel of them in her mouth. No one disturbed her. It was like being in heaven. She didn't think of a single other thing while she was

49

eating them. When good things happened, she was in them, completely, without any other thought intruding. She used the last mouthful of potato to wipe the grains of salt from the plate.

When she had finished she left the empty saucer on the step. She didn't want to go home. Rita and Shirley had discovered that a girl roughly their age lived round in the yard and they were thick as thieves with her and didn't want Evie about at any price. And as for Mom and Dad...

Evie wandered down the entry and passed the entrance to the yard, going all the way to the end where the entry branched left into the little lane behind the Warings' garden and the hens.

She saw the concrete air-raid shelter. People used them to store things in these days, when they were still standing. But Evie was thinking about the boy. Had he come out of the shelter? Might he be in there now?

There was no door anymore. Anything wooden had long gone on someone's fire. The entrance was a black hole wreathed in cobwebs, opening onto the lane to give access to the surrounding houses. A scrub of grass and weeds clung along the edge of its walls. She tiptoed closer, her heart beating hard at the thought of the dark, windowless inside of the place. She could hear the distant little noises of the hens in Mr Waring's garden.

She slipped her fingers into her mouth, because it made her feel safer, and looked round to check that no one else was in the entry. Trying to push away thoughts of the darkness and monsters and ghosts, she stepped inside.

Six

It felt cool inside. The hairs rose on Evie's arms and she shivered and stuck her fingers in her mouth. For a few moments she could hardly see, but her eyes gradually adjusted.

There did not seem to be anything much in the shelter but the dark dampness of the place gave her the creeps. She longed to have Whisky with her. She could rest her hand on Whisky's head and cuddle her. It would have been nice to have some other living thing there with her in the cold gloom. She looked around her, up at the ceiling. The corners were draped with thick, dusty cobwebs and she didn't like it.

Something caught her eye, to her right, at the back: a faint glint of light. Evie's heart picked up speed. Someone was there! She knew, immediately, who it must be, but at the same time she was scared. She wanted to run out and back along the entry but she could not seem to move.

A moment later the glint of light appeared again. Then a voice said, quietly, 'Oh. It's you.'

Evie knew it was the boy. He wasn't frightening and he didn't sound as if he minded it being her so she stepped closer. He was sitting in the corner against the wall, his knees bunched up by his chest.

'What're you doing?' she said

'Sitting 'ere. What's it look like?'

She didn't know what to say.

'What're *you* doing?'

'Just looking,' she said. Flustered, she added, 'at the chickens.'

'There ain't no chickens,' the boy pointed out. 'They're all outside.'

Again, she could think of no reply to this irrefutable truth. He wanted her to go away and leave him alone, she thought. She was about to go, when he said, 'Wanna come and sit 'ere?'

He patted the ground next to him. 'All right.' Evie was warmed by this invitation.

The boy shuffled up a bit. 'I got this mat, see.'

As Evie sat down, she felt it under her hand: the grubby flatness of an ancient doormat. Her shoulder came into contact with his. He smelt of stale wee and something sweet, sickly. Now that she was sitting, enough light was seeping through the doorway for her to see the outline of him, his pointed features, skinny legs, the scruffy hair, specs. They had a big lump of something at the corner, as if a fat insect was perched there.

'What's that on there?' she said, pointing.

'String,' he said. 'Well, cotton – sort of. I broke 'em.'

He seemed friendly, she thought. At least he had let her sit there.

'Why're you sitting here?' she persevered.

'It's my place.' He turned to her. 'You won't tell?'

Evie shook her head. She didn't know who he thought she might tell.

She felt as if she was talking a lot. With most people it seemed safer to keep quiet but with the boy she felt somehow she was the one who needed to start things off. She realized she felt safe with him.

'Those all your brothers you live with?' she said. She had seen a lot of boys coming and going. There seemed to be so many of them and she could not tell them apart. 'How many brothers you got?'

'Seven.'

'No sisters?'

'No.' He considered, then said, counting on his fingers, 'There's David, then Tony, then Paul and Ron – they'm twins – then me, then Frankie, then Carl and the babby's George.'

'Cor,' Evie said. 'All boys!' She thought of what she'd heard about the Knights. 'Have you got a mom?'

A brief pause, before he shook his head.

'She dead?'

He nodded.

'What she die of?'

He didn't answer. He shrugged off the question, staring ahead of him.

'I had some toffee,' he said, 'I've ate it all, though.' He bared his teeth at her as if this was proof. The two top middle ones were missing; the rest were small and somewhere between grey and black. His breath smelt of toffee. 'But I've got my things in here,' he added quickly. 'D'yer wanna look?'

Evie agreed, eager at this sign of friendship. He seemed to be keen to please her, the way she was always trying to please everyone as well.

The boy untied a rag he was holding cradled in

his lap and brought out his treasures one by one. 'My car...' The toy looked very old and had no wheels. 'My ciggie cards...' A dog-eared, ancient little bundle. 'Fag ends...' A handful of stubs. 'And my conkers...' A handful of dry, wizened things. 'I don't want any of that lot taking 'em off me.'

Evie was about to ask who, again, when voices erupted into the shelter, and giggles. It was too late to move.

'Come on, Dor. In 'ere!'

'Ooh, no, Terry, you sure? It's all dark and dirty in here.'

'Dark and dirty – ooh, that's good!'

There was laughter, and more giggles from the girl. 'Come on,' the lad wheedled. 'It's all right. Just come 'ere.'

'Oh, I dunno...' She seemed ready to leave. 'Can't we just go to the park, by the rezza or somewhere nice, where it's sunny?'

Evie and the boy sat still, hunched together in the corner, both petrified. Their eyes met in the gloom. They both knew to keep as quiet as the grave. The two who had come in were much older than them; the lad with very dark hair, the girl's long and lighter. She was wearing a pale frock with a zigzag pattern on.

'Come on, Dor. It's all right in 'ere.' The lad pushed her up against the wall and clamped his mouth to hers. The girl made muffled sounds of protest and freed her mouth.

'Not so hard, Terry! That's not nice. Kiss me nicely.'

'Sorry,' he said. It went quiet for a bit, but for a few scuffling noises. It seemed a long time to

Evie, sitting there, hardly breathing. After a few moments there were more squeaks of protest from the girl.

'That's enough.' She sounded indignant now. There was a slapping sound. 'Don't push it. What if someone sees?'

'Nah,' the boy said. 'They're all in having dinner. What d'yer mean, push it, any'ow? It's what you want, ain't it? You're leading me on, Dor, what'm I s'posed to do? You've got me all steamed up now.'

'You're s'posed to behave like a gentleman,' the girl said haughtily. 'Not keep shoving your hands at me like that.'

'Oh, Dor, go on.' His voice softened. 'You're a cracker, you are. You're the best girl I've ever seen. You are, honest. You get me so's I can't even think straight.'

There was another giggle.

'Come on, you like that... Just let me 'ave a feel... That's it.' There was a gasping noise. 'Oh Dor! Go on, just lie down with me here – be with me, proper like.'

'No! Are you mad, Terry! In this hole of a place! Get your hands off!'

'Ah, come on... Don't keep being like that.' He sounded angry. 'All right then. If yer not gunna lie down, I'll just have to... I can't wait for yer, Dor... You're leading me on...'

There was a scuffle, the girl's voice rising higher. 'No... NO, Terry! What're you doing?'

Then she was muffled, her sounds turning to grunts of indignation, then, perhaps, pain. Evie kept her head down, terrified they might see her

55

pale hair, but the man's back was to her and he was shoving himself hard against the girl who was pressed against the wall. He had his knees bent and seemed to Evie to writhe, making those noises she heard from Mom and Dad's room. She squeezed her eyes shut.

The noises quickly reached a climax and it went very quiet. Then they heard the girl crying.

'You're horrible, you are, Terry Wall. I ain't never going anywhere near you again. That hurt, and you've made me all wet and disgusting. No, don't touch me – *get off!*' It was a shriek.

'Shh, Dor, for God's sake. I'm sorry – I thought you wanted it. You *did* … you know you did, the way you was carrying on.'

'I told you I dain't want to go all the way,' she sobbed. 'You made me. What'm I going to do now? You've stolen my … my virtue!'

The boy sniggered. 'Virtue!'

'*Yes.*' She was hurt and sobbing, wiping at her legs with the skirt of her dress. 'What if I'm … you know…?'

'What?' He was trying to touch her and she kept pulling away.

'In the family way?'

'Oh, you're not. Don't talk daft. And don't go blabbing about it.'

'I *hate* you. I don't ever want to see you again!' she sobbed and ran off, out of the shelter. They heard her tripping tread disappear along the entry.

'Stupid cow,' they heard from the boy. He was straightening out his clothes. Then he was gone too, a brief shadow in the doorway. They heard the sound of his retreating footsteps.

Evie and the boy looked at each other at last. It felt wrong, being there, hearing all that, and she didn't know what to say. A second later, though, she heard a snicker from her right. His eyes met hers and they both started giggling. They knew something wrong had happened, something forbidden and adult that wasn't funny. But they knew that adults were usually cruel and ridiculous and did unpredictable and bad things and they couldn't seem to help themselves. His pointy face crinkled up when he laughed, wonky and likeable, and the sight of it made fizzing giggles bubble up in her. Soon they were both shaking with laughter though hardly knowing why. The boy's shoulders shook and his specs slid down his nose so he had to push them up.

'I'd better go,' Evie said in a bit. She struggled to her feet. Her legs were cramped from sitting all clenched up and her belly ached from laughing. She felt odd. Disturbed and shaken but better, all at once.

She expected the boy to say nothing, but as she was beginning to move away, he said in a rush, 'You'll come back, won't you? Sometime?'

Evie turned. She nodded.

'This is my place,' he said. 'But you can come in.'

'What's your name?'

'Gary Knight. What's yours?'

'Eve Sutton. But they all call me Evie.'

Then she stepped out into the afternoon, feeling as if she had been in the shelter for days and as if she now had somewhere to go.

Seven

February 1954

'Oh Evie,' Shirley whined. 'Don't go out. S'freezing out there. 'Ere...' Her voice was wheedling now. 'Come and play Happy Families.' She produced a pack of flimsy, dog-eared cards.

Evie stood with one hand on the door latch, two fingers in her mouth. She was almost lured in. It wasn't often Shirley offered to play with her. But Shirley was only sucking up to her because Rita was out.

'Can't.' Evie spoke with a mixture of regret and triumph. It felt good to be able to turn Shirley down, not always to be the one begging. Even so, those brief times when anyone at home chose to be nice to her were to be treasured. She twisted her mouth into a half smile, still trying to keep Shirley in a good mood with her. 'Gotta go.' Shirley scowled and Evie pulled the door open quickly.

Days-old snow was piled in brown heaps along the pavements and sagged down the slate roofs. Nearly all the neighbourhood children were out, hurling tightly packed balls of ice. There were yells and shrieks of pain. Evie had no coat and she pulled her cardigan round her, looking for Gary. Skinny, funny Gary Knight who had become her best friend. Gary who was nearly a year older than her, even though he looked such a tiddler. She soon saw him skulking along on the other side of the road, with the odd, almost crab-like walk he had, his left side leading. He moved along close to the walls of the houses opposite, as if he thought this would make him less visible. His little brother Carl was with him.

'Oi, Ducky!'

A lump of snow came flying across at him. Gary flinched out of the way and the icy lump hit Carl in the side of the face. Carl clutched the side of his head and started snivelling. Unlike most of the Knight boys, Carl was big for his age, sallow-skinned, black-haired and solid. But he was special; young for his seven years. He was like a giant toddler.

Evie hurried over to them.

'Hey, Ducky!' shouted the boy who had thrown the snowball. 'That was meant for you, not your little brother!'

Evie could hear a rough apology in the boy's voice. The lads teased Gary mercilessly, called him 'Ducky' or 'Duck's Arse' because of the odd, pointed-at-the-back haircut one of his brothers had inflicted on him. And because Gary was just Gary – off-centre and easily bullied. But it was different with Carl, who was like a big, sweet puppy. Usually the other lads teased him more gently or left him alone.

'Come on, Carly,' Evie said, enjoying feeling like a big sister, as she often did with Carl. 'It's all right. 'E never meant to 'it yer.' With her sleeve she wiped the boy's pudgy face. His ear was red and sore looking. She could see the usual Knight tidemarks up his neck and a worm of green snot

59

trickling from his nose. 'Look what I've got.' She fished in her pocket for three sticky pieces of cough candy. She loved the pungent taste of it. 'Look, one for you, Carly.'

She handed one to Gary. Carl took his and stopped crying immediately. He grinned at her, cheek bulging, slug trails of tears down his ruddy cheeks. All their hands were mauve with cold. Gary and Carl were both in short trousers. Carl's always had rings of wee round the crotch in varying degrees of dryness, like the rings in a tree trunk.

'Ta,' Gary said contentedly.

He was looking a bit better since his hair had been cut and Stanley Knight, his dad, had been forced to go and get him some more specs when the frames of his had fallen apart and he'd spent weeks squinting and bumping into things. Glasses – for free! The new ones were round, the same as the old ones, but without the lump of string holding them together.

The three of them cowered at the edge of the games, as they usually did, hoping no one would notice them, while the great mingle of children – some of them Gary's brothers – ran and yelled along the street. Evie saw Frankie, the next one after Gary, who was ten, yelling insults at some other boy. Frankie was always in trouble, walking into fights and pranks as if through an ever open door. The twins, Paul and Ron – not identical but both with the skinny, runtish looks of most of the Knights – were out there trying to push a tray along the lumpy pavement. They were fourteen but looked younger.

Anyone who mentioned Carl, or any of the Knight children, nearly always followed it up by saying regretfully, 'That poor Cathleen.'

All Evie knew was that Cathleen Knight, Gary's mom, had died having the youngest child, George, who was now going on five. She had left her husband Stanley a widower, with eight children – all boys. It was generally agreed that Stanley Knight, a thin, drooping man with an equally drooping personality and watery eyes, was not well cut out to be the head of a household even under more hopeful circumstances, let alone with no wife.

'Dreadful man,' was all she ever heard Mrs Waring say about him. Evie had heard her add, mysteriously, 'Someone ought've tied a knot in it, that they ought.' Whatever that meant. Mr Waring called him a 'feeble bloody specimen'.

Gary and Evie met, throughout the autumn, at first in the shelter and then elsewhere. She had been into Gary's a few times. Even the thought of it filled her with dread. When she walked into the two-up, two-down house the first time, she could see that it had once been a place where someone had taken trouble. Cathleen Knight – who else could have done it? – had decorated the mantle with a drape of deep blue velvet and there were ornaments and brasses on it, now thick with dust. There was some furniture: a sideboard and a meat safe, a table and one remaining chair, an upright, rickety wheel-back thing on which Mr Knight seemed to spend most of his life sagging, smoking and swiping at his sons if they came within his orbit.

The overpowering smell in the house was of

urine. Evie was used to this, but not to the extent of it in the Knights' place, which stank as if every floorboard was soaked in it. Once Gary took her up to where he slept, on the floor with his brothers in a mess of rags. There was a bucket full of wee – and worse. Evie turned her eyes away and tried not to breathe. The smell up there, in this bedwetting household, was so overpowering, it burnt the nostrils.

The boys, who ranged in age from David, now going on seventeen, down to George, were a sad, unkempt and neglected band and the inside of the house a realm of dirt and chaos. The table, whenever she saw it, showed signs of some scratched meal or other – globules of set porridge, crumbs and smears of lard and dirty plates. Their clothes were whatever came to hand, and they seldom saw water let alone soap.

'I don't know how those boys haven't been taken off him,' Evie had heard Mrs Waring say, tutting each time she set eyes on any of them, in their ragged mix of clothing. Neighbours handed old clothes on to them, when they could. The women sometimes took round offerings of food to supplement the bags of chips and loaves of bread and lard Mr Knight fed them on otherwise.

Therefore, cold though it was, Evie did not want to go to the Knights' house – nor her own.

'Shall us go to the shelter?' Gary asked.

Evie thought of the freezing gloom of the shelter. All through the late summer and autumn they had met there and sat talking and giggling, hearing the clucks of the hens. She had discovered Gary was obsessed with toffee, which any spare copper went on, hammered off a block in the sweetshop. He was an infectious giggler, tickled by the least thing. They had taken great care every time they went – going round the long way, down an entry further along the road and doubling back along the lane so that the other kids wouldn't follow.

Evie shook her head. It was too cold to go there today. But she had no other ideas.

Gary had started at the big school in the autumn. They had never been to school together. Evie didn't mind school, though she had not made a best friend. The other children seemed to veer away from her. One girl told her she smelt. She spent a lot of time wandering about dreamily at the edge of the playground on her own. Nowadays, she pretended Gary was with her and talked to him in her head. Since the first day she and Gary had met in the shelter they had kept coming back. It was their place. They never talked about anything much, not about home. And there wasn't much to do. But they told jokes and laughed and messed about, out of everyone else's way. Then Gary started bringing Carl sometimes.

Other days, they hung around the Warings' door hoping to see Whisky. Sometimes the Warings had one of their married daughters there and they wouldn't want other children around. But if he was in the right mood on a Saturday, Mr Waring helped them make toys. He had given them two cocoa tins and a twist of string to make a walkie-talkie. And after some persuasion, Mrs Waring had said that as the old pram was no longer needed they could have the wheels. The Warings had an electric fire now, so she didn't have to go and get the coal in it anymore and her eldest daughter had a newer pram. So Mr Waring had helped them build a 'moke', or go-kart. It was a good one too and he had watched them play on it, sitting on his doorstep with one leg crossed over the other, smoking and making sure none of the other kids snatched it off them. Gary and Evie had had the time of their lives on it, giving Carl turns as well, and their brothers Frankie and George who begged turns. Now Mr Waring had tucked it away in his brew house in the garden, for the winter. So that was a no-go.

Through the last crunching of his sweet, Gary said, 'We could build a fire.' He rattled something in his pockets. 'I got matches.'

'What with?' Evie said.

Gary's eye wandered. 'We'll find summat.'

They exchanged looks. Evie shrugged. 'Come on, Carly,' she said. 'You come with us.'

Carl looked up at her in his trusting way. 'All right,' he said slowly. As they set off, he slipped his freezing little hand into hers.

The three of them slid away from the others, checking that no one was following before they slipped into the entry. It felt no warmer in the shelter than outside. They could see the ghostly swirl of their breath in the air.

Gary peered round in the shadows, in the hope that there would be some bits to make a fire out of, but there was nothing.

'Told yer,' Evie said.

'Never mind, we can light the matches. That'll keep us warm,' Gary said.

They all squeezed into the corner. When Gary

lit a match, Evie saw his face and Carl's lit up for a few seconds. Both of them had their bare knees drawn up close. Carl's eyes held little flames and looked solemn. Gary's specs reflected the light and his grin showed his wonky teeth.

'Ow!' He dropped the matchstick as the flame reached his fingers and it went dark again. Carl laughed and Gary started giggling as well. Evie could just make out their faces and she began to laugh too. It never took much to set them off.

'One day,' Gary said suddenly, 'I'm gunna go and live at the seaside. You ever been?'

'No,' Evie said. ''Ve you?'

'Nah. S'nice there, though. I seen pictures. Nicer'n here. I'll light a big bonfire on the beach!'

Evie sat with her shoulders pressed against Gary and Carl's. Gary kept striking matches. They tried to believe it was warming the deathly chill of the shelter. Evie stayed in this moment, not thinking about it being Saturday, which meant Dad would come home drunk and Mom'd be furious and... She kept her mind on now and giggled when Gary lit another match and let the light burn to his fingertips before he dropped it to the ground between his legs. Now was all that mattered.

Eight

Late that Friday night, Mom was beside herself with rage. The girls had already crept up to bed when their father's footsteps were heard along the street. They knew what to expect. But this time he was not singing.

Evie lay on her lumpy mattress in the icy dark, waiting. She had chilblains and her toes felt like hot, itchy sausages.

'Here we go,' she heard Rita say, trying to sound full of bravado, but betraying the fact that she was scared. The lack of singing was unnerving. He was quiet as the grave except for the weaving footsteps out in the frosty street.

'Where the hell've yow been?' Mom erupted at him the minute he approached the threshold.

An aggressive reply was all they heard, but they could not make out the words.

Evie stiffened, waiting for the shouting, the sounds of their few remaining crocks breaking against walls, his long-congealed dinner flung against the stove, the yelling and screaming.

But there was a brief lull, words being exchanged, then a howl of rage from Mom.

'You what? Who is she? You...' A string of insults followed, then a roar from him, a thud, a yell of pain.

'I ain't staying 'ere with yow, you bastard!'

Mom's feet came thudding up the stairs. Some-

66

one outside at the front was shouting for them to 'Shurrit, for Christ's sake!' but this was drowned out by Mom erupting into the bedroom.

'Gerrup, all of yer. We're going to Vi's.' She was slapping them awake.

'Oh Mom,' Rita moaned. 'It's perishing out there. Why do we 'ave to?'

'Do as yer cowing well told!' Evie felt a kick land in her ribs and she moaned. 'Gerrup you, yer little rat. I cor stay 'ere with 'im any longer.'

'Oh, for God's sake, Irene, now what?'

Auntie Vi's voice came at them out of the dimly lit house. The smell of cigarettes wreathed out to them. Vi's hair was hanging loose over some pale garment.

'Just let us in, will yer, Vi?' Mom begged her. 'I'm starving out 'ere.'

They had walked like people with damaged limbs, slipping and waving their arms, trying not to come a purler in the road. The icy, smoky air stung their nostrils as the darkness, only broken by an occasional dim street light, folded its cold arms around them. There was hardly anyone about. It had felt to Evie, in the shadowy streets, as if they were the only people in the world.

Vi stood back in silence. Evie could imagine her face, the lips pulled tight, the frown. She was fed up with this. But they would soon be wrapped up on Vi's floor, in this house which always felt warmer than their own. And in the morning, maybe Uncle Horace would give them a half-penny, or some sweets...

She stumbled in and onto the floor, her feet

numb, almost asleep even before she lay down. Rita and Shirley bedded down to one side of her. Voices continued around her.

'Irene, it cannae be helped. We cannae just stick around here so that you can ship up when you feel like it. My mother's sick – we're moving back up there. It's all sorted out. You're gunna have tae get a grip – go out and get a job yourself if you can't rely on your feller to keep you and your weans... Ray's a drunken, womanizing sod and he's no going tae change...'

The last thing Evie remembered was the press of the button on the cushion against her cheek.

By midday the next day, after they got home, Mom and Dad were all lovey-dovey again. Especially as Dad had been moaning about his work and Mom found another way to get round him.

'I'll go out and get a job, Ray,' Mom said, voice honey-sweet in her hungover husband's ear. She knelt on the hard floor beside his chair, stroking his chest. ''Ow about that? Then yow won't 'ave to earn all the money. We can pull together, can't us?'

Evie heard her father grunt something back, which ended in 'good wench'.

Mom would do anything so long as she had his attention, even if it meant her going back to work, which she had previously put on airs about. She'd even sent Evie to buy a few rashers of bacon and a big fresh loaf for dinner – on the strap, as usual. Everyone was tired and subdued. Rita and Shirley didn't have the energy to be nasty, Dad was hungover and Mom, for once, was happily in his good books, standing at the stove as the rashers spat and sizzled, booming out 'No Other Love' at the top of her voice. She loved Perry Como.

Just before dinner, there came a knock on the door. Dad was snoozing by the fire, the girls' mouths were watering in expectation and the Sutton household looked almost like a place at one with itself.

Evie stood behind her mother as she loomed in the doorway. 'Yeah. What d'yow want?'

Through the gaps, Evie made out a faded-looking woman in a macintosh and black beret, with round specs like Gary's. The weather had warmed a little and a gentle drizzle was falling.

'Good afternoon,' she said, standing with her feet neatly together. Evie saw brown lace-up shoes. 'Something smells nice, I must say!'

Mom was not impressed by this overture. She folded her arms across her huge bosom. This was never a good sign.

'You have children, dear, do you not?' the lady asked tentatively, as if wondering whether Mom might have forgotten whether she did or not.

'Yeah.' Mom sounded suspicious now. 'What about 'em?'

'Nothing to worry about,' the lady assured her. 'I'm from the local church. I'm just going round the neighbourhood to invite local children to our Sunday school. I wondered if any of your children would like to come along? It gives them something to do – a bit of fun and activity with others. And some Sunday peace for you.'

''Ow much does it cost?'

'Oh, there's no charge, dear. And there are activities for a wide range of age groups. It's nice for them – something to do, in the warm.'

Evie waited for the explosion that must come. Mom had no time for church – that was another thing she was rude about to Mrs Charles, that she was a devout churchgoer. All church people were stiff-minded hypocrites according to her. But to Evie's amazement, her mother uncrossed her arms. The words 'no charge' acted like a charm.

'You mean,' she said with an unctuous politeness foreign to her children's ears, 'you mean my girls can come for Sunday afternoon?'

She was already calling out behind her before the lady could reply. 'Reet, Shirl, Evie! You'll go with this lady, won't yer? Tomorrow – to the church?'

Evie crept to the door and peered out past her. The lady was very thin, her mac belted tightly round her.

'Hello,' the lady said, catching sight of her. She gave an enchanted smile. 'What a lovely little girl you have.'

'Oh ar,' Mom said, not really listening.

'Can my friend come?' Evie asked.

'Oi,' Mom interrupted. 'Don't go being cheeky to the lady.'

'Of course she can,' the lady said. 'What friend? Where does she live, dear?'

'Over there.' Evie nodded towards the Knights' house. 'His name's Gary.'

'Yes, you just tell him. Now, you need to come at two o'clock sharp.' She told her to come to St

John's Church and the name of the road it was on. 'I'm Mrs Bracebridge, dear. I hope to see you there tomorrow. Two o'clock – don't forget!'

With a smile at Evie, which made her tired-looking face seem younger and light up almost into prettiness, she set off along the street towards Gary's house.

'There, d'you 'ear that, Ray?' Mom went across and nudged her husband awake. 'There's a lady come, taking the kids off of us for the afternoon tomorrow.' She leaned over him, a purring, seductive note in her voice now. 'So we'll have the house all to ourselves – 'ow about that then?'

Nine

Autumn 1954

Evie dawdled along the road from the new big school in Osler Street, in the warm September afternoon. It was her birthday today, the day she turned eleven, and she was excited, but she had hung about after school to make sure Mom would be home from work when she got there.

Upstairs under her mattress was a present: a bar of rose-scented soap she had bought when Dad was in one of his well-oiled moods, handing out joeys and sixpences like, Mom said, 'Lord Muck'. Mom didn't mind so much, now she had a job herself, making 'keckles' as she called them, at Bulpitt's. And Evie had saved up her bits of change and bought the soap. Today she was going to give it to Mom and surely then she would be pleased and be nice to her?

''Ello, Mrs Waring!' she called, passing the house. Mrs Waring was leaning against the door frame, arms folded, as if taking the air. Whisky was lying out in the shade on the pavement and Evie stopped to lean down and stroke her.

''Ello, Whisky girl. You're lovely, you are.' The old dog gave a lazy grunt in acknowledgement.

'All right, are yer, bab?' Mrs Waring asked kindly.

'It's my birthday today,' Evie said, straightening up.

'Is it?' Mrs Waring said. 'Well, many happy returns. Here, I'm sure I've got summat in here you'd like.' She beckoned. Evie waited and Mrs Waring emerged a few seconds later with a slice of cake. 'It's nothing much, bit of Madeira, but here you are.'

'Ta, Mrs Waring, that's ever so kind of you!' Evie said. She smiled and Mrs Waring looked fondly at her.

'That's all right, bab. You get it down yer before one of the others has it off you.'

The cake soon disappeared between Mrs Waring's house and her own. The front door of number twenty-nine was ajar and Evie pushed it open and took in the scene inside. To her surprise, Mom, Rita and Shirley were all sitting at the table. Evie's mind raced. Rita was about to start a new job but had not been at work today. And of course Shirley had beaten her home. Were they waiting to say happy birthday? She saw the silver and red of Kit-Kat wrappers on the table. Kit-Kats! A treat for her, for her birthday?

As soon as she walked in, they all grabbed the red and silver wrappers, screwing them up in their hands and looking at each other, laughing a bit, as if they all had a secret. They didn't say anything to Evie so she went on upstairs. Maybe they'd give her one when she came down with Mom's present. She fished about under the mattress and pulled out the little cake of soap she had bought, wrapped in a brown paper bag.

'Here, Mom.' She presented it downstairs, feeling her sisters' scornful eyes on her. Would this be the key, the thing she was forever looking for that would unlock her mother's heart into love for her? And were they hiding a Kit-Kat for her as a surprise? Surely in a moment someone would bring one out and say, 'Here, this one's for you, Evie'?

Her mother looked at her and then at her sisters, as if they were all sharing a joke which Evie didn't know about. As it was still warm, Mom was in one of her summer frocks, her bare arms big and pink.

'What's this then?' Mom's tone was mocking and curious at once. She could never resist a present.

'I bought it for you,' Evie said. She heard Shirley give a snigger.

Her mother's hand explored inside the bag and brought out the pink soap. She sniffed it and looked pleased. Then she tightened her lips. Evie could feel something in the air, something between them all that she was not part of.

'Nice. What's all this in aid of then?'

'It's...' Evie began, growing more uncertain.

Wasn't it a nice thing for her to have done? Wasn't Mom pleased? 'It's my birthday. So I bought you a present...'

She wanted Mom to melt and say, 'Oh, what a surprise!' and 'But it's *your* birthday. You shouldn't be buying me presents,' and, best of all, 'Come 'ere, kid,' and pull her into her arms. That was her dream of what should happen. What Mom did in front of other people sometimes to show what a good mom she was.

'Ta,' was all she said, but in a mocking tone. She reached towards Evie. Evie waited for a pat, for something. Her mother slapped her cheek, pretend playful, but the slap was hard and edged with spite. 'It's nice. Now bugger off, all three of yer. I want a bit of peace.'

There was no sign, or mention, of any more Kit-Kats.

Evie stood outside, her cheek stinging. For a few moments she nursed the hurt inside her, then put it out of her mind. She caught sight of Gary giving Carl a turn in the moke, shoving it along the road as fast as he could, his shirt tails flying. Carl's swarthy little face was fixed somewhere between terror and rapture.

'My go, my go!' Five-year-old George was yelling, jumping up and down on the pavement.

'Go on, Ducky, give us a go!' other kids were shouting. Gary was more popular now he had the go-kart.

On his way back with Carl, Gary looked up and saw Evie. He released the moke and it trundled further without him before crashing into the kerb.

74

'Gary!' Carl was yelling.

'Get Frankie to push yer,' Gary called to him. 'Come on,' he said to Evie. 'Let's go and get us some rocks. You got any money? I found a farthing!'

'A halfpenny, that's all,' Evie said.

The trick was to go and buy sweets off old Mrs Harris at the far end of Inkerman Street, because she was hard of hearing. Now rationing was over it was like heaven in sweet shops. They stepped into the crammed little corner shop, with a *ting* of the bell. Mrs Harris never seemed to be able to hear the bell but it *tinged* all the same. Mrs Harris sold a variety of things and the shop had a musty smell, laced with rubber and something metallic. Mrs Harris was sitting behind the counter knitting.

'Oh!' she exclaimed, as she always did. 'I never heard you come in.'

Evie stayed by the counter while Mrs Harris talked to her.

'You letting your friend choose, are you? Well, that's nice. You have got pretty hair, my dear. I'm knitting this for my lad, Bert – well, I say lad, he'll be forty next year...' There was no need for Evie to say anything.

They handed over their coppers for the few sweets Gary laid on the counter and scooted out as fast as they could, giggling as they ran down the street.

'D'yer get some?' Evie said. Home was forgotten now, and Mom. She was with Gary.

'Yeah, tons!' From his shirt, Gary pulled a bar of toffee, grinning ecstatically. 'Let's get to the shelter and scoff 'em all!'

He was having difficulty running, the pockets of his shorts were so full. Evie got the giggles seeing him waddling along.

'We left Carly behind,' Evie said in the shelter, feeling guilty as Gary emptied the loot out of his pockets.

'Frankie can look after 'im for a bit,' Gary said, shoving liquorice into his mouth until it was bulging. Both of them adored liquorice.

'We stole it,' she said solemnly. 'That's a sin.'

Their eyes met. Both of them were thinking about what Mrs Bracebridge at the Sunday school would say. She was so determined to believe the very best of them. They went every Sunday now because they could stay indoors in the church hall and play games and there was a drink of orange squash and a biscuit. Mrs Bracebridge was always there with some other ladies and the tall vicar in black and they always spoke nicely to everyone.

''Ook,' Gary said indistinctly, black spit dribbling from the corner of his mouth. 'I go' these 'n' all!' Two sherbet dabs.

Evie felt a grin spread across her face. Soon they were in fits of laughter, mouths crammed with sugar. The sight of Gary's creased-up face always made Evie laugh even more. At least this felt like a birthday present.

'Ah, there you are, Eve dear!' Mrs Bracebridge saw her come in.

It was two months later and Evie had had to come to Sunday school on her own. There were children spread out in groups round the wide space, some at small tables, others on the floor, playing games of Ludo and Jack Straws, drawing pictures. Mrs Bracebridge came across the room, wearing a grey skirt with big boxy pleats swishing round her legs. She always smelled of lavender. 'I thought perhaps you weren't coming today.'

Mrs Bracebridge was the only person who ever called her Eve. 'You've missed our Bible story for today,' she went on. 'But would you like me to tell it to you again?'

Evie slipped her hand into Mrs Bracebridge's. She didn't care if other children told her she was a babby. She didn't care whether or not she heard a Bible story. But she did like Mrs Bracebridge's kindly attention. It was the other thing that kept her coming here, week after week.

'Where's young Gary?' Mrs Bracebridge said as she drew Evie onto a chair beside her.

'He's got a bad chest,' Evie said.

She had gone to call for him. Standing outside the Knights' house, she could hear noises from inside, the hum of a large family, like a beehive. The door was ajar and she pushed it open. Her nose wrinkled as she climbed the stairs. At first she could hardly make Gary out amid the muddle of rags, a bleached-out eiderdown and an old coat which made up his bedding on the floor. It was a moment before she caught sight of his tousled hair.

'Ducky?'

Gary raised his head. Without his specs on he looked like a half-blind little rabbit. He groped for his specs and pulled the wires over his ears.

'*Don't* call me Ducky,' he rasped.

'You poorly?'

77

He nodded, coughing as he sat up. He looked dazed and feverish. Evie wasn't sure what to say.

'You ain't coming then?' Mrs Bracebridge said you shouldn't say 'ain't'.'

'Nah.' Gary coughed and coughed, before sinking back down again.

Mrs Bracebridge looked at her through her spectacles. 'Oh, poor boy. We must say a little prayer for him, mustn't we?' She seemed about to say something, stopped, then started again. 'Is he ... all right? Otherwise, I mean?'

Evie nodded. She wasn't sure what Mrs Bracebridge meant and was glad when she picked up her well-thumbed Bible, with faded gold along the edges of the pages. She wanted to lean on Mrs Bracebridge as she sat next to her, to put her cheek against her arm, in its soft-looking, lilac-coloured sweater, but she didn't dare.

Evie didn't listen as she read, even though she found the general sound of Mrs Bracebridge's voice soothing. She looked round the room, wondering if she might do a jigsaw puzzle afterwards.

'So you see,' Mrs Bracebridge finished, 'what wonderful things the Lord can do.'

Evie looked up at her. Whatever the wonderful things were, she had not heard a word of it.

'Are you a teacher?' she asked. The way she read, she seemed like a teacher.

Mrs Bracebridge smiled, the smile that made her face, with its chapped, pink cheeks, seem younger.

'I was a teacher, dear, yes, before I married. I gave it up then, thinking that... Anyway, my Herb... Mr Bracebridge, is not in the best of health, so I stay at home to make sure things are comfortable for him when he gets home. That's my vocation now.' She looked keenly at Evie. 'Do you think you'd like to be a teacher when you grow up, Eve?'

Nothing could have been further from Evie's thoughts. 'No.' She shook her head. She saw that she had disappointed the kindly lady.

Again, after a hesitation, Mrs Bracebridge said, 'Would you like me to put your hair in plaits, d'you think? It's all over your face rather.'

Evie shook her head, then changed her mind. 'All right.'

Mrs Bracebridge fetched a little tortoiseshell comb from her black handbag and very gently teased out Evie's hair, which was now long and loose on her shoulders.

'I have a little bit of string, luckily,' she said.

Feeling her touch, Evie remembered that Mom had done her hair, once or twice when she was much younger. Times when Mom was in a good mood and wanted a little dolly to dress. An ache of longing filled her for a moment. She enjoyed the touch of Mrs Bracebridge's fingers.

'Your mother must be very busy, mustn't she?' Mrs Bracebridge asked, in a casual sort of voice.

Evie wasn't sure so she just said, 'Yes.'

'And you've two sisters, dear – is that right?' Rita and Shirley had come to Sunday school once, but never set foot in the place again.

At last she had finished the hair plaiting. She swung Evie round gently and smiled at her.

'There. Don't you look neat and tidy?' For a second she touched Evie's cheek with the palm of her hand and her fingers lingered there. 'Lovely,' she added.

'Miss, miss ... will you do my hair?' Two other girls came running up.

'I hadn't been planning to open a hair salon,' she said, laughing and seeming pleased. 'But all right, just this once.'

Evie looked at Gary across the big space of the church, all decorated for Christmas. He had been sick again last week and she was happy that he had got better in time to be here for this, amid the smells of damp stone and hymn books and the fusty aroma of bodies in thick winter clothing. Her own outfit was not warm, however, and she was trying not to shiver in the white cotton dress that Mrs Bracebridge had slipped over her head. There was a scratchy train of white gauze pinned to the top of her head and flowing down over her shoulders for her angel wings, and a band of silver tinsel round her forehead.

'Don't you look a picture, dear?' Mrs Bracebridge had said once she had assembled Evie's costume. She stood back and looked rapturously at her. 'Now, you're the head angel because you're the eldest.' As the children shuffled into line to go out and begin, Mrs Bracebridge had put her arm round Evie's shoulders for a moment and given her a squeeze. 'Lovely,' she whispered. 'So lovely.'

Evie had thought Mrs Bracebridge sounded almost as if she was going to cry.

Gary, with Carl next to him, was opposite her in the nativity line-up, both in shepherds' outfits, heads swathed in stripy cloths and long brown robes reaching down to and – in Gary's case –

80

below the ankles. Gary had tripped and fallen flat on his face on the way out to begin their Christmas performance and caused a muted ripple of laughter among the audience for a few seconds as he scrambled into line again. His glasses winked under the lights. He wore a very serious expression and was holding a stick as a crook. Both he and the crook had an appearance of lopsidedness, as if he might keel over at any second. Carl's headdress was slipping forwards so that you could only just see his enchanted smile.

Mary and Joseph already had their baby – a one-eyed doll – and the assembled animals, shepherds, kings and angels all stood round. The organ gave what sounded like a dyspeptic grunt and burst into life, the sound rumbling round the church. There was a soft sort of swishing as everyone stood up and started singing, 'Hark the Herald Angels Sing!' Evie sang out. She loved singing. She saw Gary vaguely moving his lips. His thoughts seemed to be miles away.

She didn't want the nativity play to end. It was like being in heaven, here in the shadowy church with its beauty and mystery and with the voice of the tall, kindly vicar, Mr Power, telling them all how nice they looked. And there were all the pretty costumes, the music and the feeling of goodwill. Of Christmas bringing something new. Mom hadn't come to watch, of course, although Mrs Bracebridge had called specially to tell her about it and ask her to attend.

'I ay going in that church on the orders of that dried-up old busy-body,' she'd said, as Mrs Bracebridge left. 'What's 'er after, any'ow? 'Er ay

81

even got any kids of 'er own.'

The hymn ended in a blast of sound. There was a moment of silence and stillness before everyone burst into talk and handshaking and offering Christmas wishes. The children filed away to change into their normal clothes. Evie felt a pang of anti-climax as she wriggled back into her old frock and pulled on her baggy cardigan.

'You all did a marvellous job!' Mrs Bracebridge swooped down on her as the other helpers and children were milling round. Her plain face beaming, she patted Gary and Carl on their heads cautiously, as if worried she might catch something. 'A very happy Christmas to you all!' she said. Then Evie, startled, found herself being taken, just for a moment, in Mrs Bracebridge's lavender-scented arms.

The children went home with presents. Gary and Carl had little metal cars – Carl was beside himself with excitement: 'Look Evie, look, mine's green!' – and Evie had a notebook with spongey paper and five tiny crayons: red, yellow, blue, green and black. Pleased, she pushed it into the pocket of her dress.

The three of them went out into the icy darkness, the church a bulky shadow behind them. They hurried along Hyde Road towards home. Carl was singing tunelessly to himself. There was a Christmas Eve feeling in the air, one of expectation, even though none of them had much to expect. But Evie kept hearing the words Mrs Bracebridge had said softly in her ear as she embraced her, words no one had ever said to her before: 'Bless you, my darling child.'

Ten

January 1955

The moment she set foot through the door from school, her mother was on her, seizing her by the hair and dragging her to the table.

'What's this? What've yow been saying to people, yow sneaking little rat?'

She yanked on Evie's hair so that her neck snapped back and Evie yelped at the pain, her scalp burning.

'Yes, you can put it on when you want! What've you been telling 'er, eh?' Another yank, then she let go and shoved Evie towards the oil-cloth-covered table and the sheet of pale blue paper that lay on it. 'What the bleeding 'ell is *that?*'

Evie felt panic waiting not far away. Usually now she was attuned to seeing things coming with Mom. Trying to slide her way out of any trouble before it happened. But this was something she'd not seen coming and she had no idea what it was.

She saw small, neat copperplate writing:

24 Clarendon Road
Edgbaston
Birmingham
2nd January, 1955

Dear Mrs Sutton,
I have had the pleasure of meeting your daughter

Eve at the Sunday school at St John's Church. Eve is a delightful child and has been a pleasure to teach and work with. However, I have become aware that your situation as a family is not an easy one and I am wondering whether I might offer a solution which may ease things.

My husband and I have not been blessed with children. Though this was not our choice we have come to believe it to be the will of Almighty God, who has, until now, freed us to do other good in the world. Mr Bracebridge and I have prayed at length before communicating with you and now we feel that the time is right to lay our offer before you in the hope that it will be accepted in the kindly spirit with which it is intended.

We would like to offer to adopt your daughter Eve and bring her up in our Christian home with all the love and comfort we have to offer a child, to care for her and educate her as we would have done a daughter of our own.

We realize that this is a decision of great weight for you and we do not expect an immediate answer. We do hope and pray, however, that you will give our offer, and all the advantages it would entail for Eve, due and favourable consideration.

With kind regards,
Mr Herbert and Mrs Mary Bracebridge

Evie read and reread the blue handwriting, at first unable to take in what it meant. Mrs Brace-bridge offering to *adopt* her? But what did that mean? She had scarcely any time to think at all before Mom was on her again, yanking her round to face her and bellowing into her face. Her breath stank of raw onion.

'Did yow put 'er up to this, yow lying, sneaking little bitch? What've yow been telling 'er, eh?'

'N-nothing,' Evie tried to say, which was the truth. She had never said a word to Mrs Bracebridge or anyone else about home – barely even to Gary. Gary seemed to understand without her having to, but how did Mrs Bracebridge know anything? 'I never said nothing.' She raised her hands to defend herself, waiting for blows to fall.

'So, yower own family ay good enough for yow, is that it? You wait til yower father sees this,' Irene raged at her. But Evie could hear worry in her voice as well.

Just then, Shirley came in from school. Evie caught sight of her face, seeing their mother planted in the middle of the room, hands on hips. There was a mixture of fear and smugness – Evie was the one getting it. Shirley slid in along the wall and disappeared upstairs.

'Right,' Mom said. 'I ay 'aving this. You come with me. We're gunna go and see that dried-up old bitch and put her right about a few things.'

'No! Mom, you can't!' Evie said, filled with horror at what her mother might come out with to genteel Mrs Bracebridge. 'Don't go down there ... please!'

'I'll do what I cowing want – and you're coming too.' She hoiked her brown and white coat on and dragged Evie outside by the arm. Evie was still wearing a grey coat that Mrs Bracebridge had given her. She half fell down the step as Mom yanked at her.

All the way, Evie felt her mother's iron grip on

85

the top of her left arm. She did not know where Clarendon Road was and didn't know if Mom had any idea either, but that didn't stop her. Mom wove along the street, cutting a swathe like a tank between neighbours and children. As they reached the end of the street, to Evie's horror they saw Mrs Charles turn the corner and begin walking towards them. She was carrying a bag and wore a neat, dark red pleated skirt and a short black coat.

'Ho, what're you cowing staring at, eh?' Mom bawled at her, despite the fact that Mrs Charles had not even looked in their direction.

Mrs Charles lowered her head even further, making a small hissing noise between her teeth, but said nothing. Mom wasn't satisfied with that.

'Don't yow go making your jungly noises at me!' she yelled as Mrs Charles receded behind them. 'Yow want to get back where you belong, sambo!'

This was just the beginning of an hour that made Evie feel she might actually die of shame. It was at least a relief when they left the part of Ladywood where they lived so that no one knew them. Her mother was walking with fast, furious strides, all the time gripping Evie's arm so that she was forced to break into a trot to keep up. It seemed a long way, along streets of houses she had never seen before. Mom ignored everyone who dared to look at them after Mrs Charles, but she kept muttering about 'bleeding nosey buggers' and people who had nothing else to do but poke into other people's business.

The dreaded moment came when they reached number twenty-four Clarendon Road. Evie prayed as she had never prayed before that no one would be in.

Her mother marched up to the door, ignored the brass knocker and hammered on it with her fist. Evie stood beside her because she had no choice. Her arm felt bruised and sore. She forced her head down as she heard the door open, unable to cope with the thought of seeing Mrs Bracebridge's bewildered face.

'Oh ... er, good afternoon,' she heard Mrs Bracebridge say, sounding flustered.

'I've got summat to say to you,' Evie heard Mom begin. She cringed. Inwardly, she was like a rabbit taking refuge down a long, dark burrow. She heard her mother begin to launch into a barrage of insults at Mrs Bracebridge – how dare she, who did she think she was... The insults swarmed and Mom's belting voice rang along the street, but after the first outburst Evie did not take in any of the words.

Eventually, when Mom had finished haranguing Mrs Bracebridge, she dragged on Evie's arm again and the words started to reach her at last.

'Come on, you, we're going 'ome. And you're not going near this interfering old cow anymore – ever. D'you 'ear?'

Only then did Evie raise her head, and she caught sight of Mrs Bracebridge standing at her door in a straight grey dress, her hands to her cheeks and wearing an expression of utter shock and anguish. Evie could barely take in what Mrs Bracebridge had been suggesting – adopt her? She wanted to give the woman comfort somehow but did not know how and Mom was already dragging her off along the street.

'That's the last time yower going to that cowing church,' her mother decreed as they began the route march home. 'These Holy bloody Joes, think they know it all... And you...' Her venom was directed at Evie now. 'A cowing disgrace, that's what you are.'

A cold feeling settled over Evie, a dry sense of inevitability that Mrs Bracebridge and Sunday school, the best things in her week, had now been taken away.

II

Eleven

November 1959

The bonfire was on the new patch of waste ground at the bottom of Inkerman Street, where the 'development' had begun. They had knocked down several blocks of terraces, leaving a raw, open space of rubble, old foundations and twisted wire which became a quagmire when it rained. The land was now an open cut-through, where kids played amid the broken glass and dog muck and learned about knocking things down. There was no sign of anything else being done except more demolition all over Ladywood. When, people wondered, was something constructive going to begin? What was the plan exactly? And if their houses were knocked down, where would they be re-housed?

Tonight, the open space came in handy for a bonfire. Wood was in short supply and everyone around had been storing old bits of scrap for weeks. Someone had brought in a couple of van loads of twigs and gorse from the countryside to use as kindling and there was a good pile of stuff to be burnt.

Evie could see the sparks already flying high into the darkness as she walked down Inkerman Street with Gary and Carl. The younger kids had been round shouting 'penny for the guy' and the white-

91

faced rag doll stuffed with sawdust lay slumped on top of the pile. The flames were already licking up round him when they arrived and his inked-in face seemed to wear a look of anguish.

People were turning out from all around, some with plates of food they had cooked at home. The delicious aromas of hot chestnuts, potatoes and sausages mingled with the smoke. Evie knew her mom and sisters were there somewhere but she stuck with Gary and kept away from them – especially as Rita was with Conn, the feller she reckoned she was going to marry and who Mom was rude to because he was a freckly ginger Irish lad. Conn seemed all right to Evie – and if he'd take Rita off their hands, that was a favour so far as she was concerned. Rita thought she was the most important person in the world now that she was *engaged*, even though there was no sign of a ring. Shirley did not seem to have a boyfriend, but there was a regular supply of lads sniffing round. Evie, still the one they picked on, the outcast, moved around her family, trying to please and avoid trouble and not expecting anything much.

But as the years passed and she grew, she began to experience new hungers and longings. She knew there was love somewhere in the world and she wanted it. In the coppery, flickering darkness, amid the shouts and shrieks of pleasure, she turned to look at Gary. Gary who had long been her friend, the one person she could always rely on in their struggling lives. Gary was seventeen now and she sixteen. He was nearly a head taller than her. He looked much the same except that he had filled out very slightly and had different specs, with dark frames, in the usual state of disrepair and held together with bits of sticking plaster or string. But his shirt was usually hanging out, his trousers baggy and worn and his hair too long and chopped unevenly round his face. There was something rather sagging about Gary, with his funny crab walk. He always looked as if he badly needed taking care of, which was the truth. But he was the one forever looking after Carl, who had grown into a sweet, lumbering bear of a boy.

Lately, Evie had found herself thinking about Gary – not just as the Gary she had always known, but as a boy, a *man*. Even though he was seventeen, it was startling to think of Gary as a man. He was still just as likely to trip over his own feet as not. All these years they had been mates, a refuge for each other when each of their families were of little use to them. And if there was one person in the world who could make her laugh through difficult times, it was Gary.

They had always knocked around together and sooner or later other lads had started to call out, 'That yer girlfriend, Ducky?'

The first time it had happened, when they were thirteen and fourteen, her eyes met Gary's and they both laughed. It all seemed silly. What were they on about? Gary was her mate. And so it had been, for ages. But as time passed, her feelings changed and she began to think, well, we've been together all this time, maybe that's where we belong. Gary was what she knew. She felt safe with him. What could be more obvious and natural? But Gary never seemed interested in her, not in that way. Other boys were keen on her and she was forever being told she was pretty. But they were never boys who she even liked or felt anything for in return. She felt safe with Gary. More and more she started to want Gary to be the one who wanted to go out with her. Her feelings now were all confusion.

Last summer, her first summer after leaving school, something had shifted and now, although they still saw each other, things often felt awkward. It had been a warm September evening and, as usual, she and Gary were hanging about together with not much to do. They had been at the Warings'. Whisky was a very old, white-muzzled dog now but still soft and loving. Mr Waring still had his chickens. They hardly ever went near the shelter now, with its odd memories and cold dampness.

But that evening, as they patted Whisky goodbye, Gary suddenly said, 'Shall us go to the shelter – have a look? Someone else might've took it over by now.' It felt like something for old time's sake, now they were older.

They never got as far as the shelter, though, because when they got into the back lane, deserted, with its walls and weeds, Gary stopped, halfway along, all in a rush.

'Evie ... hang on a minute, will yer?'

She paused, slightly ahead of him, and turned round. She was wearing a mauve cotton frock with a white collar and a belt. It was a little tight on her – her curvaceous body was developing so fast now – and suddenly she saw him looking at her in an odd, intense way, as if taking in what she actually looked like, standing there before him in the hazy evening. She felt naked suddenly, as if every line of her body was enlarged. Her bosoms had grown and were pushing at the fabric of the dress; her hips were wide, her thighs generous. She had feelings now, that her body ought to be *wanted,* though she hardly knew what she felt. And him looking at her like that didn't feel bad. It felt ... exciting.

'What?' she said, and it came out sounding cross because she was embarrassed and unsure.

'I...' Gary swallowed and she sensed, rather than saw, his Adam's apple go up and down. 'C-can I ... I mean.' He was wringing his hands. With brusque assertion he said, 'We ought to have a kiss, that's what.'

They just stood there for a few seconds, both of them astonished by this development. Stiffly, they walked into each other's arms. It was the most awkward thing. Gary was bony and tense against her, and tremulous as a new-born chick. Evie felt suddenly motherly, as if she was much older than him. They fumbled for each other's lips and pushed a bit with their tongues. She felt Gary move his hand up and down her back.

He stepped away, looking down at the ground.

Was that it? Evie thought. She felt a twinging ache at the side of her breasts. Was that what all the fuss was about? There must be more to answer this yearning she felt. Had they got it all wrong? Things felt unfinished. But she knew then, and had felt since, that it was the being wanted that mattered more than what actually happened. That was how it seemed to her. Rita was wanted by

Conn and it seemed to mean everything.

It took Gary a moment before he could look up at her and his cheeks were flushed pink. He shrugged. 'So that's it then.'

'Is it?' she said. And laughed. They both did.

And they had not kissed since. Now, walking beside Gary in the darkness, with Carl in tow as usual, clumping along behind, she started to feel put out and resentful. After the kiss – was that really a kiss? – Gary had seemed to avoid her. Then things had eased somehow and they often had a chat, but she didn't know where they were with each other anymore.

All Gary could talk about nowadays was some bloke he'd met who came into the garage where he was now working as a mechanic in Ryland Road. A bloke called Pete. Pete was a Ted and Evie was already sick to the back teeth of hearing about him. Pete's record collection, Pete's bike, Pete this, Pete that. And now Gary was starting to dress like a Teddy Boy as well. He had bought himself a pair of drainpipe trousers – too short in the leg, of course, being Gary.

'I'm gunna save up for a waistcoat next,' he said as they walked along. The trousers looked ridiculous because they made his skinny legs look even thinner but he swaggered along seeming mighty pleased with them.

Evie rolled her eyes.

'You could dress like a Ted,' Gary enthused. 'There's girls do – 'ave yer seen 'em?'

'I don't want to,' Evie said grumpily. 'And anyway, it's all stale cakes, that – it's been about for years.'

'No it ain't! It's just changing a bit – more American stuff. Pete says he thinks it's a better thing – not just looking backwards like the old-style Teds.'

As if I give a monkeys what Pete thinks, she wanted to retort, but instead, she said, 'I just don't think it's me, that's all. Shall we get a hot spud?'

'Taters – and toffee apples!' Carl cried. He was twelve now and still in many ways like a little child. As loveable as one too – he still sometimes wanted to hold hands. Evie felt as if he was her little brother as well.

There were potatoes cooked in the fire, hot chestnuts. Evie bought toffee apples and she gave one each to Gary and Carl.

'Ta,' Gary said, without much enthusiasm, but Carl said, 'Ta, Evie!' and beamed.

They stood amid the crowd, the flames gilding the sky and lighting up the wrecked shells of houses, broken brick walls and bits of painted surface or wallpaper. The fire was in full spate now, crackling and roaring, sparks whirling up-wards. Evie could feel the heat of it on her face. A nice smell came off the burning twigs. Something cracked in the fire, like a shot, and they all jumped and 'oohed'. Somewhere in the distance, at the edge of the wasteland, someone was playing a piano and people joined in singing old hits from their youth – 'Daisy, Daisy' and 'Knees up Mother Brown'. Gary muttered something about didn't they know any better songs. He was all 'Rock Around the Clock'. Evie knew this was because of Pete and so immediately she said that she liked the old songs. People started to let off rockets and jumping Jacks, kids screaming and jumping out of the way. Carl gasped when there were bangs but someone handed him a sparkler and he was enraptured, drawing loops of snowflake light on the dark.

Evie pulled her coat round her, wishing she had better shoes. Hers were thin on the bottom, and the cold seeped through. But the chill went deeper than that. She felt as if Gary was so far away from her, as if not her friend anymore. She felt so lonely, after all the years of him being her pal, like a devoted puppy, that she reached out suddenly to take hold of his hand. It was thin and cold and she wrapped hers around it.

Gary turned to her, surprised. He smiled, but it was a strange, awkward smile and Evie felt she had done something wrong. It made her feel worse and she let go, looking ahead of her, not facing him.

A few minutes later, she heard Carl, through a mouthful of toffee apple, pipe up, excited.

'Gary! Look, it's Pete!'

Quite close to them, the shadows moving on his face, she saw Gary's new best friend moving towards them. He was a tall, slender boy with dark hair, deep-set eyes and a long, pale face. He was dressed in his full Ted outfit, the drainpipes and jacket, and he kept his hands in his trouser pockets, moving with a masculine swagger of his hips, elbows jutting as he slipped through the crowd, like a snake, Evie thought.

Something in her had rebelled against Pete the moment she met him, a couple of months back. He had never been actively unpleasant to her, but acted more as if she was not there at all. There was something about the way he could not meet her eye, something closed and secretive that always made her feel shut out. When he was there, she felt miles away from Gary, as if he and Pete had a secret male understanding from which she was excluded. She had never felt this before with Gary, despite all his brothers and all the other boys around. He had just been her mate, just Gary.

Something had happened to Gary. She could sense a pulsing excitement in him whenever Pete appeared and it aggravated her beyond words. Anyone would think Pete was God, she thought sourly. She just couldn't see what it was. All right, so he was a Ted – it wasn't as if there weren't plenty of others about. He didn't seem especially interesting or funny or exciting. Why the hero worship? And come to that, what on earth did Pete see in Gary? Did he just need someone to worship him?

'Pete! Over 'ere!' Gary hailed him.

Pete's sinuous walk brought him over to them.

'All right, mate?' Gary asked, in his warm, sweet way. She could see how excited he was that Pete had come. Pete lived somewhere in Edgbaston.

'Yup.' Pete nodded back, then nodded abruptly to Evie and Carl. He drew a packet of cigarettes out of his pocket and lit up, offering Gary one but none of the rest of them, Evie noticed. She felt even more cross, even though she didn't want one. Not off him, anyway. He drew on the fag with short, nervous puffs, not meeting anyone's eye.

'Where you been then?' Gary was saying.

'Just ... you know, about,' Pete said mysteriously.

99

He stared ahead of him. Already Evie felt invisible, as if she didn't count.

'D'you want to come and get a tater?' she whispered to Carl.

Carl nodded, always one for food if it was on offer.

In the firelight they watched the potato lady put salt and a knob of butter on the potatoes, which smelt delicious.

'There yer go, bab,' she smiled, handing it to Carl. Everyone was sweet to Carl; you couldn't not be.

'I wanna go back and see Gary now, and Pete,' Carl said, and he hurried away, not looking back to see if she was following.

'Charming,' Evie muttered. She was about to follow when she thought, what's the point? I'm not wanted in *that* department. Most of the fireworks had been let off by now anyway.

She drifted away, feeling more desolate than she could even understand. There was nowhere else to go, even though this was her night off work. She'd best just go home.

Twelve

She was working at the Tower Ballroom, by Edgbaston Reservoir. She had had other jobs – at a factory, and a shop. She liked walking to the 'rezza' for work, into Edgbaston and past the sooty brick stack of Perrott's Folly. At her school, Follett

100

Osler, they had told her that Abraham Follett Osler had been a glass maker in Broad Street, but that he was also keen on clocks and on weather forecasting. He had started using the folly tower as a weather observatory. Someone else, at work, told her that the Ballroom had once been a skating rink, before it became a favourite for dances and other sorts of entertainment. For the first time Evie had more of a sense of the wider city and a glimpse of history.

She worked in one of the kiosks in the foyer, selling tickets. When she arrived for an evening shift on these winter nights, it was nice to see the welcoming lights, reflecting in the water of the reservoir. She liked working evenings – it kept her out of the house when Mom and Dad were there. And she came across a lot of different people – it was lively and sociable.

On dance nights people queued outside, togged up in their finery. There was a happy atmosphere of letting off steam and having fun. Evie saw plenty of people but she didn't have to spend too much time with any of them and that suited her. Her pretty, strong-boned face with its Cupid's bow lips and her golden hair, falling long and thick on her shoulders, were all an asset. She enjoyed using them to charm people – people who would be gone in a few seconds. It was easy. She could smile, sell them the tickets, wish them a good evening and move on to the next one in the queue.

Tonight was her Saturday shift and she was feeling blue. She looked nice, she knew, in neat court shoes and a black and white dress in zigzag stripes that hugged her curves. She smiled, selling tickets to happy couples in their party outfits and dancing shoes, tapping her foot to the music from the Ballroom as the customers jigged and laughed. But as the music floated through the foyer, she ached with loneliness. She wanted to avoid everybody; but she also wanted desperately to get close to someone. A special someone. Everyone else seemed to have someone.

A gaggle of lads came in a bit later, all older than she was and wanting to pick up girls. They chatted to her in loud, forceful voices. They told her she was gorgeous, begged her to come and dance.

'I'm not allowed,' she said, forcing a smile. 'I've got to stay here.' And crawled back into her shell, hardly meeting their eyes. They didn't really mean it, she knew. No one really wanted or liked her – they only pretended. Like Gary.

Even Mrs Bracebridge, who had asked for her all those years ago, had not put up any sort of a fight for her – that was how Evie saw it. Mom had been outraged over Mary Bracebridge and had banned Evie from ever going to the Sunday school again. For the best part of a year, Evie didn't see Mrs Bracebridge and didn't go near St John's. Because she wasn't going, Gary never went either. Then there came a point when she knew Mom didn't care what she did as long as she was out of her hair. Mom wouldn't notice if she went back there, would she?

She and Gary returned one Sunday but it was not the same. There was hardly anyone she recognized. Mrs Bracebridge greeted her kindly, but she was distant, as if Evie was someone she barely knew, like all the others. Evie no longer felt special or cared for and the hurt of this would have cut deep into her, had she let it. But she didn't. Everyone rejected you in the end. So what? Mrs Bracebridge was just a silly old woman. She never went back.

This Saturday, two days after bonfire night, she did her work feeling low and shut into herself. She was the youngest of the girls working in the kiosks and sometimes she had a laugh with the others, but not tonight.

'Cat got yer tongue, Evie?' the woman next to her called across during a lull. 'What's up with you?'

'Nothing,' Evie said. She looked away. Why couldn't people leave her alone?

She was trying not to think about Gary. About how angry she was with him. What was so flaming special about Pete? Why had Gary kissed her that time? She was full of confusion. OK, so he was really into Pete, Pete was his new best friend, or so it seemed. But why should that stop him having a girlfriend as well? It wasn't like Gary to be mean but it felt as if that was what he was being. Mean and stupid.

A swell of music rose from the Ballroom, then stopped amid clapping, cheering and catcalls, and she imagined all the couples in there, wrapped round each other amid the smells of sweat and perfume, all having a good time. She thought of Rita with Conn. Mom was coming round to the idea of Conn now they were actually engaged. And Shirley had grown up into a real looker with her sculpted cheekbones and dark eyes like Dad's.

Shirley had no shortage of male admirers.

Evie chucked a handful of change into the till and slammed it shut. Sod everyone. Sod Gary too. What good would he ever be to her anyway? He could hardly dress himself without making a mess of it. It was no good ever trusting anyone. You were better off on your own.

All the same, she still wanted to see Gary. Home was empty of any kind of sympathy. Her father still caressed and lashed out at them alternately and unpredictably, whether drunk or sober. Mom she still tried to please, to keep the peace, still hoping that one miraculous day Mom might actually like her, say something nice to her and claim her as a daughter.

But whenever Mom got it into her head, rightly or wrongly, that Dad was playing away, it brought back the whole business with Nancy and her boy and that, of course, was Evie's curse. She had been born a girl. She was the cause of all Mom's ills and resentments. She could never do anything right. And Rita and Shirley had been schooled to push Evie out too. It never seemed to change.

Since Mom had started working at Bulpitt's making kettles, she had gained not only a whole new set of people to fall out with as well as the neighbours, but some money of her own so that she was always dressed up to the nines. She was damned if Ray was getting his hands on her money. She dyed her hair with peroxide every week, spent Saturday afternoons scouring the Rag Market for bargains and varnished her nails bright scarlet. She had gained weight as she reached her late thirties and was an even more massive, forbidding and brassily glamorous matron. Dad could still scrub up when he put his mind to it and people said, when they were together, that they looked like a pair of film stars. Marilyn Monroe and Clark Gable!

Evie sometimes felt proud of them, when they were dressed up. Proud but sad. Yes, they looked a picture, but she would rather have had them drab and kind like Mr and Mrs Waring any day.

As Christmas came closer, they decorated the Ballroom with streamers, tinsel and holly and the place felt very festive for all the parties and dances. Evie dreaded Christmas more each year. There was nothing good to expect from it and it meant being shut in with her family, who went further out of their way to be mean to her the more time they spent together. She envied other people their excitement. She found herself wishing that the Ballroom was open on Christmas Day, to give her an excuse to be away.

And then, a few days before Christmas, when Evie was at work, along with a lorry load of drinks being delivered to the bar, in came someone tall, with wavy brown hair and large brown eyes, who appeared in the foyer seeming uncertain. He looked across at her and hurried in her direction.

Thirteen

He came loping towards her, holding a sheet of paper. He had to stoop to speak into the kiosk and she saw a long face, lightly freckled, with a bewildered expression.

'Er...' He seemed shy and his cheeks went pink. 'I'm looking for the office.'

Evie smiled, amused by how flustered he seemed. She saw how nice his hair was – thick and clean – and he was well spoken. He looked so wholesome and somehow innocent that she immediately felt that he was different from her, almost foreign.

'Over there.' She pointed.

He turned, obviously feeling silly for not having seen the right way to go in the first place. 'Oh ... yeah. Thanks.'

She watched him moving away, long legs in grey trousers, long, thin arms. Something about him appealed to her. He looked defenceless, like a baby bird, even though he was handsome and moved quite gracefully. But then she was distracted by someone carrying in a crate of bottles and forgot about him.

But he appeared again the next day, without the piece of paper, after his working hours must have finished. There was a wrestling match on in the Ballroom and a rowdy queue had already formed for tickets. As she was serving a customer, Evie became aware of the boy at the back of her line. She glanced at him and away, annoyed to feel her own cheeks flaming pink. She guessed he had come to see her. He didn't look like someone who would come to see the wrestling.

Soon he was second in line.

'Ta. Have a nice evening,' she said to the middle-aged couple at the front of the queue, both wearing thick winter coats. The woman looked oddly excited at the prospect of watching wrestling, Evie thought. Maybe it was the idea of seeing men with not much on. Her eyes followed them away from the kiosk. Her shyness, her sense that the boy was somehow different from her made her want to seem aloof and pretend she had not seen him. At last she had to look.

'Hello,' he said earnestly. There was something sweet and decent about him. It was impossible not to like him.

'You were here yesterday,' she said briskly. 'Forget something, did you?'

'No,' he said. 'I...' The impossibility of what he had to say seemed to overwhelm him. He was also under pressure from people queueing behind. 'I, um... Well, I came back because I wanted to know...' He wrung his hands. 'I wanted to ask ... if you'd come out ... with me, I mean. Er ... for a drink?' He looked down then, seeming mortified.

'Tonight?' she said. She was pleased but was not going to show it. 'Can't, can I? I'm here, working. As you can see.'

'Yes,' he said foolishly. 'I mean ... later? Or another day? I just thought... I just wanted to get to talk to you.'

This was so disarming and he looked so embarrassed that she relented.

'I'm off tomorrow. What about then?'

He brightened. 'Would you? I don't live all that far away. We could go into town – or somewhere,' he added quickly, obviously wanting to please. 'Where do you live?'

'Oh, quite a way away,' she said. The lad looked a bit genteel for Inkerman Street. 'Look, why don't we just meet outside here?'

'All right. Six o'clock?' A smile played at the corners of his lips, waiting to break out. 'What's your name?'

'Evie. Sutton.'

'Evie,' he repeated, and walked away, looking like someone who has just rubbed a lamp and something wonderful has jumped out of it. He didn't think to tell her his own name.

It was cold out the next night, everything blurred by fog. At the furthest reach of the Ballroom's lights, she saw someone standing looking out across the water. So, he had come. She had wondered, nervously, if he would. But now, walking out and seeing him, Evie felt a sense of defeat. He was a nice lad – too nice for her. Why was she bothering going anywhere with him? She stuck her hands in her pockets and her head down, feeling almost sulky as she walked towards him.

''Ello.' She sounded grumpy, a bit resentful, but he didn't seem to notice.

'Oh Evie!' he said, turning. 'You came!'

His apparent astonishment made her relent and smile. 'Said I would, didn' I? What's your name, anyway? You never said.'

'Didn't I? Oh dear. I'm Ken Heaton.' He thrust a long-fingered hand at her and she took it and shook it, even more amused.

'You're a funny one,' she said.

'Am I?' He stared down at her through the gloom, then, good mannered, seemed to gather himself. 'A drink then?'

They walked a few streets, then found a seat, pressed in at the back of a pub, amid the fug of bodies and beer, but glad of the warmth.

'So ... you work for the brewery?' she asked, when he had bought drinks – Dubonnet and lemonade for her and a half of ale for him. She eyed his drink. 'A half? Don't drink much, do you?'

'Oh ... no.' He sat with one elbow on the table. 'Drinking at all is a sin in our household. My mother and father are strict Methodists. They're horrified that I'm working for Ansell's. But it's not forever. I'm just trying to think what to do. I'm their only son – well, only anything. No sisters either.' He took a sip of his drink and a thin line of white remained on his upper lip which made him look foolish and disarmed her. A cheer went up from the crowd at the dartboard across the room and they both glanced in that direction, then looked at each other and smiled.

'What do they think you should do then?' she asked, trying to get the measure of him. He was out of a different bracket from her, she could see. She wasn't sure how to talk to him.

He sipped again, swallowed. He was drinking fast and she could see it was nerves and this made her feel a bit better.

'Oh ... what *they* really want is for me to be a minister.'

'What, like a vicar?' She had never known a single person with an ambition like that before.

'Yes. I'd most likely be a lay preacher first, then go on to be–'

'A what?' she interrupted.

'Lay preacher. You go round the circuit preaching, but you're not a minister.'

Her bafflement deepened. 'What's a circuit?' She thought it must be something like a dog track.

His face creased into an attractive smile. Something softened in her a fraction.

'It's just a group of churches. Look, it doesn't matter, 'cause I'm not going to do it anyway. Church is all right, you know. There're some nice people. But not day in, day out... What I'd really like is to be a farmer.'

'A farmer?' She started laughing. 'What, in the middle of Birmingham? How're you going to do that?'

Ken picked up his drink, shaking his head. 'I've no blooming idea really. Well, actually I do – you have to go to an agricultural...'

As he was speaking, the band, who had been greeted by cheers as they came in, started up. There were five lads, a skiffle band with guitars and one of them banging on a box, starting off with the *Six-Five Special* song.

Ken beamed, seeming delighted, and they both jigged along for a while. He leaned close to her ear and shouted, 'No washboard!'

Evie smiled. The skiffle bands played on all sorts

of homemade stuff. They listened to a couple of numbers. They were good – full of energy. The pub was filling up even more. Again, Ken leaned closer.

'Shall we make a move? Can't hear a word in here.'

He helped her into her coat like a gentleman and when they were out in the foggy darkness, he said, 'I'd best not keep you out too long. I s'pose they're expecting you home?'

Evie made a non-committal sound and Ken stopped. They were near a street light and she could see an intent look on his face.

'I've hardly found out anything about you. Tell me, Evie, about your family. Have you got brothers and sisters? What are they like?'

'I've two sisters,' she said, tightening inside. She didn't want her family anywhere near Ken. She didn't know what *she* was doing anywhere near Ken.

'And?' he laughed at her clam-like communication.

'Well, they're older than me. And I've got a mom and dad.'

'Where does your father work – as we're exchanging information? Mine's in an engineering firm – office work, though, accounts and such.'

'Oh ... Docker's,' she said, adding vaguely, 'Paint factory.' Dad was on deliveries now, driving the trucks, but she didn't say so. She wanted Ken to imagine him as something a bit higher up in the pecking order.

'You must come and meet mine one day,' he said, then added, as if he'd been too forward,

'Sorry, Evie ... we've only just met.' He stepped closer and, daringly, put his hands on her shoulders. She realized, with a wave of need, that she wanted him to kiss her, as if to undo that kiss of Gary's which had meant nothing.

'Only...' He looked down into her eyes from his gangly height, sweet and intense. 'I just think you're smashing! I really do. You're the prettiest girl I've ever seen and... I really want to see you again. When can we get together?'

She felt carried away on his enthusiasm. He was so safe and innocent and kind. And being wanted, being adored like this, was so alluring. A wash of warmth and affection for him went through her. She liked the way his long face looked when he smiled – happy and foolish at the same time. And all he seemed to want was to gaze at her.

'I'm working tomorrow,' she said. It would be Christmas Eve.

Ken put his head back and sighed. 'Oh, and then it'll be Christmas, and then Boxing Day! Oh, I don't know if I can stand it. Aunties and uncles... We'll have to wait 'til it's all over, I suppose.' He looked down at her again. 'But knowing you're there – that'll make it all right.'

Evie looked steadily back at him. She felt unsatisfied. They both got stuck for a moment and then she said, 'You gunna kiss me then?'

'What now? Already?' Ken looked surprised, seemed flustered for a moment. 'Well ... yeah! If that's all right.'

'Not here,' she said. 'Too many people.' There were revellers coming in and out of the pubs. 'I'll show you.' She felt excited and in command, leading him towards Ladywood as he'd said he'd walk her home, taking his hand as they wandered through the foggy streets. Before they reached Inkerman Street, she pulled him gently into an entry and soon they were locked in each other's arms, lips pressed together.

'Oh Evie!' Ken exclaimed when they finally parted and walked on. He sounded drunk, much more than half a pint of bitter would warrant. 'Oh my! You're just... I'm seeing stars!'

Evie giggled, but felt deeply gratified. Kissing Ken had been so much nicer than kissing Gary. Ken held her close in his long, gentle arms and his lips were soft and tasted of beer. He kissed her in a lingering, tender way which made her feel something she had seldom ever felt before – honoured and cared for and precious. She was reeling even more than he was, she thought, but she could think of nothing to say.

This was life. How things were meant to be.

At the end of the street she said, 'We're nearly there – I live a bit further up. You might as well go back now.'

'Oh Evie,' Ken said adoringly. 'D'you know, the moment I saw you, when I walked into the Tower, I thought, that girl is for me. You're so beautiful,' he added earnestly. 'Beautiful in body and mind.'

'Thanks,' she said, though wondering how Ken thought he knew anything about her mind. She didn't know what else to say back. 'See you soon. Sat'dy?'

'I'll be willing the time away,' he said. She knew he was still watching her as she walked away and his gaze felt like a caress.

Fourteen

January 1960

Ken stood at the corner of Inkerman Street, blowing a kiss along the road towards her.

Evie paused outside number twenty-nine and waved. Someone blowing her kisses – what a thing! She was astonished by Ken's devotion to her. Though everyone said she was pretty and she was softly spoken and tried to speak nicely the way Mrs Bracebridge had taught her, she never felt as if she was an attractive person. She always felt bad inside. In a way she didn't believe in his love. Everything about it felt unreal, her walking out with this sweet, gentle boy. She wasn't good enough for him and she was convinced that one day he would realize it.

As soon as Christmas was over Ken had turned up at work and wanted to see her every moment possible. They had already been out for a few more drinks and Ken was waiting for her to have a whole Saturday off.

'Then we can go somewhere, can't we? Into town, or out somewhere nice.'

She kept waiting for it all to go wrong, for him to see the bad in her. He couldn't really want to be with her. But they'd been out to the pictures – Ken adored Westerns – and for a few drinks and she had enjoyed it. Ken seemed to adore her and

114

being adored was a heady novelty. As she walked into the house that evening, she forgot to wipe the smile off her face quickly enough.

They were all there, round the table with the fire going and a proper fug up of sweat and beer and fags – Mom and Dad, with Shirley at one end of the settle. Next to her were Rita and skinny Conn, ginger-haired, pale as a fish, forever under Rita's thumb.

Mom was in her finery – a scarlet dress, red lipstick and nails to match. Rita and Shirley each had their best dresses on, Rita in yellow and black stripes. Just right for her, Evie thought – like a wasp. Shirley looked classier, in a moss-green dress, her dark locks curving down round each side of her face. She sat with her cheek resting on one arm, looking down at the table, and only raised her eyes to look at Evie. Shirley was good at being quiet and mysterious. The real mystery, Evie thought, was why, of the two of them, it was Rita who had a steady boyfriend.

They all turned to stare at her, except her father, who was knocking back his beer from a glass he must have walked off with from the pub. It felt as if their eyes were scraping over her. She could feel them, as always, waiting to get at her in some way.

'Where you been then, eh?' Rita demanded, smirking at Conn. 'Dirty stop-out!'

'Just out,' Evie said, avoiding her eye. 'With a mate from work.' Although she had been out with Ken quite a few times since Christmas, she had not breathed a word about him. She had invented a girlfriend who she was suddenly pally with instead.

Evie thanked God she hadn't brought Ken back with her. What would he think of this place – the smell, the litter of cups and crumbs and fag ends on the table? His own mom and dad sounded prim and proper, all kippers and curtains and embroidered tablecloths, no doubt.

'Oh, a mate again, eh?' Rita went on in her spiteful way, finding anything she could seize on. Rita would pick a fight with her own shadow and Evie usually took the place of that shadow, however much she didn't rise to the bait. 'And who might *that* be then?'

Evie perched on the bottom step of the stairs to slip off her work shoes. They were black court shoes, nothing fancy, but the best she had to keep the cold out. Even so, her feet were blocks of ice. She rubbed them, feeling the tingle of a new chilblain, trying to ignore Rita. Her father, who had been splayed in his chair, sat up abruptly and gave a rasping belch. Everyone sniggered.

'Don't cowing laugh at me!' he said, but could not be bothered to make an issue of it and sank back again.

'Cat got yer tongue, has it? Rita was still on at her. 'Who d'yer go out with?'

'Babs,' Evie lied, not even knowing anyone called Babs. She wanted to tell Rita to mind her own sodding business but it wouldn't make things any better, especially in front of Conn. Rita always showed off more when he was there. And what a prat he was, Evie thought. He must get a thrill out of being bossed around.

'Oh, *Babs!*' Rita cried mockingly, looking at Conn and waiting for him to join in with the laughter. Shirley was giving her a sly smile. 'Who's Babs then? You frightened to bring 'er home, are yer? 'Fraid of what we might say to 'er? 'Ere, you ain't one of them lezzies, are yer, Evie?' She roared with laughter at her own joke and Mom and Shirley joined in.

Mom gave a belly laugh but added, 'Don't be stupid, Reet.' She sobered for a second. 'How d'yow know words like that? We ay got any of that, not in our family.'

'Leave 'er, Reet,' Conn said, feeble as usual.

'What d'yer mean, leave 'er?' Rita snapped. 'Whose sister is she anyway? Don't you tell me to leave 'er.'

Conn subsided, folding his long arms across his skinny chest in its bright blue jersey.

'Don't you tell me to leave my own sister!' Rita pulled herself bolt upright, the wasp attacking now, wanting the one-sided fight to go on.

'I never,' Conn protested, even more limply.

'Shurrit, the pair of yer,' Mom said, leaning forward to fill up her cup with ale. Her feet, in stockings, bulged out of her red shoes. Evie badly wanted a cup of tea but did not wish to draw attention to herself. The teapot was probably cold by now – they had moved on to the beer. So she knew the only way she could get one. She'd have to play servant – as usual.

'Anyone want a cuppa?' she asked, moving over to fill the kettle.

'A lezzy cuppa!' Rita snorted and then laughed loudly at her own joke.

'Shut it, Reet,' their father put in.

'We oughta have a telly,' Mom said. 'When're

we gunna get a telly, Ray?'

Dad grunted, making no commitment.

'Go on, when are we?' Mom persisted.

'Don't need a cowing telly, yer daft cow.' Evie saw her father give one of his sudden grins of charm. 'Yer got me to look at, ain't yer?'

'Huh,' Mom snorted. 'Yow'm like the back of a bleeding bus.'

'Go on, Dad!' Rita nagged. 'Go on, get us a telly. You never get us anything. I wanna watch *Opportunity Knocks*. And *everyone* else's got one...'

'No they ain't.' Dad bestirred himself to sit straight again to contradict her, then flopped back as if worn out by this exertion.

Another ding-dong ensued. Evie quietly made the tea, relieved that this had distracted them from her. She stood by the stove thinking about Ken and the look in his eyes when he had kissed her goodbye. Her lips tingled with the kiss. It was nothing like that kiss she had had with Gary, so awkward and... It had not felt right at all. A pang went through her. Ken was lovely, he really was. But she was still hurt by Gary and she missed him.

She saw Gary now and again, but usually only by chance. And then he was usually with Pete.

The Knight family muddled on from year to year. The oldest boy, David, was married and lived not far away with his wife and two daughters. The second boy, Tony, who was nineteen, had disappeared a couple of years back, saying he was going to Liverpool, and nothing had been heard since. Everyone said he must have gone to sea. The others muddled on, leaving school and getting work in local factories. Frankie, fourteen, was the next one due to leave.

Gary had told Evie that he met Pete when he came to the garage to get his motorbike fixed. He lived in Edgbaston, and the pair of them could often be seen roaring round the neighbourhood, Gary riding pillion behind Pete, whose face was always stern and tense looking, his arms braced as they slewed round corners. Evie had never once seen Pete smile.

She had not put two and two together, not by then, even though there was gossip and speculation.

'What's that lad want with our Gary? Posh lad like him?'

Gary, at seventeen, still looked young for his age even though he was tall. There was something defenceless and childlike about him even now. Pete must be eighteen, Evie guessed.

She'd come across them a few times in the neighbourhood, not on the bike, but going along the road. Pete, in his Ted clothes, quiff of hair, drainpipes and jacket, striped tie and tiepin. He walked with a loose-limbed strut, one hand in his jacket pocket, the other with a fag wafting round. And Gary copied him like a spaniel – the fags, the clothes, which never looked anything like as smooth on him because Gary, crab walking along as ever, just wasn't smooth.

He would greet her cheerfully, trailing smoke as he waved.

'All right, are yer, Evie!'

'All right, Gary,' she'd say. They'd stop now and then but couldn't seem to get further than 'How's

119

the family? How's Carly?' these days. She'd tried talking to Pete but he seemed snooty and he couldn't meet your eye. What did he want with Gary? She had to admit, he was nice looking, or would have been if he wasn't forever scowling, but he couldn't find anything to say to her and she soon gave up trying.

If that was what Gary wanted, well, that was that. And he did look happy, she thought, hurt at this realization. He had always been a laugh, Gary had, managing to find the funny side of things. But now she could see something new in him. He stood taller, walked differently, with more confidence. He looked more like a man.

Fifteen

Over those first weeks of walking out with Ken, Evie slowly gave in to the idea that he actually wanted to be with her. He was with her every moment he could be. Often she stepped out of work at the Tower Ballroom quite late but still found him waiting outside, wanting to walk her home.

'You don't have to stand out in the cold for me!' she said sometimes. But Ken insisted there was nowhere on earth he would prefer to be.

'Why d'you like me?' she asked him one night. She was not fishing for compliments, just baffled by him seeing anything in her.

'Why?' They were walking along in the dark, his

arm around her. 'Well … 'cause you're pretty and … oh, I don't know.' He squeezed her shoulders. 'I just do. You're everything a girl should be, that's why.'

'That's what you think,' she said, elbowing him playfully. Suddenly, full of devilment, she broke away from him and ran off down the street. 'Catch me then!'

She couldn't run fast in her work shoes and Ken was soon upon her.

'See?' he said, pinning her by the arms.

'See what?'

'That's why I like you. 'Cause you're full of life.'

And she did feel full of life. She felt herself blossoming with Ken, falling for him despite feeling that it was all a dream and could not last. His sweet devotion was gradually breaking through to her. He kept looking at her as if she was a miracle, sang songs to her – *why am I so starry-eyed?* – as he gazed deep into her eyes.

'When can I see you again?' was always the question he asked when they parted, after a visit to the pictures, when they'd sat holding hands in the Lyric or the old 'Ledsam' in Ladywood in front of a weepy – Ken didn't mind weepies as Evie was sure some boys would – or one of his Westerns. Whenever they were galloping about on the horses he couldn't keep still and kept jiggling in his seat until she nudged him and mouthed, 'Stop it!', grinning at him. He longed to ride a horse, to own a horse. Ken seemed to have been born in the wrong place. His dream, strange as it seemed to her, was to go to agricultural college and live on a farm.

'It's just what I've always wanted,' he told her one night, over another drink. 'Mom and Dad aren't keen either, but they say that if I still want to go after I've held down a "normal" job, as Dad calls it, for a couple of years, they'll help me – once I've turned eighteen.'

'Oh.' Evie couldn't imagine this. 'Where would you go?'

'I dunno yet,' Ken said. 'I'll have to look into it.' He pushed his hair out of his eyes and gave a lopsided smile. 'I s'pose I should get on with finding out. Mom always says I'm one to let the grass grow under my feet.' He grinned. 'I s'pose that's what farmers do!'

Evie found herself hoping that the grass would grow long. Surely if Ken went to college he'd go away from her and never come back? Already that felt unbearable.

They tried going dancing at the Tower, on one of her evenings off, but Evie didn't have much experience of dancing herself and Ken was hopeless. They stood in the crowd of Rock Around the Clockers and Ken attempted to do the moves with such a grim expression of concentration and such a hopeless result that soon Evie was in fits of laughter.

'Come on,' she shouted, pulling him to the edge of the jostling, sweating crowd. 'Let's have a drink instead.'

'Sorry.' Ken was very downcast. He looked down at himself despairingly. 'I think my arms and legs are longer than they were meant to be. I've no coordination.'

'Never mind,' Evie said. And she really didn't

mind. She preferred times when she and Ken were alone, when he held her close and they kissed and he whispered sweet things to her. *You're my baby, you are...*

One night, as they stood kissing goodnight in the winter shadows of Inkerman Street, Ken drew back from her a moment and said in a rush, 'Oh Evie. I think I love you. I *know* I do.' His voice was full of feeling and she felt a fizzing explosion inside her of amazement and happiness. He loved her! For the first time in her life someone loved her and had said so!

'I love you too,' she said solemnly, hardly knowing what it meant, but it felt so exciting to be able to say it. It felt as if life had begun at last.

And now she was hooked on Ken, on love. She could not get enough of sitting close to him, of cuddles and kisses and laughter – anywhere they could find. As the spring came and the evenings lightened, they walked until they could find a park – the reservoir was a favourite and Summerfield Park if they had time. All she wanted was Ken, him and no one else, his arm round her as they walked under the trees, him pointing out birds and squirrels. He knew the names of all the birds. And kissing her, wanting her and her alone. It was bliss.

But inevitably they could not stay in their own world together forever.

'I want you to come and meet my mom and dad,' Ken said, when they had been walking out for a couple of months.

'Not yet,' she begged him. She had a terrible fear that Ken's parents would think she was not good enough for their son.

'They won't bite, you know,' Ken said, guessing her fears. 'They're very nice. They take everyone as they are. And when you come down to it, I'm no great shakes myself. They'd have liked me to go to the grammar school, but I made a mess of the eleven plus.' He rolled his eyes but she could see he minded. 'I think they thought I'd be a doctor or something brainy like that – fat chance!'

Evie laughed, pleased that Ken had not got into the grammar school otherwise she probably would not have met him.

'Anyway, apart from that I want you to meet Molly.'

Molly was Ken's dog. A cocker spaniel, he had told her. Brown, with the softest of ears. Evie was much more keen to meet Molly than Mr and Mrs Heaton.

He kept asking her about her own family, but the thought of Ken, Mom and Dad all in the same room filled her with horror and shame. She could already imagine the snide remarks Rita would make and how rude Mom would be. It would be like throwing Ken into a tank of man-eating sharks.

'Why won't you let me meet them?' he kept asking. This time it was on a cold February afternoon when they were walking home. It was one of the rare Saturdays Evie had off work. They'd been in town, to a coffee bar called El Sombrero in Horsefair, sitting in the steamy warmth, sipping coffees, the jukebox playing the latest hits. 'Are you ashamed of me?' He was teasing but she could hear the doubt in his voice.

'Not ashamed of *you*,' she said. She longed for a family she could be proud of, who would welcome Ken, with good manners. To have the kind of mom who would bake a cake. A mom like Mrs Waring. Or like some of the neighbours who had been so kind to her in Aston, Mrs Booker, Melly's mom, and that pretty Italian lady, Mrs Morrison.

'Look, your mom and dad sound like nice people. Mine just aren't very...'

She watched her feet move along the blue bricks of the pavement as she struggled to find the words. Suddenly she wanted to pour everything out, how Mom always fell out with everyone, how loud and rough she was, how she had locked Evie out at night, several times when she was small, to sleep on the step... *My Mom doesn't like me...*

Thinking about saying it, for the first time she knew how clearly it was true. She doesn't like me. She never has. Mom has always *loathed* me. In those seconds without expecting it, she was choking with sadness. When the tears came it was with deep sobs. She had not cried for so long, she scarcely knew what was happening.

'Hey!' Ken, moved, pulled her gently into his arms. It was only a moment, like a small gush from a tap where the pipes are air-locked. But after this brief outlet of emotion, she was wiping her eyes. She never could seem to cry much.

'What's the matter?' Ken said, seeming disturbed. She was usually the one joking and being light-hearted about everything.

'I didn't know I was going to do that.' Feeling a bit stunned, she looked into his eyes, which were full of tender emotion, and tried to smile and lighten up. 'They're just... Not everyone's mom and dad are nice, that's all. I don't know if I want you to see, that's all. I want to get away from them and never go back.'

Even as these words poured out, they astonished her. Was that what she wanted? Yes, it was! She wanted to walk and keep walking.

'Oh Evie!' Ken was half laughing now, hugging her. She could tell he didn't believe her. He thought she was exaggerating and making a drama. 'Nothing can be that bad! I bet they're nice really – 'specially as they had you! Look, maybe we should just go and see them and get it over with.'

Frustrated, she pushed him away and looked up at him.

'You don't believe me, do yer?' She was almost shouting at him in the street. 'You don't know what they're like! I'm serious, Ken. You just think everyone's nice like you.'

Ken looked shocked at her tone, and hurt. 'Look, I'm sorry. I...'

'Never mind.' She turned and walked on, furious – both with him and with herself for letting this be a cause of her falling out with Ken. He caught up with her, looking upset. 'Evie, I'm sorry.'

'It's all right.' She forced a smile. 'Just take my word for it, will you?'

A week later, she went for tea with Mr and Mrs Heaton.

Ken lived in what seemed to Evie a very big house, three storeys high, in Stirling Road, Edgbaston. As they walked there that afternoon, she realized with a pang that it was only a few streets away from Mrs Bracebridge's house. For a moment she ached with regret, recalling the lady's hurt, shocked expression that day. Imagine if she had really gone to live with loving, sweet Mrs Bracebridge. What would her life have been like?

She didn't let herself feel nervous about Mr and Mrs Heaton. She pushed the feelings away, walking beside Ken like someone with all the confidence in the world.

When the door opened, Ken's parents were standing there almost as if they had been waiting behind it. As Evie took in Mr Heaton's tall, thin appearance rather like Ken's and his mother, a small, dark-haired, attractive lady, there were outbursts of furious barking in the background which made them all smile as they said nervous 'hello's.

'That's Molly, wanting to meet you,' Mr Heaton said in an over-jolly sort of way. Evie noticed that he spoke differently. Ken had told her that his father was from Lancashire. He laughed. 'There's no stopping her. Ken, you'd best go and let her out before she takes all the paint off the door.'

'Hello, dear,' Mrs Heaton said, smiling. 'We're very pleased to meet you. Come on in. I hope you don't mind being at the back? The parlour takes such a lot to heat up – we only use it in the summer.'

Evie suddenly felt desperately shy and awkward. She knew she must be on her very best behaviour and talk nicely, the way Mrs Bracebridge had tried to teach her. 'No ... that'd be very nice, thank you.'

As she followed the Heatons along the tiled hall

127

to the back room, Ken rushed ahead. A door opened and a moment later a bounding, jumping, writhing Molly appeared, tobacco coloured, with a silky coat. Evie couldn't help laughing as the dog leapt at her, licked her hands, hurled her body at Evie's legs and generally made a racket.

'Well, I hope you like dogs?' Mrs Heaton said.

'Yes.' Evie smiled, stroking Molly's silky ears as she calmed down. 'I do.'

'You couldn't not like Molly,' Ken said. As he and Evie sat down in two armchairs, the dog leapt into his lap, then into Evie's, then back again and she laughed, delighted.

Mrs Heaton bustled in and out fetching little plates of sandwiches – fish paste and egg – and filling the teapot. Everything felt very formal to Evie. There was a fruit loaf on the table, a sponge cake dusted with icing sugar and a pile of pale green plates and little tea knives beside them. Evie looked at it all with astonishment. So much food! Her mouth was already watering at the sight of the cake with its seam of jam in the middle.

She had two slices when it came to it and said to Mrs Heaton, 'Could you give me a recipe for that? It's lovely.' She spoke softly, very politely, desperately wanting Mr and Mrs Heaton to think well of her.

Mrs Heaton looked surprised. 'It's only a simple Victoria sandwich, dear,' she said. 'I'm surprised you've never made one? Does your mother not bake?'

Bake? Evie thought. She almost laughed.

'Oh ... I didn't realize,' she corrected herself quickly. 'It tastes so nice I thought it must be something different.'

As they drank tea from the pale green cups and saucers and passed the food round, Evie took in the room. The fireplace was surrounded by pretty flower-patterned tiles with a dab of red in them and of course there was the glow of the fire, but everything else – the chairs and curtains, the rug by the hearth – were all in some shade of fawn or pale green.

Mr Heaton sat on an upright chair with his long legs braced apart. Ken had told her that his father worked in the offices of an engineering firm 'doing the books' as he put it and was also a Methodist lay preacher. He seemed a nice man, she thought, but she found his attention rather overwhelming.

'So, young lady,' he said, 'why don't you tell us about yourself? What does your father do for a living?'

Evie, with a mouthful of bloater sandwich, could not utter a word for several seconds.

'Dad,' Ken protested. 'Leave her be. Let her finish eating at least!' Evie noticed Ken sounded different with his mom and dad. More proper, sort of, as if he was trying to please them.

'Sorry, lass,' Mr Heaton laughed, sitting up again. 'Didn't mean to rush you.'

Evie felt panic rising in her. Ken was smiling encouragingly but she really did not know what to say.

'He works at Docker's,' she managed.

'Ah, yes, the paint people,' Mr Heaton boomed. 'A good firm. I remember the night they were bombed – about '42 I think it was...'

129

'Our Ken tells us you live in Inkerman Street?' Mrs Heaton said.

She nodded, wondering nervously what other questions might be coming. But in the end, Ken and his parents supplied most of the conversation, about Ladywood and the Tower Ballroom and then about Ken wanting to go to agricultural college and about Mr Heaton's preaching, which he seemed to be able to talk about almost indefinitely. Evie begin to relax – it was clear she would not have to say anything. Every so often Ken looked across at her from his armchair and gave her a smile or an encouraging wink. He seemed so happy that she was there, as if there was no better place to be. And after a while, Molly slid off Ken's lap and came and sat gazing adoringly at Evie.

'You've made a friend there,' Mr Heaton laughed.

Gratified, she stroked the dog's head and she rolled onto her back to have her tummy tickled. It was all very strange and rather stiff, but they were all right, she told herself. Was this what it meant to have a proper family?

Afterwards, as Ken walked her home in the dusk, he seemed happy. 'They're so nice, my mom and dad, aren't they?' he said proudly.

'Yes,' she agreed. She didn't feel his enthusiasm. Truth to tell, she'd found so much attention a bit oppressive, and the feeling that she must watch her manners. It was not what she was used to. But she could see they had meant well and the tea had been lovely. 'They're very nice,' she added.

Ken was so happy. 'They liked you – I could see straight away,' he said, drawing her into his arms.

Sixteen

A few days later, it was Rita's turn to cook tea – one of her watery stews. Mom hardly ever cooked if she could help it. The new telly, bought on HP, was nattering away on the side. Rita suddenly dashed from the room, a hand over her mouth.

Evie had the sense to stir the stew instead of letting it stick to the bottom of the pan. Just as *Blue Peter* was ending, Rita came back in looking pasty and unwell.

'Shove it,' she snarled, elbowing Evie out of the way. 'You'll only burn it.'

Evie stepped aside. There was no point in saying anything. Rita stood glowering into the saucepan. Evie knew better than to ask. If it had been Shirley, she might have done. At least Shirley was half-way human sometimes. But when it came to Rita, she didn't really care what was the matter with her.

When Shirley and Dad got back in, Rita almost threw the food at everyone and once they had a plateful, she slammed the spoon down. Her pale face wore an odd expression.

'Right,' she said, standing over them all. 'I've got summat to tell yer.'

Everyone looked at her, narrow-eyed, whippet-like, at the end of the table. For a second Evie felt sorry for her. Rita had hardly ever been nice to her, but she could see that she didn't have much of a life either. She was even more at Mom's beck and call than the rest of them.

'Spit it out then, wench,' her father said, through his first mouthful of the stringy cagmag beef.

'Conn and me, we're getting wed,' she said defiantly. She paused for effect, then leaned back slightly, a hand stroking her belly. 'I'm in the family way and Conn says that Mrs Hennessey says we'll 'ave to do it proper, 'im being Catholic, like.'

Mom's head shot up. 'Yow dirty trollop!' But it was half-hearted. There was a wedding on the way.

Rita leaned over the table, glaring at her. 'I'm getting wed, ain't I? And Mrs Hennessey says–'

Conn's mom was a thin, browbeaten-looking lady and a fierce Catholic.

'Yow may be getting wed, but yower still a dirty wench,' Mom said, scraping marg onto her bread. 'Whatever that Irish cow says.'

'Oh, leave off 'er,' Dad said. ''Er said they're getting wed.' Then he looked suspicious. 'Who's gunna pay for that then?'

'You are, Dad,' Rita said and started laughing so much that even Shirley cracked her face and the rest of them couldn't help joining in at the sight of his stricken expression. 'Father of the bride.'

'Shotgun wedding more like,' he retorted. 'Well, yer won't be getting much out of my ribs, wench. Quick in and out and down the pub – none of that church carry-on.'

'It's a quick in and out's got 'er in this mess in the first place,' their mother observed, guffawing loudly at her own joke, her belly shaking.

'We've gotta go to church,' Rita argued. 'If

132

you're Catholic, you gotta do it.'

'Some Catholic 'e is,' Mom sniffed. 'Still...' She changed her tune. 'If 'e's gunna marry yow, after getting yow in the family way...'

'No more'n you was yerself, Irene,' their father remarked. 'As I recall.'

Their mother opened her mouth to retort but for once thought better of saying anything and instead filled it with a scrap of bread.

Evie thought about Mr and Mrs Heaton, imagining them listening in on this conversation, and her cheeks flushed with embarrassment. It was all just impossible!

''Ere, Evie's gone all red,' Rita crowed. 'Dain't you know where babbies come from yet then, Evie?'

'We're still trying to work it out,' their father said and he and Mom laughed like drains. Evie looked down at her plate.

'What about you, Evie?' Rita needled her. She seemed very pleased with herself now. She was getting married. 'You gunna marry old Gary then?'

'What? That Nancy boy?' her father snorted. 'Can't see 'im marrying any wench!'

Evie looked up, startled. She had heard other mutterings about Gary, since Pete had been around, people seeing them roaring up and down the street on Pete's Norton. But even now it was only just beginning to dawn on her. Did that mean...? Was Gary ... one of *those?* Those people who were called nasty names? Gary and Pete... Gary was certainly besotted. But she was only just beginning to realize what that might mean.

133

The thing she had not wanted to recognize and the reason why Gary was just ... different.

In a way she didn't want to know. And she didn't want to hear anything her family might say – about any of it. With a bursting sense of oppression, she thought, me and Ken should just run off together – where no one would ever find us.

A few days later she was just setting off for work in the late afternoon when someone overtook her, walking at a furious pace, and she saw it was Gary. He wasn't looking to his left or right and had his head down, his legs working like pumps in his black drainpipe trousers.

She watched for a second, in two minds, then called, 'Gary!'

He glanced behind and gave her a stricken look before turning and marching onwards again. Evie saw from his look that he wanted her to follow – or at least would not object if she did.

He hurried on along the street and with a glance – the old habit – turned into the entry they always used for the shelter. It was an age since they'd been there and Evie was certain other kids must have taken it over by now.

Though she needed to get to work, she went after him, along the back lane with its weeds and rubbish. Gary had already disappeared into the shelter.

Heart pounding, she stepped into its gloom, and the old familiar damp smell. There was a sharp, burnt stink as well – more kids making fires in there perhaps – but she was not interested in looking round. She wanted Gary, wanted him to talk to her. He had been so distant for so long, so caught up in Pete, but she had a feeling that now he wanted her.

He was standing a few feet away, his back to her, shoulders hunched. She could see the backs of his arms, bent up as if his hands were over his face. Then she made out that his shoulders were shaking.

'Gary?' she said softly. 'It's me. What's up?'

He let the sobs come then, bent over, distraught.

'What the matter?' As there was no reply she dared to touch his shoulder, wanting him to straighten up so she could see his face.

To her astonishment he righted himself in a sudden, thrusting movement and flung his arms round her. He lowered his head so that his forehead rested on her shoulder and as her own arms tightened round him, she could feel all of his thin body shaking with emotion.

'Hey, Gary!' She stroked his back, letting him cry for a few moments, touched that he had turned to her to let out his feelings. Dear old Gary. 'It's all right,' she murmured to him. 'That's it. You have a cry if you want.'

Eventually he raised his head, seeming stunned. His face was red and wet, his specs all steamed up, and he took them off to wipe his pink-rimmed eyes.

'Sorry,' he said, pulling away and wiping his sleeves down his cheeks. Now he was embarrassed.

'S'all right,' she said, trying not to think about the time ticking by and about where she ought to be. 'What's up, Gar?'

His face crumpled again. 'It's Pete. He's...' He shook his head as more tears came, but more gently this time. He struggled to find the right words. 'He's... I mean, I'd never... I'm *true* to 'im, like that...'

Evie felt unusually grateful to her father for his blurted words. *Nancy boys.* So yes, she was beginning to have an idea what *like that* truly meant for Gary.

She tried to look calm, as if all this didn't disturb her, men with men and all that, even though she had barely begun to know it and believe it. But this was dear old Gary, so heartbroken and vulnerable in front of her. She knew deep down, from a host of memories and impressions, that Gary did not want girls, had never wanted them. She thought of his kiss, the way he had seemed to be forcing himself and it feeling all wrong. Well, if that was the way he was...

'D'you mean he's got someone else?' she asked.

Tears welled and rolled down Gary's thin cheeks. ''E says it wasn't anything, it dain't matter, that sort of thing. Not as if it's gunna give anyone a babby, is it? he said to me. But that ain't the point!' Gary was full of hurt and outrage. 'If you love someone, you love 'em, don't yer? You don't just go off with someone else just like that.'

Evie couldn't help hoping Pete was gone for good. She had never liked him. Ever since Gary was with him she had felt shut out and abandoned, even though she now had Ken.

'But,' she said, trying to get to the bottom of this. 'You mean he's left you?'

136

'No, he hasn't gone. But he just likes...' Gary drew in a long breath through his nostrils, raising his head as if against a horrible thought. 'He likes playing about – having a lot of ... having a lot of other blokes... I can't stand it, Eves.'

Evie stared at him, unsure what to say. It sounded horrible. Pete was horrible, she thought. Why didn't Gary just tell him to get lost? She felt out of her depth and clueless in all this. But poor Gary – she didn't want him to know her real thoughts.

'But he wants you still, does he?' she asked carefully.

'Yeah,' he conceded, looking down then, so sadly that she wanted to hug him again, but that moment had passed.

'Well,' she said, knowing she must go and get to work. 'That's all right then, ain't it? He still wants you?'

'But I want him to want *just* me,' Gary said desperately.

She searched for something comforting to say. 'P'raps he will. P'raps he just needs to grow up a bit.'

Gary looked back into her eyes then. 'D'yer think?'

She nodded. 'Yeah ... well, could be, couldn't it?' she offered, not really having a clue.

He sniffed and gave his lopsided smile, looking more like the old Gary. 'Ta, Evie.'

'S'all right. I've gotta go, though – got to get to work.' She wanted to say that it was nice to see him, why couldn't they meet up more, or something, but he was wrapped up in his own feelings and as they parted at the end of the entry, all he said was, 'T'ra, Evie.'

Cheerful as she could manage, she said, 'Tara-a-bit, Gary.'

Seventeen

April 1960

She saw Gary a number of times in the next few weeks, but only in the distance. Whatever had happened with Pete, they must have made it up. A couple of times he waved at her, beaming from the back of Pete's roaring bike. She was glad for him, but it still gave her a pang because she did not trust Pete. She felt that he was bad for Gary, who she had lost again after those moments of him confiding in her.

At home, all anyone could think about was Rita getting married. Conn's family took over the arrangements which – whatever Dad thought about it – meant a proper Roman Catholic wedding at St Peter's and a dress that would prevent Rita from showing. The whole thing was arranged in a big hurry and soon they were all traipsing into the church, Mom and Dad dressed to kill and on their best behaviour. Evie wore her best dress, a pale blue one with pink flowers on it and a nicely shaped bodice. She was frozen all the way through as the April weather was still chilly, but people kept saying how nice she looked.

Rita wore a long white dress with a frothy net skirt ample enough to have hidden most things. She looked as pretty as she was ever going to look and seemed to get away with it. And Conn stood looking gawky and delighted in a stiff suit. They processed in on a wave of fag smoke from all the men waiting outside until the last minute and swept out on a wave of incense, as Mr and Mrs Hennessey. Evie, watching their departing backs, smiled at the thought that Rita would now be leaving home.

The weather warmed and Evie and Ken spent every spare moment they could together. All the time she was making excuses as to why he should not come home with her, though she'd been to his house a few more times. Ken had shown her his childhood trainset. Mrs Heaton always made a nice tea and she had taken to laying out a jigsaw puzzle. The latest one was called 'Happy Days at Work', showing a group of women in coloured frocks next to a double-decker bus in a pleasant street with a church. It was easier than just sitting there talking and there was Molly to break the ice as well. But Evie much preferred seeing Ken away from the house. Usually on her evening off they would go to town, to the pictures or to a park if the weather was good enough, where they could walk arm in arm and have a kiss under the trees.

'I've got the day off on Saturday,' she told him one spring evening when they were sitting in the Kardomah, one of their favourite coffee shops, next to the Great Western Arcade.

'At last!' Ken beamed. 'It's ages since you had a

Saturday off. Tell you what, let's have a proper day out – right out of Brum. Go and see some farms!' He half stood and kissed her lips across the table.

'Ken, not here!' She pulled back, giggling. 'Nice jumper by the way.' He was wearing an enormous sludge-green cable-knit thing which made him look wider than usual.

'I know.' He shrugged, making a comical face. 'Mom knitted it. Have to wear it, don't I? And why shouldn't I kiss you? No one minds. But I want you all to myself.' He leaned towards her again for a second, kissing the tip of her nose. He was like a puppy in his enthusiasm for her.

'Well, you'll have to wait 'til Saturday,' she said coyly.

They woke to sunshine. Evie, already washed and dressed, opened the front door, almost unable to believe it, smelling the spring-like promise of the air and seeing each fragment of colour in their soot-darkened street – every white glint of sun on windowpanes, every doorstep polished with cardinal red, the dull, dusty hues of the doors – all lifted by the bright light. Excitement bubbled through her. She got her things ready, gathering up her bag.

Shirley was sitting at the table in her nightie, yawning and drinking tea, a magazine spread in front of her. Mom and Dad still weren't up and their father's snores could be heard rising and falling from upstairs.

'Where're *you* going?' Shirley asked eventually. There was a snide edge to her voice, but she was less forceful without Rita there. Now Rita and

Conn were living in a couple of rooms above a pet food shop in Nelson Street, close to Conn's mom and dad, Shirley had lost her main ally and companion. It was peaceful without Rita constantly making trouble.

'Just out,' Evie said, not meeting her eyes. Should she take a coat? She might be cold without one. 'Town – the shops,' she said. She hardly ever went shopping now. Instead of mooching round C&A and Woollies with a few shillings to spend after she'd handed over some of her wages to Mom, she spent every spare moment with Ken. But she had found time to buy a pair of jeans and she was proudly wearing them now, with a white blouse and pink jumper. 'Wear something you can walk in,' Ken had said. She didn't have anything, so she had bought some cheap plimsolls.

'You're always out,' Shirley remarked, with an edge of accusation.

Evie went to the door, coat over her arm, and looked back at her sister. 'So?' she said. 'What's it to you?'

She closed the door behind her on Shirley's glare. As she walked off down the road, a smile spread across her own face at the thought of a whole day ahead with Ken.

Eighteen

'So where're we going?'

'You'll see.' Ken teased her until she stopped caring where they were going. They were together, she was on Ken's arm and the whole day stretched in front of them. It was amazingly warm, her jeans were thick and she had to stop to peel off her jumper and tie it round her shoulders. By the time they were sitting on a train together, she was rolling up her sleeves, cursing herself for bringing the coat.

There was hardly anyone on the train as it was early on a Saturday and they were heading out of town. 'I'll carry it for you. I've got my camera as well.' He nodded towards his knapsack on the seat. 'I can get some nice snaps. And I bought sarnies.'

'Oh, you think of everything!' she said, laughing at how middle-aged he was in some ways, while being sweet and kind. 'Picnic, eh? Come on, where're we going?'

'Wait and see. Now come 'ere, you.' Ken nudged her forwards so that he could put his arm round her and drew her close to kiss her, deeply absorbed in her. She found the effect she had on him exciting.

As the train slowed to a stop at another station he surfaced, almost as if from sleep, and looked out.

'A couple more stops to go,' he said, turning to her. He looked at her, an intensity in his eyes. 'God, Evie.' His eyes moved over her body. 'You're some girl, you are.'

She felt a give inside her, a hitch of desire. Up until now, though Ken was full of admiration for her, he had always been restrained and gentlemanly, kissing her but drawing back. But in that moment she felt something change. She looked at Ken, a frank, giving look. He gazed back at her, then had to look away, as if her look was too much for him.

'ALVECHURCH.'

They climbed down, onto the platform of the country station, which was bathed in sunlight. A few people were waiting on the opposite platform to go into Birmingham, but on their side, it was only them. Once the train moved away again, it was so quiet she could hear a breeze in the trees behind.

'I've got a map,' Ken said, unfolding it.

Evie saw a well-worn map, covered with browns and green, criss-crossed by red and green roads. She didn't mind where they went, and would just let him guide her. What was now between them – desire, unspoken, but insistent – veiled everything.

Ken folded the map and looked at her. Solemnly, he took her hand. 'Come on then,' he said. They walked hand in hand as they headed along a road lined with hedges and fields.

'I've never been out of town before,' Evie said.

Ken looked astonished. 'What, never? Don't you ever get out for walks?'

She shook her head, smiling at him. 'Told you. We're not that kind of family. I'm a townie through and through.'

The wide spaces, fields dotted with grazing cows or striped with green shoots, made her feel strange. It seemed empty and dull to her, but she didn't want to say this to Ken. And it was a lovely day, the air fresh and warm and only a few puffs of cloud in the sky.

'I just can't imagine that,' Ken said, sounding almost sad. 'We used to go off for a good walk nearly every weekend – Mom and Dad and me. And I went with the Scouts.' He looked ahead, towards a thick clump of woodland. 'This is what I want – to live out here, on a farm, with all this.' He swept his arm to take in the view. 'And animals. Growing your own food. Nothing like it.' He fumbled in his bag and brought out the camera and snapped a picture of the view.

'Aren't you going to take one of me then?' Evie said, affronted.

Laughing, Ken turned to her and obliged. 'I've only got twelve shots – I'll have to save some for later.'

He took her arm and they set off again. She liked the feeling of him close to her, but his words were rankling.

'So, why d'you want to come and live out here?' She could hear herself sounding aggressive because she felt there was no place for her in his plans.

'Well, I want to be a farmer – or at least work for one to begin with. I don't want to spend my life living in a town, with filthy old factories everywhere. I want a cottage with a garden, where I can grow things and have a dog and chickens... And' – he glanced at her, realizing he was being tactless – 'you as well. In our own little house, with a nice big table to sit everyone round.'

Evie smiled, slightly mollified, but her heart sank at the thought of living surrounded by fields and trees.

'I don't think I'd be much good,' she said, feeling cast down.

Ken looked round. 'So where would you live if you could live anywhere?'

She struggled to think. Apart from Aston and Ladywood she hardly knew anywhere else. She thought of Gary's dream, all those years ago. 'By the seaside. What if you had a farm by the sea?'

'Maybe.' Ken chuckled. 'Better wait and see, eh?' He put his arm round Evie's shoulder. 'Here, let's go along there.'

There was a footpath between two fields, just wide enough for them to walk twined together, Ken's arm round her shoulders, hers reaching round his waist. She could feel the wiry strength of him. Walking like that, close, feeling each other's warmth, changed things again. Evie wanted him, wanted to be close, for their kissing to go further. She knew he wanted it too, but neither of them could say because they knew they shouldn't, that it was wrong.

The mood changed between them suddenly and for a time neither of them spoke. To break the silence, Ken stopped her and moved to kiss her. It was still only just gone ten and no one else was about. He put his bag down and, with an intense

145

look, drew her close. They stood in the breeze, warm lips pressed together, bodies finding their way closer. A bee buzzed somewhere low down, rooks were scraping in the trees beyond and it felt as if they had the whole world to themselves.

Ken drew back again and gave her a long look, as if he wanted to say something but could not think how to begin. All she could think about was wanting him, being pulled more and more into those feelings as if nothing existed except now. Nothing else. No thought, no consequences.

He took her hand. The path led into the woods. They followed it for a time, a well-worn path in dappled shade, then turned off it through the trees, along the woodland floor littered with leaves and twigs.

When they could tell that they had gone far enough, where they could only see trees and more trees on every side, Ken stopped. Neither of them said anything. It was as if each of them were waiting for the other to say, *No, don't, we mustn't,* to try and put a stop to the wanting. Evie was partly ashamed of what she wanted. But she saw in that moment that she regarded herself as bad and Ken as good, and that if they did wrong together, it would make him more like her.

Neither of them spoke and Ken looked at her longingly, as if asking permission. Seeing the look in her eyes he reached for her coat and laid it spread on the leaves. Gently, he pulled her to the ground with him and she went gladly, her knees ready to give way.

And all she could feel in this floating moment was that this was the most important thing she must ever do, as if each of them must guarantee the other, claim them, and keep them tied and close forever. There was nothing and no one else except this and now: Ken's hands moving hungrily over her body. Every move was about removing layer upon layer so that their skin could be close with nothing in between and eventually Ken's urgent voice saying, 'Can I, Evie? Can I ... please?'

They lay afterwards, holding each other. The breeze seemed louder in the trees.

Ken still seemed in a kind of trance. He gazed and gazed at her, running his hand over her white body, the curve of her belly, and she shivered.

'I've thought so many times about what you'd look like,' he said in an awed tone. 'I can't believe it. I knew you'd be beautiful, but you're much more than I thought...'

Evie lay, listening. It was a wonderful feeling to be so worshipped. The very sight of her had sent Ken into a taut desperation for her which moved her. He was so sweet and loving. She had never been adored like this, ever before. Her body felt strange, the memory of him pushing up inside her, the remaining wetness between her legs, the tight feeling of the skin of her lips, her cheeks, where he had kissed and kissed her.

'Here.' He noticed the goose pimples rising on her skin. 'You'd better put something on. You'll catch cold.'

'And you,' she said, giggling. 'Your thing's gone all wrinkly. And what if someone comes?'

While they were dressing they heard a dog barking somewhere in the distance and their eyes met with desperate mirth.

'Hurry up!' she hissed, throwing Ken his trousers, tingling with the danger of it. 'Get them on, quick!' She was already hauling up her jeans.

Both laughing and now fully dressed, they lay down again, cuddling up to get warm. Somewhere a voice called, 'Billy! Billy!' twice, but they never saw anyone.

They wandered through the woods and fields, each thrumming with what had just happened. They picked bits of stuff out of each other's hair. Ken held tight to her. Every so often he turned to her with a look of amazement and said, 'God, Evie.'

Once he said, blushing, 'That was ... you know, your first time... I am right?'

'Yes.' She went pink as well. 'Course. Couldn't you tell?'

Ken shrugged. 'How? It was my first time as well.'

They ate their sandwiches when they came to the canal, watching a few boats go up and down. The sun glanced off the water and a breeze blew the surface into ripples. Evie looked at Ken beside her, his long legs bent up in front of him, his good-looking face in profile. He was only just needing to shave and there were a few little bits of stubble round his chin. She could see his jaw moving as he chewed and she felt tender towards him. He's mine now, she thought. Really mine. They would be together forever now, that was what it meant.

A moment later, almost as if reading her thoughts, Ken, staring ahead of him, said, 'Evie, why won't you let me meet your mom and dad?

148

Mine like you – you know they do.'

She had noticed that Mr and Mrs Heaton were warm and welcoming to her, but she still wasn't sure if they really thought she was good enough for Ken or just doing their Christian duty.

'I've told you.' Thinking about home, about Mom and Dad, was like a cold shower on this warm day when she had never felt so loved. 'They're just not ... they're not like yours. Just believe me, OK?'

Ken rubbed her back playfully. 'Oh, I'm sure they're all right. You're just getting in a stew about nothing. And anyway,' he said, serious now, 'what if we're to get married?'

Her head shot round. 'What?'

'Married, the way people do. I mean, we've just...' He blushed. 'You know, done what only married folk are supposed to do.'

Ken used words like 'folk' sometimes which she found quaint.

'So...' He paused gravely and she gazed back at him. Marriage – someone to love her and live with her? She had thought one day perhaps, but...

'But we're not old enough,' she said, frowning at him.

'We might think about it, though, mightn't we?' Ken was saying. 'In a couple of years or so anyway, when we're older. Maybe when I've done my training and I'm more settled. We could be engaged. We don't have to tell anyone – but *we'd* know, wouldn't we?'

'Oh Ken!' She was brimful of happiness suddenly. 'Shall we? It can be our secret. And then when we're older–'

149

'I'll buy you a ring!'

'Oh Ken! I love you so much,' she said, almost crying for joy. 'I never thought anything as nice as this could happen – ever.'

It stayed beautiful and warm all day. They wandered the countryside talking about their plans. Ken took pictures of animals, of farms, of Evie. She insisted that she take one of him so that she could have one when they were developed.

Later in the afternoon, Ken came up close, kissing her neck just beneath her hair, and whispered, 'I can't stop thinking about it. Let's do it again.'

And the melting, hot sensation filled her all over again. It all seemed different now, not even wrong. They were promised; they would be husband and wife. They found another remote spot at the back of a half-empty barn and made love again, more slowly, lingering over it. As Evie lay beside Ken afterwards, his arms round her, she found herself filled with a sense of rightness, of amazement, as if this being wanted, giving herself, was what she was made for.

Rolling over, she looked down into Ken's eyes, surprising herself with her own heartfelt words.

'I love you, Ken. I *do.*'

Ken's long face lifted into a rapturous smile. 'Do you – really?'

'I do. I never...' Tears came to her eyes. Tears that were strangers. 'I never knew there was anything so nice.'

She could see he was moved. 'Come 'ere,' he said, and cuddled her close. 'God, I love you, Evie girl.' Held in his arms, there on the musty old straw of the barn, she felt she had found everything she needed.

Nineteen

December 1960

'Filthy little bitch!'

Mom towered over her, in a glorious rage. God, how she was loving it, Evie could see, even as she cowered, ready to beg her not to be angry, not to be nasty but please, please to help her.

They were downstairs – just she and Mom, who was wrapped in her checked coat over her night-dress. Evie stared down at her mother's beefy legs, her feet pushed into a pair of pink sling-back slippers, too narrow for her feet. Evie, in her nightdress, crouched on the chair, hugging herself.

'Yow think I cor see the nose on your face, but I can see yower bally all swole up. What kind of noggen yed d'yow tek me for?' She came up close, her arm raised, and Evie shrank back, but she was hard up against the table. Dad and Shirley had gone to work so there was no one to save her – not that they would anyway.

'Ow far gone are yer?'

Evie shrugged, staring at the floor. 'I dunno. Quite far, I s'pose.' All these months of trying not to see it or believe it.

Mom's hand slashed across her face and she

cried out at the usual blast to her ear, the pain jarring her neck, the skin of her face smarting.

'Ow, Mom, don't!' Too late, she put her arms up to cover her head.

'Ow, Mom, don't!' her mother mocked. 'You should've thought of that before you let that nancy boy have 'is way with you an' all. I never thought 'e 'ad it in 'im. But I tell yer, I'm gunna 'ave his guts for garters now, that I am.'

It took Evie a moment to catch on what her mother was talking about. Gary. Mom thought it was Gary who...

'Mom, no!' She brought her arms down again. 'It's not Gary's! Me and him never... He's not... I mean...' She stumbled over the impossibility of talking to Mom about anything in a reasonable way.

'Well, that don't surprise me,' her mother said, while nevertheless looking surprised. 'Bent as a nail that one.' She stood upright, folding her arms in magnificent self-righteousness. 'So if it ain't that little runt's, whose is it?'

Evie lowered her gaze to the floor. 'You don't know him.'

'Ho, don't I? Well, why not?' She bent forward again. 'Sounds as if you know 'im all too cowing well, though, yer saft wench! Who is 'e? You'd better get 'im over 'ere and I'll tell 'im what's what. 'E's got to marry yer, or else!'

Numbly, Evie said, 'He will. He doesn't know – about the babby. He's *nice*,' she appealed, looking up at her mother at last.

'Well, if 'e's that cowing nice, why've I never set eyes on 'im, eh? You'm a sneaky little bugger, yow

152

am. Our Reet 'ad Conn round 'ere every week. But you, oh no! I s'pose you think yower too good for us?'

'No, Mom...' Evie pleaded. She was feeling shocked and terrified herself. Only now had she fully grasped the fact that she was expecting a baby, that terrible thing that you were never supposed to do if you weren't married. All this time she had tried to pretend to herself that it was nothing, that she was putting on a bit of weight, had a bit of wind, that this could not really be happening. Since she hadn't told anyone anything, nothing about it seemed real.

If only Mom would be nice, just this once. Desperate for her mother to support her, to be kind, she said, 'Look, I'll get Ken to come over and see you. You'll like him – he's ever so nice. And I know he'll do the right thing. He keeps talking about us getting married anyway.'

'Well, yow'd better get 'im in 'ere to ask yower father – do it proper. And you, yer little trollop, you keep yowerself covered up. I don't want them blobmouths out there canting about us.'

'I will, Mom,' Evie said humbly. She slipped away upstairs, thinking that over all, this had not gone too badly. The thought of Ken coming over was awful. She could imagine his face as he looked round, not just at the house, but at her family as well. Compared with Mr and Mrs Heaton, they were so rough. She didn't think Ken would mind about that because he was so nice about people. But Mom? Mom was another matter. A shudder went through her as she climbed the stairs. It had to be done, though. There was no way out.

Once her mother had dressed, in between shouting abuse at her, she left for work. Evie was alone in the house. It was still early, the streets full of mist. She crept – out of habit, as if trouble might still be lurking – down to the kitchen and brewed another cup of tea from the lees of the last pot, stirred in three spoons of sugar and took it back up to bed.

As she sipped her tea, sitting back against the wall, she could feel the twitching from within her belly that had become harder to ignore. At first, in early summer, she had at times felt mortally tired, more than ever before. Her monthly periods were never very regular and she put it all down to evening work catching up with her and trying to keep her relationship with Ken a secret.

And there had been plenty to keep anyone else from taking any notice of her. On the first day of July, Rita gave birth to a baby boy. Conn's mom had wanted to call him Joseph and Rita, who seemed to want to gain the approval of all of Conn's family, agreed that Joseph would be his name. Evie had felt sorry for Conn and his mom, Mary Hennessey. Did they have any idea what they were taking on with Rita? But to her amazement Rita seemed to be going all out to be a true Hennessey and was talking about becoming a Catholic, something so beyond the ken of Mom and Dad that they barely even commented on it.

On the other hand, Rita was back and forth from Nelson Street, demanding attention for Joseph. She would settle herself downstairs on Dad's chair, which she now seemed to think she had the right to occupy, and queen it over everyone. She ordered Shirley and Evie about and demanded bottles of milk to be heated up – none of that disgusting feeding it yourself business – and spent her time there generally being bossy. Rita had become even thinner having the baby, her cheeks gaunt and her body like a pole.

Evie drank the last of her fast-cooling tea, put the cup on the floor and sat back. Grey light seeped in through the window. She pulled up her nightdress and looked at her pale drum of a belly. There were twitches from within. She stared with astonishment. For heaven's sake, she was big – really big! All this time she had been trying not to look, drifting along and pretending to herself that nothing was happening...

She and Ken had only made love a couple of times since their day out, back in the spring, because it was so difficult to find anywhere to go. She wanted it as much as he did, the closeness, the attention and excitement of it. They had managed it one summer evening in a park, quickly, in a scrub of bushes, breaking into giggles when it was over. Another time in an alley, standing up in the dark, which was not very good but better than nothing. Not once had they worried about babies, or trying not to have them. It wasn't something Evie had given thought to, as if she was living in a dream. Starting a baby took ages, was what she thought, and she felt safe because she knew she and Ken were going to get married.

She pulled her nightdress down and lay back, wishing Ken was here now, the two of them alone. She cuddled her thin pillow. It hit her then. Now they would be together – like Rita and Conn! She would tell Ken and he would have to break it to his mom and dad, but they would promise to get married straight away. She had turned seventeen at her last birthday and Ken was a few months older. That would be all right, wouldn't it? They could rent their own little place – even a room would do if she could only get away from here. And she'd be Mrs Heaton.

'Mrs Eve Heaton,' she said. Then added, 'Mrs Kenneth Heaton.'

It was all terrifying, but exciting. And soon she would be a mother – a proper mother, not like Mom. She lay looking at the cracks along the ceiling, thinking, I want to be like Melly's mom, Mrs Booker, or Mrs Waring. I'm going to give her everything. Somehow she knew it was a 'her'. She was full of a sense of being grown-up suddenly and of wanting to make everything right.

She lay wondering about her own mother. Mom seemed to have no one. *Why haven't we got a Nanna, Mom?* This had always met with a snapped reply: "Cause you ain't, so shurrit.' Whoever Mom's family were, over in Netherton, in the Black Country, she had no idea whether they were still alive. Whatever the case, Mom had left and never gone back. And now Auntie Vi and Uncle Horace, the only people Mom had ever turned to, had gone to Scotland. For a second she felt a glimmer of understanding of her mother's feelings about her own birth. It had been years before she knew the reason why Mom was so bitter and hateful towards her – Dad's unfaithfulness with Nance; Nance's baby boy. Dad always wanted a boy, or said he did.

It wouldn't have suited Dad having a boy anyway, she thought. A boy might have stood up to him. Dad wouldn't have liked that; he enjoyed being the cockerel in a cage full of hens. It wasn't nice for Mom, but none of it was my fault, was it? She didn't have to hate me... I was only a babby... Tears swam in her eyes. All she had wanted, all her life, was for Mom to love her and show some warmth towards her.

She thought about Ken. Now she had someone who really did love her. Ken was good and kind. He was better than all of them. And when she saw him tomorrow, she'd tell him, and then they would be able to be together.

Twenty

All evening, as she worked at the Tower, she knew Ken would be there to meet her after her shift as he usually did, even though she finished quite late.

'At least I get to see you,' he often said. 'And we get a chance for a chat.' And a kiss and a cuddle as well, he could have added.

As the evening passed she grew more and more nervous. She kept practising in her head what she was going to say to him.

When she saw him wave to her, out in the cold darkness, her heart started pounding. She had fastened her coat round her swelling belly, wondering now how he could not have noticed anything.

'Ken–' she began to say as they set off, his arm round her shoulder. But he had news himself and broke in, excited.

'Dad's been helping me look into agricultural colleges,' he said, a big smile on his face. 'I reckon they'll have to help me a bit, but they've come round to the idea that that's what I want. Another year or so and I'll be able to go – get some proper training.'

Evie hoped he could not see the tension in her face as she tried to sound encouraging. She was suddenly sick with worry.

'That's nice,' she said, trying to control her voice. 'If that's what you want.'

'Oh, it is.' He squeezed her shoulder. 'I'd hate to be stuck with this brewery job forever more.'

He'd go off to his new training and leave her! She was half choked by panic, but managed to fight it. Why was she being silly? If they were married and had a child, she could work, somehow, couldn't she? They'd manage and pull together. She watched the dark shapes of her feet moving along the pavement with a feeling of unreality, not knowing how to begin to speak to Ken – about any of it.

He noticed that she had gone quiet and peered round at her.

'You tired?'

'Yeah,' she said, keeping her head down. 'It's been a long day.' Then she looked up abruptly and said all in a rush, 'Ken, stop. I've got summat to tell you.'

They stood next to a workshop, all shut up and quiet by now. She drew in a gulp of air.

'Hey,' Ken said, seeing that she was upset. 'Come on, what's up?'

'I...' She looked into his eyes, pulled him close to her. 'I mean, we...' She stumbled. 'Ken ... we're... I'm expecting.'

'Expecting what?' He seemed bemused. God, he didn't even know the meaning of the word.

'A baby,' she whispered. 'A baby – yours.'

He stood staring at her. She could just make out, if not his actual expression, the tense seriousness settling over him. He put his hands on her shoulders.

'What d'you mean?' His voice was hoarse. 'Are you sure? How d'you know?'

Ken had no sisters or other family with children. Mr and Mrs Heaton were obviously not the types of people to discuss where babies came from with their only son – or at least not in any useful detail. Not that her mom and dad had ever gone into any of this either. Her only knowledge came from living in cramped, thin-walled houses. And Rita. Why had she not thought more about Rita?

'It's kicking me,' she said. 'It must have been that first day, when we went out to the...' She didn't need to remind him. 'I'm well on. I never knew – not 'til just the last few days. But now ... here, feel. I'm getting big.'

She took his hand and undid the button of her coat to slip it inside. Ken, like a man in a trance, pressed his palm against her swelling stomach.

'See?' She wanted him to say something. She

was very scared. 'Our baby, Ken. In there.' She didn't know if she was pleased, but she wanted him to be, for his face to light into a smile.

'God,' Ken said. Then again. 'God. Oh Evie.' He pulled his hand away as if afraid. 'Are you sure?'

She nodded, wanting him to say all the things she needed him to: that he loved her, that they'd be together always. And at last he began.

'Well ... if that's... I mean, we'll have to get married, won't we?' he said. It came out like someone trying to sound as if he knew what he had to say.

'Oh Ken!' She was overjoyed, relieved, flinging her arms round him. 'I love you, I do! I knew you'd be nice about it!'

As they walked to Inkerman Street, though, he went very quiet. He was shocked, she knew. It felt as if he had gone and left her all alone, even though he was still there.

'Talk to me, will you?' she said.

'Well, what d'you want me to talk about?' Ken snapped. 'I'm just trying to... I mean, *God...*' He stopped, a hand to his head. 'What the hell are Mom and Dad going to make of all this?'

She felt chilled at the thought of Mr and Mrs Heaton's tight, respectable household.

'They'll want us to get wed, won't they?' she said uncertainly. 'They're church people, so that's the right thing to do.'

'Well, yes,' Ken said. But he sounded angry. 'In a few years' time, when we've been courting for a good while and ... not when you've... Not with a baby already on the way. That's not right, is it? We should never've... You said... I mean, you

160

seemed...' He sputtered into silence.

She felt he was blaming her. Was it her fault, all this? What had she said? Was there something else she should have done – refused and told him not to touch her when he had begged? She had a horrible feeling inside her, a shrivelling, as if she was dirty and small. They were on opposite sides again – he was good, she was bad. What was she doing walking out with a respectable lad like Ken anyway?

'Sorry,' she half whispered, a sense of despair settling over her. 'But I don't know what we can do now. It's too late.'

'No, look, sorry.' Ken turned to her, contrite. 'Come here.' He held her, stroking her back. 'It's just a shock. Look,' he said, pulling back after a while. 'We'll see this through together. Just you and me. I love you – I *do*.' He paused, then said with great solemnity. 'So, will you marry me, Evie Sutton?'

Mom couldn't leave the subject alone. Evie was grateful for the loud babble of the television, otherwise it seemed the whole street would know.

When she came out with the fact of Evie's condition in front of Shirley, while the four of them were all milling about downstairs, Evie saw her sister's face crease with disgust.

'What're you looking like that for?' Evie dared to say. 'It's a babby, not a lump of muck.'

Shirley was at the stove – now Rita had gone she and Evie took it in turns. She gave one of her slinky, film-star shrugs and turned away again, behind her hair.

Mom was getting warmed up, goading their father to join in, though he had just got in and was flat out in his chair by the fire.

'Fancy that one getting a bun in the oven,' she said, sitting complacently by the table. 'I'd never've thought anyone'd go near 'er with that face on 'er. Is 'e blind then, this bloke? Oh, I know, I bet 'e's some old bag o' bones who can't find anyone else!' She gave her bellowing laugh.

Evie stood miserably by the fire. Her back was aching and her feet so cold she could hardly feel them. She saw Shirley's shoulders shake in response to this but to her surprise, her father piped up, 'Oh, leave off 'er, wench. Give it a rest, will yer? That wench is bonnier than you ever was and you know it so shut yer cake'ole.'

Evie straightened up with astonishment at this outburst and in the second or two it took before her mother erupted like a geyser, she stared at her father. Was that what he really thought? He was never the one who was mean all the time, like Mom. He just never took much notice of any of them.

But Mom was off. 'Bonny – *er?* That little rat? And I s'pose you think that slag's boy, *Raymond'* – her voice dripped with contempt – 'is "bonny" as well 'cause 'e's of your stock, even if 'e's got a face that'd stop a clock!'

'Oh, shut yer gob, Irene,' Dad said wearily. 'Give yer arse a chance.'

Which did nothing to shut her up. Her parting shot as Evie took herself upstairs was, 'And 'e's supposed to be marrying 'er – huh! That'll be the day!'

Evie turned at the bottom of the stairs. 'He's already asked me – yesterday,' she announced. 'And I said yes. So you'll soon be shot of me.'

She saw the look of shock on Shirley's face. Her mother sobered up abruptly.

'Wha'? You're getting wed? You cor do that at your age without asking yer father, you know. 'E'd best get 'imself over 'ere. And I 'ope they've got a bob or two, with you in the condition you're in.'

'*They're* very respectable,' Evie said. 'And they live in Edgbaston. In a *nice* house.'

She left the room with a feeling of triumph. Ken was going to speak to his mom and dad tonight. And then – she tingled with excitement as she climbed the stairs – Ken could meet Mom and Dad at last to show them what a nice boy she was marrying. They'd be on their best behaviour now if they thought they were getting her off their hands to a family with some money behind them. She and Ken could start making plans for their life ahead – and she'd be free.

Twenty-One

Evie expected Ken to come rushing back to her the next day, but she heard nothing from him. Nor the day after. It was the last days before Christmas and there was the usual rush on. What with work and their hours being so different, it was always difficult to meet. She tried to make excuses for him. But Ken usually would have managed it.

She began to panic, to lose faith in Ken. Where the hell was he? Surely she would see him before Christmas? He wouldn't just not come? She remembered last year when all he could think about was when he would next see her.

On Christmas Eve a note arrived from him saying he was ill.

'I'm so sorry not to see you before Christmas,' it read. 'I'm laid up – temperature's been 104. See you very soon. Love Ken xx'

But the note made her worry more. It did not sound quite right. She was on tenterhooks waiting for them to resolve things now she had faced up to what was happening. They needed to be making plans. She told herself that the note was short and empty because he was ill. *See you very soon.* The two days of Christmas felt like an eternity to her. But at least once Christmas was over Ken would be better and they would sort everything out.

Mom had decided that her daughters were too old for even the minimal amount of effort she once used to go to, so apart from a bit of beef for Christmas dinner, there was not much in the way of a celebration apart from not having to work and being able to watch the telly. It sat on Mrs Garnet's sideboard and was on almost all the time, the test card showing and music tinkling out much of the day.

Evie could not concentrate on anything. Even if they were all sitting there in front of *Juke Box Jury* or *Billy Cotton's Christmas Party,* all she kept thinking about was Ken and the baby. She was in a fever of wanting to make plans but she became

164

more and more terrified that Ken did not feel the same. That note he had sent – had that just been an excuse? Was he really ill? Her mood sank. Did Ken really want to be with her or not? She started to believe Mom's constant goading.

'Where is 'e then, this cowing Romeo? No sign of 'im, is there? I s'pect 'e's cut and run if 'e's got any sense.'

Rita and Conn came round for a while but all Rita did was look down her nose when she heard about Evie and say, 'Oh, is that so?' And then she ignored her. Rita wanted all the attention on her and baby Joseph.

The two days seemed eternally long and she was beginning to be taken over by a piercing sense of doubt. She wanted to run round to the Heatons' house, but knew that would be a disaster. Had Ken abandoned her? That was what men did, wasn't it? It was what Dad had done to Nancy when she had his child.

Two days after Boxing Day she was once again alone in the house. Everyone had gone to work. She had just got dressed, slowly, in an old skirt which she could barely get round her now and a jumper, to do some chores in an attempt to keep busy. All she could think about was Ken. Surely he'd be better by now? He'll come later today. He'll come and meet me. He *will*.

It was a freezing day of bright winter sunshine. She was sweeping out the downstairs room when she heard running feet outside and a hammering on the door as if someone wanted to knock it down.

'Blimey,' she said, going to it with the broom in

165

one hand. 'Where's the flaming fire?'

For a second she thought it might be Ken, but she already knew Ken would not bang on a door like that.

Outside, she saw Carl, Gary's brother. Carl was nearly fourteen now and was starting to grow tall but he was the same solid lad, a dark helmet of hair round his still childlike face. His trousers looked too big, the hems dragging on the ground. He was breathing hard, almost sobbing, and he could not keep still, his arms flailing, feet moving in agitation.

'Eh, Carly, what's up?' Evie said. She propped the broom by the wall and stood back. 'Come inside.'

'No!' Carl shook his head vigorously. 'You gotta come, Evie.' He came up the step and took her by the sleeve. 'Come! Gary wants yer.'

'Carl,' she protested. 'Stop pulling me, I'm coming. Just slow down and tell me what's happened.'

She managed to get the front door shut as Carl seized her arm and started hauling her along the street towards the Knights' house.

'Is Gary at home, Carl?' She knew Gary was supposed to be at work at this time.

'Yeah. Come *on*.'

Evie had not been inside the Knights' house for a long time. Carl kicked the front door open and before she was even inside, the stink of the place hit her and she could hear sobs from the back room. Gary had always been a blarter and now he was crying as if the world had ended.

She had a moment to notice that the back room

166

of the house was as squalid as ever. There was one remaining curtain slewed half across the window, chinks of light piercing through it. The table was strewn with things and the room stank of mouldiness mingled with urine and cigarette smoke. Gary was hunched on a chair next to the unlit grate, his hands over his face, fingers shoved up under his specs.

Carl pointed at his brother in a stricken way, as if Evie might not have noticed the figure in front of her, shoulders shaking with sobs.

'Gary? GARY!' she almost shouted, when he seemed too lost in himself to hear her.

She went and squatted by the chair, knees wide to accommodate her girth. She didn't want to kneel because the floor near the grate was strewn with ash and who knew what else. Laying her hand on her old friend's knee, she looked up at him.

'Gary – look, calm down. It's me, Evie. What's the matter, eh?'

Gary surfaced and took his hands from his face. He looked as if he was emerging from somewhere far away, his eyes red behind his wonky specs, cheeks wet with tears. He took off his smeary specs and pulled his arm across his face. For a moment he sat quiet, then, as if with memory dawning on him again, said, 'It's Pete,' his face crumpling as he started to sob.

'What about him?' Evie decided her legs would not stand squatting down there. She hauled herself up and as Carl watched helplessly, pulled up a little stool from by the fire. She sat beside Gary and waited.

167

'He's ... dead...' Words jerked out between the sobs.

'Oh Gary, no!' She felt the shock. She had thought it was going to be Pete misbehaving again; moody, unfaithful, self-absorbed Pete. Another of their tiffs. But now she was moved by his grief. 'God. How? Was it an accident on his bike?'

Gary was shaking his head. 'No. They don't know.' The words jolted out of him. 'They found the bike on Christmas Eve. No one'd seen 'im, not for days. And then...' He cried again for a few moments at some new thought. 'I only know because one of the other lads who knew 'im came and said... I mean, I was closest to 'im and I never knew 'e was dead for all that time. It's *wrong*...'

Evie put her hand on Gary's back, trying to be comforting, not knowing what to do or say. She realized in those seconds that until now she had not taken Pete seriously. Not really seen that poor, hungry Gary was utterly devoted to him. She had never liked Pete so she had dismissed him from her mind. She thought, what if it was Ken? Worry knifed through her again for a moment. It was a relief to be distracted from her own life by the tragedy in Gary's. She felt Carl's presence, just standing there behind her.

'D'you know where he was?' she asked gently.

Gary lit a cigarette with shaking hands, took a deep drag on it and blew the smoke upwards, the cigarette nipped between his finger and thumb.

'Stourbridge. Near there somewhere.'

'Stourbridge?' She barely knew where it was.

'They found him – his body...' Tears rolled down Gary's cheeks again. He took another drag then coughed at length. His lungs sounded bad. 'He was in the river.'

Evie gasped. 'Oh my God, Gary. He was drowned? Did the bike go in, or...?'

Gary was shaking his head. 'I told yer – the bike was just there, on the bank.'

She didn't like to ask the next question. Pete must have killed himself. In that split second she thought how every time she had seen Pete, with his swaggering, sulky appearance, he had looked unhappy.

'They're saying he done it – you know, topped himself. But 'e *wouldn't* 'ave. 'E'd never've! 'E wouldn't 've gone and left me. Someone done it to him, I know they did. Pete was murdered!' Gary punched his own thigh so hard that he yelped. ''E'd never leave me. If 'e was gunna to top 'imself, 'e should've taken me with 'im!'

'Oh Gary, don't say that!' Evie said, horrified by this extremity. She felt shut out by the force of his rage and grief. Gary was so upset there was no chance of a calm conversation with him. Had Pete been murdered? Did the police think so? Or had he taken his own life? She had no idea what to think and she could see she was going to get no sense out of Gary the state he was in at the moment.

Carl suddenly moved in and wrapped his arms round Gary from behind, his own cheeks wet with tears.

'Don't cry, Gary,' he implored. 'Don't. Don't.'

This, of all of it, brought tears to Evie's eyes. These loveless boys in their rotten home. But then, Gary had had love – or thought he had.

And now it was gone.

'Look. Come on, you two,' she said, standing up. She felt like their friend and mom all at once. 'There's no one in at ours. Come on over and I'll make you a cuppa. Get you out of the house for a bit, Gary.'

Gary gently pushed Carl off and stood up, obedient as a little child. 'All right,' he said in a tired voice.

'You both s'posed to be at work?' she asked.

Gary shrugged. 'Yeah.'

'Come on.'

She led them across the street. Gary cried all the way, Carl holding his arm as if he were an invalid. Evie sat the two of them at the table, cut them a piece of bread and marg and brewed the tea. Gary made as if to refuse, but she insisted.

'Eat,' she ordered. 'You'll feel a bit better.'

Gary looked up meekly at her. 'All right.' He took a bite, then another, then gave a twisted smile which did not reach his eyes. 'Ta, Evie.'

Twenty-Two

'All right, lad, all right. I can see you're upset.'

Mr Hooper, the mechanic who Gary worked for, stood in the doorway of his little workshop, wiping his hands on a rag. He was a squat, middle-aged man in dark blue overalls, head thinly covered by faded ginger hair.

'In the normal run of things, I'd er...' He

170

stopped, leaning against the door frame, seeming unable to think what he might do in the normal run of things. 'But you've had terrible news, I can see. Just make sure you're in in the morning.' He looked at Evie. 'Good job you brought yer girlfriend with yer, lad.'

'Thanks, Mr Hooper,' Gary sniffed, tears welling in his eyes again. It would have taken a heart of stone not to be touched by his sagging, lightning-struck appearance. 'I'll be there in the morning, without fail.'

The gaffer at the factory where Carl had a little holiday job as a sweeper-upper and general gofer told him to get started straight away. Carl did as he was told, with a backward glance at Evie and Gary like a puppy who has had a thrashing.

'Ta, Evie,' Gary kept saying as they walked home. 'You're a mate.'

'S'all right,' she said gruffly. Then she nudged him. 'We've always been mates, eh?'

'You're my best mate,' Gary said earnestly.

She was about to say, what about Pete? but thought better of it. She must keep his mind off Pete. In any case, she could see now, as she had never quite seen before, that Pete had been some-thing else altogether.

'Can you stick around with us?' Gary asked miserably. 'I can't stand being on my own. Or with the others.' He nodded towards the house. 'They don't ... you know, don't get it. Except old Carly – 'e's all right.'

'I've got to go to work this afternoon,' Evie said. 'But it'll be all right 'til then. Come on, let's go down to Monument Road. I'll treat you to some chips. I'm starving.'

She didn't tell him why she was so hungry – not then.

As they walked along the street together Gary said, 'I can't stay here. I've just got to get out and go somewhere else. Somewhere which won't make me remember him.'

She spent every spare moment that weekend with Gary, trying desperately not to think about Ken. Why had she heard nothing more from him? Was he really ill or was that just an excuse? All she could do was to fear the worst. He had spoken to his mom and dad and they had told him never to see her again. This thought left her numb more than anything. It was what she deserved. All she had ever deserved. She had always known really that Ken was too good for her. But she didn't want to believe it. What she would do if this was the truth of it, she could not think at all. As the hours passed, the more anxiety gnawed at her, though she poured all her sympathy into Gary, trying to take her mind off it.

All Saturday she was torn between wanting to go out with Gary to distract both of them, and wanting to stay in because Ken might come. But there was still no sign of him.

She was working that evening. She had gone to the Rag Market and bought a loose dress which she wore to the Tower now, hoping to goodness it would disguise her swelling front. Luckily she stood behind a counter. All that evening she worked to the sound of dance music, selling entry tickets, counting change, sick with anxiety. Surely tonight he would come and be waiting there for her?

But she knew she could not believe in anything anymore. Nothing felt real, not even the baby, even though she could feel it kicking. One minute she expected Ken to turn up just as before, for everything to be as it had been; the next it felt as if she would never see him again, as if she had never had this good thing in her life and it had all been a dream. She was never meant to have anything good or be happy. Life was not good to someone like her.

Even so, she left the darkening building that night with her pulse racing. That spot where he stood waiting – let him, please God make him be waiting for me...

But there was no one there.

By the day Evie was growing more frantic, not knowing what to do. She could not sleep. She kept imagining things. Ken had died of a fever. He had told his father and they had forbidden him ever to see her again. He had deserted her. Oh God, where was he? Why didn't he come?

Looking after Gary was a way of staying out of the house and away from Mom's constant sniping at her. Where was this husband to be of hers then? It was like having a knife gouged into her every time Mom opened her mouth. She and Gary wandered about in the freezing evenings, had a drink or two while the pubs were open, the Christmas spirit passing them both by. Gary talked about Pete. She did not talk about Ken or the baby. While she was with Gary she could pretend none of this was happening. She just had no idea what to do next.

But by the evening of New Year's Eve, she could not stay out any longer. It was cold, she was tired out, her feet aching and frozen. Gary went home to his father and brothers, still swearing he was going to make the break and get away, though he seemed to have no idea to where that might be. Pete had talked about going to America but Gary thought this was a bit far.

As soon as Evie got in, her mother started on her, shouting over the telly.

'Oh, you're back, are yer? Thought yow might've been out sorting out this gunshot wedding of yours. I s'pose yow cor find 'im? Run off from yow, 'as 'e?'

Evie said nothing, forcing herself to keep her temper under control. Shirley looked up from her magazine and eyed her with what Evie chose to think might be sympathy, though it was hard to tell.

Shirley had scarcely said a word to her since they had known Evie was pregnant. She was walking out now with an older man who had an Austin Cambridge which sailed up to the door to pick her up. Apart from the car, all Evie knew was that he had clipped hair and a sporty moustache. Shirley refused to tell anyone anything about him however much Mom kept on, even his name. This was an attitude Evie could well understand, even if Shirley was a smug cow.

'Tea ready, is it?' Mom demanded from her chair.

'It's already *on*,' Shirley snapped, slamming her

copy of *Woman's Own* on the table. *'The Queen's thoughts on life today,'* Evie read on the cover. 'It's Evie's turn anyhow. Get Evie to look at it.'

'No,' Evie corrected her, peeling off her coat. 'It's not my turn – I did it yesterday.'

She was just hanging her coat on the back of the door when there was a knock. Unprepared, she went and opened up. Ken. He looked almost paralysed with fear. In those seconds Evie could see their house from the outside: the shabby door opening straight off the street, the frowsty stink, their cramped room with undies hanging for all to see by the fire. And this, set against his parents' neat terrace, the little front garden with bits of box hedge in pots, the hall and the tidy rooms behind...

'Evie, can you–'

'Who's that?' Mom bawled. 'Tell 'em to sod off – we're 'aving our tea.'

'No one.' Evie grabbed her coat and stepped straight back outside again, slamming the door. 'Quick,' she said to Ken. 'Let's get down the road.'

But she had seen the look of horror on his face.

It was not until they were round the corner, in Reservoir Road, that they slowed at last. Ken touched her arm to stop her.

'Evie. This is no place to do this, but I don't know what else to do.'

She just stared at him numbly. She knew already, by the cold, inevitable feel of things, that this was not going to be happy. He was not going to pull out an engagement ring and go down on one knee. Too many days had passed. But she could still not abandon hope, not yet.

'Did you speak to your mom and dad?' she asked, trying to stop her voice trembling. And then it didn't work. 'Oh Ken! Where've you been?' She burst into tears. 'I've been worried sick. I don't know what to do, and Mom's been on at me non-stop.'

She wanted him to take her in his arms and tell her that everything was going to be all right.

Ken looked terrible. She saw how pale he was. He seemed thinner, as if in the past week he had shrunk, under some sort of torture. He did truly look as if he had been ill.

'Are we going to get married?' she asked. And then, a glimmer of anger lighting in her, 'You've got to marry me, Ken! What'm I going to do? It's your baby!'

He seemed to wither before her. He put his hands in his trouser pockets and moved back from her, just a step, but that step said everything. He spoke staring at the ground.

'I can't.' The words seemed to struggle out of his mouth, as if they were put there by someone else and did not fit. 'I just...' He looked up at her. 'My father says, if I go off with you, they won't let me go to agricultural college. In fact, they'll cut me off altogether – throw me out, they said. So I won't have anything – not for me or for any of us.'

'You've got a job,' Evie said. But already she could see it was hopeless.

'But no future ... not the future I want.' His face creased and she thought he was going to cry but he fought it off. 'I feel so terrible, Evie. They were so furious, Mom and Dad. I've never seen them

176

like that before – even when I didn't do well in the exams... So disappointed – heartbroken. It was awful. They said ... they said awful things. About me – and about you as well. I don't want to say. But can't you see it's hopeless? We can't get married like that, with them feeling like that about us. We should never've... It's not right... And you did ... well, you led me on...'

'What?' She didn't know what to say. 'What d'you mean?' Had she? Was it her fault? She was filled with terror suddenly. All this disgust everyone felt for her. Ken's parents had turned him against her and he was going to leave her all alone so that he could carry on with his nice life.

'They're Christians, aren't they, your mom and dad? I thought they wanted people to get married and do the right thing, not have you just run off?' Her voice rose. 'Ken, you can't just abandon me! What'm I going to do? This...' She laid a hand on her belly. 'This is your baby as well as mine. Don't leave me – please!'

Ken was weeping now as well. 'It's not that I don't love you, Evie.' He came close as if to put his arms round her, then lowered them, drew away again. 'I do, and I feel so bad about what's happened. But can't you see it's the wrong time? What sort of life would we have?'

'I don't know. We'd have to work and...' She stared at him in horror. He didn't love her at all. If he did, he'd never go and leave her. 'We'd have to do what other people do – work and bring up our baby, and–'

'I'm sorry.' He shook his head, final and quick now as if this was something he just had to get finished. 'I can't Evie. Maybe it's selfish of me, but it'd mean giving up my whole future – the future I want for myself. Look.' He reached into his jacket pocket. 'They don't want you to be without help with, you know – when you have the baby... Or not...' He was completely out of his depth. 'They've given me this – for you.' He held out a white rectangle towards her.

Evie kept her hands by her side. She was so stunned, so hurt and afraid, she could not think what to say.

'Take it, Evie.' He sounded angry now. 'For God's sake. I'm sorry. I'm so sorry...' He kept crying, pushing the envelope at her, not looking at her.

'What is it?' she whispered.

Ken came close, looking round to see if anyone was listening, and she despised him for this. Voice very low, he said, 'It's fifty pounds. To help see you right.'

'How will that "see me right"?' she said, dazed. 'It's a baby, Ken.'

'Look, just bloody take it. *Please.*' He grabbed her hand and pushed the envelope into it. He had done it and she could see he hated himself but that now he was desperate to get away. For it to be over so that he could live his life: the life he really wanted.

Silent, she tucked the envelope in her pocket. Fifty pounds – a few weeks' wages – for him to be rid of her.

'Evie...' He stood before her, agonized, longing to be off. 'I really am so, so sorry.'

'So am I,' she said. She was not crying now. She

178

felt empty as a husk. But as he moved away, thin and scurrying, she yelled after him, 'Keep it in your sodding pants next time, Kenny boy!'

Slowly, in the dusk, she walked home, dazed and empty. The only thing clear in her mind was that if the envelope tucked under her hand in her coat pocket contained the money Ken had claimed it did, on no account must Mom have any idea of it. Beyond that she had no thought. Tomorrow felt years away at that moment. There was no tomorrow, only the present.

She stepped into the house. The family were sitting round, the three of them. No Rita today – on Sundays she was with Conn's family.

She had only set foot in the door when Mom looked up, and through a mouthful of stew, said, 'So, is 'e marrying yow?'

Her father's dark eyes turned towards her and, lastly, Shirley's.

Evie stood in her coat. Her hand, in her pocket, brushed the envelope. She raised her chin. 'No.'

'You what?' Mom stopped chewing. She got to her feet, slowly, like a cow getting up in a meadow. She started, across the table, low, getting louder.

'So 'e's leaving yow to carry 'is bastard child? Too bleeding good for the likes of us, is 'e?'

For one crazed moment, Evie thought her mother was taking her side. But no.

'Well!' Mom banged a fist on the table. 'Yow needn't think yower gunna stop round 'ere and feed off the rest of us. Miss High and Mighty ... yower no more than a dirty little ho!'

'Irene, for God's sake,' Dad said, trying to intervene. Shirley's mouth was hanging half open, her eyes wide.

'No, Ray, leave this to me. We cor 'ave 'er bastard darkening our doors. I've 'ad enough with this 'un. 'Er's given me nobbut trouble ever since 'er were born. Yow can pack yower bag and get out of 'ere, Eve Sutton, if yow ay gunna change yower name. Go on, go! You ain't got no family 'ere anymore. And don't you gainsay me, Ray.' She held up her clenched fist. 'Don't you say a bloody word. It was you sired this little bitch in the first place. I never wanted 'er and for once, you can cowing well do as I say.'

Twenty-Three

And she was alone in the dark street, in her hand an old cloth bag they usually used for carrying meat and veg back from the shops into which she had crammed a few of her belongings while Mom ranted.

Her voice still rang in Evie's ears, all the things she had called her, as if a lifetime of her loathing had bubbled over like a vile cauldron. And Dad had just sat there, saying, 'Eh, wench...' and nothing more effective. Even Shirley had come out of her shell to look shocked. 'Mom ... you're not really going to turn 'er out, are yer?' They were paralysed in the face of Mom's rage, all her own hurts, her deafening hatred being hurled at Evie, propelling her out of the door.

180

'Mom,' she had tried to beg. 'Don't! Where'm I gunna go? It's dark out there – and it's freezing. I'll go back and see Ken, make him change his mind...'

But she knew it was hopeless. Her mother was a tidal wave of retribution. And she was relishing her hatred. Her face, lipstick lips and plump, pitted cheeks, wore a look of exultation as she ordered her youngest daughter-who-should-have-been-a-boy out of the house and her life. For a moment Evie thought Shirley might stick up for her more, come with her even. But no. She sat tight, letting Evie disappear into the night.

Stepping out, again she had a feeling that none of this was real. But once she had walked to the end of Inkerman Street and turned the corner, the realness of it came to her with a crushing force which halted her on the pavement. She was having a baby, not married, a disgrace. And Ken, who she had thought loved her, *really* loved her... Her chest ached. A man walking past eyed her, as if he was about to speak, and a blush spread over her. He thinks I'm ... one of those... A woman standing on a street corner. A shameful, dirty woman – wasn't that what she was? She heard Ken's voice, *You led me on.* Maybe she had. She was a dirty, bad person. Hurriedly she moved on.

The cold of the night seeped into her as she walked, with no destination in mind. I can't stay out in this, she thought. And the weight of everything seemed to fall on her: Ken's back walking away, her father and sister turning their eyes away, the streets around her and the huge, uncaring sky. She had always felt alone, except for during those months with Ken, when she thought he loved her enough to do anything to join his life with hers. Now, the aloneness was complete, echoing round her like a sentence.

For a second she thought about going to Gary. But that house, all those boys, and Mr Knight with his wandering hands... It was more depressing than being out here. Auntie Vi and Uncle Bill were the only other family. Scotland. She hardly knew where it was. And Auntie Vi didn't want her. They had brought enough trouble to Vi's door in the past. But there was no one else.

Head down, she wandered along Reservoir Road, passing blokes coming and going from the pubs. Bursts of noise came to her as pub doors opened, adding a waft of ale and fags to the already smoky air. Her feet were frozen. Almost colliding with someone, she looked up for a moment as the bloke muttered, 'Watch it.'

Seeing the street ahead, she was struck by a sudden inspiration. This route, along Reservoir Road, was the way she had gone all those years ago when she had been to Mrs Bracebridge's house, before Mom was so rude and nasty to her. Her heart sped up. Mrs Bracebridge had liked her, had been kind. She was a good Christian lady. She had even offered to take her in, back then, to give her a home. Maybe now she could go to her for help – at least for somewhere to shelter tonight. Tonight was quite enough to think about for now.

She hurried again, along the street towards the neat terraces of Clarendon Road.

In the darkness she was unsure which house it

was after all this time. Twenty-two? Twenty-four? There was something about this one that looked right, except that it had a deserted feel to it, the front windows dark and swathed with nets.

Legs trembling, she mounted the step, felt for a knocker, banged it twice. It did seem like the right place. She stepped back and waited.

Let me in, please just let me in, she whispered to the forbidding wood of the door. Oh, to be inside. To belong inside somewhere and for always. Her heart ached, an actual pain in her chest.

A sound came from inside, the tiny rattle of a lock. It seemed to take an eternity before the door opened on a chain. She saw a pale face through the crack and could just make out that the woman's hair was caught up in a net.

'Who is it?' She sounded frightened.

'Is that you, Mrs Bracebridge?' She moved closer.

'Yes.' If anything, the quavering voice sounded even more worried.

'It's...' She felt the ache in her chest grow and tears rising but she swallowed them back. 'I don't know if you remember me. My name's Eve Sutton. I used to come to the church, like – to Sunday school.'

'Oh? Yes,' Mrs Bracebridge said, her voice firmer now. 'Eve. Yes.'

Evie heard the chain being taken off the door and it swung open. Mrs Bracebridge was dressed in a long, dark-coloured garment, her face a thin wedge of white above it.

'Sorry, Eve, only you have to be careful. I didn't know you at first. You've grown up, a good deal.'

183

Her voice was warmer now, though cautious. 'What did you want, dear?'

'Mrs Bracebridge, I...' Her voice started to shake. 'I'm in trouble. I'm sorry... Can you help me?'

Mary Bracebridge stood for a few seconds, as if calculating what she should do. *Jesus always welcomed strangers.* She had told Evie that, more than once. The outcast, the foreigner, the people no one else wanted.

She stood back and ushered Evie inside.

'I've got money,' Evie told her, sitting in the back room, a cup of sweet, comforting Ovaltine in her hands. 'I don't want to make trouble. And I've got a job. Just over at the Ballroom.' It was very near to here. She looked down at herself. 'For the moment, anyway.'

Mrs Bracebridge had made herself a little cup of Ovaltine as well, and was drinking it like a person recovering from shock. Which, Evie realized, she might well have been. Now they were in the lit back room, she could see that Mrs Bracebridge was wearing a navy and purple weave dressing gown and ancient sheepskin slippers, her hair in curlers under the net. Her face looked much the same, though the flesh sagged a little on her thin neck.

'It's nice to see you again, dear,' she said carefully. 'I was sorry about what happened – you know, when you were little. It was kindly meant.'

'Oh, I know,' Evie assured her. 'My mom's...' She looked down, unable to find quite the right words, or at least words that she might say to Mary

184

Bracebridge without scorching her ears off.

In the silence, she heard someone upstairs give a cough.

'And you say you're coming up to eight months?' the woman asked, with a kind of bracing courage for discussing difficult things. 'And the father is ... reluctant to take on his responsibilities?'

Evie nodded. Her face had already turned varying shades of puce telling Mrs Bracebridge about this. She could see her internal struggle. *Judge not, that ye be not judged.* 'There's no one, Mrs Bracebridge,' she admitted. 'Otherwise, I swear, I wouldn't have brought my troubles to you. Ken ... that's the father. He – at least his mother and father – paid me off.' She couldn't keep the acid out of her voice. 'I dain't tell my mother or she'd've had the money off me. But I've still got nowhere to go.'

Mrs Bracebridge took her cup, with twining ivy leaves round it, to her lips and sipped. She returned it to the saucer with a sigh and looked into Evie's face.

'You're still lovely, dear, to look at.' She hesitated. 'You do know I really wanted to adopt you, Eve? I would have brought you up as my own. Herbert and I ... we couldn't... We had a home, an empty home, and a lot of love and care to spare.'

For the first time, Evie felt her throat tighten and her eyes fill with tears.

'I know,' she said. 'I wish–'

'But now,' Mrs Bracebridge said, cutting her off, 'things are very different. My Herbert is most unwell. He already suffered with his nerves and a few months ago he had a turn – a stroke they call

185

it.' She sat a little straighter, as if to gain strength in discussing it. 'He's paralysed down one side. He couldn't speak for a while, though now he can – a little. I am looking after him and...' She looked across at Evie sorrowfully. 'We can't have anything else disturbing him. The slightest thing, and he is...' She shook her head. 'He's just not a well man.'

'I'm sorry,' Evie said. She had never met Mr Bracebridge. But she was sorry. Mrs Bracebridge was so transparently good and she did not seem to have much of a life.

'You can stop here tonight, dear, of course, so long as you're quiet. I'm not going to turn you out. But I'd prefer that Herbert does not know.' She got up and took Evie's cup along with her own. 'I can find a few bits of bedding for you. And in the morning, we'll see what else can be done.'

When she had found some blankets and a pillow and instructed Evie to settle on the soft hearthrug, she turned at the door and stood looking in at her.

'Thank you, Mrs Bracebridge,' Evie said. 'You're very kind.'

'Goodnight, dear,' she said softly, closing the door, and in her voice, Evie could hear all the inflections of love and regret.

Twenty-Four

January 1961

They stood side by side, Mrs Bracebridge's brown lace-ups beside Evie's old black shoes, in this terrifying house, with its enormous tiled hall and imposing staircase.

'You'll need to leave now,' the young nun said. She was very polite to Mary Bracebridge. 'I can show her where to go.'

Even Mrs Bracebridge seemed overawed by the sheer expanse of the building after her own little terrace. She was wearing a powder-blue macintosh and a see-through plastic hat which tied under her chin as it was drizzling outside. She turned to Evie, her eyes full of sadness, as if she felt guilty for leaving her.

'Well, dear,' she said gently. 'I must go. I'm sure you'll be all right.' She sounded uncertain. In a whisper, as the nun had started to walk slowly up the stairs, she added, 'The sisters are very good.'

Don't leave me, please don't! Evie wanted to beg. If only Ken were here, to put his arms round her and help her, to look into her eyes and tell her everything was going to be all right. Recollection came to her like a stab. Ken was never going to be there. Ken did not want any part of all that was facing her. She swallowed and reached for a breath, feeling the weight of her distended belly.

She was queasy with dread.

'Thank you, Mrs Bracebridge,' she whispered, dry-eyed. 'Thanks ever so much for helping me.'

Mrs Bracebridge looked for a moment as if she might embrace her, but she stepped back, her eyes still meeting Evie's for a lingering moment. She didn't say, come and see me afterwards, let me know... Nothing like that. After a few seconds she gave a nod and said, 'Goodbye, dear, God bless you.' She turned and Evie heard her footsteps and the heavy door closing behind her.

She was alone, in this place Mrs Bracebridge had organized through her church, this forbidding house with a name Evie had no idea how to pronounce. All she knew was that it was the mother and baby home in Moseley and that this was where she would now have to stay until after the baby was born. It felt like being sent to prison.

'This is where you'll sleep.'

The nun pushed a door open high up in the attic of the house. Evie was panting from climbing all the stairs to what had obviously once been the servants' quarters, and she could smell polish and disinfectant and something cooking – meaty but not especially appetizing. The nun's face was plain and fleshy under her veil, her manner clipped and definitely not friendly.

Evie saw a long room with a window at one end letting in sad grey light. It contained six black iron bedsteads, three along each side, each covered by a washed-out green candlewick bedspread and with a wooden chair beside it. Hers was the middle one on the left. Nervously she looked round the room. She had to share with all these strangers – what would they be like? It was a frightening thought.

'The others are downstairs at present,' the nun said. 'In fact, it's nearly dinnertime. I'll take you back down once you've left your things.' This was more of an order than a suggestion.

Leaving her bag was the work of a moment. She put it on the bed and followed the nun's – she was sure – disapproving back down the stairs.

Those first few days were a sea of faces, of meeting her room mates, of questions, of numbness. The house contained a dozen girls, some heavy with child and others who had already given birth and were there to feed their infants for a while before they were delivered for adoption. These girls looked deflated, their bodies adapting back to the separation. Some of them were in a terrible state, weeping on and off all day as their full, sore breasts did their work but reminded them constantly that this giving of themselves would soon no longer be needed or possible. Their babies would be torn away from them. One of them, a dark-haired girl called Dora, seemed as if turned to stone.

The days were spent on chores in the house, eating, resting and some recreation together. Outside was a wide garden, but it was too wet and cold to go out. Evie gradually got to recognize the nuns, some gentle, some obviously judging her to be fallen and of no account. She could see moral superiority in their eyes. She didn't really care. They were mild medicine compared with her mother's hands and mighty gob. She made faces behind their backs, which amused some of the others, and didn't let their icy looks reach her at all. In any case, despite the fear and loneliness of the first few days, there was a surprise at Lahai-Roi, as the house was called, a gift of something unexpected which came as a wonder to her: the other girls.

The silent, sad girl Dora slept in their dormitory but she left within a few days. On each side of Evie were girls who were still expecting, like herself. To her left was Jen, mousey-haired, nicely spoken and so slender that her pregnancy looked like a strange growth jutting from her. On first sight of her and the others, Evie guessed they would all be snobbish but she was wrong. The situation they were all in brought them closer. Jen, a precious only child from Leamington Spa, had been sent away by her parents.

'So,' she explained to Evie as they perched on the edge of their beds the first night, 'they wanted somewhere quite far away from everyone we knew in Leamington, that's for sure. I don't even know if there is a place like this there... They're telling people I'm on a holiday.' She looked towards the window. Her face was gentle, with neat, modest features and a rose-bud mouth.

'We only did it once,' she said, looking back at Evie, her eyes filling with tears. 'I mean, it was silly. I didn't know him all that well. Actually, he's a friend of my father's – younger than Daddy but still quite a bit older than me. I suppose he sort of talked me into it. I hardly knew what he was going to do 'til he'd done it. When they found out they forced me to say who the father was – oh my goodness!' She rolled her eyes, laughing and crying at once. 'You've never seen such a kerfuffle.' She shook her head. 'I don't half feel silly, though. And, sort of *cheap*. The way they talked to me... And of course *he* doesn't want to know now.' She looked across at Evie. 'What about yours – did you love him or anything?'

Evie put her head on one side. Ken. Sweet, affectionate Ken. Angry, hurt as she was, she knew he was not a bad person. He was scared and young and didn't know what he was doing. Just like her. And sometimes she ached with missing him, before the pain of his betrayal came to her all over again, his blaming her for everything that had happened. She was the one having to do this, not him.

'I thought I did. I thought he loved me. Just...'

'Not quite enough to stick around?' Jen said with a wry expression.

Evie nodded, giving a sad smile. 'Yeah. That's about it. His parents didn't want me either.'

'Like Rhoda.' She nodded at the empty bed the other side of Evie. 'That tall, interesting-looking one. That's a sad story. Not that she shows it much. They were both madly in love but the parents won't have it, not at any price. She's only eighteen. How old're you, Evie?'

'Seventeen.'

'Oh my! Are you? You look older! I'm twenty.' She rolled her eyes. 'Still got no sense, though.'

Just then the other girl, Rhoda, arrived. Rhoda was tall and rangy looking with heavy brows and full lips, both of which seemed to take up most of her thin face. It was not a pretty face, but one Evie found she kept wanting to look at in fascination. She was very heavily pregnant and was walking leaning back slightly.

'Who's got no sense?' she demanded, rummaging under the thin pillow for her nightdress. Her voice was deep and rich. Evie realized she was rather posh and immediately felt on her guard.

'None of us, by the looks of us,' Evie said.

Rhoda stopped what she was doing and burst out laughing. Evie felt gratified that she could make her laugh. 'Can't argue with that,' she said. She came round the bed and sat down. 'You're Eve?'

'Evie. Usually.'

'When's it due?'

Evie shrugged. 'Two or three weeks. Not sure. What about you?'

'Any sodding minute.' She rolled her eyes and the three of them laughed. Evie was taken aback by her language. 'Anyway, welcome to "Tears of the Living Well",' she said, and seeing Evie's puzzled expression, explained, 'That's what Lahai-Roi means. It's from the Old Testament.' With another throaty chuckle, she added, 'Cheerful that, isn't it?'

Despite the fear and heartache all around her, those weeks in the home were not all unhappy. She got used to the rooms, the food, the distant sound of the babies from the nursery on the first floor, the way they rang a little bell when one of the girls gave birth – one ring for a boy, two for a girl – and the others would all look at each other.

Evie grew close to Jen and Rhoda also, in the short time she was there. Rhoda kept swearing – in both senses of the word – that as soon as she got out of this place she was damn and blasted well going back to Tom, the father of her child, and everyone else could sod off and leave them alone. She would elope if necessary, to Gretna Green. Within three days of Evie being there, Rhoda went into labour and was delivered of a little boy. During the time afterwards, they could see her wrestling to keep up her front of bravado and resistance to being pushed around. But at night, she wept and wept. Hearing her heart-broken sobs, the other girls got out of bed to comfort her, sitting round her in the darkness.

'He's so beautiful. He's mine,' Rhoda cried. 'Mine and Tom's. I hate my bloody parents. *Hate* them.' She thumped the mattress beside her head. 'They can afford to let me keep him. All they can think about is what other people think. *Stupid,* narrow-minded people, all shut into their little social conventions. I don't even know most of them. Cowards, *all* of them.'

Stroking Rhoda's shoulder beneath the thin candlewick, Evie met the revelation that there were other people who loathed their parents. Jen didn't say she hated her mother and father, but all the same, they had seen fit to send her off miles away to preserve their own reputation. This was an eye-opener to Evie.

She lay awake for a long time afterwards, thinking about all the people who had made up her life. She didn't want to go over what had happened with Ken. That hurt too much. But she kept thinking about her family. Sharing a room with Rita and Shirley as she grew up had meant an almost constant vigilance against their spite. It had been like a game to them, she thought, so normal that until now she had barely given it a thought. She could not walk across the room without Shirley sticking a leg out to try and trip her up; could not do anything without Rita's jibes about her looks, or anything she did. They ganged up with Mom to leave her out and be nasty to her. She thought of her birthday – the day of the Kit-Kats. And here, it was so different. The girls were kind and sympathetic to each other.

She could see that her sisters were nothing but the result of training by their mother. Everything always revolved round Mom and her feelings. Mom's loathing of her, all stemming from Dad and that woman and her son, and the fact that she was a girl, meant she had recruited Rita and Shirley to her side. She had shown them nothing but an example of how to be nasty. Even though she disliked and distrusted her sisters, Evie could see that this was the truth. It made her feel very sad. And Dad had never been any good – not to any of them. He just did what he wanted and sod everyone else.

Thinking of her mother, despite everything, there was all the old longing. Love me, please. Can't you just love me? All those times she had tried to please her, to get her to be nice, just for once... She felt the child moving inside her body and she wondered, frightened now after seeing Rhoda's grief, how she was going to feel after the baby was born. Would she love it the way Rhoda did her little boy? A wave of longing came over her. If only she could keep this little baby and bring it up. She would give it everything she possibly could and she would love it and love it...

A possibility leapt into her mind. Could she keep the baby? She had the money that Ken had given her. That would last for a while. Then she'd get a job, find someone to look after him.

She thought of Mary Bracebridge. That morning, dressed and ready, before they set off, she had said to Evie, 'I'm sorry not to be able to give you a home, my dear. I would have done once, you know that. But things are different now.' In the light of day, Evie had seen that Mrs Bracebridge looked aged and exhausted.

'But I want you to remember something. I get the impression you have not had a lot of love in your life.' Her eyes were kind. And she had a message to deliver. 'Just remember that whatever happens, the Lord loves you. You are, as the hymn says, "ransomed, healed, restored, forgiven". Just go on after this, dear. You have a good heart; I could see that in you when you were a child. Pray to the Lord and he will strengthen you.'

'Yes,' Evie had agreed humbly. 'All right.' She didn't really think she would, though. Surely God didn't bother with people like her?

Lying in her bed now, with its squeaky springs, she decided it was worth a try.

'Dear God...' She faltered. It felt a bit like writing a letter. Hardly knowing what she was asking for she went on, 'Please let me keep the baby. Please.'

Twenty-Five

Jen's baby came earlier than expected and she vanished into the delivery room. Eventually, they heard the two rings of the bell that the home used to announce the arrival of a baby girl. Evie and Rhoda looked at each other.

'Poor old Jen,' Rhoda said gently.

Evie was the only one of the three of them who had not yet passed through this experience, though there were two more girls in their room who were waiting as well. She found herself spending more time with them. Rhoda was in the nursery every moment she was allowed, nursing her baby son, who she had called Edward. In between she seemed unable to sit still, pacing with frustration, saying she was going to run off with 'my little Eddie', but never actually doing it and crying stormily. Evie sometimes sat beside her, stroking her back and trying to think of something to say.

Jen returned to their room the evening after the birth looking pale, with dark rings of exhaustion under her eyes. Her whole body seemed to sag. The others greeted her warmly and Jen raised a smile which left her eyes looking dead and sad.

'You all right?' Evie said as Jen sank down on her bed with the cautious slowness of someone whose body is very sore.

Jen nodded stiffly.

Evie felt awed. Jen had now passed over to the other side. She knew what it was like and Evie both wanted and did not want to know this.

'You had a little girl?'

Again, Jen just nodded, as if speech was too much to risk.

Rhoda came round and sat on Evie's bed, her black hair loose down her back. 'What've you called her, Jen?'

Jen shrugged and, seeming to come to life, said angrily, 'What's the point in me calling her anything? They'll only take her away and call her something else, won't they?'

'No,' Rhoda insisted with her usual passion. '*You* must give her a name – the name you want her to have. That you'll always remember her by.'

Jen made a twisting motion with her head and shifted on the bed, wincing. 'I'm so sore,' she said, looking down at herself.

'From the feeding?' Rhoda said. Evie was glad she was there. She was not sure what to say to Jen.

'From everything,' Jen said tearfully. 'All this bleeding. It's horrible...'

She lay down, curled away from them as if making herself as small as possible.

Evie and Rhoda's eyes met and Rhoda shook her head sadly. Evie looked at Jen's slender back in her pale nightgown. In a few weeks, Jen's baby would be gone, given away forever to strangers. And Rhoda's boy. And... She lay a hand on her drum of a belly. And hers...

But despite the flickering movements inside her, which had become the twitches and kicks of a child almost full-term, still none of it felt quite real.

'Do get on with it, Sutton.' The nun who had shown her into the house stood at the foot of the staircase. 'We want them dry, quickly, not soaking wet all day!'

Evie clanked the heavy mop bucket down onto the next step.

'Bossy bitch,' she muttered. The harsh smell from the bucket of dirty water mixed with disinfectant and the rotten old stink of the mop all turned her stomach. However heavily pregnant you were, there was no let-up on the chores. Her job today was to sweep and mop the brown linoleum of the enormous staircase, from top to bottom. Her belly was heavy and her innards felt sore and dragged down. All she really wanted was to go and lie down.

She wrung out the mop, working it across the step until she heard footsteps moving away and knew she was no longer being watched. She was not bothered by the nuns. Some of them were kindly and one or two she liked; others were sour and cold in their attitude. But none of it mattered. It wasn't as if she was going to be here all that much longer.

What she was going to do *after* she just could not think. She could not imagine *after*.

She had finished the top half of the staircase and began working her way down the wide flight which led into the hall. One or two people passed up and down, some saying, 'Sorry, Evie!' as they trod all over her handiwork.

'S'all right,' she muttered. For a moment a warm feeling filled her. It was nice in some ways living in this place where people knew her name and there was a lot of kindness and fellow feeling among all the girls because whatever background they had come from, they were all facing the same disgrace and heartache.

She kept thinking about Rhoda. Rhoda was the sort of girl who lived in a big house in the country and rode horses. Evie would never ever have met her in any other situation. But today was the day when the adoptive parents were coming for Rhoda's baby – this afternoon at two thirty, to be precise – and she could do no more about it than any of them.

When the babies left the home, in the arms of strangers who were to be their new parents, the girls were told to go and wait in the basement, in the room next to the laundry, out of the way. It was deemed best that they did not see the parents who were taking on their child. They were not to upset them. As the time drew nearer, Rhoda had gone very quiet. She knew, and they all knew, that she was not going to keep her baby. But that morning she had been frantic.

'I can't.' She was pacing up and down the room, looking as if she had not slept at all, dark smudges under her eyes. 'I can't let them take him. I can't stand it.' Tears poured down her face and she clutched at her chest. 'It's tearing at me. I can feel my heart actually breaking.'

'Oh Rhoda,' Evie said, feeling her own rare tears welling in sympathy. It was so hard to watch her friend's agony and know that there was nothing any of them could do about it. There seemed nothing they could do about anything. For all Rhoda's brave talk about keeping her boy, her parents were dead set against it. So far as everyone knew, she was in France working looking after someone else's children, which seemed to Evie a cruel lie to tell. And she had heard not a word from Tom, the man who was supposed to love her so much. Evie thought sourly that she hadn't heard a word from Ken either, though she also knew that Ken would have no idea where she was. And Ken had walked out of her life, she had watched him do it, whereas Rhoda had clung to the belief that there was hope.

As Evie lifted the mop bucket to move it further down the stairs she felt something give inside her. Liquid poured down her legs, the warm gush of it soaking her underclothes, and she cried out. Her waters!

If she had been at home, she would not have known what this was but by now she had heard so much talk. Girls who she had heard say, 'I thought I'd wet myself – you know, spent a penny...' She leaned over, propped up on the mop handle as the liquid ran down into her shoes and seeped around her feet. She gasped, feeling sensations inside her like a dam breaking, slowly, slowly...

Someone was coming up the stairs behind her. 'Evie? You all right?'

It was Jen.

Evie turned to her. 'It's starting,' she said. 'My feet are all wet. Help me. What do I do?'

She stood staring down at a dot of light reflected in the mucky, shifting water of the mop bucket as

Jen's footsteps hurried away to get help.

'Right.' It was the same nun again, something white in her hands. 'Any pain?'

Evie shook her head. Not pain, not exactly.

'I see. Well, in that case, tie this on yourself.' Evie saw that she was offering a wodge of towelling, like a large napkin. 'You can mop up after yourself and finish the job. And Cairns,' she said sternly to Jen. 'You go and finish whatever it is you're supposed to be doing.'

Jen's eyes met Evie's for a sympathetic moment before she obeyed. It made Evie feel less alone, seeing that kindness in them. The nun stood over her as she had to undergo the humiliation of hitching up her skirt and trying to pin the napkin on somehow, over her soaked underclothes. The wet and the bulk between her legs felt shameful and being watched by those cold eyes made it even worse.

'There you go,' the nun said as Evie at last tugged the hem of her baggy frock back down. 'You're not in labour yet so get on with it.'

Evie, having no idea what labour felt like, began her mopping again. 'Sour old cow,' she said to herself. 'You sodding try it.' But though she tried to be defiant she felt frightened and very much alone.

The pain started soon after, a clenching so fierce across her abdomen that she could only clutch the banister and whimper, caught up in it, until it passed.

One of the sisters walked her down to the delivery room, to a hard white bed. Hands undressed her and forced her limbs into a shroud-like robe. She lay on the bed and realized that there was no longer anyone else in the room.

'What do I do?' she whispered to the air as the latest pain seeped away. 'I don't know what to do. Help me. Please help...'

When the next pain seized her, she rolled over and drew her knees up under her so that, her backside sticking up, her head was sideways on the hard mattress and the bulge of her belly between her knees. It felt the right thing to do. As the pains intensified, she heard cries coming from her as if from someone else, like an animal moaning, sounds she had never made before, even when Mom lashed out at her or Dad shoved her across the room. These pains were much longer and more mysterious, feeling as if they would tear her apart.

It was terrifying. Is this how it was supposed to be or was something wrong? Jen and Rhoda had said it hurt like hell, but she had not really believed them until now.

If only someone would come and be with her and tell her what to do. She found herself even wishing for her mother, for someone familiar, to stay beside her.

In the lulls between the pains, which pressed her down onto the bed like a crushing weight, she turned on her side and stared at the wall. The lower part was covered in chipped, mustard-coloured tiles. Halfway up, the wall was roughly whitewashed brick. She came to know some of the marks on the tiles, making patterns with her eyes. One of them looked like the lopsided features of a face made from little spots of an ominous reddish brown. The face seemed to keep her company.

Now and again the sister came in to check on her, said, 'Ah, not ready yet then,' or something similar, and vanished again. She had full lips and dark eyes. She was not unkind, except when once she came in and found Evie at the height of one of the pains, crouched forward, taking the weight on her arms.

'What on *earth* do you think you're doing?' she snapped. She gave Evie a shove. 'How dare you display yourself in that position. Get over onto your side!'

Evie lurched, moaning, onto her left side. 'I can't...' she gasped. 'Am I going to die?'

'No, no, of course you're not.'

As soon as the woman had gone Evie moved back onto her knees again.

She didn't know what the time was and soon she had no idea how many hours had passed. The pains grew worse until all she was aware of were the clenching bouts of agony with shorter and shorter spaces between them, until she could think of nothing else. And she was alone – as she had always been.

Twenty-Six

She came, when Evie felt she was beyond exhaustion, forcing her apart, bursting into life with a snuffle, a scream.

Someone else was in the room now, another of the nuns with a round face and smiling eyes.

'A little girl.' Two rings of the bell. And there was joy in the nun's voice for which Evie would always remember her with gratitude. Joy for a life, not this constant sense of shame and judgement.

The baby was whipped away, washed, weighed and Evie, also being washed and prepared, felt strange and empty.

'Can I see her?' she said, several times, until they brought a bundle wrapped in a towel and she saw the face of the new person who had travelled inside her all these weeks. Seeing her, the crumpled, perplexed-looking face with little flecks of white sticky stuff at the corners of her eyes, her mouth open and searching, Evie was filled instantly with love and longing.

I know her, she thought. It was the strangest feeling, as if in some way she recognized this little person. She's *mine*. The thought of Ken did not even cross her mind at that moment. She came out of me and she's mine. And I'm going to call her Julie. My little Julie.

'You can feed her soon,' the kindly nun said. 'You can see that's what she wants, can't you? It's good for them to have your milk straight away. Sets them up well.'

Sets them up, Evie thought later, as that tiny mouth tugged and sucked on her breast and her innards bucked and clenched in reaction. She was setting her daughter up for a life without her. For the first of many times that week, she found tears pouring down her cheeks. Suddenly, she could cry, as if Julie had pierced into a well of tears waiting inside her.

By the time she returned to the attic dormitory, Rhoda had left the home. There was another girl in her bed, heavily pregnant.

Jen was still there and Evie saw her both in the dormitory and the nursery where the two of them spent every moment they were allowed, nursing their babies. Jen had called her little girl Patsy. They were only supposed to go there when the babies needed feeding and to help look after and bath them, though the nuns wanted to limit the time they spent there.

'They don't want us to get close to them,' Jen said when they were down there together for the first time. There was a large room containing half a dozen cots and chairs for the mothers to sit on and suckle their little ones. 'I know it's meant to be for the best, but if I have to give her up, at least I want to be able to spend every moment I can with her before...' Her eyes filled with tears as she looked down at Patsy. 'I want to remember *everything.*'

Evie felt just the same. As she recovered from Julie's arrival, she realized that despite all the

205

pain of it, she had had what was thought of as a 'good birth'. She had not needed stitches and Julie weighed over seven pounds and was healthy, with a thin fuzz of light brown hair. Evie recovered quickly and the soreness of the birth wore off. She had plenty of milk and Julie fed happily and soon gained weight.

'You seem to be a natural at this, don't you?' Jen sighed. Her little Patsy had been slow to feed and she often cried. Julie, however, was the round-faced picture of a contented baby. She lay in Evie's arms, eating and snoozing with a confidence that suggested all the good things in life would come to her, which was what made Evie weep most of all.

She sat on the low wooden chair in the nursery as spring light poured in through the window, gazing and gazing at her child in devoted astonishment. Every morning she woke aflutter with excitement. Julie! She would rush down to the nursery almost afraid that she had dreamt her, that something so sweet and good could not be true – not for her, Evie Sutton.

And Julie was nothing to do with Mom or Dad or her sisters. They did not even know she existed. The one good thing, Evie thought bitterly, was that Mom and Dad would never be able to get their hands on her. And yet she was also filled with longing – to have a child with loving grandparents, a good family. For everything to be different.

She tried not to think about any time except now. These precious moments when she sat and nursed and cuddled Julie and lost herself in the feel and look and smell of her. This was all she was going to think about. She wanted to shut out everything else. Today she had a little girl and she was called Julie.

'I can't! I can't give her up!'

The time was approaching for Jen's baby to be adopted. Most of the infants stayed for about six weeks before the adoptive parents took them, allowing them to have a good amount of their mother's breastmilk. As the time drew close, Jen could no longer pretend to herself that this was not going to happen. She grew distraught.

'I hate my mother and father,' she sobbed, in the darkness of the dormitory.

Evie felt her way across to Jen's bed. The other girls were asleep, or pretending to be, and the room was lit only by shreds of light round the edges of the door. Evie put her hand on Jen's shoulder, sick with pain for Jen and dread for herself. This was the thing she did not want to think about – that soon this would be her.

'All they want,' Jen raged, 'is for things to be exactly as they were before. They won't have people gossiping about us and Daddy can run his precious damn business. And I'll have to be cheerful and pretend nothing's happened – or that I think it's all for the best. And it isn't for the best – it's hell!' She was becoming hysterical, throwing herself about and thumping the pillow.

'Shh,' Evie whispered, 'or they'll be up.' Shivering, she reached over and pulled a cardigan round her shoulders.

'They don't care about me,' Jen ranted, though in a hoarse whisper now. 'All they care about is what everyone else thinks. Why can't I keep her?

They want me to send her away to strangers – it doesn't matter what I feel about it or whether they'll treat her well. They just want... Evie...'

Jen sat up suddenly as if something had bitten her. 'Look, you want to keep Julie, don't you? Why don't we do it together – you and me? We could rent somewhere ... and we could work somehow, or one of us could, and pay the rent or whatever needs to be paid. And we wouldn't need anyone else, would we?'

For a few seconds Evie's heart leapt with hope. Yes, that's what they should do. They could keep their little girls and they would grow up together like sisters and she and Jen could be friends and look after each other.

She could feel, rather than see, Jen's expression fixed on her in the darkness, almost deranged with hope.

'We *could* ... couldn't we, Evie?'

Already Evie could see how hopeless it was. She had money from Ken – what seemed like a lot of money, tucked away in her bundle of things. She had never told Jen about this. She could still hardly believe in that money herself. But even if they lived on it, it would soon dwindle away to nothing. Jen had no idea. She was used to a much better life. And really, she hardly knew Jen. Though she liked her, Evie had no desire to tie her future in with her. And they would end up in somewhere like Aston or Ladywood on a yard, in one room even, where the rent was rock-bottom – with two babies...

'Jen, I don't think you'd like it, where we'd have to live. We'd be very poor.'

'I shouldn't care!' Jen's hand gripped her wrist. 'I'll live in a hovel, a cave – *anywhere,* if I can keep my baby!'

There was a sudden knock on the door and a figure appeared, a veil and long garment in silhouette.

'What's all this noise in here? Sutton, get back into bed, now!'

Evie scuttled back to her bed and the door closed. Her mind was racing. She adored Julie, every finger and toe and breath of her. But how would she manage? Did she want her little girl growing up in the sort of places she had grown up in – when she might be adopted by people who could give her something so much better? The thought tore at her. The idea of never seeing her again was an agony. But when she thought, really thought, about keeping her and trying to bring her up, she knew she was not up to it. Where could she go? She had no one – no one she really trusted. And how could she live? She had seen mothers bringing up babies. She knew how hard it could be. And Julie, her beloved Julie, deserved more than this.

'Evie!' Jen hissed at her.

'Shh,' one of the other girls said, with sleepy irritation.

Evie raised her head from the pillow, close to tears at the hopelessness of it all. 'Jen ... we can't. You know really. No one'd let us anyway. We just can't.'

And she lay listening as Jen sobbed until the sounds turned to sniffles and at last she slept.

Three days later, baby Patsy's adoptive parents arrived to take her. Jen went to the basement and emerged later, once it was all over. Evie saw a car in the drive, but nothing more. She took Jen in her arms and her friend wept, grief contorting her whole body.

'I'll never forgive my parents,' she said, her face strained and hard. 'They've got enough money. We could have brought her up. I'm going to leave home the moment I can.'

The next day, an expensive car slid to a stand-still outside the home and Jen got in it. Evie never saw her again.

Three weeks later it was her turn to sit in the room next to the laundry. Three more weeks of feeding, dressing, holding her little Julie. Three weeks in which the bleeding after the birth dwindled and her body began to feel as if it was returning to normal. Except for the milk still gathering in her breasts.

Every hour of every day of that three weeks was filled with dread. She kept trying to pretend to herself that the day would never arrive. When she could push any thoughts from her mind about what was to come, she had moments of perfect happiness, holding Julie, pretending that this was how life was going to go on. But each day seemed to fly by faster than the last and soon it was two days before, one day before...

The night before they were due to come for Julie she was awake all night, going over and over in her mind what she could do. Was there any way she could make this not happen? She dreamt of creeping down to the nursery and stealing away with Julie. But there were night staff, and she would never get out and, even if she did, where could they go? She wept in despair at the thought of the two of them out there on the streets in the winter cold. All she prayed was that morning would never come, that even if she had to stay lying here, desperate and praying for a way out, at least Julie was in the nursery below her, her little girl safe and asleep, knowing her mother was near her...

But morning came. Evie walked into it exhausted, every nerve of her body screaming for help. Don't take my baby! It was like having a part of her body ripped away. She told herself that the only way she could survive the day was to see nothing, hear nothing, feel nothing. That's what she had to do – become a cold, unfeeling statue. By the time she thawed out, Julie would be gone...

All morning she begged every second, every minute to drag into eternity, but time did not oblige her. Before dinner, she held her little girl for what she knew would be the last time. As she did so, pressing her cheek against Julie's, feeling her rubbery little limbs, breathing in the scent of her, she tried to make herself go numb, but it was impossible.

'I love you,' she whispered in her tiny ear. 'I love you so much. I always will. Don't forget me, please.'

She sobbed and sobbed so much that Julie's little face was wet and the nun in charge of the nursery came hurrying to her.

'Come on now, Sutton, this won't do. Hand her

to me.'

'No.' Evie clung to this little bundle of life, this beloved child who had come from her body and who was the only thing she had in the world. 'Don't take her, please, sister.' Her voice rose. 'Let me keep her. I'll be good... I'll find somewhere... I've got some money...'

'Don't be ridiculous!' The nun pulled Julie away from her, sounding panic-stricken. She tried to make her voice kinder. 'They're coming for her in two hours' time. Now go and get your dinner, Sutton.'

Evie knew really that it was hopeless. She could not eat a crumb. Two hours later she sat surrounded by the steamy, soapy smells of the laundry. This was the chair where all the girls sat to be parted from their babies forever. Pressed between her palms was a pair of white knitted booties Julie had worn while she was in the nursery. She had slipped them into the waistband of her skirt the day before and taken them from the nursery. They had a little drawstring of wool that tied round the ankle.

She knew what was happening upstairs. A couple who had been unable to have children had applied and been granted leave to adopt Julie. Matron, rather to Evie's surprise, had said to her, 'I wouldn't normally mention details, but your daughter is very lucky, Eve. The couple who have asked to adopt her are very nice people. You don't need to worry. She will lack nothing and they seem very kind.'

In the two days that had passed since, this information had sat inside her like undigested

212

food, feeding her hopes while making her twist with pain. Better parents than her, that was what Matron meant. What could she have given her? Julie would have a good life, would lack nothing.

In torment she sat rocking back and forth on the chair, picturing every second of what was happening upstairs. They would be in Matron's office. Now, they would be walking to the nursery – no, Julie would be brought down to them, in the very best clothes, all spotless and white. They would be handing her over, the mother smiling down, astonished at how lovely she was, this fair-faced child that had cost them no blood or pain. And now they would be walking out to their shiny car, carrying *her* little one, *her* flesh and blood.

Julie. My little Julie. She ground her fingers into her thighs, shaking with sobs. There was still time; she could hurry out, take her back. Every ounce of her body felt as if she wanted to run, to scream out to them, *No, you can't have her, she's mine!*

But she couldn't. She knew it was no good. A feeling went through her as if she was being broken, actually rent apart from the centre of her chest. She folded forward on the chair, one arm clutched tight around her, the other hand pressing the little bootees to her lips, to muffle the anguished sounds which rose, forcing themselves out of her.

The next morning, carrying her cloth bag of belongings, she stepped out of the home and walked to the Moseley Road. Everything felt alien and distant, as if she had been away from it for much longer than a few weeks. It was a cold,

February day, a wind blowing which threatened rain. She stood for a moment. She had her envelope of money tucked in her bag, a few coins of change and nowhere to go.

Putting her head down against the wind, she headed for the nearest bus stop.

III

Twenty-Seven

1962

The long street of terraced houses curved between the Stratford and Ladypool Roads. Early morning light brightened the windows on one side of the street as Evie stepped out from her lodgings to go to work. She took in a breath of the crisp winter air, closed the door behind her and walked towards the Ladypool Road. Now she had been living here all these months, it was coming to feel like home.

A few days ago she had had her hair cut, and it was now curling under at the ends, a side parting slanting the hair across her forehead. 'You've got ever such nice hair,' the girl who cut it for her had said, enviously. Evie thought sourly that her thick blonde hair was the one good thing her mother had ever given her. It made her feel a bit better, having her hair cut. As if she was beginning to feel young again.

Under her navy coat she wore a plain grey skirt, a pale yellow blouse and a blue jersey – old clothes and cheap, for going under an overall at work. She had gone for another Saturday spree at the Rag Market for them, half hoping, half dreading to see Mr and Mrs Booker or some of the family she had known in Aston. When she saw their business in the distance – DANNY

BOOKER, SHEEPSKINS AND LEATHERS, SLIGHT SECONDS AT BARGAIN PRICES – she veered away. Why would they want to see her? On one of her trips she caught sight of Gladys Poulter standing at her stall over at the far side of the market. You couldn't miss Gladys – she always stood out with her vivid, almost gypsy-like looks – and today, instead of her usual black, she had on a scarlet blouse. She looked very handsome and Evie felt a pang of longing. But she did not have the courage to go and see her either. Why would any of them want to give her the time of day?

As she walked amid all the other people hurrying to factories and shops, a voice called to her.

'Evie! Wait for me!'

Evie turned to see Carol Rough, one of her workmates from the factory, running to catch her up, her curly brown hair bouncing as she ran, breath clouding on the air.

She smiled. Carol was a pale, sweet-faced, slender girl with dreamy blue eyes. She had come to work at Coopers Mackie factory shortly before Evie. The factory was one of the hundreds of metal bashing firms housed in filthy old Victorian buildings round the centre of Birmingham. This one was on the first floor of a building, up a narrow staircase, its grimy windows looking out onto a side street just off Digbeth, not far from the great blue-brick railways arches which spanned the area. When Evie first arrived, Carol had been asked to 'show her the ropes'.

'Ropes ain't going to be much use to you in here,' she'd said, winking as the gaffer of their workroom turned away. She led Evie over to the row of machines for turning the tips of the steel needles. 'Your hands'll get sore, I'm warning yer – them shavings can cut your fingers to ribbons if you're not careful.'

There were eight girls working in a row on a bench along the windows, in mucky overalls, feeding the steel rods of varying sizes upright into the machine. This spun the rods round, with oil running down them, so that the bottom end was sharpened to a point. The metal shavings were caught underneath and Evie found Carol was right. When you went to transfer them into the waste box, they were rough and sharp and she had cut her fingers many a time on them.

'Oh yeah, you have to watch that.' Carol smirked at her that first day as the oil in the machine suddenly sprayed out all over Evie, even getting her in the face.

'Ergh!' Evie jumped back, cursing. 'Sodding thing! Well, thanks for telling me! All this for some flaming knitting needles.'

'Oh, they use them for other things,' one of the girls said.

'Well, what?' Evie asked crossly, wiping herself down with a rag as the other machines still banged and whirred away.

The girl shrugged, laughing. 'I dunno. Who cares? It's a bit better than stamping, that's all I know.'

The girls put them back in boxes and they went off elsewhere for coating and to have ends put on them.

They were a rough and ready crew, standing all

day on the dusty old floorboards. By the end of each day Evie's feet ached, her hands were often cut to ribbons, she stank of oil and her neck was stiff. But she had become good friends with Carol and a couple of the other girls in the factory over the past year, working side by side, meeting up in coffee bars after work or going to the pictures. Carol had been the best thing about this miserable year. She still lived with her parents, not far away in Balsall Heath, and sometimes invited Evie home. Mrs Rough, her mom, was a kindly, welcoming lady and Carol, the baby of her family, had two brothers.

'Happy New Year! D'you have a nice Christmas?' Carol asked, panting as she caught up.

'Oh yeah, ta,' Evie lied. 'You know – just quiet, like, back at home.'

Though Carol was now her best friend, Evie had never been entirely straight with her. She had told Carol that her family had moved back to Manchester because that was where her dad was originally from and his mother was old and needed him. Though she had gone with them, she had missed Birmingham and the wages were better here (she had no idea if this was true but it sounded like a good reason) and wanted to come back. She had two sisters, both married with children up there. This, at least, was partly the case, though she painted her sisters as the sort of family she would have wanted to have – nice and a bit of a laugh, the way Carol's seemed to be. Of the real truth about where she was from, she said nothing. About what had happened and her aching heart. About Julie.

Here was a new place where no one need know anything much about her. She was determined to wipe clean the whole experience of her life and begin again. The only person she felt badly about was Gary. Poor Gary. The last time she saw him he was in such a state. She couldn't help feeling she had let him down by vanishing. But she had had her own pain, her own suffering. What else, in reality, could she have done for Gary?

'God, it's cold,' Carol complained, blowing on her green woolly-mittened hands. 'They say it's going to snow tonight.' She peered up at the clear sky. 'Don't look like it at the moment, does it? Anyhow, our mom says d'you want to come over for tea at the weekend? We're already sick of the sight of her Christmas cake!'

Evie laughed. 'Wants me to come and eat it up for her, does she?'

'She likes you.' Carol looked soberly at her. 'And now our Maureen's got married she misses having more girls in the house.'

Evie felt a lift of happiness at this. Her Christmas had been so solitary and sad and now someone wanted her. However lonely she often felt, at least Carol was friendly to her.

'Course I'll come,' she said. 'It's nice of her.'

She had not spent Christmas completely on her own, because Mrs Hardy, her landlady, a widow, was alone herself. She had one grown-up son, Len, who had emigrated to New Zealand with his wife. Len was her main topic of conversation – about how proud she was of him, his grammar school achievements, the good jobs he had been

221

given – and how betrayed she felt at his departure. The other lodger in the tall, spacious terrace was a morose secretary called Barbara who had taken herself off back to her parents in Astwood Bank over the holiday.

Mrs Hardy was a plump, homely lady in her fifties, with faded blonde hair swept back into a pleat and blue eyes. As well as needing the rent money, she was rather a nervous person and did not like to be alone in the house at night. She had been very glad Evie was staying for Christmas and plied her with food and sherry. Evie in turn felt looked after, even though she said very little to Mrs Hardy about herself.

Mrs Hardy had been a stroke of luck. The day she left the mother and baby home, Evie had boarded a bus in Moseley hardly knowing or caring where she was going. After a few stops, on impulse, she got off again in Balsall Heath and wandered the streets for quite a time. In Sparkhill, she saw a sign in the window of a house. It was not the first sign she saw saying 'Room to Let' – some added 'No Blacks' or 'No Children' or both – but it was the first that seemed to beckon her. She liked the look of the house and of Mrs Hardy, whose husband had gone to the Far East during the war, leaving her with Len, a young lad at school. He never returned.

Her room was at the back, looking over a long strip of garden edged by roses and flowering trees – lilac and laburnum, bright mauve and yellow in spring. The room was plain, with brown linoleum covering the floor and brown and yellow striped curtains. Other than the bed, there was a chest of drawers, a small wardrobe and a table and chair by the window.

That day, when Evie arrived, she looked into the room and knew it was a place she could be. It was well away from Ladywood and it felt safe and comfortable. She put the cloth bag down on the chair and reached into it for the little white booties she had taken from the home: the wool which had lain softly against her little girl's feet only a few days before. All of it, the experience of having Julie, her arrival in the world, holding her and feeding her, still felt so close to her. And her baby's face was clear in her mind. Not having her near was like having her skin torn away. There was a pain of grief and longing in her all the time and she felt she would never be complete again without the warm weight of a child in her arms.

She lay on the bed, head on the pillow, and held the little booties against her face, breathing in their scent.

'Julie,' she whispered, her body aching with loss. 'Julie, Julie.'

The rent was ten shillings. She gave Mrs Hardy an advance on it out of Ken's money and with a few pennies more she bought a pad of good-quality Basil Bond writing paper and envelopes, as well as a pencil, rubber and sharpener.

At that time her body was still producing milk. Every so often, especially if she thought of Julie, there would be that almost painful tingle at the sides of her breasts and the milk would come down. She was horrified at the way it wet her clothes and at the thought that people would notice and she bought a length of muslin and some cotton wool and made pads to line her bra. At night she still sometimes woke bathed in sweat and all of it was a reminder of what her body had been used for, what it should still be doing for her little girl. Every night she lay in bed sobbing, her breasts wet and aching, cuddling the pillow, or her rolled-up cardigan – anything to feel that her arms were not empty.

She had no photograph of Julie, no picture to remember her by except that in her mind. During those days, as well as finding herself the job at Coopers Mackie and getting used to Mrs Hardy and her rules about meals and noise and hot water, she sat with her notebook at the little table by the window in her room.

She tried to sketch Julie as she remembered her, tearing the drawing up, sometimes weeping in frustration. One Saturday, bright and alive with the feel of spring outside in the garden, she ripped up yet another sheet of paper.

'I can't draw – I'm hopeless,' she said, distraught. Scraps of paper were scattered on the bed. She would put them on the fire downstairs. These were something she did not want Mrs Hardy, or anyone else, to see.

She rested her chin on her hands and stared out at the row of houses behind. A ramshackle hen coop in one of the gardens added another pang to her already aching heart, reminding her of Mr and Mrs Waring: two more people who had shown her that kindness was possible. Memories of home flooded back to her. She had tried not to think of any of it since she left. Her mother's words, her bullying hatred. I'm never ever going back there, she had said to herself over and over.

She stared down at another sheet of blue paper, willing Julie's face to appear on it by the force of her longing. Again, she tried with her pencil – the curve of a cheek, her little nose, closed eyes, loving every line, trying to will her back into flesh. For once something seemed to go right. She drew only her baby's head, with a soft line at the neck suggesting her clothing. It was working! Hardly daring to do more in case she spoilt it, she shaded in a tiny fuzz of eyelashes, a hint of hair, the faint outline of an ear.

Yes. It was her. It was what she remembered. She wrote 'Julie, my beloved daughter' in the corner. This sheet of paper now felt like her most precious possession.

'I'll never forget you,' she whispered, stroking the paper cheek with her finger. 'Whatever they call you and wherever you are, you'll always be my little girl. I'll think of you every day and you'll be forever in my heart.' An ache began in her throat, and more tears washed her face. 'I'm sorry I couldn't be better for you. I'm so sorry.'

In one of the envelopes she had already, with bitter feelings, put the rest of the money from Ken. Yet it was also a cushion of safety for when she needed things. Why shouldn't she have some nice things? He was getting on with his life all right no doubt.

Into another envelope, she slid the folded picture of Julie. She did not seal it. She wanted to look at it again and again. She tucked it right at the back of her top drawer, under the few underclothes. After closing the drawer she stood holding the handle, not wanting to let go.

Twenty-Eight

At first she thought about Julie almost every moment of the day, sick with the pain of separation. She did her best to put on a normal face to the world and hide her misery, but she felt she would never be able to forgive herself or smile again without having to force her face against its will. She kept getting out her little drawing from its hiding place and gazing at it, stroking it until the lines were blurred and she had to go over them again.

As the weeks passed, her milk dried up and the reality of Julie's physical presence receded, and she began to find that there were times in the day when she was not thinking about her. The memory of her baby would suddenly jar back into her mind, flooding her with guilt. How could she not be thinking of Julie? How *could* she think of something else? She became afraid that she would forget. But she was aware that already she no longer knew exactly what Julie looked like. Julie was gone, and she had to believe that it was to a better home than she could ever have given her.

All through that year, she had tried to live quietly. She had made friends with Carol and some of the other girls in the factory and listened to Mrs Hardy's reminiscences. Mrs Hardy was pleasant and was company of a sort. Evie was grateful to her. In the evening they often sat in the back room with its table covered by an embroidered cloth, armchairs by the fire, the mantel displaying her wedding portrait, the sepia smiles of a younger Mrs Hardy and 'Arthur', solemn-faced with a neat moustache, and the photograph of Len at about sixteen, fair-haired and smiling. Mrs Hardy rarely asked her lodger anything about herself, which suited Evie very well. And being someone who could listen made her feel needed.

'It's very nice having you here, Eve,' Mrs Hardy would say sometimes, surfacing from her own preoccupations. 'That other girl' – she nodded her head upwards towards Barbara's room – 'doesn't seem to like company.' At Christmas she had shaken her head and said, 'You're such a pretty little thing. I don't know what you're doing sitting here with an old lady like me.'

'I like a nice quiet life,' Evie told her. 'I'm a bit of a home bird really.'

But as time passed, she was not always sitting in with Mrs Hardy. At first she did. But she became more and more restless, driven by a hunger inside her. And by her own anguished thoughts. She could not stand sitting in her room for long. Some evenings she went out with Carol and the other girls. But other times, she found herself buttoning up her coat, stepping out of the house and, at first, just wandering about.

Sometimes, at weekends, she walked for hours. Balsall Heath and Sparkhill felt quite like Ladywood, which was both a comfort but also a source of pain and regret. There were the jagged wastes of bombsites filled with weeds and rubble and puddles, the rough open spaces of rubbish and dumped old cars busy with dogs and kids, soon filthy however much their moms sent them out in clean clothes. There was the wasteland where tinkers had moved in to camp, which Evie skirted round; there were the new tower blocks going up, stark and sharp-edged against the sky.

She walked streets of tightly packed terraces, some of them backing onto yards, just like the ones she had been brought up in. Doors stood open, children milling in and out. Some, however poor, were neat and scrubbed clean, from the front step to the proudly mended furniture and fresh curtains. Others, she could tell from a glimpse or a whiff of staleness and neglect, were like the houses she had been reared in – unkempt, shabby, crammed full of people, with dodgy plumbing and even dodgier electrics. Some housed families who either couldn't, or wouldn't, cope with so many kids and all the burdens of life.

The smells coming from doorways of this neighbourhood were now full of a mixture of people who had lived there all their lives and incomers from Ireland, Pakistan, the West Indies... There was the musty stink of the old houses themselves, mingled with cigarette smoke and scouring powders, coconut and scented hair oil, curry spice, urine, chimney smoke, drains... Houses teemed with children of varying colours in clothes of varying colours, spilling into the streets in knots: wrangling, chanting, laughing, sweet-sucking, squabbling, energetic kids.

One afternoon she was walking along a street in Balsall Heath when she saw, perched on the front doorstep, a little girl of about five years old, with waxy white skin and fair hair tumbling over her shoulders. Her elbows rested on her knees, hands cupping her cheeks. She seemed lost in a dream world while the other children played along the street.

They've shut her out, Evie thought, with a sharp twist of memory. She felt again the coldness of the step against her own backside, her own sense of abandonment. As she drew closer, the little girl sat up, lowering her hands as she saw Evie watching her.

''Ello, lady,' she said.

She seemed happy enough, Evie thought as she said hello back. She looked a perky little soul with a trusting smile on her face. Is that what Julie would look like, in a few years' time? As Evie walked level with the door, she saw that it was open and a plump, pink-faced woman in an apron was sitting on a chair just inside, a cigarette jutting from her lips, hands busy in a white bowl in her lap. She looked up, hearing her daughter say something.

'All right, bab?' she called out, removing the cigarette. 'Who're you looking for?'

Evie was filled with longing to be taken in by this kind lady, to be sat down, given tea and motherly advice. But she could not pretend.

'No one, ta,' she said. 'Just passing.'

She went to the next corner shop for cigarettes – she smoked off and on. She had been using Ken's money to buy treats in an angry, why-the-hell-not sort of way. She bought a bar of Dairy Milk for comfort, sucking each sweet, melting square to make it last.

Sometimes in the evenings, when the gnawing inside her took over, she would creep downstairs and along the dark hall, not wanting Mrs Hardy to notice her slipping out. If Mrs Hardy ever said anything, she'd make an excuse. 'I'm just popping out for a smoke,' at which Mrs Hardy would reply, 'Why don't you go out to the back, dear? You don't need to stand in the street like that.' Usually she escaped without her noticing. She felt bad doing it, but she could not help herself.

She would wander, looking at the lit windows of houses, feeling left out and bereft. It felt as if everyone but her had a home to go to, a room to sit in with the lights on and laugh with people they loved. She would hear laughter and chatter from pubs and one day she stepped inside one. Nervous at first, she raised her chin and asked for a port and lemon, daring herself onwards, driven by something she could hardly understand. I just want a bit of a life, she told herself. I'm young and free – why shouldn't I go out and have a drink?

Being young, blonde and pretty, she immediately attracted attention. She was never alone for long. Some longing inside her that she scarcely knew was there must have come off her like a scent. Meeting men, she discovered, was not difficult. More nights than not, she went out, dressed up in a little black wool dress and black court shoes. Black looked good against her pale hair and skin and the dress flattered her curvaceous figure.

Paul was one of the first. He was twenty-one and worked at a firm in Cheapside. Paul was someone you could have a laugh with. He was also fair-haired, a nice-looking lad with blue eyes and a careless outlook on life.

'Come on,' he'd say on a Saturday night. 'No work tomorrow – let's make a night of it.'

She walked out with him for a while, went to a few dances. And then with Barry, a quiet, intense young man who had just finished an engineering apprenticeship. Evie never took much notice of what they told her. If she could not find in them what she was looking for within a few dates, she withdrew. And the men, who were also looking for something if they could get it, never got far with her. She would let them kiss her, have a cuddle in the dark, allow their hands to wander – but no more.

'You're so gorgeous,' they'd groan. 'I want yer, Evie. I've never met a girl like you before.' All types of flattery and persuasion.

'*No*,' she'd insist, withdrawing. 'I'm not like that. I dunno what you take me for, but I'm not that kind of girl. Marriage first – do it right. No hanky-panky.'

And sooner or later, she left them, before they could leave her. Every time she felt terrible – empty and sad. But she kept going back for more. However much she longed for all of it, to be held and loved, to lie with a man and feel the force of him wanting her, she knew after Ken she was never ever going to let anyone do anything to her unless it meant more. No more money sealed in an envelope, no more bye-bye have a nice life and walking off. Never would she go through that again – a baby, her baby, being handed over to strangers.

She wanted the real thing – marriage and babies. Someone who would give her everything she needed. All the same, she liked the feeling almost of danger, the company, the drink, which made her halfway forgetful and feel as though she was melting.

One night, she was coming out of the Drovers' Arms in town, on the arm of a bloke who had taken a fancy to her. Les. Alan. One or the other. As they got to the pavement, she caught sight of a familiar face approaching along the street – familiar and unmistakeable. Mrs Poulter, the powerful matron of the yard of her childhood. She must have been going home, late after the markets. Their eyes met, just for a second, and Evie had a terrible feeling of her blood pumping too hard round her body, as if she had been caught in a criminal act. She turned away and said something to the man, laughed loudly. When she looked back, Mrs Poulter was gone, but her gaze stayed with Evie, and the feeling of shame it brought with it.

And not long after, just before Christmas, she was with a man she met in one of the pubs round Sparkhill and they'd had a few drinks. When they left the pub he started to get amorous. He was a bit older than most of the others she had been with – well into his twenties – a solid bloke who told her he was a bricklayer.

He flung an arm round her shoulder in the street. Others were turning out into the cold night, warmed by Christmas spirits of one kind or another. Evie, who was half drunk herself, paid no attention to where they were going. She was getting used to wandering about with blokes. One street looked very much like another but she always found her way home in the end.

'You're a nice'n, you are,' he said, leaning round to kiss her. He had a moustache, she remembered later. It prickled against her lips. 'Lovely wench, you are.' He kept muttering, weaving along. 'Come 'ere...'

He pulled her into an entry between two factories and pressed her up against the wall, kissing her, his lips hard and forceful, his mouth tasting of whisky and bad teeth. She soon realized that the man was very drunk and that he was making short work of her, his hands up her dress, tugging at her clothes, mind on only one thing. He took it for granted that she was going to give him what he wanted and quickly. As he thrust his body against her, she knew that she could be anyone, any piece of female meat.

'No,' she started to say, cursing herself for having drunk so much. She felt swimmy in the head and nothing was clear. 'Stop! Gerroff of me now, will you!'

She grabbed at his hands, trying to pull them out of her clothes, but he was very strong.

'What?' He drew his head back and she could hear the aggression. 'What d'yer mean, no, yer stupid bitch? What the hell're you playing at?'

'That's enough. I don't want this.' She started trying to scrabble away from him. 'I never said I'd do that with you.' She managed to move away, pulling her clothes together. 'Not that. I never meant–'

His hand lunged at her, catching her cheek-bone, and her face jarred. She cried out with pain, clutching at her cheek.

'You're asking for it, out on yer own! Go on, piss off then, yer stupid bint...'

I've got to get away, she thought, frightened of him now, of what he might do. Within seconds another blow came, a crack to the side of her head, and she lost consciousness.

When she came to it was still dark and she was freezing cold. She was lying on her left side, her cheek pressed against the hard ground.

Oh my God, she thought. Where am I? She felt about her. Rough bricks, grit, glass. The entry. The man. What had he done to her? The main pain was in her head, a heavy throb on the left side. As she slowly sat up, feeling sick, she realized that though her left knee and elbow were sore where she must had fallen, she was otherwise all right. Her clothes seemed to be intact. He had not taken advantage of her after he had knocked her head against the wall.

All she could think about then was that she had to get home. Thank heaven it was Saturday tomorrow and she didn't need to get to work.

She dragged herself to her feet and the moment she was upright her insides bucked and she bent over, retching, her head throbbing. She straightened up, spat and let out a moan, leaning against the wall. She heard a voice.

'Someone there?' A beam of torchlight pierced her eyes as she turned. 'You all right, miss?'

A police constable was standing at the end of the entry. He sounded very young. Evie staggered towards him. Immediately she knew she didn't want to tell him anything. She wiped at her cheek with the back of her hand, knowing there was blood on it.

'I fell,' she said. Her voice sounded slurred. It wouldn't seem to behave. 'Can you tell me the way to the Stratford Road from here?'

The young man looked worried. In the end he insisted on walking her home. Once she got walking, she realized she was not badly hurt, though she felt very groggy. Her head was sore but it cleared a little as they walked from street lamp to street lamp. She could see ice forming on the pavements.

'What time is it?' she asked him.

'Nearly midnight.' He seemed shy of her, or was it frightened? She wasn't sure. It had been nearly eleven when they left the pub. She hadn't been lying there for too long.

'Will you be all right?' he asked, once they got to Mrs Hardy's house.

'Yes. Ta. I've got a key,' she said.

After bathing the cuts on her face, Evie at last sank into bed, all of her hurting, her feelings very low and sober now. He could have killed me. She wondered if her head was all right but did not know what to do except sleep it off and hope that would do the trick. She was disgusted at herself, shocked and frightened by what had happened, by the way she could feel herself slipping down and down into somewhere lost and dark. To that policeman she must have looked like... Well, she could imagine what he had thought. And she knew how she must have looked to Gladys Poulter as well. Dear God, what was she becoming?

She lay filled with despair, but she hadn't the energy to cry. Falling asleep, hugging her sore body, her head aching, she thought, I must get a hold on myself. She would have to make up something to tell Mrs Hardy tomorrow...

Over Christmas she made herself stay in and keep Mrs Hardy company. And it was soon after that – not in a pub – that she met Jack Harrison.

Twenty-Nine

February 1962

'Here you are, bab, have another bit of cake. It won't keep.'

Evie smiled and held out her plate. They were all round the table at Carol's house and Mrs Rough had stood up to cut more slices off a fruitcake so solid and stuffed with fruit that it looked as if it would last forever. The marzipan and icing combined were almost an inch thick.

'You could've sent that on an Antarctic expedition, Eileen,' Mr Rough remarked, somewhat muffled by a sticky mouthful. He was a rangy man with dark clipped hair and a curling moustache. 'They wouldn't need another thing 'til they got home.'

'Shush, Bernard.' Mrs Rough flapped a hand at

him good-naturedly. She was a comfortable-looking lady, hair permed into tight red-brown curls and wearing a brown woolly dress. 'That's it, our Evie, you eat up. Have a nice Christmas with your family, did you?'

'Oh, yes, ta,' Evie said, smiling up at her.

Evie loved the cake, and being with someone who fed her, and, even more, she loved being called 'our Evie'. It gave her a tremor of happiness inside every time she heard it. Carol's family had taken to her. She was always welcomed warmly and they weren't nosey. Carol must have told them a bit about her, but they didn't keep asking her too many questions. They went about their own business, were pleased to see her and let her be. For her own part, after what had happened with the man before Christmas, she had decided to take herself in hand and stop going out wandering about, behaving like a loose woman. What she needed was a proper life, she told herself. She had had a narrow escape. And now she was happy to be sitting here with this friendly family.

The afternoon was chill and foggy and they sat round the table in the cosy back room of the Roughs' little terraced house, the red and white check cloth over the yellow formica table laden with food. The telly chattered on the sideboard. Evie could see its light and shade flickering to her right. The gas fire was pumping and every face was pink. As well as the stout Christmas cake, Mrs Rough had made luncheon meat and mustard sandwiches, bridge rolls with egg, and laid out Kit-Kats and Skippy bars and angel cakes and bowls of crisps, so that, as Mr Rough observed,

237

trying to put down a cup was like playing a game of draughts. Mr and Mrs Rough were at each end, Evie on one side and Carol squeezed next to her brother Paul on the other.

'Where's Tony?' Evie asked, aware that she was sitting in his seat. Tony was the eldest, well into his twenties and still living at home, working for Tangyes in Smethwick. Tony was a lively, confident man, always laughing and joking, whereas Paul, two years younger, was shy, seemingly in Tony's shadow, and hardly said a word.

'Oh, he'll be in,' Mrs Rough said. 'He's off out tonight – with that pal of his. He said he'd come by first, though. Now, I'll fill the pot up again. Have a Skippy, Evie.'

'God, Mom, let her finish her cake first,' Carol protested. 'I know you want us out the way so you can watch your show.'

'No I don't!' Mrs Rough protested, but giving a lopsided smile to mean she did. They all knew she was devoted to *Dixon of Dock Green* on Saturdays, *This is Your Life* on Sundays and *Coronation Street* in the week – and nothing must get in the way.

Evie smiled at Mrs Rough, enjoying her. She was so different from her own mother it was hardly believable and it warmed her heart.

Just as the kettle was coming to the boil again, they heard the front door open and male voices booming in the narrow hall.

'Ah, here's our Tony now,' Mrs Rough said, rather unnecessarily. In seconds, the boys burst in.

'All right, Mom?' Tony said, swooping down on

238

a meat sandwich and chewing with relish. Evie saw his strong jaw working. She smiled shyly at him.

'Eh!' Mrs Rough protested, slapping him fondly on the arm. 'What about your pal? Helping yerself first. Here yer go, bab. Want a sandwich, Jack?'

'Yep, ta very much.' The room felt suddenly even more crammed as the lads stood over them full of male energy, joking and teasing Paul, trying to get a rise out of him.

Tony's friend had a deep, distinctive voice and Evie turned to look. She saw a tall, slender, vivid man, his brown hair shorn neatly into a short back and sides, but longer at the front, sweeping across his forehead. His face was thin and pale, the eyes dark and intent. It was a face she couldn't stop looking at. He stood leaning one elbow on the wall to the side of the tiled fireplace. As she looked across at him, their eyes met.

Evie saw him take her in, then look away as Mrs Rough was talking to him, offering him tea and cake.

'No, ta, Mrs Rough,' he said. That voice again. She kept looking, while trying to pretend she wasn't. She saw him glance back at her. 'We're off out with some of the lads. Just come for a quick wash and brush-up.'

'You've got room for a cup of tea,' Mrs Rough instructed, handing him one.

'Mom!' Carol said, obviously mortified. Evie could see her blushing and wondered if she fancied her brother's friend. She hadn't said much about him but Jack's presence was a force in the room.

'Oh, all right, ta then,' Jack said easily, taking the green cup and saucer. He smiled and the face became even more interesting.

'You can't get away from our mom without being fed,' Tony told him, laughing. 'It's no good even trying.'

'Go on, lad, have an angel cake with that,' Mrs Rough insisted, thrusting a plate at him.

Jack stared at the little cakes with their daubs of icing and shrugged helplessly, taking one. As he looked up, his eyes met Evie's laughingly and lingered, just for a second, before his glance moved away. His looking at her had made her breath go shallow. There was something electric about Jack Harrison, as she later found out he was called, standing propping up the mantelpiece, his jacket draped over one shoulder like a resting wing. Even the way his hair was cut, the shape of it over his ears and round his neck, felt right, as if there was something in him she had recognized.

Almost as if she had sensed something, Carol said, 'All right, Jack?' As if claiming him. Evie wondered again if she fancied him and wanted him to pay her attention. But he didn't seem interested in Carol. Carol was sweet looking, but not striking. She always wore her hair nicely, but she was mousey and homely like her mom.

Every so often, Evie felt Jack's glance return to her, then dart away again, looking but not wanting to be seen doing it. She knew she looked nice. She had put weight back on after Julie and all the strain of it. Her bobbed hair curled under nicely and she had on a straight black skirt and a pale yellow blouse. She knew the outfit flattered her,

240

but as she was sitting down, this could not be seen.

The boys stayed long enough to drink a cup of tea and then Tony was saying, 'Come on, best be off soon.'

By the time the lads came down, ready, they were clearing away tea. Evie had got up from the table. She was alert for the sound of the boys' feet on the stairs. As they came in to say goodbye, she turned, feeling the satisfaction of her own shape, her femaleness, the fact that now she was standing up. Jack's eyes immediately swept her up and down.

'Tara-a-bit!' Tony called to them. 'T'ra, Mom. T'ra, Evie.' He nodded at her.

'T'ra,' she said, looking at Jack.

Jack nodded back, murmured a goodbye, and the two off them wheeled away, like a couple of horses, full of pent-up, muscular energy.

A couple of days later, Carol caught up with her on the way to work again.

'Hey,' she panted. 'You'll never guess what?'

'What?' Evie said without enthusiasm. It was early and freezing cold. She was bundled up with her coat collar round her ears and a woolly hat pulled right down. Her chest was tight in the icy air.

'That pal of Tony's – Jack Harrison. He's been asking about you.'

Evie felt a lurch of excitement, a feeling she had been pushing away ever since she had laid eyes on Jack. She had been trying not to think about him, even though he kept barging his way into

241

her thoughts day and night.

'Oh,' she said, very casually. 'Has he?'

Carol elbowed her hard. *'Oh, has he?'* she mimicked. 'God Evie, he couldn't keep his eyes off of you.'

Evie wondered if Carol was jealous, but she didn't seem to be.

'He's nice looking, isn't he? Our Tony says he's ever so clever – going places, that one. He's twenty-six, you know! Anyway, he was beating about the bush a bit, Tony said, but he wants to meet you – if you want?'

Evie took this in. 'He's a bit old, isn't he?' she said, taken aback to realize that Jack was eight years older than her. The lad she was walking out with at the moment, Pete, was only nineteen. But now, in comparison with Jack, he seemed like a boring child.

'Oh, that doesn't matter!' Carol said. 'Our dad's nearly ten years older than Mom. It makes no difference in the long run. Jack's a bit of a lone wolf anyway. At least, he's not got anyone, a girlfriend, I mean – not so far as I know. He lives in digs somewhere – off the Hagley Road, I think.'

Evie hesitated, wanting to clear the air. She was excited that Jack had taken a fancy to her, but she didn't want to spoil her friendship with Carol.

'I'm not treading on your toes or anything, am I?'

'Oh … no. I mean, he's a cool cat, that one,' Carol said, in her sweet way, though, Evie thought, trying just a bit too hard to sound as if she didn't care. 'But no, he's *too* much of a cool customer for me. And anyway, it's you he's after, isn't it?'

Hearing it put like that, Evie felt a happy excitement swelling in her for the first time in a very long time.

Thirty

She met Jack the next Friday evening. The arrangements were made through Carol and the other girls at work all got to hear that Evie was going on a date and kept teasing her as they stood in a row along the workbench, feeding the steel rods into the spinning machines. *Go on, what's he like, Evie? Carol says he's a proper looker...*

'Ooh, aren't you scared?' Carol kept saying. 'I'd be a bag of nerves, meeting him!'

Evie shook her head, trying to be mysterious. 'Not really,' she fibbed.

All week her heart kept speeding up each time she remembered she was meeting Jack Harrison. She kept forcing her mind back to work in the room's dingy light. If she wasn't careful, she was going to get her fingers caught in one of the vicious machines. She lay in bed every night that week, imagining how the meeting would be, what she would say and trying to predict Jack's responses. She could picture him clearly, with his lean, chiselled features. He made you feel there was really *someone* in the room, a person whose presence you could sense, like an animal that gives off a roving energy.

They had arranged to meet in town outside the

243

cathedral, which was easy for both of them as they would be coming in on different buses. Evie hoped she would be there first so that she could calm down and prepare herself. So that she could see him walking towards her.

But it was pouring with rain that evening and her bus crawled along the Moseley Road. I'm going to be late, damn it, she thought, peering out through the streaming windows. At least I've got an umbrella. But it was not a good start. She was almost running most of the way from the stop to the cathedral and arrived feeling sweaty and flustered. She wondered for a moment how she was going to find him in the ill-lit gloom, but almost immediately she saw a slender figure step forward from a doorway on Colmore Row, where he had been sheltering. He had the collar of his coat up, shoulders hunched, but he strode towards her, with that energy she remembered. She could see the orange tip of a cigarette.

'Here,' she said, raising the umbrella. 'Come under here.' Being the first to speak made her feel bolder.

'Ta.' He ducked under and she tried to hold the thing higher but he was several inches taller than she was. 'Here, you'd better have it,' she said.

He took the umbrella in his left hand, let the cigarette fall from his lips and trod it into the pavement. To her astonishment, he brought his right arm around her back and pulled her close to him.

'Oh!' she said, then felt silly.

Jack laughed, looking round at her, eyes full of amusement. 'Only way to walk under one of these, in't it?'

'I s'pose so,' she said. In seconds, Jack Harrison had his arm round her! She imagined telling Carol when they were at work on Monday.

'Let's get inside,' Jack said. 'Kardomah all right?'

'Yes,' she said breathlessly, trotting through puddles to keep up with his energetic stride.

They didn't talk much, not until they were inside the steamy atmosphere of the coffee house. As they walked in, there was a tune playing which she could not name but it brought Ken back to her with a shock of pain such as she had not felt in a while. Drawn by the music, things spilled into her mind – home, Ken, Gary – but she forced them all away and smiled at Jack as they found a table near the front window. She hung her coat on the chair.

Jack fetched coffees and she watched him, the clipped hair, the set of his shoulders in his work jacket. He looked neat and strong and somehow right. The music changed and she felt better, seeing Jack carrying the two cups and saucers back to her, slowly, trying not to spill them.

'Thanks,' she said. Jack sat down, searching inside his jacket for his cigarettes and flinging a packet on the table. He smoked Senior Service, not the cheapest, Woodies or the Park Drive ones she tended to buy. Class, she thought.

He lit up and offered her one, which she took, feeling better for something to do with her hands. She had put on her black dress which she knew looked good against her pale hair. A touch of lipstick – not too much; a good flick of mascara on her lashes. She felt acutely aware of everything physical about herself, her chest pushing at the close-fitting material of the dress, the spread of her hips on the chair, as if her skin were suddenly sensitive all over. And she was acutely conscious of him: the wet hair, one strand pressed flat against the side of his forehead, his thin face with prominent cheekbones, the blue, searching eyes. It was as if everything was turned up, more brightly coloured.

'So ... you work with Carol?' he said, smoke clouding from his lips as he spoke.

'Yeah.' She held her hands out, marked with little red cuts. 'Very glamorous.'

He nodded, drawing on the fag again.

'Carol says you live with a landlady,' he said. 'What's she like?'

'She's all right.' Evie flicked ash onto the grimy brass ashtray. Evidently he had been asking about her. This pleased her. 'There's her and there's Barbara the secretary. Miserable, she is – hardly says a word. But Mrs Hardy's all right. She's got no one else so she likes the company.'

Jack looked levelly at her. 'Haven't you got a mom and dad?'

Evie's eyes met his. In those split seconds she struggled to decide what to say. The story she had given Carol was that they were in Manchester. But this was different. She didn't want to start – because it felt as if something was starting – by telling fibs. And it felt safe talking in here, cosy behind the steamed-up windows, most of the tables full, the place alive with chatter and the clink of spoons and the hissing coffee machine behind the bar.

'Yeah,' was all she said, looking at the cigarette in her hand.

'Yeah?' Jack sat back, watching her, as if gauging her. 'What does "yeah" mean?'

'Let's just say we don't see eye to eye.'

He nodded, seeming reassured. 'Got out from under my old man the minute I could,' he said. 'I ain't been back there in years.'

Evie's pulse speeded up. Someone else who knew. Not like Carol who would never understand why you would just leave your mom and dad and never go back. She decided it was her turn to ask questions.

'Why? What's he like?'

Jack took another sharp drag on the cigarette. Not looking at her, he said, 'Oh ... you know.'

'Do I?' She laughed. But she did know, or could guess.

He flicked ash. She thought he wasn't going to say any more. But then he sat back.

'Our mom, she was scared ever to do anything but take his side. Ted, my brother, went into the army, soon as he could. My sister got out, married a man she should never of but there you go. Then I went, came down here.' He shrugged. 'Serves 'em right.'

'Where do they live?' she asked.

'Wolverhampton.' Another flick of the cigarette. 'They can be in cowing Australia for all I care.'

Her snort of laughter seemed to startle him and he grinned slowly.

'Why're you laughing? Most people, if you say that, they go, "Oh dear. Oh that's awful..."' He mimicked expressions of concern. '"Don't you think you should go and try to make it up with them?" All that sort of happy families claptrap.'

Evie sipped her coffee as he spoke. It was weak but hot. She wiped a curve of froth from her upper lip with her finger, feeling him watching her.

'Go on then,' he said.

'What?'

'Tell me. About yours – where are they?'

Truth spilled from her. 'Promise you won't tell Carol?'

His shoulders inched up and down dismissively. 'Yeah. Course.'

'Ladywood. I told her they were in Manchester.'

'Ladywood? What, and you never see 'em? When d'you last see 'em?'

This was hovering too close to details she would not go into. Ever.

'Oh...' She slid into vagueness. 'Months. I don't get on with our mom.' She flicked ash savagely. 'She's never liked me. She's all right with my sisters – Rita and Shirley. But me...' She tried to brush it off, make it funny. 'I dunno. I think I was born with a curse or summat, like Cinderella.'

Jack was watching her intently. He didn't say anything for a moment, just reached forward and stubbed out his cigarette, leaned his elbows on the table, hands clasped under his chin. Suddenly he was quite close to her.

'Why would she be like that to you?' he said, seeming genuinely puzzled.

'Oh, she wanted me to be a boy – something to do with my dad and some other woman,' Evie told him. 'That's what she said anyway.'

'I've been out with a few women,' Jack said.

248

Evie was taken aback by this turn in the conversation, as if everything had shifted. 'I won't pretend I haven't. But the minute I saw you, I...'

She was touched at seeing how uncertain he was suddenly, and by the force of what he was saying. She looked down in confusion, into the cup of greyish coffee.

'Evie?'

She only just heard him in the racket of the room and looked up. 'You know I'm only eighteen?' she said.

Jack sat back, sucking in air. 'I must admit, I thought you was older than that. I'd've put you at twenty or more. But what's it matter? You're just ... well, you're lovely, you are.'

Evie felt a blush rising through her, as if her body was responding to the almost insane excitement she felt at the longing she could see in him. He wanted her.

'I'll be nineteen in a few months,' she said.

Jack laughed suddenly. 'Yes, I s'pose you will.' He pointed at her cup. 'Want another one?'

They sat chatting all evening, Jack telling her about his job making hydraulic equipment, his ambitions. He said he wanted to go and work abroad. Canada, he said.

'Why?' she asked. 'Why Canada?'

'There's loads of people going over there – 'cause of the oil. Lot of jobs going; good money. And it's different over there. More space, more opportunities. Not like this tatty bleeding hole.'

'Would you really go and live over there?' she said.

'Oh yeah,' he replied. He gave her a challenging look. 'Wanna come?'

She smiled slowly. 'Maybe.'

Evie had never met anyone who said things like this before. He had ambition and drive and she felt taken along with it – not like with Ken when she had always felt he would leave her behind.

After, she talked a bit about places she had worked, stretching the time a little to cover her missing months, so that it sounded as if she had moved from the Tower Ballroom to where she was now without any gap. Julie... No, she could not talk about her. She would never be able to talk about her without flooding the table with the tears dammed up inside her.

Outside, it had stopped raining, though the roads were full of puddles and the sound of dripping from gutters, lamps and trees.

'I'll walk you back to your stop,' Jack said.

Feeling more at ease now, he put his arm round her again, even though they had no need of the umbrella. Within yards of the coffee shop, he stopped on a corner and turned her towards him. He said nothing, but even in the dark she could feel the force of his eyes on her and his arms pulling her close. She turned her head up, loving being held, longing to be kissed. His kiss was a surprise. Her lips remembered Ken, a nervous beginner; other men's fumblings since. But this was different, more urgent, filling her with excitement. She felt Jack's hand at the back of her head, fingers exploring her hair as they clung together.

When they separated, it was like being woken from a dream.

'I s'pose we'll have to go,' he said, sounding resentful.

Within yards they had stopped and were kissing again. In this fashion, they made their way slowly to the bus stop.

'Look, there's one there!' She started to run, pulling on his arm, trying to fish for change in her pocket as she did so.

Jack tugged her to a halt outside the bus. 'Tomorrow? Come out with me?'

'Yes!' she cried. And leapt aboard.

The driver, a middle-aged man, looked witheringly at her, but she beamed back at him. Her whole world was lit up by Jack Harrison! She already knew that the future would contain him, that everything had changed.

. . . .

IV

Thirty-One

May 1964

'There. Last one.'

Evie clicked shut the latch of the suitcase, stood it next to the others and sank down on the bed. Their rooms, in this house in Smethwick, were bare of almost all their belongings and instead there stood this row of new black cases.

She got up and went to the window, her steps echoing on the boards now the room was empty. Yanking up the sash window, she rested her elbows on the sill and looked out at the now familiar street. It was a warm spring morning, the breeze carrying the usual whiffs of oil and industrial grime, tinged with brewery smells and refuse. She could hear the ragged blare of a trumpet somewhere nearby, signalling that the scrap metal man was coming round. She looked across with sudden fondness at the soot-begrimed bricks of the houses, the scruffy old slates covered in moss and dirt, things sprouting through in places. There came another elephant-like blast on the trumpet. A car passed below in the quiet street, slowly, as if the driver was looking for something.

Soon, they would be far, far away, she and Jack, this man to whom she had pledged her life. Far away in a strange place. The dream, his dream to which she had joined herself, in this moment filled her with grief. She had never known anywhere but Birmingham, and now Smethwick. Birmingham was home – its factories and shops, pubs and people. They must be mad to leave and throw away everything they knew! But she asked herself how many close friends she really had. Now her job had changed and she and Jack had moved over here, she hardly saw Carol and her family. A twinge of regret passed through her, closely followed by panic and the queasiness which had possessed her for the past few days.

She laid a hand on her belly. The sick feeling was familiar. If it were not for that, she would have put it down to nerves about the journey. But she was becoming sure it was something else. Could it be? This was not something she was going to tell Jack – not until she was really sure. But it made the new life she was facing just a little less fearsome. Because maybe, soon, in the strange, new place they were heading to, there would not just be the two of them. They would be three; they'd be a family. And there was nothing in the world she longed for more than that.

Everything had changed for Evie when she met Jack Harrison. Jack, full of energy and drive, slender, fresh-faced, handsome and older than her. From the start, she had looked up to him, was so proud to be seen out with him. She saw girls look at Jack all the time, but he seemed to be mad about her, gazed at her with those intent blue eyes of his as if he could not drag them away from her. She had never had anyone pursue her with such force and determination. And she felt exactly the same about him.

'You're the most gorgeous wench I've ever seen,' he'd say, pulling her close to him. She liked him calling her 'wench', half joking and half as if this was just the kind of woman he wanted – not a dolly bird, or a fragile little thing, but a proper woman, broad, strong and capable. It reminded her of her father in his occasional good moods when he had noticed her, patted her head and said, 'There's a good wench.' A thought like that could give her a pang as well, the old pang of longing for love. But she didn't need Dad now – or any of them. She had Jack. The way Jack kissed her, urgently, holding her as if she was a rock he had found to save him, and his dazzling gaze into her eyes, made her forget everything else.

They soon began spending every possible moment together. Jack seemed quite happy to come over from Smethwick night after night, on the bus or his bike. He would meet her after work. Every time she saw him waiting on the corner of the Moseley Road, tall and handsome in his work clothes, a bag slung over his shoulder, giving off that energy which he seemed to transmit, she was filled with gratitude and excitement. She would run to meet him, not seeing anyone else who was on the street, flinging herself into his arms. They often forgot completely about their tea and Mrs Hardy would present her, huffily, with a plate of something-or-other congealed under gravy when she finally got in.

The age gap which at first she had been conscious of melted away. It didn't seem to matter. Jack made no secret of the fact that he could not stand his parents and said he had left home and was never going back.

'My father's a copper,' he said, on one of their first nights out when they were getting to know each other. They were in the Old Moseley Arms in Tindal Street, tucked away in a corner. Even as he mentioned his dad she could hear the tightness in his voice. 'Some blokes can go either way, I reckon. You become a criminal or you join the police. He's a head case. Dunno if it was the war or what. He was in Palestine. Never talks about it, so...' He shrugged. 'Anyway, Mom just dances round him. Scared of him. Never goes against anything he says or does, even if it means...'

'Did 'e lamp yer?' she asked, moved by what she could see in his eyes. Lost boy, like Gary.

'Just a bit,' Jack said, with iron in his voice and a look which made her want to put her arms round him and comfort him.

'I used to do anything I could to try and please him,' he said. 'Make him stop. In the end I could see that whatever I did, it would make no difference.'

'Like me.' Evie knew she would not tell Jack the real reason she had to leave home. She spoke shyly to him at first, but right from the beginning she knew she could be honest – except for that one thing. Not about Julie, who was locked tight in her heart.

From the very start it felt as if the two of them, together, were a fortress against the world. She could face anything with Jack.

And he raised her up, gave her new ideas and more ambition.

'Why're you working in that factory?' he asked her. 'You're clever, you are. You could be doing something better than that. Work in an office, get some training. The more you know, the better you get paid – and you can go anywhere then. Get a job in Canada, not just stay stuck in this bloody place. Mr Richards, my gaffer, he says I could get a job over there no problem. I know all about the machines, see – pumps and that, for the oil. They're sitting on a gold mine over there and there's people going over in droves. I want to see the world, I do, not just stay stuck here.'

'You really want me to come as well?' She asked this when they had been together a few months. She was wondering if he meant to go off and leave her, like Ken had.

'Yeah.' Jack sat forward and gave her his intent look. Once again they were sitting in a coffee bar. 'That's if you're up for it. In a year or two. Everything's opened up. We could have a much better life over there.'

With his encouragement, she went to work in an office. She had imagined herself as an office girl, learning to type, even doing shorthand, but she got herself taken on as a trainee comptometer operator with Midland Red buses in the Bullring. At first she was afraid she would not be able to keep up, but the work was all right, though punching numbers in made her fingers ache. But she soon got used to it and liked most of the other girls she was working with, rows of them in front of the big machines.

She lived and breathed Jack. When they parted, she felt an actual physical ache of separation and

counted down the hours until they were back together again. She loved his energy, the way he
was full of schemes, full of enthusiasm for her.
Whenever they were together they ended up in
each other's arms, wrapped close together, kissing and touching. She loved stroking the hair at
the nape of his neck, because it felt soft, vulnerable, like a baby's. But even though she so often
felt weak-legged with longing for him, she was
very strict.

'I'm not going the whole way, not if we're not
married,' she told him.

They had been walking out for nearly three
months when they had this conversation, on a
warm May evening, in Cannon Hill Park. They
were wrapped round each other as usual and Jack
had whispered, 'You're driving me mad, I fancy
you so much. I'm getting so I can't think of anything else.'

When she drew back and gave her answer, she
saw Jack look startled. She realized he was used
to girls falling into his arms, because Jack could
charm anyone into doing anything he wanted.
But this time, even though she was crazy about
him, she wanted to be sure.

'What if you got me in the family way? What
then?' An ache began in her throat. All the sadness of the memory, of loss. She wanted him to
know, to understand how it felt, but she knew
somehow that he never could.

'Oh ... yeah.' He laughed. She did not like him
laughing – not about this. He put his arm round
her shoulder and they walked along, beside the
water and the preening geese. He seemed to be

thinking. After a while he said, quietly, 'They should never've had kids.'

'Who? Your mom and dad?' She was glad he had spoken because she had wondered, with a rising panic, whether he was angry.

'Yeah. Dad any road.'

She wasn't sure what he was trying to say and, in any case, Jack always got very moody when he mentioned his dad, so she brought the conversation back to what was really on her mind.

'I love you, Jack.' She looked up at him, wide-eyed. 'But I'm scared. I don't want to be left with a baby. I've got no one else but you.'

'Who said anything about leaving?' Jack said. 'I'm nothing without you, wench. Look ... what if we was to get married?'

'Married? Oh Jack! D'you mean it?' She was so excited, so amazed, she was jigging up and down in his arms. Everything was perfect. This was everything she had ever wanted! 'Oh, d'you mean it? It's so soon!'

'Yeah. I do.' He ducked down suddenly and was perched on one knee. 'Miss Evie Sutton, will you marry me?'

'I will,' she said solemnly, though her grin was already spreading wide, a huge excitement fizzing inside her. 'Yes Jack. Course I will!'

They made preparations. Since Evie was living in Balsall Heath they decided to marry there, where they could most easily have the banns read. Neither of them went to church but Jack told her that if he was anything he was Church of England and Evie thought she must be the same.

261

The question of her family haunted Evie at this time – both Jack's and her own. When she told Mrs Hardy she was getting married and would soon be moving on, her landlady smiled in a pained way, trying to be nice while obviously worried that this was all being done in such haste.

'Have your family given their consent?' she asked. 'You are underage, aren't you, dear?'

Until this moment, this had not crossed Evie's mind. Panic filled her. Did this mean she could not marry Jack without going home and asking Mom and Dad? She and Jack were hoping to marry in October, by which time she would only be nineteen. She could not bear the thought of having to wait another two years until she was twenty-one. The thought of going home gave her a twinge of regret now and then. If only she had a nice family. If only things were different... But she knew straight away that she was not going back.

As if blown there on her thoughts, while she was in town, dreaming of clothes for her wedding, she saw a familiar figure appear before her one day in Grey's department store. Evie was mooching about in the women's clothing department, immersed in the fantasy of a new dress and soft underwear and new stockings for her wedding day. She planned to spend the rest of Ken's money – her pay-off. That was still how she thought of it, with a bitter, enraged feeling which almost made her want to throw it away. She didn't need their hush money! But she knew that was stupid. Ken's life had presumably gone on as it would have done if none of it had happened, unperturbed except perhaps for a few guilty pangs. And Ken would have felt guilt, she knew. He was a nice, dutiful boy. There would be these few painful shadows of guilt in a blameless life. She, on the other hand, had been cleaved apart, mind and body and spirit, moulded into someone else, who knew the grief that only the loss of a child could bring. She had earned that money. After all she had lost, she was damn well going to have something nice.

She was looking through a rack of pretty dresses when someone caught her eye across the racks of clothing. The store was crowded but the person leapt into her attention, even though she was turned to face the other way. All Evie saw was thick, shoulder-length hair, sage green wool across the shoulders, a flick of the head, but she knew almost by a second sense that it was Shirley.

Her heart began to pound. Her first instinct was to run across. Shirl! It's me! Of anyone in her family, Shirley was the person she would have been gladdest to see. Shirley, the one who had been all right to her – sometimes. She was suddenly swelling inside with curiosity. How was everyone? Rita and Conn and the babby? Mom and Dad? And the neighbours – Gary and Carl, Mr and Mrs Waring. All that had been familiar, had been her home.

Tugged by a longing for something she belonged to, however much it caused her pain, she hurried after Shirley, who was moving away towards the main doors. In those moments she wanted her mother, her sisters, her old childhood life; wanted everything to be new and fresh, for them to come to her wedding, to wish her well and forgive her, to love her, *love her...*

Shirley disappeared. It broke the dream. Other thoughts rushed in. The day Mom threw her out, Shirley had not intervened to help. Never said a word. And Rita would certainly not have done. They did not care for her, did not love her and never had. Mom was mean and nasty and had tutored her sisters into being the same. She stopped abruptly, full of the grief of reality.

'Oi, watch it,' a voice said behind her.

'Sorry.' Evie stepped aside, taking refuge in a rack of winter coats. She wanted to break down and howl, right there in Grey's, to weep from the depths for all she had never had. Could it never be better? Could she never have that love, not ever in her life?

'Tell 'im your parents are dead,' Jack said. 'That's what I'd do.' Jack's age was not a problem, only hers.

After deciding to get married, they spent the early autumn making hurried plans. They met almost every evening, walking out or in pubs, depending on the weather. Tonight was a wet September evening and they were back in the Old Mo again in Balsall Heath.

'Would you?' Evie said doubtfully. They were on a bench, backs to the wall, and she pressed her shoulder against his, wanting to be close to him, to be with him at all times. He was all she had, but she didn't mind that, so long as she had him. 'It's such a big fib, though. S'pose he finds out?'

'He won't,' Jack said confidently. 'Why would he bother? Any road, you could tell him you're in

264

the family way – he'll marry you like a shot then.'

'Jack! That's another lie!' she laughed, though with a tremor of excitement at hearing him talk like that about the thing she most wanted, as though it was what he wanted as well. She linked her arm through his. 'It seems bad, all these fibs, and to a vicar as well.' She looked into his face. 'Are you going to ask your mom and dad? To the wedding, I mean?' She wanted, really, a proper wedding, not this hole in the corner thing of theirs. She wanted someone to be glad for them.

Jack almost choked on his beer. 'Mine? Not on your life! All I want is to get far enough away from them, and this flaming place, that I never have to see any of them again. I wanna start again, have a house, a new life, not this miserable bloody tat over here. It's different there. You can be someone else.'

Be someone else. More than ever before, Evie felt herself leap and catch at the string of this idea. Start again. A new person, a new life, married to Jack. Seeing Shirley had left her raw, aware suddenly how close she was to her old home, terribly close, yet with an agonizing distance gaping between her and them. She wanted as much distance as possible – from the risk of running into them, from the feelings it gave her.

'Oh, let's, Jack! Let's go. You're so clever, you could do anything. We can start all over again – just us, away from everyone.'

Thirty-Two

'Oh my God!' Evie gripped Jack's hand, terrified but excited as the plane launched itself from the runway and her stomach turned in a queasy somersault. 'How on earth is it going to stay up in the air?'

'Aerodynamics,' he whispered enigmatically, tearing his fascinated eyes away from the window to look at her for a second. She wondered if he knew, really. Maybe he did. Jack knew a lot of things. She didn't really care, so long as it was going to be all right, leaving the ground, leaving everything.

She swallowed hard, trying to fight off the nausea rising in her, and leaned round to look with him, both watching as they climbed through a swirling mist, up into sunlight, the clouds spread below like a frozen, woolly sea. And after a time, once the Boeing had lifted higher and there was nothing much to see, Evie sat back to admire the air hostesses in their blue uniforms. They're so glamorous, she thought wistfully. I wish I'd done something like that. But she knew she couldn't have. She certainly didn't know anyone from Ladywood who had ever done anything like that.

Evie had imagined at first that they would cross the Atlantic by ship. That was what you always heard about when people went over there, a sea

266

journey taking days and days, like a voyage in a storybook.

'Oh no, we don't need to do that,' Jack told her, with the usual confidence he displayed in his knowledge of everything, especially everything new and fast. 'We can fly now. Just think of that, wench. You and me, flying!'

And now the day had arrived, so strange and dream-like still, and here they were, soaring above the ground, leaving everything they had known all their lives, except each other. And except... She laid a hand on her stomach for a moment and gave a secret smile.

Sitting back, she closed her eyes, drained of energy. After the weeks of preparation, the scrimping and saving, the planning and dreaming and excitement of heading into the unknown; after the journey to London to queue at Canada House; after the job applications and Jack being offered work, and all of it seeming like a dream from which they would one day wake – now it had begun at last. They were moving to this new country, this new life, in Rosette, Alberta, Canada.

Already things felt new. She was wearing the outfit she had bought to travel in – a pink skirt, in crimplene because it didn't crease, a white short-sleeved blouse in broderie anglaise, a pale blue cardi and white shoes. She lifted her right shoulder and rubbed her cheek against the cardigan's softness for reassurance. She had had her hair cut, styled with a deep parting at one side, brushed across her forehead. The finishing touch was a pink lipstick to match the skirt. She wanted to look her best to arrive in a new place.

Unfortunately, she was not feeling her best. Pray God her acid stomach would settle down later in the day.

She kept hold of Jack's hand because she needed to; his strong fingers were linked loosely with hers, as if he did not. Between us, she thought, we've hardly a soul to say goodbye to. Carol had promised to write and she knew she would miss her and her family. But apart from her...

Julie ... I'm leaving her behind. It was a second of sheer grief, that she could not be near wherever her little girl was, as if in moving away she was betraying her. But that's stupid, she told herself. Julie doesn't even know who I am – and I don't know where she is. Evie could not watch over her, even if she did think of her always, several times a day, every day... And knew that she always would.

She had to stop thinking like that. Her new life was beginning – with Jack. She thought about how her life would have been if she had not met him. Would she still be living with Mrs Hardy? It felt too miserable to dwell on. And now, though she had not said anything to Jack yet, she knew that there was this other reason for her feeling so exhausted, aside from all their preparations for the journey. She knew the signs – the queasiness, the way things smelt and tasted stronger than usual... Every time she thought of the new life inside her – and she was almost certain of it now – a thrill of excitement went through her.

They had married in a church in Smethwick. The vicar, an old man with a grey bush of hair and an air of having seen it all before, showed no interest in her age and married them with no objection when they said they lived within the parish boundary.

'I reckon he thought you was over twenty-one already,' Jack said as they emerged from the vicarage, hand in hand and giggling.

Evie asked Carol Rough to be her bridesmaid. Her brother Tony was Jack's best man and apart from them and a handful of work friends, there wasn't anyone else to come to the wedding. The Roughs invited Evie to stay the night before the wedding. She took her leave of Mrs Hardy that day, as she and Jack were to move into their rooms in Smethwick.

'Well, dear,' Mrs Hardy said, stiff with disapproval. 'I hope you'll both be very happy.'

'Thanks for everything, Mrs Hardy,' Evie said. 'I'm sorry to leave.' This was not true at all. Mrs Hardy seemed very disapproving of her getting married. And it's none of her business, Evie thought.

So Evie bunked up with Carol on her last night as a single woman in the Roughs' little terrace, grateful to Mrs Rough for mothering her and to all the family for their kindness.

'Dad's mate Ron's going to run us all over to Smethwick,' Carol said. 'And I can do your hair for you, help you get ready, like.'

Carol was a homely soul but she was very good with hair and her own mousey waves always looked nice. At first light she sat Evie on a wobbly wooden chair in front of her mirror in the tiny bedroom with its big dark cupboard and chest of drawers. Skilfully she arranged Evie's

269

hair into a stylish pleat. Evie tried not to wince as she felt the scrape of Carol's comb against her scalp and her locks were pulled this way and that. Mrs Rough popped her head round the door every so often, still with her curlers in, and said, 'Oh yes, that's nice, Carol,' and other encouraging remarks. Each time, she brought in a gust of cigarette smoke and frying bacon and music from the telly.

'There you go,' Carol said once she was satisfied, administering hairspray all over it so that they both coughed. 'You look a treat.'

'Oh,' Evie said, turning her coiffured head this way and that, gazing in wonder. 'I've never had it like this before. It looks...'

'It looks bostin!' Carol said. 'Though I says it myself. You look really glamorous, Eves, like a film star.'

It was true. Evie had already done her make-up. Her strong cheekbones were emphasized with a touch of rouge, her lashes drawn up with mascara. The stylish hairdo flattered the shape of her face. With a pang she saw how much she looked like her mother, only younger, softer, prettier. Her big blue eyes were alight with excitement. She had never felt like this before – new and grown-up, desirable and in charge of her life.

'Thanks, Carol.' She beamed at her friend in the mirror. 'I'd never've managed anything half as nice by myself.'

'Well, it's your wedding day – you're not supposed to be by yourself.'

'No.' Evie looked up at her. She felt as if she had always done everything by herself. She smiled. 'I s'pose not.'

Carol tutted. 'You're a daft one, you are. Come on. Get yourself dressed.'

As Evie laid out her clothes, Carol gasped.

'Oh, haven't you got some lovely things!' Carol had her best dress ready to put on, in cornflower blue wool, and it looked sweet on her but Evie's dress was in a different league. She picked up one of Evie's stockings. 'God, Evie! You must have been saving forever for those!'

'I have,' Evie agreed, making a joke of it. 'I've been living on bread and water!' She wasn't telling Carol where she had got her juicy sum of money from.

'Look, I'll go out and let you get changed,' Carol said. 'I'll go and check Uncle Ron's not going to be late with the car.'

Glad to be alone for a few moments, Evie looked at all her new clothes. She had blown all Ken's money on an expensive silk dress, some lovely underclothes to go with it and a little black patent handbag. She had not chosen a white confection to wear. In all conscience she would have felt a hypocrite putting on white. Instead, she chose a silky dress the colour of milky coffee and edged with black. It was by far the most expensive thing she had ever had and she knew it looked good on her. She put on the new lacy knickers and cami-sole and fastened her stockings, then slid the dress over her, careful to avoid getting make-up on it. It seemed to flow over her like cool water, flattering her every curve. She had a marvellous feeling of luxury, knowing she was wearing something that made her look truly beautiful.

She stood in front of the mirror, trim, curvaceous, turning this way and that, and feeling all the silky garments move against her skin. When she smiled, she saw a pretty, happy woman smiling back at her.

'Thanks, Ken,' she whispered, her gratitude sarcastic with bitter, sad, regretful feelings. 'This one's on you.'

Everyone exclaimed as she came downstairs.

'Look at you! You're glowing!' Carol said. 'Must be love!'

'Oh bab, you look a picture,' Mrs Rough said tearfully. She was standing ready, in a dark green coat and hat, and looked a comforting sight. 'Doesn't she, Lewis?'

Mr Rough smiled bashfully and made noises that indicated agreement.

'Thanks, Mrs Rough, Mr Rough,' Evie said. 'Thanks for having me to stay – for everything.'

They squeezed into Ron's Austin and drove across Birmingham. It was a bright October Saturday, crisp leaves on the ground after a dry few days. When they got to the church, Evie saw Jack waiting outside, standing very straight, and looking self-conscious in a grey suit, Tony already at his side. For a moment it seemed to Evie that Jack looked hard and forbidding, but as they drew close, Tony said something to him and Jack's face cracked into his infectious smile which made her spirits soar.

There he is, she thought, brimming with excitement. He came. He wants to marry me. She only realized then that she had been worried he would have got cold feet, was going to let her down...

272

But no, there he was, waiting. Her man and the life ahead of her.

They stood side by side in the echoing church and made promises to keep until death did them part.

That night, since they had no plans to go away anywhere, it was their first night in the new lodgings in Smethwick. The rooms looked out over a side street and every stick of furniture was shabby, but it was home, for now. Jack had taken her hand as soon as they were up in their private room, leading her into the bedroom gallant as a prince, and it felt as if the two of them were acting out a story.

'Now you're mine,' he said, urgently pressing his lips to hers. 'Mine at last.'

The feel of him running his hands over her in the silky dress came back to her now. She squeezed his hand at the memory of his face as he looked into hers that evening, full of longing, is if to say, *We belong together.* She had been so in love with him, possessed by him almost, and she was just as in love with him now.

She had been nervous, wondering if Jack would realize that this was not her first time. But he had been far too caught up in himself to notice. It was only afterwards as they lay snuggled close that the ghosts of her life came back to haunt her. She started to feel frightened.

'Jack?' She raised her head from the pillow and looked down at him. 'You won't ever leave me, will you?'

'What?' He was drowsy and content. 'What're you on about? We just got married, dain't we?'

'I know, but...' She felt very emotional suddenly. 'We've hardly got anyone. You're my family now, Jack. If you was to leave, I don't know what I'd do.'

'C'm'ere, you daft wench,' Jack said, pulling her into his arms. 'Where's all this come from all of a sudden? You're my wife, and we're good together, aren't we? I love you, Eve Harrison. You're gorgeous, you are – and you looked like a princess today. We don't need anyone else, do we? Sod 'em all if they don't want you. You have to learn to look out for yourself in this world. We're going places, you and me.'

'Oh Jack, I do love you,' she said, lying in his arms, warm and reassured. 'You're everything to me, you are.'

Within weeks of their wedding, Jack had started making plans for Canada. What was the point in waiting? he argued. They were married. They might as well get on with it. And she was completely caught up in his vision, in the idea of this great adventure. Her family seemed further away than ever now she was married. She had a different name. She was Evie Harrison, not Sutton anymore. She was with Jack, and she would go with him anywhere. After all, she had nothing much to leave behind here in England. Except Julie...

Much as she adored Jack, she had to face the fact that she had secrets she was keeping from him. She thought of Julie still, constantly, praying that she was all right, calculating, week by week, how old she was, imagining how she might look and sound. But each time, with a stabbing pain, she collided with the truth that if she was to appear to Julie, now or at any other time in her life, her daughter would not have any idea who she was.

'Welcome to Canada!'

She was surprised and touched by how welcoming the customs officials were at Toronto, the first place they set foot on Canadian soil. But although the people were warm and kindly, the weather was cool, the sky iron grey and heavy with rain. Evie had thought Canada would be all sunshine and beckoning spaces. Instead, all she had seen of it from the airport windows was flat, grey and sodden and she felt low and homesick looking out at it as they waited for their flight to Edmonton.

While they were waiting around, though, they met another English couple, a big, strong-looking man and his pleasant, freckle-faced wife, who said they were on their way to a place called Devon, near the Leduc oil-fields. They chatted for a while about where they had come from and what they were planning to do and it was reassuring and made the place feel less foreign.

'Maybe we'll run into each other!' the woman said as they parted, getting on the plane.

By the time they reached Edmonton, more than four hours later, it was pouring with rain.

'Well, folks,' the pilot announced in a genial tone as they circled the airfield, preparing to land. 'On a good day this place doesn't look too bad. But as it turns out, this is not a good day.'

All Evie could see, stepping out, was an area of endless, rain-lashed flatness and the few drab buildings of the airport. It was desolate beyond words. Was this the golden land they had been promised? But she said nothing to Jack. She was in any case too tired and bewildered. They put up in a small, sterile hotel in the city, which she was too exhausted to take in.

First thing next morning, she had to rush along to the bathroom, her body wringing thin bile from her. She stood, panting over the whitest washbasin she had ever seen, her head throbbing, mouth full of sour sickness.

'You all right?' Jack said as she came back into the bedroom. 'You're white as a sheet.'

She was surprised he had noticed and she longed to tell him. But not yet. Let them get there. Let her be sure she really was expecting, that nothing was going to go wrong. She felt superstitious, as if speaking about it would make it not true.

'I'm just a bit tired,' she said. She sat back down on the bed and forced a smile, though she felt like crying. She wanted familiar things round her. If only they were back home, even if that meant their dingy rooms in Smethwick. But it was too late now.

'Soon be there. Just got to get a train.' He squeezed her hand, but she could see that his mind was racing ahead in excitement. She felt a moment of panic at having to travel even further, as if she was on a long cord which was still attached to home. If she pulled on it any more, it would snap, leaving her cut off from everything. In that moment she wanted to beg that they just turn round and go back again.

276

Thirty-Three

They asked directions to the railway station. People were kind and they were soon on their way to Rosette, where, Jack assured her, they would be met by a man called Don Sorenson, from Jack's new employer, the Rosette Tube Company. He was to show them to the new home which he had kindly organized for them.

The journey took them across a flat prairie landscape blurred by rain. Evie gave up trying to make out anything more of this endless new country, so big that it made her feel dizzy. She dozed leaning against Jack's shoulder. He was glued to the window, gazing out hungrily. When she woke, the weather had changed and there was bright sunlight as they reached their destination. It seemed like a good omen.

They hauled out their cases onto the platform of a whitewashed station building, bearing the sign 'ROSETTE'. A handful of other people got off with them and the silver train, which Evie thought looked like a tin can, moved away towards the west. For a second she wanted to call out to it, Stop! Don't leave me here! She reached for Jack's hand. She had put on a pair of comfortable slacks for travelling in, but now they had arrived she felt rather scruffy.

The other passengers moved out of the station by walking straight across the tracks. Evie and

277

Jack glanced at each other, both feeling foolish. It would never have occurred to them that they could just walk across like that. Once they had gone it was very quiet. The tracks stretched away on either side.

'Blimey,' Jack breathed, looking round. He sounded excited, but also – just as she felt – stunned by the strangeness of it, by all the changes that had come upon them so fast. They stood side by side, next to their luggage like lost children. Evie felt the acid burn in her stomach and no coherent thought formed in her head. All she really longed to do was to lie down.

They looked around them. Behind them, along the margin of flat unsown land, electric wires slung between wooden poles extended away along the tracks, thrumming in the breeze. The sun was bright, the sky pocked by a few fast-moving white clouds. Evie felt it through her clothes and it seemed to be blowing away everything she had ever known or held dear.

Across the tracks were a few low, station buildings, and beyond they could just see other buildings which must have been the edge of the town. Though it had a name and they had things waiting for them – the Rosette Tube Company, a man, somewhere, called Don Sorenson and their belongings coming by sea – Evie felt she had arrived in a place that was nowhere. Never before had she been anywhere so open to the sky, so spread out, with such a feeling of being half made. All her life she had spent in a built-up place, the old parts of a city. Now she felt as if she had come to the bleak ends of the earth.

She wondered if Jack was feeling the same because he turned to her, as if uncertain, and took her hand. Evie squeezed it, happy that they were in this together, both feeling uncertain.

'Well, hey there! Hello!'

A figure appeared walking with a casual stride along the opposite platform, a stocky, bearded man in an open-necked white shirt, grinning, a hand raised. His hair and beard, the colour of rusty leaves, glowed in the light. He clambered, bear-like, across the tracks towards them.

'Hey, folks! Welcome to Alberta!' Close up, she saw the man had grey eyes and a strong jawbone and looked as if he was built from tree trunks. Beside him, Evie thought, Jack appeared as if tacked together out of kindling. He shook each of their hands and his felt very thick and strong.

'Here, let me give you a hand with those bags,' he said. 'That's OK, come right on over the track. There won't be another train coming this way for a good while yet.'

'Ta ... er, thanks. Thank you,' Jack said and she heard the eagerness in his tone as they set off across the track. They both seemed like little children compared with this bear of a man.

'Come on,' Don said. 'I'll give you a ride to your new place. I hope you're going to like it!'

'Oh, we will. I'm sure we will,' Jack said. 'Thanks for, er, you know, sorting it out for us.' Never had Evie heard him so full of a childlike desire to please.

'Not at all. We're glad you're here,' Don said, in a formulaic way, yet it did not feel false. There was a warmth to the man.

His car, parked at the front of the little station, was a flat-shaped vehicle in bronze, with a wide radiator that looked like bared teeth, as if the thing might be about to eat you. 'Meteor' she read along the front of the bonnet.

'I'll put your bags in the trunk,' Don said. He smiled at Evie. 'Here, Mrs Harrison.' He opened the front-passenger door, confusingly on the right-hand side, and held it open in a courtly way. 'You sit up beside me.'

He settled them and their things inside. Evie was relieved to sit down again as she was feeling terribly queasy and was finding it hard to concentrate on anything. As they drove, she only took in a vague impression of this strange, low-level, boxy town with its straight roads, because she was worried she was going to be sick. She drew in deep breaths and Don Sorenson talked to Jack alarmingly over his shoulder. His Canadian accent felt like a fresh wind blowing.

'Tell you the truth, Jack, the company's really eager to have you,' he said in his sunny way. 'Rosette Tube is doing well – oil is booming in Alberta, of course – but we need all the expertise we can find. You're going to be a great asset. Oh, and you'll need a car.' He laughed, facing forwards again, to Evie's relief. 'Here, the car is king. We can soon get you fixed up.'

About twenty minutes later, after passing through the middle of the little town where they saw churches, shops, a glimpse of the lake lined with trees, they moved into more suburban roads and stopped outside a white clapboard house. So far as Evie could see it was one storey high, with steps leading up to the door. Along the street were other similar-looking houses, some with cars parked outside.

'Well, here we are!' Don announced. 'Your place for now. We always try to fix people up when they first arrive, but of course, if you don't get along with it, you can look for somewhere else. But it's a pretty nice place. And Edith's done a fine job getting in a few things for you.' They gathered that Edith was Mrs Sorenson.

'Looks nice,' Jack said enthusiastically. He was going to be enthusiastic about everything in Canada. All Evie could feel was the strangeness. And relief that she had not been sick in their host's very clean car.

This is what you wanted, she told herself fiercely. A new life.

'I'm sure we're going to love it,' she said as the nausea made her innards lurch. She swallowed hard and gave Don Sorenson a dazzling smile, wondering how quickly she could get into the house, to a lavatory.

'I sure hope so,' he said, somehow bashful, as if the country was a lover he was introducing them to.

She just made it, bile rising in her as she leaned over a spotless white lavatory, hoping to God they couldn't hear. But the two men were busy talking. She gulped down some water, wiped her face and felt much better. There was a mirror and she looked at her pale face, her hair flat and in need of a wash after all the travelling. But she looked much as usual, which was reassuring because everything felt so different. God, she thought desperately, I hope I *am* going to like it. So far it all felt so strange and empty.

'You're going to have to,' she whispered to her reflection. 'You're here now. Mrs Harrison with her husband and...' For a moment her hand flickered protectively over her belly and she managed a smile.

They were both amazed at the house. It was compact: one storey with a kitchen, a bathroom, a living room and two bedrooms. Don pointed out features to them before he left. When Jack mentioned the height of the house off the ground, he laughed.

'Oh, you haven't seen a Canadian winter yet. We have snow right up to the windows and over. You better make sure you stock up on plenty of warm clothing.'

When he had gone, leaving them a bag of groceries, the two of them explored the place, excited as children. They were amazed by everything and Evie's spirits lifted. What a lovely house – she had never seen anything like it before! The living room was already furnished with rugs on the wooden floor, armchairs, patterned pink and grey, a wooden table and chairs and a big wooden sideboard. The kitchen was brighter and cleaner than any they had ever seen. Evie looked inside the cupboards, thinking of all the ways she would arrange the shelves in the larder unit which stood in one corner, astonished at the white brilliance inside the refrigerator.

'They must really want you, Jack,' she said. She saw him differently suddenly. He was someone clever, in demand. 'They've made it so nice for us. And look – I can't believe this bathroom!' She went to view it properly. A whole bathroom to themselves, all new and clean. It had patterned linoleum on the floor in dark blue and turquoise patterns. They had their own lavatory, bath and washbasin and a little white wooden stool, a rail on the wall for towels. It felt like a palace. Jack came to stand beside her and she could see the pride and pleasure in his eyes.

'Oh Jack, it's lovely,' she said.

'That's Canada for you.' He flung an arm round her shoulders, looking into their new bathroom. 'Better in every way.'

'And look, there's a little patch of garden outside!' she said, excitement filling her. It was a bare rectangle, but there was grass and a little fence and they could make it nice. She didn't know a thing about gardens but she would learn. She was about to say, 'It'll be lovely for the baby.' But she bit back the words. Should she tell him? Soon – she would tell him soon. At the moment his mind was fixed on settling here, on Canada. She wanted the moment to be right.

They stood looking out of the front door. The street was quiet. It was warm and Jack unbuttoned the top of his shirt and lit a cigarette.

'When you think of what we've come from...' There was wonder in his voice. He angled his head back and blew smoke into the air above him. 'Thank Christ we got out of there.'

And in those moments, having seen their bedroom with its double bed, the living room and her new, neat little kitchen, all she could do was agree with him.

Jack turned to her and took her in his arms. He removed the cigarette from his lips and kissed her.

'Well, Mrs Harrison. We're gunna be Canadians!' Already he sounded different, trying it out.

She looked back at him, uncertain, but again she smiled. 'I s'pose we'll have to learn to talk different, won't we?' she said.

That night Jack made love to her with more force than usual, with a frantic kind of energy. Straightening his arms as he came, he put his head back and let out a cry, as if of triumph. For a moment he was lost in his own thoughts and sensations, before righting his head and looking down at her.

'You all right?' She smiled up at him. She had found it exciting, this reaction, but was not sure of it.

'This is me.' He was still moving in her, enjoying himself, gently circling his hips. 'I've arrived. This is really me.' She knew he meant here, Canada, all of it.

'Good,' she said. 'Good, my love.' She pulled him to her, holding him close, hoping to goodness that in the end she was going to feel the same.

Thirty-Four

That first morning Jack disappeared, full of eagerness, to the Rosette Tube Company. Don had said take a couple of days for goodness' sake, get settled in. But no. Jack wanted to get in to work, get cracking, he said. Don laughed and said he would call by and give him a ride.

Evie was glad of his hurried departure because once again she was feeling sick. She had made Jack breakfast from the supplies Don's wife had left for them – eggs and toast, which she certainly couldn't face herself.

For a moment she had wanted to cling to him and beg him not to leave her alone in this strange place, feeling like this. But of course, she did not do it. This was a big day for him. She could feel the tension in his body as she kissed him good-bye.

'Good luck,' she said. 'Knock 'em dead.'

Jack grinned and kissed her again. 'Don't get into any mischief, will yer?'

She watched him with the front door open a crack so that Don Sorenson could not see her in her nightie. Jack, in his new black trousers and shirt, his fast, muscular walk, raising a hand to Don. Going off into his male world of work. Jack's world which did not include her. She felt a pang, a sense of being left out. But she smiled as well, proud of him. Then she allowed herself to crawl groggily back into bed.

As her stomach buckled with nausea she felt lonely and desperate lying in the silent house. A couple from next door had come round the evening before to say hello – both in their forties and pleasant. But apart from that she had no idea who was around her. How was she ever going to get started on this place feeling like this? Last time, with Julie, it had not been anything like this bad. But of course Jack didn't know about last time. He didn't know about this time either. For a few minutes she pressed her head into the pillow of this new wooden-framed bed and had a cry, feeling very sorry for herself.

As she wiped her eyes, a thought struck her, fully for the first time. Here she was, with her husband, who had come to do a job in Canada, so many miles from home that it might as well have been on another planet altogether. Their coming here was all about Jack – but what was *she* going to do, here all on her own?

Another twist of queasiness reminded her: she was not alone. Not even alone in this room, because a small, beginning of a person had taken root and was developing inside her. She laid her hands side by side, like a little roof over her stomach, feeling the soft warmth of her flesh.

'Julie...' she whispered, stroking her hands back and forth. 'No, I know you're not Julie. And I'll never ever give you away – not like her. You're mine, and whatever happens, we'll be together, my little one.'

Filled with new, determined thoughts, she got up, first to be sick, then to begin on building a new life for a family. Because whatever Jack or anyone else wanted, that was what she hungered for more than anything.

Once she was dressed and had managed to eat some toast, done under the eye-level grill of the newest cooker she had ever seen, she felt better. Cup of tea in hand, she opened the back door. The day was already warm, the sky a hazy blue. Stepping out onto the strangely wiry grass, she looked around, at the neighbouring houses, all similar to their own, and wondered nervously who might live there.

I could plant roses, she said to herself. But where do you get them from? What do you have to do? Helplessly, she thought, I don't know the first thing about gardens... To the child growing inside her, though, she whispered, 'But I'll learn. I'll make it nice for you, so you can play...' She felt dreamy in the warm sun.

'Hello!'

Evie jumped, only just managing not to spill tea all down her. For a second she could not tell where the voice was coming from, then realized someone had walked round to the side of the garden. A young, slender woman in a pale blue skirt and chocolate-coloured short-sleeved shirt, her dark brown hair cut in a bob. 'Sorry,' she said, laughing. 'I didn't mean to make you jump.'

Evie realized the accent was English, though different from her own. Smiling uncertainly, she walked towards her. Between the white palings of the fence, she took in that beside the woman stood a little child and that from the curve of her at the front, she was clearly expecting another. She was carrying a round dish, covered by a white plate.

'Am I glad to see you!' the woman said. She held out a hand across the fence and they shook. 'We could do with a few more Brits in this neighbourhood, I can tell you. Though there are quite a few of us scattered about town. I'm Cath, by the way. Cath Laker. And this is Robbie.' She looked down at the little boy.

Eve was overjoyed at the warmth of this greeting. A neighbour. A friend! She already felt desperate to make the woman like her.

'I'm glad to see you too,' she said. 'We just got here. And I got up this morning and thought, what the hell am I s'posed to do now?'

Cath laughed. Evie thought how nice looking she was, with her brown eyes and sallow skin.

'I know the feeling – well, except I was just about to have Robbie by the time we got here, so I wasn't in a fit state to do much anyway.'

Evie was on the brink of saying that she too was expecting and that this was how she felt but she stopped herself. It was strange how much easier it would have been to blurt all this out to a stranger than to say it to Jack.

'D'you want a cup of tea?' Evie said eagerly. 'That's all I've got really – I don't even know where the shops are.'

'That'd be nice. And I can show you. That's partly why I'm here. David – my husband – said you'd both arrived and I knew you'd be in a tizzy. Don't I remember it!' She came in through the side gate, carrying the dish and leading the little boy with the other hand. He had dark hair like hers and a sweet, wondering expression. They followed Evie into the house. 'What's your name?'

'Oh, sorry.' Evie turned from running the tap. 'Evie Harrison. My husband's Jack.'

'Well, Evie, I'll take you to the shops, if you like, a bit later. But I made you a pie.' Cath wrinkled her nose. 'It's bottled plums.'

'That's ever so kind,' Evie said. Tears pricked her eyes for a second and she blinked them away.

But Cath noticed.

'You might not think it's kind when you taste it.' She made a wry face. 'I'm a lousy cook. Don't worry, I'll show you everything.'

'Thanks,' Evie said, making the tea in a pan as there was no teapot. 'That would be such a help.'

'You'll get settled.' Cath picked her little boy up and perched him on her hip. 'But Canada takes some getting used to, I can tell you. Everyone thinks it's going to be more or less like England and it isn't at all. I didn't think I'd survive the winter when it arrived and it goes on and on... Long after the snowdrops are out at home there's snow and more snow. It takes an age to get out of the house.'

'I'd better get some more clothes,' Evie said. 'We've only got what we brought with us so far.'

'Oh, you've got a while yet,' Cath said. 'The summer's only just getting going, and that's *blistering*.'

They talked and drank tea, sitting at the table in the living room, little Robbie cuddling on Cath's lap. Evie ate a slice of Cath's plum pie and it was pretty terrible and soggy but the kindness of it meant most. She learned that Cath and David were from Bromley, in Kent, that nearly everyone who came here now was working in the oil industry or something to do with it, and that there were a few Brits scattered across Rosette, as well as the Canadians and others from Ukraine and Germany and Scandinavia, which Evie gathered meant Norway and Sweden.

When she told Cath she was from Birmingham,

Cath joked, 'No, really? I'd never've guessed!' It seemed as if they were already making friends and Evie felt a great deal better, even though the pie made her stomach feel terrible.

'I've just got a few chores to get done,' Cath said, getting up to go. 'But I've got the car today. I'll take you out and show you the fleshpots of Rosette!'

By the time Jack came home that evening, Evie had been introduced by Cath, in another enormous, American car, to the town of Rosette, its main street of shops, its pretty expanse of water known as Lake Glass, with a church spire reflected in it which Cath said was something to do with the Ukrainians – 'not sure which kind of church really,' Cath admitted. 'But a lot of life happens round the lake in summer because it's the nicest part of town for picnics and so on.' They drove past the squat warehouse that contained the Rosette Tube Co. in the north of the town, and Evie bought some food from one of the stores.

As she was trying to think what she needed, Cath appeared with another woman beside her.

'Evie, this is one of our number in the neighbourhood – Bea Henshaw. Meet Evie, our new arrival.'

Evie saw a young woman with blonde hair loose on her shoulders, a neat, bird-like figure and kindly blue eyes. She was also, very obviously, expecting a child.

'Hello, nice to meet you,' she said. As she talked, Evie could tell that she came from somewhere northern and that there was a lovely warmth about her. 'You just arrived?'

'Yesterday,' Evie said. 'I don't really know where I am yet.'

Bea chuckled. 'I'm not surprised. Takes a good while before you stop feeling like that – I found, anyway. Listen, Cath, I'm due at the doctor's in a minute. But bring Evie round for a cuppa soon, eh?' She touched Evie's arm. 'Nice to meet you, love. We'll get together soon.'

Her wiry little figure hurried away. As they drove home, Cath explained that Bea was a nurse who had been working until recently at Rosette Hospital where her husband was also a doctor.

'Course, she's far more worried about having a baby than the rest of us. Knows too much, I s'pose. Ignorance is bliss the first time, for most of us. She's a real good sort, Bea is,' Cath said. 'You'll like her.'

Evie had already decided that she did. Rosette, however, she found very strange as they drove along. There were all the usual things of home – shops and houses, factories and timber yards – and yet it felt so low-lying and spread out and somehow unfinished.

'The roads are very wide,' she said to Cath, gazing out as they drove along a street of shops. Some of the buildings looked pretty, she thought, with canvas awnings draped from the windows, and some with wrought-iron balconies. There were cars and 'station wagons' parked along the street, like she had seen in American films back at home. The sun brought out the vivid colours of everything.

'On a really clear day you can just see the

291

Rockies,' Cath said. 'Just the little tips of the high ones. It's a bit hazy today, though. They look magnificent when you can see them.'

Evie peered out to the west but could not see anything. But she decided she liked Rosette that day. Or at least that she could get used to it. And Cath's friendly company helped, and meeting Bea. All in all, she felt much better.

Back in their neighbourhood, Cath helped her unload the car and then said, 'Come on. You come round to mine now.'

The inside of Cath and David's house was much like hers and Jack's, except that as they had already been in Rosette for eighteen months, it looked established and homely, with Robbie's toys in a corner and a high chair and coloured crocheted rugs on the backs of the chairs.

'Tea OK?' Cath said, as Robbie ran in and went to his toys.

'Yes,' Evie replied. 'I don't much like coffee. I try because it's all coffee bars at home, isn't it?'

'You all right?' Cath said, looking closely at her. Evie had had a moment of faintness, having to hold on to the back of a chair.

'Yeah. Ta.' She sat on one of the chairs by the table. In a moment of longing, of not being able to resist confiding in this new friend, she looked up at Cath. 'Thing is ... you're not the only one who's expecting.'

'Oh, isn't that lovely!' Cath clasped her hands together under her chin, beaming. When she smiled, she had very even, white teeth. Evie thought how pretty she was. 'Your first! When's it due, d'you think? That's nice – our kids can be friends!' Evie felt warmth steal through her at this reaction. She ignored the comment about it being her first and smiled, as if with first-time nerves.

'I'm only about three months gone.' She realized she must not sound too sure about anything. 'I think anyhow. I feel quite bad some of the time. The thing is, Jack doesn't know yet.'

'Oh, you're saving it, are you? I did that, the first time – just to make sure. Didn't want him all disappointed if, you know, anything went wrong. But when I started being sick this time of course David spotted it straight away. Oh, your husband's going to be so excited!'

Cath hugged her briefly round the shoulders. She smelt of something nice: talc or perfume. 'David was like a big kid himself when I told him. It makes them feel they're real big men.' She laughed and went back to making the tea. 'Oh, that's made my day, Evie, it really has!'

So when Jack came home Evie was full of excitement. He had had a good day and was happy and he wanted to know everything she had learned about this new country. Evie knew she would soon tell him about the baby, but for now there was enough to say about her day in Rosette. She talked all about Cath and how they went shopping and met Bea and Jack said he'd met David Laker, Cath's husband, at work and he was a nice bloke. Evie said that Cath told her that the best way to getting along in Canada was if you like sports, especially ice hockey.

Jack listened, seeming keen to absorb everything that there was to learn about their new home. She even noticed he sounded a little different, already

293

tinged with Canadian. Cath, Evie realized, hardly sounded Canadian. Just a little maybe.

'Well, we'll have to see what we can do, won't we?' Jack said. 'There's a hockey rink in town, I know that.'

Evie beamed at him. He was happy, she could see. They needed him at the works. He was where he wanted to be. And at that moment she was overflowing with love for him and wanted to be here too, where things were so nice and everyone she had met so far had been so friendly and kind and seemed to accept her. She was truly starting to get hooked on the Canadian dream in which she would be a new person, truly someone on the inside and not left to sit out on the cold step.

Thirty-Five

A few evenings later, the two of them fell laughing in through their front door.

'Call that a pub!' Through his chuckles, Jack's voice held a tone of bewilderment. 'I've never seen anything like it!'

Evie giggled, happy that they were having a laugh. Sometimes recently it had felt as if he was very far away from her. He was trying to alter himself to fit in with the Canadian way as fast as he could. Sometimes it scared her, as if he was easing away from her – and they had only been in Canada for a couple of weeks.

She kept telling herself that she must put him

first. He was the one earning the money after all – good money as well. But he barely asked what she had been doing. He just took it for granted that she was there, putting a house together, giving him his dinner when he turned up. She had had some very lonely moments in the long, empty days. Her one comfort was the thought of the baby growing inside her, the family she and Jack were going to make. And soon she was going to tell him the news...

And at least tonight it felt as if the two of them were united. And she had had an unexpectedly enjoyable evening.

'They're so funny about drinking,' she said, turning a light on in their living room, so bright, so clean and new. It struck her still, every time she came in. 'It's like a dirty secret – bottles all wrapped up in bags if you want to take them home.' The other women had been telling her about it. 'Daft, isn't it? D'you want a cuppa?'

'All right.' Jack threw himself down in a chair. 'Christ, I could do with summat stronger after that, but that'll 'ave to do.' He sounded like a Brummie now. Like her old Jack.

Evie made tea and snuggled up beside him on the sofa, relaxing as they digested the evening's experience. Most of this week Jack had come home and talked about his workmates – blokes with names like Bill, Red, Harry. Some were Canadians born and bred, but just as many were from all over, drawn to Canada by the new Alberta oil finds. Most of these men she had not met until this evening and then, as it turned out, only for a few minutes.

Canada was already full of surprises: rice was eaten not just as a pudding! And everything was so enormous and spread out. But the so-called pub, a little bar off Main Street, had come as a real shock. For a start, men and women had to enter through separate doors and drink in separate rooms. A few of the blokes from work had asked Jack along. The wives went too and Evie had found herself separated from Jack and among a group of women she had never met before. At first, in the simple room, sitting round tables on wooden chairs, she felt very insecure.

Cath was not there, no doubt because she had Robbie to put to bed, and Evie didn't know a soul. She was full of all her old uncertainty as she sat down with them, on guard as she had always been with her sisters, waiting for trouble and rejection. What would they think of her? She was so much younger than most of them and they would think she was rough and that she didn't belong. But she had been overwhelmed by how welcoming they were. They gave her tips about life in Canada and treated her like a younger sister. She had relaxed, felt less shy and had a laugh with them as her confidence grew. They were all surprised to find out that she was not yet twenty-one.

'Oh, you're such a sweet young thing,' one of the older ladies, in her forties, said, patting Evie's hand. It was only later in the evening that Evie realized the woman was Don Sorenson's wife, Edith. 'We'll have to keep a little eye out for you!'

It had all been gentle and friendly and it made her feel so much better. People seemed to be easy-going and kind. Maybe she could even fit in.

Like Jack said, they could leave their old lives behind and start afresh. She felt hopeful tonight.

'All this business about drinking sitting down,' Jack said, shaking his head in bewilderment. 'I mean, I was sat there, with a beer. After a bit, I got up to go and talk to Don over the other side, picked up my glass and the waiter comes over. Oh no, sir, you're not allowed to carry your own drink across the room!' His voice was incredulous.

Evie laughed. 'I never thought it'd be this different. I mean, they all speak English. But nothing's the same at all.'

She was enjoying this moment, both of them puzzling out their Englishness versus the new Canadian way. She kicked her shoes off, tucked her feet under her and cuddled up to Jack. It felt lovely sitting like that, just the two of them. Should this be the moment she told him about the baby?

A warm, expectant feeling stole through her and she turned to Jack, the words ready on her lips. But just as she opened her mouth, Jack pushed himself more upright and looked down at her in the intense way he sometimes did.

'It's different, but it's *good*,' he said. Her mind jerked back to the track of their former conversation from which she had long moved on, leaving him behind. It was as if he needed to repeat that he had made the best choice in coming here. He relaxed back again and gave a rueful smile. 'Could do with a decent pub, though! Any road, Bill and Red and some of the others asked me out on a fishing trip with them.'

Evie felt a pang, like a chill. She felt herself withdraw. The fishing trip was only for him, obviously.

'Oh. That's nice.' He didn't notice her flat tone. Once again he was caught up in his male world. 'When?'

'Sat'day.'

'You going?'

'Yeah, course!'

He didn't ask her what she was going to do all day. She felt distant from him again suddenly and decided her news could wait.

But soon she could not keep it to herself any longer. She picked her moment: that Saturday morning, before he was to go off on the fishing trip.

The mornings were easier for her now. The sickness had died away and she woke aflutter with excitement. Jack was still asleep and she slipped out of bed into the already warm morning to make tea in the tin teapot and two white mugs she had bought in town. She carried them to the bedroom, placed them on the cheap little deal chests of drawers on each side of the bed.

'Wakey-wakey.' She looked down at him, his handsome face lost in sleep, and thought how lovely he looked. She kissed his cheek, feeling the prickle of stubble. 'Someone's going fishing.'

This thought woke him abruptly. He stirred, smiled. 'I made some tea,' she said, climbing back in beside him. A shaft of sunlight fell across the bed.

They sipped tea, warm and close. When she judged he was awake enough, she put her cup down and linked her hand with his.

'Love? I've got summat to tell you.'

'Umm?' He did not sound especially curious.

Her heart pounded now. 'Thing is, I... We...' She watched his face, anxious for the response.

Jack gave a laugh. 'Well, come on, spit it out. Can't be that bad.'

'We're ... I mean, I'm in the family way, Jack.'

It took seconds for him to grasp her meaning. 'What?' He stared at her. 'You... What, a *kid*, yer mean? You can't be!' He pulled the bedclothes back and looked in bewilderment at her body. 'There's nothing there!'

Evie laughed at the sight of his face. 'I'm barely four months gone yet. You don't just get big straight away, Jack, the babby has to grow.'

He looked really pole-axed. 'But...'

'But what?'

'Well ... I mean it's quite soon, isn't it? I never thought it'd happen this quick.'

'Jack, we've been married months, and it's not as if we've taken precautions every time, is it? You're not exactly keen on those rubber things.' This was true. And there were also times when she had not reminded him...

'But I just never... I thought it just took a bit longer, like.'

'I don't know what made you think that, love,' she said, the amusement dying in her eyes as a coldness filled her again. This was her news, the most important news she could ever tell him, but Jack did not look pleased. He looked really put out.

As she was speaking he swung his legs out of bed and was sitting with his back to her. She felt horrible, shut out, as if she had done something terribly wrong and this was all her fault. A lost, vulnerable feeling came over her at the sight of him turned away from her, as if she was alone in the world all over again. She wanted him to hold her, love her, tell her he was happy, that it was what he had always wanted.

He sat for a moment, saying nothing.

'I mean,' she said huskily, 'you want kids, don't you, Jack? It's what everyone does, isn't it? All those men – Red and Bill and whoever, they've all got children. It's what you do. It'll make you fit in, won't it? And...' She could hardly speak for the hard ache in her throat. 'It's the best thing that's ever happened to me. I really want a family, Jack – a *nice* family, of our own.'

Hearing this, he turned, looking at her as if thinking about it.

'Yeah.' After another pause, he said, 'I s'pose you're right.' He nodded. 'Yeah. A kid ... well, well. I s'pose that's the right thing. And it'll give you summat to do, won't it?'

Relief coursed through her. 'Oh Jack!' Tears ran down her face. 'I'm so happy. I want to be such a good mother. I can hardly wait 'til she arrives.'

'She?'

'Well ... or he. I don't know! Oh, give me a cuddle and tell me you're glad too?'

He came onto the bed and held her, resting his chin on her head. She could hear the rhythm of his heart, smell his warm, man smell, feel the strength in him. Her man. He would look after her and they would be a family.

'How long have you known?' he asked.

'Not long,' she said.

'Right. Well. Better get used to the idea.' He released her gently, seeming stunned but coming round to the idea. 'Canadian kids, we'll have.'

He gave her a final kiss, though it felt perfunctory, before getting to his feet.

'Best get going,' he said.

She sank back onto the pillow, still needing more from him. 'Jack ... I love you.'

He turned, managed to meet her eyes. He still looked shocked, she thought. 'T'ra, kid,' he said.

Evie smiled at the closing door. Jack was never a great one for pouring out his feelings. But he was pleased, she told herself. Of course he was.

Thirty-Six

Those early weeks in Canada were exhausting. Expecting a child added to the fatigue of coping with new places, new faces, and all the other strange things she had to get used to.

The few things they had had shipped over arrived at last and they now had all their clothes and a small number of knick-knacks: cheap ornaments that she had not been able to resist buying in Birmingham. There were a pair of orange-brown china corgis which she thought were sweet, a china girl with a garland of flowers round her head and a little pale green vase. She arranged her treasures round the house.

Added to that was their new car. She gasped with amazement when Jack appeared in it, sitting in the passenger seat beside Don Sorenson, wearing a grin from ear to ear.

'How d'you like this nice little Chevvy, gal?' Don said, getting out. He patted the car's pale-green-painted boot – trunk, he would say, Evie had already learned. 'Young Jack's got to get his licence but that won't take long. I'll give a hand and then you folks'll be on the road!'

'How're we going to afford that?' she asked, when Don had gone, sweetly saying he would walk home, that it would do him good.

'Oh, it's on the strap,' Jack said airily, walking round the car, gazing at it with devotion. 'Hire purchase, they call it. We can afford it. It ain't new, but it's in good nick.' He squatted down, staring at the hub caps. Then, sounding Canadian, he added to himself, 'It sure looks good.'

It was true. The car was astonishing – so big and comfortable looking. Jack soon learned to drive and they gradually got to know the town – the central streets with shops and the pretty area around Lake Glass, where churches and houses reflected in the still water and where families had picnics and played games in the parkland. There was the south-east section where Jack worked, lines of factories, but not crammed in close like in Birmingham. And there were residential streets like their own, wide and quiet and lined with low-rise houses. At the far end, away from town, the houses petered out into farmland and the road joined the main highway towards Calgary and the Rocky Mountains.

Over those first weeks, as well as the company wives, Cath introduced Evie to some of the other women in the neighbourhood and she soon belonged to a group of women who were to become her best friends and the support of her life in Canada: Patsy, Jean, Lois and Cath and, of course, Bea – especially Bea. Evie had taken to her straight away and the two of them had really hit it off. If only she had had a real sister like Bea, Evie thought.

Bea had stopped work now as she was soon to have her baby and she had exchanged her nurse's uniform for slacks and comfortable, informal clothes, which most of them wore. Bea, with her Cheshire accent and friendly, kindly ways, had quickly become very important to Evie. She and her husband Stan lived in the next street, in a house like Evie and Jack's, with a little square of grass at the front and a grassy yard at the back.

Cath and Bea soon drew Evie into a circle of women, mostly British, who met in each other's houses and had young children. They passed the time together, drank tea, talked about home and, as Bea put it, helped 'keep each other from going off our rockers'.

'I remember when we first came here,' she told them one afternoon when a group of them were chatting together in Bea's homely living room facing out to the yard. 'Stan and I, being English and everything, thought we'd go out for a walk. So we went off out into the fields.' She got to her feet and mimed two people striding along with absurd determination. 'It was the summer and I had a frock on. I stopped to look at some flower or other and the next thing I knew, I was covered! I mean my legs were black – it was *horrible!*'

303

'What was it?' Evie said, shuddering. The others all laughed.

'Black fly – *thousands* of them. Ugh.' Bea held her fists clenched up to her chin, mimicking her frozen horror at the time and the others all laughed. It somehow looked even funnier because she was quite heavily pregnant.

'Well, that was a lesson,' one of the others said.

'Oh, there've been plenty of those.' Bea subsided back into her chair. 'You don't want to go wandering off out there, Evie.'

'I'm not one for going for walks like that,' she said, thinking with a sinking heart of the bleak, endless prairie beyond Rosette's rough boundary. 'I'm a townie, me.'

'The biggest lesson, Evie,' Bea went on, 'is the Canadian winter. *Oh my.* You've no idea what you've let yourself in for.'

Evie was always hearing dire warnings about the winter – how long it went on for, how deep the snow, how cold the weather, how mothers spent half the day just dressing their children to get them outside. Soon, she thought, she would be doing the same.

'I'll have to buy some more clothes,' she kept saying.

'Oh, you *will*,' they urged. 'Layers and layers. And you're having a winter baby!'

She had asked Cath not to tell everyone she was expecting until she was ready. But when they eventually heard she was going to have her first baby, the news was greeted with cries of enthusiasm and everyone hugged and kissed her.

'It's going to be a cracking baby,' Bea said, hugging her, 'what with your looks and that handsome husband of yours!'

Evie felt special and truly part of the group.

She built up a picture of the town through their eyes. Everything seemed to revolve round the 'League' as they called it, the social centre of the veterans, the Royal Canadian Legion. There was the library, the churches and the curling rink. She had to learn curling, they told her. It was fun and got you moving in the winter. For the men there was fishing and icy hockey games to play, or at least to watch.

The only thing that was awkward was when they all asked questions about her family and how they felt about her being so far away. It was easier just to say she had no family. These women felt more like sisters now and she knew that when the baby came she would have help and people from whom she could ask advice. They were so kind and to her amazement they all seemed to accept her. She was part of a group – on the inside. It was the best feeling she had had in a long time. With a shock, she sometimes felt she was closer to her women friends than she was to Jack.

Thirty-Seven

November 1964

'There you go, dear. Here she is, a lovely little girl!'

It was four o'clock in the morning, after Jack had driven her to Rosette Hospital between the snow banks which rose up on each side of the road like white giants in the moonlight. Evie had groaned and gasped through the contractions as they crawled along. Jack kept saying things like, 'Hold on, for God's sake,' sounding really alarmed. He kept snatching anxious looks at her as she writhed around. In between the pains she giggled at the sight of his face because she knew she was not ready to give birth – experience told her there was road left to walk yet – only Jack was not used to this and did not know it.

She had laboured through the night. Compared with last time – a last time that no one knew about except her, or if the staff of Rosette Hospital noticed anything they did not say – it was a very different experience. The pain was the same – the rolling, thunderous waves of it. But inwardly, Evie knew that this time she could keep the person that she was about to meet. This time it was all approval – she was a married woman. Nothing was shrouded in shame and grief. Not like with her poor little Julie. Just as she had carried the baby with joy, she gave birth with hope.

She was encouraged by friendly Canadian accents as a tiny being forced itself out and into the world.

'Here you are, Mrs Harrison, meet your beautiful little girl.'

The smiling nurse swaddled the child and Evie reached hungrily for her, could hardly believe that at last she was holding the real, solid weight of her. And her weight in the world was allowed because a momentary vow in a church had changed everything. She took one look at the crumpled, mouthing face and sobs wrenched up from inside her as she took in the sight of her. She was everything for which Evie had yearned for so long and she burst into gulping tears.

'Oh dear, oh dear!' The nurse seemed quite put out. 'There's no need for all that, is there, Mrs Harrison?'

'But she's just so lovely!' Evie wept, tears falling onto the baby's cheeks. 'I can hardly believe it.'

'She is.' The nurse softened. 'And you've done very well.' She patted Evie's shoulder. 'A good weight too. Almost eight pounds. She's a beauty.'

Beautiful didn't seem a big enough word. Evie gazed and gazed at her. She was everything. She was the world. Later she could remember nothing much about being cleaned up in the hospital, or other details. Just the baby, there in front of her, her mouth suckling and a feeling of completion, as if a raw gap in her was being filled.

Then people began to come: Jack first, later that day, when both she and the baby were washed and rested. Seeing him come along the little ward, which held only eight beds, Evie sat up, eagerly, grimacing at her soreness which she had almost forgotten.

Jack looked bashful and out of place. He leaned down in a stiff way and kissed her. There were melting snowflakes on his coat and his cheeks smelt of cold.

'You all right, wench?' he asked gruffly.

'Yes. And she's fine. She's so lovely, Jack.' She wanted him to be brim full of joy, the way she was. At least he's here, she told herself. What more could she want? 'They'll bring her in for us in a minute. She's due for a feed. Is it snowing again?'

'Yeah.' He sat by the bed in his coat, looking masculine and handsome and uncomfortable in this place of women. He seemed not to know what to say next, but just then one of the nurses came in carrying the baby. Evie held her arms out for her. She hated being parted from her little girl even for a moment, haunted by the fear that they might take her away...

'Here she is.' She held her out for Jack to see. He peered down at the face, her swimmy eyes open, trying to take things in. 'Isn't she the most beautiful thing you've ever seen?'

'No, wench.' He joked to cover his uncertainty. 'You are.'

'Oh *Jack!*' She wasn't sure whether to be pleased or cross.

'Yeah, she's all right,' he conceded with a brief smile. 'Looks a good'un.'

'D'you want to hold her?'

'No, you're all right,' Jack said. 'Not now. It's

you she wants, isn't it?'

He seemed uncomfortably fascinated as she latched the baby on to feed, wincing at first.

'Hurts a bit,' she says. 'But it'll get easier.' Then added quickly, 'Or so they say.'

Jack nodded, seeming unsure where to look.

'I thought we'd call her Tracy,' Evie said. They hadn't talked about it. Jack had never seemed all that interested. She could see that the baby had never felt real to him until now – maybe not even now.

'All right, yeah,' he said.

'I mean ... we don't want to call her after either of our moms, do we?'

They both laughed then.

'Tracy Harrison,' Jack said.

'What about a second name?'

He looked hopeless. 'I dunno. You choose.'

Evie thought back. Not after any of her own family, that was for sure. People who had been kind passed through her mind. Mary Bracebridge. Melly Booker and her mother Rachel. Dolly Morrison. Old neighbours from way back.

'What about Rachel?'

'All right, go on then,' Jack said.

He didn't seem to mind either way.

'Oh! So it's a little lass!' Bea came into the ward at her energetic speed. She was wearing scarlet trousers and snow boots, and her cheeks were rubbed pink by the cold. Evie felt her friend's strong arms round her and found herself being kissed. Tears filled her eyes.

'I can't seem to stop doing this,' she said,

between laughing and crying.

'It's your hormones,' Bea said, sinking into the chair and pulling off her scarf and unbuttoning her big navy duffle coat. She rolled her eyes in her comical way. 'Don't worry, I was just the same. Like a flaming dripping tap I was. Oh, now it's my nose instead!' She groped in her coat pocket for a hanky. 'It's so warm in here.'

Evie laughed again. It felt so wonderful having a friend like Bea. She knew Bea missed her own mother being all the way over here and Evie had tried to do everything she could for her when she had her baby back in August. Bea had had a tiny little girl called Clare and had shrunk back almost instantly to her normal, bird-like size.

'Well done, you!' Bea was saying. 'I bet she's gorgeous. And I'm glad it's a girl – the two lasses can grow up friends, can't they? Are they going to let me see her? I suppose it's not feeding time yet?'

'Not for a bit, no,' Evie said. Out of everyone she knew she was most eager to show Tracy to Bea. 'Depends how long you've got.'

'Can't be out too long.' She pulled another face. 'I've left her with Stan. That's the blind leading the blind all right. And I'll have to get back and feed her. She's a proper greedy guts. But anyway' – she sat forward and looked into Evie's eyes with warm concern – 'how did it go?'

'It wasn't too bad,' Evie said. She shared some of the details. Everyone, Bea included, thought that this was her first baby.

'Sounds as if you're a natural,' Bea said. 'Like shelling peas.' Bea had had a hard time having

Clare, though she made light of it.

'Oh, I wouldn't say that!' Evie said, her memory of the wrenching pains still fresh in her mind. 'It had its moments, I can tell you.'

'Well, you look flipping fantastic.' Bea grinned. 'Mind you, you haven't started on the broken nights yet, have you? But eh' – she was serious suddenly – 'it's worth it, isn't it? I never knew I could feel like this.'

She was teary and smiling at the same time and Evie was soon the same. Oh yes, she knew all right.

Bea stayed for a bit but had to get back to feed little Clare.

'Thanks for coming to see me,' Evie said, still amazed at the kindness she experienced from everyone.

'Oh, I'll be back.' Bea winked at her and squeezed her shoulder. 'And well done again, chuck. I'll come tomorrow and see if I can meet the little lady. But I'm glad you're all right, Evie.'

Evie smiled fondly as she watched Bea depart, wrapping her scarf round her again. She lay back, exhausted. Most of the other women had visitors with them now, husbands and friends. With a pang she thought, I wonder what Jack's doing. I wish he'd come. Why isn't he here? She missed him suddenly, with an almost unbearable longing. Surely he must be dying to see his daughter again? So far he had only caught the smallest glimpse of her.

She was starting to feel really sorry for herself, but a few minutes later she saw Cath coming along the ward and she sat up, immediately cheered. She was also well wrapped against the snowy cold and had brought ginger biscuits.

'I made these for you. They're probably dreadful, but I never seemed to be able to get enough to eat in hospital!' she said. Her baby, another boy who they called Joe, had been born in July.

Evie was touched by the way her friends had come rushing in so soon. They all understood how it felt. They were kind.

Later she lay back in bed and, once more, began thinking about her life. She had everything she needed. She felt a little bit sore that Jack had not come in again, but he was probably busy at work and having to fend for himself, she thought. He was a good husband, he was making a success of his job, of Canada – and now she had her own baby at last and all these warm-hearted friends who really seemed to care about her. Tears of joy ran down her face.

The early weeks of Tracy's life were the happiest Evie could ever remember. Jack was doing well; they had more money than they had had in their lives before, along with their house, their car and a good life with friends in their neighbourhood in Rosette. Above all, Evie had her beautiful daughter.

Tracy was an easy, happy baby. Evie would not have especially minded if she hadn't been – having Tracy at all was all that mattered. As it was, the first days back at home were a time of bliss. It was the height of winter, the snowed banked up outside, but she had no reason to go out. Her women friends offered to fetch things from town.

They brought round cooked meals and kept her company. They encouraged and petted her, mothered her.

Over time she had hinted to them more of the truth about her own family. They were shocked to hear even a few of the things she told them and Bea and Cath were protective of her. The two of them had given Evie a present of a rocking chair padded with colourful flowery cushions, which she sat in to feed Tracy. She had it in the bedroom and from it she could see out to the back, the snowy rooftops beyond.

Jack was at work, but the women were there, in and out. Evie had never felt so loved in her life, and the only shadow was her nagging feeling that she did not deserve this loving shelter, that it would soon be snatched away and she would once more be left out in the cold.

She was also a little hurt that Jack did not seem all that interested in Tracy. If she talked about her, he would try and seem interested. He would hold her occasionally if Evie handed her over because she needed to do something. Eventually, feeling down about it because she wanted him to feel the way she did, she mentioned it to Cath and Bea, trying to make a joke of it.

'Jack still hardly knows one end of a baby from the other,' she said. But the joke did not work because she found she had tears in her eyes. Bea patted her arm.

'Don't fret, Evie. Mine's no better. It's just not the same for them. Stan's a good father really but he just seems to feel he has to work even harder rather than pay us any attention. He spends *hours*

313

at the hospital.'

Evie was reassured that it wasn't just Jack. All she wanted was to devote her days to Tracy. She sat for hours holding her, feeding and kissing her on the rocking chair in their bedroom, in the snowy light coming through the window. She would stare at the baby's plumping cheeks, her down of fair hair and her solemn, roving gaze and was utterly in love. Nothing else mattered. When Jack came home she would wrench her attention to him, do the wifely things of asking after his day and try to listen to the answers.

But amid the joyful reality of Tracy's life, there was one sadness she could not escape. For all the hurt she had experienced from her own family, Evie kept thinking about them. It was four years now since she had left home, that terrible, frightening night. She knew she could never forget her mother's words. But even so...

Rita and Conn must have at least a couple of kids by now, she would muse, as she sat feeding Tracy, rocking gently in the chair. And Shirley, might she be married with children as well? Those kids would all be Tracy's cousins. And what about Mom and Dad? If she was to go to Mom now with a grandchild born within wedlock, might Mom be different? Might she be nicer and treat her like a proper grown-up person?

Now Evie was a mother again, she found herself thinking about that woman who was her own mother. Irene Sutton. Mom, who had taken up all the space. Mom, so loud and rough, so easy to anger, so insulting to people when there was no call for it. Why was she like that? They all knew about Dad's long flutter with Nance because Mom had never let any of them forget it.

It couldn't have been easy, Evie found herself thinking. Having me, knowing Dad was carrying on with *her*, and Nance having a lad by him. Worrying he was going to walk out. God, I'm surprised she didn't flaming *kill* him.

She felt a harsh sort of sympathy with her mother. She imagined if it was Jack and the thought was terrible.

'You're such a silly moo,' she muttered to her mother, holding Tracy against her shoulder. 'Why did you put up with it?' But Dad always got round her somehow. Twisted her round his fat, hairy fingers, she thought. Mom talked tough but she was terrified of Dad going off.

Would she ever say this now, if she saw Mom again? Be able to talk to her woman to woman?

But other memories of her mother and father came fast behind: their almost constant brawling, the drinking, the way neither of them seemed to be able to think anything through or control themselves. Mom's just like a child, she thought. Like a great big overgrown kid. Loathing, pity and longing mingled in her. Longing for this woman who had blocked out the sky with her bulk. Who was so needy, so childish and impossible but who, in the end, was her mother. If only she could go back there, see them for an hour or two and then escape back here.

But that wasn't possible. Some of the other women said that homesickness in Canada could be treated by the 'thousand-dollar cure' – the family returning to England for a holiday.

'As often as not,' Bea told her, 'they realize they're better off here. They remember why they left in the first place.'

She thought about writing home. But no – it was a scab not worth picking again. Mom could barely read anyway. No. She was well off where she was. Here she had kind friends. She was inside, not forever on the outside longing to be let in. Her eyes filled for a moment and she looked at Tracy through crystals of tears.

'You're my family now, my little darling,' she said. 'You and your dad.'

She sat dreaming of all the lovely things they were going to do.

As they became more settled in their neighbourhood in Rosette, getting used to the seasons and new Canadian ways, each of them changed. Jack had almost instantly become as Canadian as he possibly could. It was as if he had been born to the life. He was popular and sociable and by the time they had been there just a few months he had lost his Brummie accent, except sometimes at home, and joined in with everything he was invited to by his workmates.

They had a lot of fun with all their friends. They went fishing and picnicked on the lawns on the banks of Lake Glass in the summer. In winter there was curling and ice hockey games. There was a ski slope on the edge of town and it was a good place to watch the skiing and let the children run about together. Soon, egged on by his workmates, Jack had started learning to ski himself. He would come home with a glowing face, happy as anything. He had never played hockey, but he was a staunch spectator, one of the gang. Evie could see that whereas at home he had never had the chance to do anything in the way of sport, here in active, outdoorsy Canada, he was developing a new sense of himself as a man. And although at times she felt resentful of him going off with 'the boys' once again, he was happy, and she was happy with her friends and with Tracy. Life was busy and full.

Jack often invited people over at weekends and they all sat around and chatted. Some of Jack's circle were older men, veterans of the oil boom, such as Don Sorenson. Jack loved hearing about roughneck work on the rigs and about the old days. One man, Arthur, had been a wildcat oil prospector round Alberta's Athabasca River. Everyone knew there was oil there, seeping through all the sediments. You could see and feel it. It was a case of finding the best spots. Once the big strike came in Leduc, just south of Edmonton in 1947, Arthur had gone to work there. Jack never tired of hearing about it. Arthur only had to say something like, 'Well, course, I remember when the gas well went up in the Turner Valley in '26. The stuff coming out of there – phoo! It was raining rocks! Burnt for over a month...'

And they were off. The women, who had heard it all before, rolled their eyes and turned to each other to talk about their children and their day-to-day concerns.

But Evie knew that Jack wished he had been there. How he would love to have been a roving oil prospector, been part of it all at Leduc after they struck oil and whole towns, like Devon, on the

North Saskatchewan River, were built to accom-modate oil workers. If only he had been part of all this instead of growing up in the confines of a filthy industrial city working in a factory all his life. Jack wanted to be an outdoors man, a Canadian through and through. He would have been happy to be an Athabasca trucker if it meant he could be part of it.

Most of the women's lives, with their young child-ren, centred around informal meet-ups in each other's houses. The children played and learned together. In the winter the mothers wrapped them up like little fat parcels in layers and layers, to venture out into the glare of stacked snow. She found it hard going. It went on so long. She'd get Tracy all dressed up to go and then she'd fill her nappy and you'd have to begin all over again, so that hours passed before you could open the front door.

Tracy was a solemn, sweet-natured little girl. Even from a baby she looked wise for her years.

'She's one of those old souls,' Bea said, watching her as she regarded them all with round, knowing eyes. 'Look as if they've been here before.'

Evie knew what she meant. Sometimes, the way Tracy looked at her, she felt the child knew her in some way better than she knew herself.

As Tracy grew, found her legs, started to talk, Evie was more and more delighted by her company. It felt as if, day by day, a small friend was growing beside her. But as she looked at the other women and their growing families, a longing began in her for another baby. The longing grew, day by day...

By the Christmas of 1965, after weeks of feeling queasy on and off, she was certain. Jack took it better than she had expected.

'I knew we should've been more careful,' he said, when she told him at bedtime one night after he had been out with his pals and was tanked up, relaxed and in a good mood. 'We should've had belt as well as braces.'

'But you don't like belts or braces,' she said, kissing him.

Jack reached for her. Even if he did not really want another baby, he was aroused by the thought that he had created one. 'No, I bloody don't. Come 'ere, wench. Too late now any road, isn't it?'

After all, she thought, it makes no difference to him. She did everything for Tracy and no doubt it would be the same with this one. She fell asleep, blissfully happy.

Thirty-Eight

July 1966

Bea's face, pink in the summer heat, appeared round the door in the hospital. 'So I hear you've had a little lad this time!'

Evie beamed at her wearily from the bed, holding her dark-haired infant boy to her breast.

'Hello, Bea. Yes, here he is, large as life. He's

just having a guzzle, sorry.'

'Don't talk daft.' Bea came and sat beside her, smiling at the picture of happiness she saw before her. 'Oh, I bet Tracy's excited. She with Cath?'

'Yes. They're coming in a bit later,' Evie said. Tracy, skinny, blonde and active like her father, was just about old enough to understand that a new member of the family was arriving.

'What're you calling him?' Bea asked.

'Andrew – after Jack's brother.' Evie grinned. 'The nurses keep saying, "Oh, is that after your English prince?" So I said "Who?"' They laughed together.

Bea had two children now – a boy and a girl – and Cath three. Along with a number of other women in the neighbourhood, they were Evie's mainstay.

'He's darker than Tracy,' Bea said.

'Umm,' Evie said. 'Looks quite like my dad, poor little sod.' Dark and handsome, she thought, but my God, he'd better not turn out as vain and selfish as our dad.

She had still not contacted her family, or let them know about their Canadian grandchildren.

'If you have them that easily, you'll end up with a whole tribe at this rate,' Bea teased her.

'Well, I s'pose I've got to be good at something,' Evie said, forcing a smile to her face. 'I don't seem to be good at much else.'

She was putting on a brave face, but in truth, she didn't feel quite right. After she had Tracy she had been perfectly well, but today she felt hot and shivery and her head was throbbing. She had had a very disturbed night and her spirits were dragging low, putting everything in a bad light.

Sometimes she didn't think she had made much of a wife, if her husband's lack of interest in her and the family was anything to go by. Andrew had been born the day before but Jack had not come yesterday evening. He had not yet seen his son. Evie felt deeply hurt and miserable about it.

But Bea's presence was a comfort and when she asked how the proud father was doing, Evie said, 'Oh, he's happy as anything to have a lad.' So far as everyone else was concerned they were the attractive, happy couple they had always been.

But suddenly she couldn't keep up the facade any longer and she was in tears.

'Eh, love, what's up? Got the blues, have you?' Bea was all kindness. She came and put her arms round Evie which made her cry all the more.

'I don't think Jack loves me anymore,' she blurted, hardly even knowing that that was what she felt. She had been sensing him moving further away from her; he was forever out with the boys, not really interested in the children. She had kept going day after day without acknowledging how wretched she felt.

'Oh now, come on, Evie love,' Bea said. 'I'm sure that's not true. Look.' She sat down on the chair again, still holding Evie's hand. Evie saw the professional Bea emerge, as well as her kind friend. 'Sometimes it's best not to think too much about anything, when you're feeling a bit blue. You know it hits people just after the baby's born.' She reached round and felt Evie's forehead. 'Eh, I thought you didn't look too good

321

– you're burning up! Look, I'll go and tell someone. No wonder you're feeling bad. You might have a bit of an infection.'

Her busy form moved along the ward. Soon came a nurse with a thermometer and Evie realized that she did in fact feel ill and not just a bit down.

'Don't you fret about anything,' Bea told her. 'Cath and I'll take care of Tracy. We'll bring her in to see you. Everything'll be all right. Your job is to stay in here and get better.'

By the time Jack turned up that evening, Evie was feeling very ill and had a high temperature, so that she was only barely aware that he had come and he went away without even seeing Andrew.

Her body felt wracked – sore and torn from the birth and burning with fever. She still continued to feed her baby some of the time and the nurses topped him up with a bottle. Her breasts ached, her body sweated and she drifted in and out of sleep, dreaming distorted dreams – her baby was still inside her, struggling to get out; Jack had gone back to England and left her behind. She would wake even more worn out and frightened. But because of the miracle of penicillin, soon the fever began to abate.

She was aware of Jack visiting from time to time. He held her hand. As she got better, her friends brought Tracy in to see her. The first time she saw her little girl, when Cath brought her in after more than a week, it was Evie, not Tracy, who burst into tears.

'Mama,' Tracy said solemnly, and wrapped her

arms round Evie's neck.

'Oh babby,' Evie sobbed. 'I've missed you so much. D'you want to see your little brother? He'll be coming in for a feed in a minute.'

When the nurse carried Andrew in, Tracy gazed at him in wide-eyed awe. Cath laughed.

'Well, he looks bonny,' she said. 'He's none the worse for any of it.'

'Andwoo,' Tracy said, poking his face with an exploring finger. The baby winced, then gurgled and Tracy laughed.

'We'll soon be home with you, Trace,' Evie said. 'Then you can help me look after him, can't you?'

She was in hospital for just over two weeks. When they came home, Jack seemed really pleased to see them all. He had been alone for the past fortnight, with some of the women taking pity on him and bringing round meals.

He drove Evie home with Andrew in her arms and Cath brought Tracy back to the house. She left Tracy and withdrew tactfully to let them all be alone.

'You all right?' Jack asked, helping her in through the front door. She was surprised and touched by how concerned he was. He didn't like hospitals, she knew. He was happier to have her back home.

'I'm all right,' she smiled. 'No need to fuss. And I gather you've had them all clucking round you – lucky for you, eh? Now we can all be together. Be a family properly.'

'How's little'un then?' Jack looked down at

Andrew as he settled Evie into her chair. She was wearing a loose skirt and blouse that it was easy to feed Andrew in. The room was tidy and the windows open onto the garden in the warmth, letting in the scent of cut grass. She still felt weak and drifty, but she was on the mend and it felt wonderful to be home. She settled into her rocker with a feeling of luxury.

'Oh, he's all right. Been living like a king.' She latched Andrew on and he suckled happily. Tracy stood watching, fascinated.

Jack smiled. 'Want a cup of tea?'

'Yeah, go on then.'

She was amazed by the way he fussed around her that evening. He's missed me – missed all of us – she thought. Maybe my being ill was for the best. He's had to be on his own all this time. She thought back to her sense of despair in the hospital. It was because I was feverish, she thought, I was just blowing everything out of proportion.

And Jack seemed pleased that at least Andrew was a boy.

'He can learn to ski, soon as he can walk,' he joked, sitting down beside her with a mug of tea. Tracy was playing nearby with her wooden horse. 'And play ice hockey – learn it straight away, like they do here.'

'Course he can.' Evie smiled. 'This is nice,' she said, reaching out a hand. Jack, after a second's hesitation, linked his hand in hers. 'It's heaven all being together like this, Jack. You, me and the kids.'

'Yeah,' he said. 'Yeah.' He squeezed her hand and let it go. 'I just, er...' He spoke as if reluctantly, but he got the words out all the same. 'On Saturday, there's a group of the lads going up country for a fishing trip...'

Evie felt her heart sink. Today was Thursday. Surely he wasn't thinking of going away already? Couldn't he have said he would miss it this time?

'Oh Jack, d'you have to?' She was immediately near to tears. She needed him to stay with her, to look after her.

'Thing is...' He wasn't looking at her. He spoke to the open windows. 'I, er...' He couldn't find any excuse or justification. 'I said I would, yeah. There's not a lot I can do with the kids.' He made a joke of it. 'I mean, I can't feed him, can I?'

Evie tried to swallow her sense of rejection. It felt like a physical blow. She knew she ought to say that yes, of course she minded. But she never liked standing up to Jack in case... In case what? She did want to think about that. And anyway, what difference did it make now? It was the fact that he took it for granted that he was going that hurt. He didn't *want* to be with her and the kids – he wanted to be away with the lads.

All right, if that's how you feel, she thought, looking down at Andrew to hide her tears. Just sod off and leave us all then, if that's what you want.

'You don't mind, do yer?' Jack said, broad Brummie again suddenly. She noticed he did that when he wanted to get round her. 'It's only a couple of days, like. You're a good wench.'

When Jack came back from his fishing trip that weekend, which she spent with her women friends and the children, putting a brave face on it all, he was very attentive and apologetic. Evie realized that the other men – not to mention their wives – must have had a few things to say to him about going off and leaving her when she had not only just borne him a son but had been so ill.

She imagined Don Sorenson taking him aside for a fatherly chat: 'Now look here, son, Edith says you really should be back home this weekend.'

Whatever had happened, Jack was not going to say, but Evie was grateful to whoever it was. For a while Jack was more attentive and came home a little earlier from work. He even opted out of the next fishing trip and instead took Evie out for a drive with the kids in the car. They made one of their rare drives towards the Rockies. With Andrew in her lap, she watched the great spaces of the prairies swallowed beneath their wheels.

'This is lovely, Jack,' she said, as the majestic grey peaks with their folds of summer snow eased into view with the sun on them, behind the shadowy lower hills. She was grateful, ready to forgive him anything. He had two weeks all on his own while I was in hospital, she thought, finding excuses for him. Got a bit too used to the bachelor life again, silly old thing.

Sun and wind were pouring in through the car window, Tracy had dozed off along the back seat and it felt as if everything was going to be all right. A shadow fell on her thoughts, chilling her. What if it all went wrong? What if Jack wasn't happy? She thought back with shame and embarrassment to her outburst to Bea in the hospital. *I don't think Jack loves me anymore...* Bea had put it down to her being in an emotional state after the birth. Bea *was* right, Evie told herself. Course she was.

She took a deep breath of the fresh air. As she did so, she found in herself an iron sense of resolve. No more outbursts like that. Whatever happened, she was going to make her marriage work and she must never say anything to anyone that was disloyal to Jack ever again.

She turned and smiled at him as he drove and he sensed her looking and gave her a smile back.

'It's a bit of all right, isn't it?' he said. They were passing a lake, its ruffled surface icy blue. And he was being so nice. Like the old times.

'It's lovely,' she said. And it was, all of it. The beauty of it, Jack and her children close by. This was how everything should be.

Her dream was intact.

Thirty-Nine

August 1969

'We're going on a holiday!' Evie announced to the children.

'With Dad?' Tracy asked doubtfully. Now nearly five, she was still a serious, rather grown-up little girl. Evie felt a pang at the disbelief in her voice that their father would want to spend time with them.

'Yes, course with Dad,' she said in a jolly voice. 'He's taking us camping.'

'Camping!' Andrew leapt about with excitement. He was three; dark-haired and brown-eyed, but lively and wiry like Jack.

These days they hardly ever went anywhere all together because it seemed such an effort. Evie had learned to drive, but she just took the kids out around town, to the Lake with some of the others, or on picnic trips.

'They're old enough to take some of it in now,' she said to Jack. ''Specially Trace. How about we go camping?' He liked going camping with some of his mates. 'Andrew's going to be keen on all that if we start him early, isn't he?'

Jack seemed reluctant.

'We never go on holidays, Jack,' she begged, hurt by his lack of enthusiasm but trying desperately not to sound peevish. Her life had become a struggle to keep Jack happy. She was so used to it she hardly noticed anymore. It was what you did, she thought. 'Everyone else goes on holiday. They must find it funny that we never do.'

This hit home. They were not used to holidays; had never had them in their lives before. But now, if there was one thing Jack always wanted, it was to fit in.

'Go on then. All right,' he said.

Evie was excited. Apart from a few little drives out she had still hardly been anywhere in Canada. Her life had come to revolve round the kids and her neighbours in Rosette. During the first years of Andrew's life they had quickly settled into a routine.

Jack was taken up with his male world of work, of weekends fishing or at hockey games or skiing; Evie with the women and children, and all the concerns of childhood illnesses and nursery school and the daily round. She was happy, proud of her two children and immersed in them. It was all she had wanted and her children helped to heal the painful rent in her experience made by her birth family. If it meant giving Jack as much time away from them doing what he wanted, then that was what she was going to do and put a brave face on it.

She tried to tell herself that their lives were not slipping further and further apart. Some weeks she hardly saw Jack. He got up early to get to work, often went for a drink after, making sure he was home once she had got Tracy and Andrew to bed. Weekends he saw as his time to be out – fishing, hiking, at hockey games.

It was just how it was, she told herself. Men and women lived in different worlds. Bea and Cath and the others joked about their husbands and how hopeless they were in the house. Evie laughed along with them. These friends were the ones who helped her most – during the childhood illnesses and getting through the long winter days. Jack had his male world and she had hers.

When they were together, they rubbed along all right amid all the busyness, mainly because she never questioned his right to do exactly as he pleased.

With the car loaded up, they drove towards the

Rockies, heading west across the prairie towards the distant, shrouded peaks. At first the day was overcast and soon they were driving between dark, sheer walls of rock, heaped rockfalls at their feet. The lakes, in this louring day, looked like pools of liquid steel. Evie found herself feeling dragged down by it. She felt shut in and threatened by the dark mountains, by the land's endlessness, its dour, punishing moods.

But by the afternoon, the sky had cleared to a pale eggshell blue, the highest peaks peeping and vanishing with every bend in the road, some grey, some capped with snow. The steel waters lit to a vivid blue and all was transformed into something awesome and beautiful and she liked Canada better again. They all relaxed and Jack even joined in some nursery rhymes to keep the kids happy.

But camping with two little ones was harder work than she had reckoned on. There was all the putting up of the tent, the searches for water and the preparation of food on a little stove. The moments when one or other child was roaring because they had got wet, or were bitten by some insect. And that was when the weather was fine and they were not crouching inside the tent, looking out at one of the endless downpours which could block out almost everything to be seen around.

As the days went by, however hard Evie tried to keep everyone going – 'Let's all play a game! Who wants to paddle? – Jack grew more and more tetchy. It was hard to walk very far. The children were too young for long hikes. There was no private time for the two of them together, for the lovemaking that still brought them closer for a while, since they were all crowded into one tent.

In the end, hating the tension Jack was injecting into each day, Evie started telling him to go off and do what he wanted, to try and put him in a better mood. She stayed behind and had to keep the children entertained. Some days, she realized with guilty unease, she preferred it when he wasn't there. It made life easier. In the end they spent hardly any of the holiday together.

On the last afternoon, on their way home, they had a long distance to drive. They drove in heavy silence. It had not been a success. Evie looked out, her heart heavy. She was longing now to get home, for them to be able to sink back into their normal life and routine, with their friends around them. She tried to push away the sense of despair she felt that being with Jack had been so difficult.

He seemed desperate to get home. She knew better than to say anything, but she kept sneaking little glances at his frowning face, his elbows tensed as he held the wheel, driving as fast as the roads would allow. Inside her the feeling of tension and hurt was heavy, like a stone.

Part of the journey took them along a straight, seemingly endless road through lonely country, the golden remains of harvested grain stretching away on each side and no petrol station for many miles. The day was hot. Andrew started howling, bored and uncomfortable. Jack began letting out sharp, angry sighs. Thunderclouds gathered in his face.

'Shut him up, can't you, for Christ's sake!' he erupted at last.

'I'm trying,' Evie snapped back, her nerves completely frayed. For once, after the week they had had, she couldn't keep quiet. 'It's not my fault, is it? Why don't you do something to help for once? They're your kids as well, Jack. All you ever think about is yourself. And watch your language!'

She twisted round, ignoring Jack's furious muttering, to deal with Andrew. 'Come on, babby, stop that now. D'you want a sweetie?' But he was wriggling and fighting in the seat, the tense atmosphere in the car only making him worse.

'Here, Andrew,' Tracy said. 'You can have my bear. Look, he wants to play with you.' Her blue eyes full of worry, she thrust her little brown teddy at her brother, trying to get him to be quiet. Evie's heart buckled at the sight of her tousled, honey-coloured hair and scared face. Andrew didn't want her bear. He was past being pacified by anything.

Moments later the car started to bump erratically and they rolled to a halt. Jack got out to look, his face taking on an even more grim expression.

He stooped down and disappeared from view. Then reappeared. And just went mad. He slammed both hands down on the bonnet before reeling about at the side of the road, ranting at the top of his voice. Evie sat frozen, separated from him by a pane of glass and what seemed to be an ocean of pent-up feeling gushing out because a tyre was flat.

Jack was in a world of his own, not looking at her or the children. She saw him as if he was a wild stranger, this man in jeans and a red and black plaid shirt, cropped hair gleaming in the sun, lost in his rage. How nice his hair looks, she thought, the way it falls away from his parting. There he was, this man, her husband, as good looking as a film star, pacing and ranting, waving his arms and swearing. Who was he, this man she had lived with now for five years?

She heard a lot of it. Some of the words that broke out of him engraved themselves in her mind.

'Look what you've cowing well reduced me to!' Jack yelled. He was very Brummie again in his fury. 'I never wanted kids in the first place and now I'm cowing well stuck with the whole soddin' lot of yer...'

Evie's heart seemed to stop. She sat very still, clasping her hands in her lap, on her plump thighs in her navy blue slacks. She could not do anything about the fact that Tracy could probably hear every word her father was saying. The worst of it was that the children were now deadly silent. Evie could not even turn and look at them. She sat like a statue, numb inside.

After what seemed an age, Jack stopped ranting. Without even looking at them or asking them to get out of the car, he winched it up with furious movements and changed the tyre. She wasn't damn well offering to help after that. He got back in without meeting her eye and drove, in a silence that none of them, even Andrew, dared break, until they reached the refuge of home. Home, where they fled to different corners of the house, where, as the days passed, they could immerse themselves in their own lives again and try to pretend this had never happened. Pretend that a chasm had not cracked open through their home, through their lives and the lives of their children.

They went on, day after day. As usual she didn't say anything. She tried to keep everyone happy.

Yes, she told her friends, they had a lovely trip. Even the children never mentioned the shouting, the rage, as if it was a dream they had all had and now everything was back to normal.

She and Jack spent hardly any time together. He was out more in the evenings and he went on a trip almost every weekend. They made love from time to time, in a routine sort of way, but it became a rare event. She tried not to think about that. That was marriage, wasn't it? Her own mother, indiscreet as ever, had moaned about the same thing. This was what happened to everyone.

When they were together in public, they acted as if everything was well. Evie and Jack, a lovely couple. And even to Bea, she never breathed a word. She started to feel that the only way to keep things going was not to think about it. To keep living day after day. Because at all costs, she needed Jack.

But sometimes terrible things went through her mind. It would be better if he hit me, she found herself thinking. At least then I'd know he *felt* something.

Very rarely, she steeled herself to tackle him about the way things had changed. One Saturday night, during the winter after the holiday, she had been in alone all day with the children while Jack was out, as usual. He came in, after the children were asleep, seeming in a mellow mood after a drink or two. When they got into bed she said, 'Jack, we don't spend any time together now – you and me. I don't want... I mean...'

Saying it, she realized just how much sadness she had been hiding from herself all the time and a lump rose in her throat. She kept trying to tell herself that all the couples she knew were like this, but she knew it wasn't true. It felt as if she and Jack were strangers who moved around each other in the same house.

Jack was lying on his back, hands behind his head. He moved his nearest arm down so he could look at her.

'What?' His tone was not very inviting, not angry, just as if he didn't want to talk or – she tried to push away this thought – didn't care either way.

'I just...' She could hear the huskiness in her voice. 'It used to be different, that's all. You know, when we were first...' She was struggling not to cry and she couldn't look at him. 'I don't want ... I don't want you to be unhappy – with me.'

He stared at her. It was a cold stare, or at least not one containing affection. He didn't take her in his arms and assure her that everything was all right, that she was his wife and he loved her. She knew in that moment that he didn't love her, however much she longed to hear him say that he did, that nothing had changed.

'I'm not unhappy,' he said in a neutral voice and looked away again.

'You sure?' Her voice had gone small. Even if he sounded like a stranger, she wanted him to reassure her that all her dreams were not dead.

'Yeah. Course. I dunno what you're on about. Come on, let's get some kip.'

Forty

1971

It was the beginning of January and Evie was feeling hopeful. She and Jack had certainly lived through a long bad patch but it seemed to her that they had come through the worst of it.

Things aren't perfect, she thought, but what marriage is? Jack seemed to have settled down. He was still out a lot, but he was doing well at work. The Rosette Tube Co. had given him a good promotion. Nowadays when he came home he seemed more relaxed, amiable. Evie could see that it was because the children were older. Tracy was six and was at the local school, and Andrew would be four in the summer and would soon begin at the kindergarten. Things had started to feel easier.

But that was when Bea dropped her bombshell.

'Stan and I have been talking a lot over Christmas,' she told the other women as they socialized one snowbound Saturday. Some of the men were in the house too, as it was minus ten outside. Not Jack, of course. He had gone to watch ice hockey.

'Anyway ... Stan wants to move on and, well...' Bea looked round at them, Evie, Cath and the rest. Evie was startled to see tears in Bea's eyes, calm Bea who was always a comfort to everyone else. 'He's taken a job at the hospital in Calgary. We'll be moving over there soon as we can manage it.'

Evie thought for a moment she was joking. Bea, not here! But Bea was her rock, her lifeline.

'Thing is, eventually I'd like to work some shifts as well and we thought, well, while everything's changing all the time with the kids we might as well make a move now.'

But you can't, Evie almost said. *You can't just go!*
'Oh Bea, no!'

It was the reaction of several of the others as well. Bea was the lynchpin of the group and everyone loved her.

'I'm so sad about it,' she said, letting her tears fall now. 'I'll miss all of you lot like mad. I don't know what I'll do without you. But we'll still be able to see you.' Bea wiped her eyes. She looked both sad and excited. 'You must come on over to Calgary.'

But they all knew it would never be the same. No more sitting in Bea's cosy, relaxed house with all their children. They had been each other's mainstay through a lot of the heaviest days of childrearing. And Bea – competent, kindly and fun – would leave a huge gap in their lives.

Both Evie and Cath wept the day Bea and Stan left. But soon after, as if a ripple had begun, Cath said that she and David were talking about returning to England. They had never wanted to stay permanently in Canada and it would be a good time to get their kids into English schools.

337

It would take some time, of course.

'I hope it takes you forever,' Evie told her sincerely, and Cath laughed sadly.

'That's so sweet, Evie. We are going to be on our way, I'm afraid. Obviously my mum's dying to get us home. But we must all keep in touch.'

Evie had thought things would just go on, but suddenly, nothing felt the same. All the security of her friends and the help they had given each other was melting away.

Maybe we should go back as well, she found herself wondering. For the first time since the early days in Canada she had begun thinking wistfully about home. But she told herself, there was no point in thinking about it. To the children this was home – and Jack would never go back to England, so that was that.

One Friday morning in early summer, Evie was in Rosette shopping for weekend groceries while the children were playing at a friend's house. Even shopping had become a miserable thing. In the past she often bumped into Bea or Cath and had a chat. Now there was no chance of that and the place felt less like home than before.

She was bagging up her packages and tins when she saw a familiar face behind her in the queue. It was a Canadian friend of Jack's called Steve, who she didn't know very well, but he was one of the ice hockey enthusiasts who went along to all the games.

'Hello,' she said, turning to him. He was a solid, wide-faced man with smooth brown hair and pink cheeks. She couldn't remember anything about him, where he worked, but she wanted to be friendly.

He looked puzzled for a second then said, 'Oh ... hi. Sorry, you're...?'

'Evie Harrison,' she said. 'Jack's wife.' He still seemed not to know what she was talking about. 'Jack Harrison?'

'Oh ... yes, course!' He laughed. 'Sorry. Trying to put two and two together. I haven't seen you in a while.'

'You got the day off?' she said, packing the last of her tins and reaching in her bag for her purse.

'Yeah.' He looked down at his clothes and she noticed then that they were splashed with paint. 'We've got a whole pile of things to do in the house so, you know, thought we'd make a week-end of it.'

Evie smiled at the cashier and picked up her bags and turned to Steve again. 'Oh well, one of the last games of the season this weekend, isn't it? But I guess you won't be going?'

'No,' he laughed. 'I'll be hard at work. There's a couple more, though. Anyway,' he called after her as they both waved goodbye and she was pushing the door open, 'tell Jack to get himself over to a game soon. Haven't seen him in yonks!'

Evie stopped for several seconds too long while this sank in, before she remembered herself.

'Oh ... yes. I will!' She gave Steve what she realized must have been a deranged smile and waved, hurrying off.

At the car she threw everything into the back and climbed in, her blood pounding so hard she thought her heart might be about to give out. She slammed the door and sat panting, Steve's words looping round and round in her head. *Tell Jack to get himself over to a game soon. Haven't seen him in yonks...*

There was a game most weekends. Jack went religiously every weekend he possibly could. So if he wasn't at the hockey game, where the hell was he?

She staggered into the house with the shopping. Without thinking, she put some water on for tea and stood while it boiled, staring out of the window. She felt as if she was listening for the distant sounds of an earthquake, the cracking and roaring and shaking growing nearer by the second, and she couldn't stop it, couldn't pretend anymore.

Once she had sunk down at the table with her tea, she started to shake. She gripped the mug with both hands.

Haven't seen him in yonks...

Was it all a mistake? Had she not understood him all this time?

Does he even really go fishing? she asked herself. His other great weekend pastime. She thought he did. Or had until recently, because David Laker often went as well. Surely Cath would have said something if Jack had not been there? During the ice hockey season, though, he had been going to every game he could.

Her mind spun. What do I say to him? What do I do?

She had to run to the bathroom and threw up so violently that her head throbbed. She hung over the lavatory, her tears coming then, and gulping, heartbroken sobs.

'Where've you been?' she sobbed. She knelt back on the floor and howled. He had been lying to her. For months? Years? And she had known. In a way she had known, but she had not wanted to know.

Sobbing, she curled up very small on the bathroom floor, her forehead pressing on the woven mat, knees pulled up close to her chest.

Forty-One

That week, she went through the motions of her life, getting the kids ready in the mornings, cooking Jack's dinner, asking him about his day.

If you can pretend, she thought, by God, so can I. She was amazed at her own calm.

And so what, anyway? She tried to talk herself round. Jack had not left her. No one else had said anything and Jack seemed happier. Why did she need to stir things up? She could just leave things as they were – as they had been for heaven knew how long. She would keep her family together.

But if she asked him, maybe there would be some other explanation. Some reason that did not mean that her husband had left her without actually leaving her; that the life she had clung to and tended so carefully was not being ripped into rags that could never be stitched together again.

She wouldn't ask. She lay beside Jack at night while he slept. This stranger breathing beside her.

341

His smell, his familiar body. Her heart hurt – an ache in her chest that never went away. But she stayed quiet.

For days, she said not a word. She started to believe that she could keep it up forever. For all she knew he had been... Been what? All this time? Going with someone else?

Someone else. The words flared in her head. The feelings. The hurt and jealousy.

And she knew she could not keep quiet. Not forever. Not in this cold, false way where she felt like icy glass that would shatter apart at any moment.

That next Friday night he came home by five. Her first feeling, for seconds only, was to be pleased to see him because it did not happen often.

'You're back early,' she said, smiling as he came in. It was still sunny and the kids were out in the garden.

'Yeah... Well...' He threw her a smile but even then she could tell he didn't mean it, that he was nervous. Something was wrong. Not normal. Instead of going straight upstairs to change, Jack just stood. He pulled a hand out of his trouser pocket and ran it along the back of the nearest chair. His nails were clipped and clean. She remembered that: the neat half-moons of his nails. He stopped, as if preparing himself, and turned to her.

She stopped him before he could speak. Walking to the kitchen, she called over her shoulder, 'Want a cup of tea?'

Her heart – she could feel it now, banging slow

but hard. Because she wanted to be the first one to say something. And she did say it casually, calling from the kitchen, 'I met a pal of yours.' He didn't need to know that it was a week ago.

There was no answer. She came out into the living room and Jack was still standing just where he had been before.

'That guy Steve. The one you go to the ice hockey games with.' No hint of accusation in her voice, she plumped a cushion, not looking at him. 'He said to say hello. Said he hadn't seen you in ages.'

And then she looked at him, her blood seeming to stop. He was looking right back. There was a long pause before he said, 'Thing is, Evie...' He sounded very Canadian. Smooth, somehow. 'I've just got to say something. I, er...' He wiped a hand across his forehead. He had been going to say it anyway, she saw. Maybe. Or if not today, another day. But he looked like someone preparing himself. 'I've got to go. From here. I mean...'

She bent over and picked up a cardigan from Tracy's favourite doll which was lying at her feet. She thought she would never forget the soft feel of that pink wool between her fingers, so entwined it was with something hard and fractured. For a moment she saw herself from outside, as if she was watching a movie, as if she wasn't herself at all.

'I've met someone else,' Jack said. 'And I want to move in with her. Start again.' He shrugged hopelessly. 'Sorry.'

She heard herself gasp. Everything made sense. And it made no sense. *Met someone...* He didn't say

343

when. And she knew, had known, had guessed – where else would he be going? But still she did not expect that this was what he would say. That he could just break everything in a handful of words.

'Jack... No...' Her voice came out as a moan. 'No!' And, to her horror, she threw herself at his feet. 'Jack, don't leave me. You can't! I can't bear it if you leave me.' Sobbing, her head on his shoes, she clung to his legs.

'Don't, Evie, for Christ's sake!' He was getting angry, frantic. 'Stop it. The kids...'

'What do you care about the kids!' she screamed. 'When've you ever cared about them – or about me? All you've ever done is what you sodding well like. You don't care about anyone!'

Climbing to her feet, out of control, she started hitting and slapping at him, sobbing, until he grabbed her hands and managed to wrestle her so that he had her from behind, her arms crossed over her body while she fought him.

Until she saw two little figures standing at the door, watching them, silent and terrified. She saw Tracy reach for Andrew's hand.

The woman, Linda, was a secretary in one of the firms in the area – not the Rosette Tube Co., but somewhere nearby. Linda was Canadian born. She had no children. She was single. Linda was Canada. She was freedom. She was all Jack wanted.

The worst of it was that he did not seem to mind if she took the children back to England. At first she had used that as a threat.

'I'll take them back home!' she threw at him,

not believing it then herself. 'You'll never see them.'

She had no idea what she was going to do. She was in shock. Jack was like a wall sealed against her. He had set his face towards Linda and whatever she did or said seemed to make no difference.

'Jack, I love you,' she sobbed, over and over again. 'I've done my best to be a wife to you. Please don't leave – I need you. What about the kids – *your* kids?'

Again she begged, kneeling at his feet, not caring how humiliating it was.

But it was no use. He was not insulting, or unkind, he just stepped over her as if she was not there and left the house, while she sobbed with her face pressed to the rug.

At first she thought she would stay in Canada. But her tight group of friends was disappearing. All the life she wanted was disappearing. And coming here in the first place had all been about Jack. He was planning to stay in Rosette. He was very nicely off here, thank you. She did not want to start again – not here, or anywhere else in Canada, without him. Canada seemed tainted: she was burying her dreams here. It felt as if the country had turned against her and now it felt a sad, alien place.

Jack was calm reason itself. There was no changing his mind or moving him in any way. If she wanted to move somewhere else, he would help set them up. He would help them get to England if that was what she wanted. He was all helpfulness in disposing of a whole family and that helpfulness made her more bitter than anything.

'Don't you care that you won't see Tracy and Andrew?' she kept asking.

'I don't see them that much anyway,' Jack said, when he finally answered her instead of evading the question. He was so caught up in himself and his new life she could hardly get any sense out of him. 'Tell them to come over and visit when they've grown up – get to know their old dad, eh?'

She was so full of rage and hurt that she couldn't speak. Only later all the things she might have said poured into her mind, but at that moment she stared at Jack's back as he turned away, this husband who had become a stranger. It was then she knew for certain she could not stay here. They would go back to England – get as far away from him as possible. It felt as if they would all be better off without him.

V

Forty-Two

October 1971

The plane rumbled along the runway, picking up speed as if something was chasing it. Evie gripped the arms of the seat. Tracy, beside her, was watching Edmonton airport shrink away below them. Her fair hair was tied in a little ponytail and the sweet slenderness of her neck filled Evie with tender protectiveness.

She drew in deep, shaky breaths to try and quell the turmoil inside her. If the children had not been there, she knew she would have broken down. She turned to Andrew, the other side of her, her sweet, dark-eyed lad, who had had his fifth birthday that summer. He had had a haircut just a few days ago and his treacle-coloured hair was neatly clipped and very grown-up looking.

'You all right, lovey?' she whispered.

He nodded. He looked small and bewildered, in a blue jersey that was too big for him. It came halfway down his thighs, partly covering the grey trousers. The last few hours had been full of change and strangeness. Evie took his hand and he gripped hers hard.

'Look, Mom, clouds!' Tracy turned to her, full of excitement. She had never flown before. At nearly seven, it was all an adventure. 'They look like sheep!'

'Yes, they do, don't they?' she agreed, trying to sound normal, even though sick with nerves and upset.

Evie heard her children's voices afresh – both full Canadians – and panic welled up in her. What the hell did she think she was doing, running back to England, to a place neither of her kids had ever seen, where they would be foreigners, just because she had... Had what? Family who she had not seen or had anything to do with in years? She was mad. But the thought of staying in Canada now was unbearable as well. And, she thought, her hurt and rage welling up in her again, however much she had begged Jack not to leave them, not to break up the family, he had set his face away from them and never faltered. He had practically paid her to go.

Looking back now, she saw through different eyes the way Jack had left England, without a backward glance towards his family, his country. She had admired it then. Now it chilled her. He had moved on from them as he had now moved on from her. And what also shamed her was that she had done much the same. She didn't want to be like Jack.

'Mom.' Tracy was looking at her in that sharp, blue-eyed way she had. There was something fierce about the girl. She's stronger than me, Evie thought sometimes. Stronger inside. Tracy put her hand on Evie's arm, the way a secure child will, as if a mother is a wall or a piece of furniture. 'Mom!'

'What, bab?'

'Why isn't Dad coming with us?'

'Because... Look, I've told you. Your dad's busy at the moment, so he couldn't come.' The answer was so limp and untruthful, but there had to be some sort of answer for now. They had managed to keep most of their rows away from Tracy and Andrew. None of them could manage to take in all the truth at once.

The novelty of the flight soon wore off. After they had had some food, both Tracy and Andrew fell asleep, Andrew with his head resting against Evie's arm, Tracy curled up against the side.

Evie knew there was no chance of rest herself, even though she had barely slept for several nights in a row. She felt she would never sleep again. And though she was grateful for the children sleeping, for not having to pretend and jolly them along, she was left with her own thoughts now and that was almost harder: she had to face what she had done. What they had each done.

She adjusted the seatbelt which felt as if it was trapping her, and she could smell coming from the seat the sickly perfume of a previous passenger. Andrew's head lolled against her and she stroked his soft hair. Tracy muttered, but slept on. She looked so sweet, her pale hair against the crimson of her dress.

Pain tore through her. Children of a broken home, that's what they were now. It was a terrible feeling. Of all the things she could say about her own mother and father, she could not accuse them of that. Though God knew, there were times when she and her sisters had wondered why Dad didn't just go off and have done with it.

Sitting here now, hanging over the Atlantic Ocean, she thought, Tracy and Andrew have got cousins, aunties and uncles, grandparents. A

351

wave of longing came over her. They were all older now. Grown-up. Might they be nicer now? Might it all be different?

Forty-Three

I never wanted kids. Never ever – I told you...

Evie woke with a start. Jack's angry voice was hectoring in her head and all of her mind, her emotions were left behind, in those moments, in Rosette, Alberta, Canada. She took in the sight of brown curtains, a grey light straining through them; the stale smell of fags in the room. Wherever was she?

She sat up. A double bed. Beside her, still asleep, Tracy, her honey hair spread on the pillow. Andrew lay between them, with his neat short back and sides. The sight of their trusting little forms in the dim light steadied her.

They were peaceful now, after having shed tired, bewildered tears as she put them to bed in this cheerless room. She had wanted to break down and cry herself. But she had stayed strong. Had to, for them. They were all she had, her beloved children. Everything she did was going to be for them.

The room, where they had arrived last night, was in a cheap lodging house on Birmingham's Hagley Road. The stale-smelling room and its dark furniture dragged her spirits down to the dregs after their light, airy house in Canada.

She did not feel as if she was really back in Birmingham. This was not the city she knew. Even the money was all different. When she exchanged her last Canadian dollars she was given funny little pound notes, not like the ones she remembered. Instead of half-crowns and sixpences she found herself with the decimal twelve and a half pence. There was the fifty-pence piece, an odd-shaped coin, for what she knew as ten shillings. Even though she knew about the change, it made her feel like a foreigner in her own country.

Last night she had put her exhausted children into a taxi from the bus station in town. She had not been able to see much out of the window, but some of what she did see looked different. It had not occurred to her not to come to Birmingham. She knew nowhere else in this country. And she found herself aching for familiarity after their long journey, after living so long in a strange land.

She pulled the green sateen cover more closely round her, hugging her knees, longing for a cup of tea. The dream, in which Jack had felt so close again, began to fade. She wanted to hold on to it and yet push him away at the same time.

Sitting beside the children, her mind rushed into anxious calculations about all the obstacles in front of her. Jack had paid their fares, given her extra to get settled. Oh yes, he hadn't stinted in getting shot of them. But they still needed somewhere to live, a school for the kids... It all felt overwhelming, terrifying. She had to find the strength somehow. Tracy and Andrew were everything.

Soon Tracy began to stir. She opened her eyes and a look of panic crossed her face before she saw her mother. Evie put her fingers to her lips and looked down at Andrew.

'Let him sleep,' she whispered.

Tracy nodded solemnly and sat up with great care, her eyes wide.

'It smells bad in here,' she said, screwing up her nose. 'What are we going to do today?'

'Well...' Evie felt herself tighten inside. She tried to make her voice encouraging, as if it was all an exciting adventure. 'What we're going to do is see if we can find your nan and granddad, and your aunties and uncles. I've been away a long while, so you've got lots of cousins by now, I expect, Trace.'

'Who are they?' Tracy said, bewildered.

'I told you – they're my mother and father, babby,' Evie said. 'And my sisters.'

'Do they live here?'

'Somewhere, they do, yes, lovey.' She reached over and stroked her daughter's face. 'And we're going to find them, aren't we?'

After a breakfast of watery scrambled egg, which Evie could have sworn was made of powder – left over from the war, *still?* – and white toast like singed cardboard, they stepped out into the morning.

The road was gleaming wet but the sun was beginning to strain its way between the clouds. She had only had a dim idea of where she was, until the enormously plump lady running the lodging house told her that if she turned left she would soon be at Five Ways. It dawned on her that they could just walk to where they needed to go.

'Oh, we're near home!' she said to Tracy. And then wondered what she had meant. When she got to the roundabout at Five Ways, each of the children clinging to her hand, it felt strange compared to what she remembered. Some of the buildings were the same: tired and grimy looking. But it felt different. There was a wide road to the left where she remembered a narrower one. The sign on it said 'Ladywood Middleway'.

Tracy looked up at her. 'Are you lost, Mom?'

'Oh ... no.' Evie rallied herself. 'Come on – along here.'

When she had left Birmingham, seven years earlier, the bulldozers had already begun on the area, had laid swathes of it to waste and retreated, leaving rough wastelands and half-wrecked terraces, even worse than the Blitz, people said. And now she longed for something familiar. But when she tried to find Inkerman Street a terrible shock was waiting for her.

At the end of Hyde Road, along which she had trotted so many times to get into Inkerman Street, she stood in silence, too stunned even to say anything. The street was gone. The strip of cracked old tarmac led into nothingness, a chimney poking up in the distance, a couple of spindly trees. It looked like the remains of a battleground. At each side of the road were piles of scrub and red-brick rubble. She could see trees and realized she must be looking at the edge of the reservoir. Never before had she been able to see so far.

'Oh my God!' she whispered as she took it in.

There were still patches of waste ground, but in the far distance, pale tower blocks poked up like overgrown teeth in the morning haze. She looked round her in dismay at the wreckage of the remaining scraps of terraces, gaps strewn with rubble and weeds. All the places of her childhood, the houses and entries, the yards and the air-raid shelter were no more. And where were all the people now – her family and neighbours?

'Are we there?' Tracy said, frowning.

'Yes.' Evie struggled to find words. How could she explain? 'No. Well ... I thought so. But... This is where the street was...'

She turned, lost and disorientated. On Monument Road there were still things she recognized – the baths, the dispensary, some of the old shops she knew. And St John's Church, which felt like an old friend.

'See that?' She bent down and pointed it out to the children. 'I used to go in there – to Sunday school.'

They both stared. 'Don't like it here,' Andrew said in a tiny voice.

'It's all right, babby,' Evie said, squeezing his hand. She didn't know what else to say.

'You all right, bab?' A middle-aged man with a lined, friendly face stood in front of her. His chest was bad; she could hear his every breath.

'I was looking for Inkerman Street,' she said, feeling foolish.

He gave a wheezy laugh, face creasing, then coughed while they waited.

'Where the hell've you been, then?'

'Away,' she said.

'You must've been – they knocked Inkerman Street down a good while back.'

She was battling to take it in. She felt Tracy and Andrew press themselves in closer to her.

'You looking for someone, are yer?' he asked. He was kind, she could see, but she felt like crying and didn't want to say she was trying to find her whole family. It sounded bad. She swallowed, pushing away the tears.

'Where've they all gone?' she asked pitifully.

The man tried to speak but had to pause, first to let a heavy lorry grind past, pumping black fumes, then to cough, a hand banging his chest. Finally, he managed to say, 'All over. New houses, new estates. If you're looking for someone in particular, your best bet's the pubs.'

'Yes.' This made sense. 'There's still...?'

'Oh ar, there's still a fair few of them left standing, bab. Any idea which they would have gone in?' He tactfully didn't ask who.

'The Inkerman,' she said, making a face. Both of them glanced at the flattened neighbourhood. 'Or the Hyde Arms.'

'Well, you ain't gunna have much luck there, are yer?' There was a bitter edge to his joking but his face still looked amiable. 'You could try there for a start.' He pointed at a pub just visible near the baths. 'Or there's the Duke of Wellington, further along.'

'All right ... yeah,' she said, feeling as if she had slipped into a dream. 'Thanks.'

They had to wait. It was too early for the pubs to open. She took the children back to the Hagley Road and sat in a cafe with them, sipping tea while they had squash and biscuits. She would

357

have liked to walk round and round the neighbourhood, taking it all in, trying to find the
things she could remember, the survivors clinging on after the battle. That was how it felt. But
she knew the kids wouldn't put up with that.

After, they went into pub after pub. No one
seemed to know Ray Sutton, her dad, to her
amazement. She thought Dad had been familiar
with every watering hole in the area. Where's
everyone gone? she asked the landlords and the
drinkers who were drifting in. All over, she was
told. Depends.

She drifted back along Monument Road, the
children quiet and miserable. What the hell do I
do now? She thought, her mind racing. There's
no one left to ask. I suppose I could go to the
council. They might be able to tell me. The
thought was exhausting and she felt near to tears.
They'd have to go back to that frowsty lodging
house again. And it was eating up the money, but
what else... Her mind raced on.

Along the street, suddenly, she fixed on a face
moving towards her, along the opposite pavement. Years fell away. Who was it? A tall, pinch-
faced man in old clothes that looked too small,
smoking a skinny roll-up. He had almost passed
by when she clocked who it was.

'Ron?' Gary's brother, one of the twins. She
was shocked by how old he looked; he was only a
few years older than her. Seeing him stop, she
hurried across the road, tugging the children.

'Yeah?' he said suspiciously.

'It's... I'm Evie ... Sutton. Gary's friend. D'you
remember me?' She felt eager suddenly, the past

rushing back to her. She wanted to know everything about everyone, how they were, what they
had been doing all this time.

'Oh ar.' He shoved his hand in his pockets and
did not seem able to meet her eye. It made things
difficult.

'How's Gary then?' she asked. 'All right, is he?
And Carl?'

Ron shrugged. 'How should I know?'

Evie was silenced by this. But Ron was her one
chance to find out something.

'Look ... I've been away, a good while – in
Canada. Just looking for everyone – the family,
like.'

Ron looked rather more impressed by this. To
her astonishment he drew in a last gasp of his
cigarette, chucked it down to grind under the
heel of his stained old plimsoll and volunteered
sudden information. It was like watching a faulty
boiler spring into life.

'I seen yer old man, like.'

'My dad? Have you?'

'Yeah. Works at Docker's, don't 'e? S'where I
work, see.'

'Oh, he's still there, is he?' she said. 'But I don't
know where they live. Everything's gone.' She felt
tears rising again, as if all her past, unpalatable as
it was, had been wiped out.

Ron was groping in his pockets and brought
out tobacco and Rizlas. She felt her spirits sink
even lower. This was all she was going to get. Ron
did not seem prepared to be hurried. He rolled a
cigarette with impressive deftness and, once that
was done, seemed able to speak again.

'Lives down Weoley Castle.'

Evie seized on this. 'Any idea where, Ron?'

He closed one eye against the cigarette smoke. 'Dunno. But I do know it's near the Sally Army somewhere. 'Ad one of 'em come round, dain't 'e?' He gave a snort of laughter. 'Practically on their cowing doorstep, 'e said.'

Forty-Four

Before they got on the bus, Evie bought Smarties and a packet of ginger nuts. She fed them to the kids on the way, the two of them squeezed into the seat next to the window beside her. They were too tired and confused to play up. They had stopped asking where they were going.

She had never been to Weoley Castle and, unable to think which bus to catch, she had got one out along the Bristol Road which had a reassuringly familiar number – 61. They'd have to walk the rest.

Evie felt bewildered enough herself. She had come home. But was this home? Now she was back here, seven years on, finding the family and showing off her kids, seeing her sisters' kids and being part of it all, felt like an urgent need. Even if they had a grudge against her, surely they would love Tracy and Andrew?

As they travelled further out of town, things began to feel more as she remembered. The smashed-up inner ring gave way to the suburbs.

Though there was bomb damage, it was more as it used to look and there was more green space. Looking out at the passers-by, Evie thought her own clothes, her small-town skirt in chocolate-brown pleats, cream blouse and black roll-neck jumper felt old-fashioned, as if she was middle-aged before her time. She saw people in bright colours, swirling patterns. Of course she had heard the Beatles and the Rolling Stones and other pop groups, but the 'Swinging Sixties' had reached Rosette only as a distant echo. Suddenly she felt she had missed being young.

They got off on the Bristol Road and walked through to the Castle Square. Evie, tense as a wire, had to hold on tight to her temper and make encouraging noises to Andrew, whose feet were dragging all the way. The square was in fact a circle, with shops set back from the road. There was the usual array of shops – the Co-op, a hairdresser's, a bakery – and boards propped outside advertising newspapers and coach trips to the seaside.

'Is this where our nanna lives?' Tracy asked. She seemed encouraged suddenly. The pavements here were wider than in town, the houses newer. It felt more like Canada.

'Yes ... somewhere, I think. Just got to ask.'

Evie poked her head round the door of the hairdresser's. There was a strong chemical smell, hairdryers humming, the light yellowed by plastic sheets stuck to the windows. A girl with heavy black eye make-up and an air of resentment eyed Tracy and Andrew as if they might be about to wreak havoc. The Salvation Army? She shrugged – how would I know? – seeming insulted by the question. It was an older woman who spoke up from under a dryer and said, pointing, 'It's in Alwold Road, bab. Just up that way.'

More walking. They found themselves standing in front of a squat white building with a notice-board outside. It was growing warm now and Evie was sweating in her brown wool coat but she didn't want to take it off and carry it.

Andrew began to grizzle. 'I wanna go home,' he said. 'I don't like it here.'

Evie picked him up and cuddled him. 'It's all right, babby, nearly there,' she told him, hoping this was true – not sure what she hoped anymore. 'Then we'll get you some dinner, all right?' Looking down at Tracy she could see she wasn't much more cheerful. 'I think Nanna and Granddad live near here somewhere.'

'Why don't you *know* where they live?' Tracy said crossly.

Evie could not think where to begin on this. She caught sight of a lady coming out of a house across Alwold Road with a cloth shopping bag over her arm. Evie tapped the back of Tracy's head, urging her across the street.

''Scuse me!' she called.

The woman, who had been about to walk off, turned with an air of suspicion. She was middle-aged, in a stone-coloured mac, with hair tightly permed and batwing spectacle frames. Seeing Evie with Andrew in her arms, she softened a fraction. He had stopped grizzling but still looked the picture of misery.

'Sorry,' Evie said. Already she had lost all trace of Canada in her voice. The city of her birth had reasserted itself instantly. 'Only I'm looking for someone – I don't know the address but I know it's round here somewhere.'

'Well, I don't know...' the woman said, as if afraid she was about to be caught up in something she might regret.

'A family called "Sutton". Mr and Mrs... It's Ray and Irene...'

The woman recoiled visibly from her. 'Oh,' she said. *'Them.'* She peered at Evie. 'You her daughter?'

'I... Yes,' Evie admitted.

'I can see the likeness – in your face, any road.' Her tone seemed laden with criticism. 'Don't you know where she lives then – your own mother? Mind you, if she was my mother, I'd keep *my* distance.'

Evie couldn't think of anything to say. She shook her head, her cheeks burning.

'Over there – where that lad's just come out of.' The woman nodded her head in the direction Evie had just come from. Sourly, eyeing Tracy and Andrew, she added, 'Good luck to you is all I can say.' And off she went.

Another boy had come out of the house she had pointed to and the two of them – eleven or twelve years old, Evie guessed – were cuffing each other on the worn square of grass outside. She narrowed her eyes. Who could they...? The penny dropped. Was that Rita's son, Joseph? And was that another brother? The second lad was the same ginger as the older one – like Conn. She had only seen Joseph, before she left home for good. It was astonishing to see the size of him now. My nephews, she thought. A warm feeling filled her. She wondered if Shirley had had any kids.

She was moving closer when someone else appeared – an unmistakeable, corpulent figure in a bright green frock, with almost white-blonde hair hanging down shoulder-length. Evie knew her instantly, the ample set of her hips, the huge calves and that walk, lurching from foot to foot, more stiffly now than she remembered.

The woman shouted something, though Evie couldn't make out the words. She took swipes at the heads of the boys, who disappeared indoors again followed by the woman – this woman who was undoubtedly her mother.

Evie ground to a halt. Panic filled her. Mom – as she always had been. What was she doing back here, chasing some idea of a mother that never was? Some dream of a mother who would love and welcome her?

But in those seconds she gave herself a stern talking-to. She was grown-up now with two children of her own, not the lost girl who had been thrown out of home. She didn't have to let her mother push her around. Mothers didn't have to be like hers had been – she knew that now. She could do her duty, introduce her mother to her grandchildren. And, after all, where else did she have to go?

Reaching down to take Tracy's hand, she said, 'Come on.'

They were terraced houses, modern, but built on the same principle of cramming as many human beings into a small space as possible. The front strip of garden was full of trampled weeds; the door was sky blue. Limp, grubby-looking nets hung in the lower front windows.

The front door was open. As they reached the house they could hear voices indoors – boys, Mom shouting above them and another nagging female voice. Smells of stale smoke and burnt toast wafted out from the hall, the lino of which was patterned with browns and orange. There was a threadbare doormat on the step. Evie felt Tracy tighten her hold on her hand. Andrew was silent, staring.

As she went to knock, Evie heard her mother's voice: 'Get that dinner on the table before I knock all their cowing blocks off!'

Evie knocked, knocked again and finally someone, not Mom, yelled irritably, 'Who's that? Oh, I'll get it...' Was that Rita's voice?

A thin, scraggy woman came barefoot along the hall. Her hair was scraped up behind; she was heavily pregnant and swathed in a bright yellow smock dress. Seeing Evie, she stopped in astonishment, crossed her arms over her chest and stared.

'Who're...? Is that...?'

'Hullo, Rita,' Evie said. She felt an advantage, having taken them by surprise. She cuddled Andrew close to her. 'Yeah, it's me. And these're my kids. Tracy, this is your Auntie Rita. And this is Andrew. We've just come over from Canada – for a visit.'

For the first time Evie could ever remember, she had impressed and astonished her eldest sister. Rita stood, gawping.

'Who is it, Reet?' Mom shouted. 'Gerrin 'ere –

I'm not feeding this cowing tribe all on my own.'

Rita came closer to the front door, all belly and stick limbs, and looked down in wonder at Tracy.

''Ello, darlin',' she said, in a syrupy voice. 'Aren't you a pretty little thing then? I'm your Auntie Rita. Come on, babby, come with me.' She held out a hand and Tracy, not sure what else to do, took it. Evie put Andrew down and they followed. She was amazed at Rita. That was about the nicest she had ever seen her. Maybe being a mom to a few kids had changed her?

The back kitchen appeared, on first sight, to be full of boys. In fact, there were four of them, but the room was small and they were constantly wriggling and trying to thump each other. As they walked in, the bottle of ketchup went rolling onto the floor. Evie saw her mother struggling to squeeze round the table with a pan in her hand, cuffing them as she went.

'Mom!' Rita cried. 'Guess who's 'ere! It's Evie! And look, you got more grandkids!'

Evie saw her mother's gaze swivel over to them. Her instinctive eye assessed that Mom had not been drinking – or if she had, not much. She was in control. She had gained a lot of weight. Her clothes strained around her as if she was tied into her dress like a parcel. Her face had slackened, its pink and white flesh softer and more jowelly, yet she still had a little girlish air, as if she might dance on tiptoe or fall into a tantrum any moment.

She took in the new arrivals. Evie felt Mom's presence in the room, the old force of it. She faltered inside. Gripping Andrew's hand, she told herself not to be stupid.

'Hello, Mom,' she said coolly. 'We've just come over from Canada – for a visit, like.' She wasn't going to tell them the truth, not yet – maybe not ever. And certainly not now, in front of the kids. 'This is Tracy and this is Andrew. Your grandchildren.'

Her mother appeared to melt at the sight of Tracy's sweet, intent face. She put down the pan, containing tinned spaghetti, and came round.

'Ooh, more grandkids for me then!' She made it sound as if it was a race she was winning. 'Ain't you a pretty little thing, eh?' She laid her lardy hand on Tracy's head for a moment. Evie saw her wedding ring, so embedded she could surely never take it off. Tracy gave a strained smile. 'Oh, and another lad as well!'

'These are my boys,' Rita said immediately, not wanting to be left out. 'Joseph, Sean' – she pointed at each – 'Jimmy and Wayne. And this one...' She looked down at her swollen belly. 'This'd best be a girl. Ooh, I'd love a girl to dress. I'm not going through all this again. I've said to Conn, come January, when it's all over, you've 'ad yer chips, mate. You can tie a knot in it.' She gave a chesty laugh, not sounding as if she meant it.

The boys all looked remarkably like Conn – red-haired and freckled, except for the youngest, Wayne, who must have been Andrew's age and was dark, more like their own father. A lot like Andrew, in fact. The two youngest boys eyed each other. Evie's two were uncertain, as yet. They watched as Sean noisily sucked spaghetti between his lips. The end of it went into his mouth in a rush, flicking sauce onto his face, and he giggled. Tracy and Andrew laughed as well.

'D'you want some spaghetti on toast, babby?' Rita bent over Tracy and when she nodded, Rita shooed her older two boys away from the table. 'You can eat standing up – these are your cousins and they've come a long way.'

Evie was amazed by this. And even more so when Rita turned and said rather piously, 'It's the most important thing, family, ain't it? Want a cuppa, Evie? And some spaghetti – or beans?'

'Oh, yes please,' Evie said. She felt a surge of hope. Maybe they could put all the past behind them, be a family in a new way?

Her mother had sunk down on what was clearly always her chair, sideways on to the table, legs spread in front of her. She pulled her ciggies from a pocket and lit up.

'Want one?' she asked indistinctly, holding out the packet.

'Oh ... no. Thanks.'

'Sit 'ere.' Mom pulled out the one spare chair, between her and Tracy. It had a pink plastic seat.

It was very strange being close to her mother again. Evie knew every line of her, the heave of her stomach pushing up the pea-green dress, the mighty white calves, feet half spilling out of flat white shoes. And that face, the big cheeks and full lips, faded red with old lipstick; her smell of sweat and cheap perfume. Her breathing was heavier now, almost a wheeze. Evie felt her body tingle, as if warning her of extreme danger. It was an old familiar feeling but it shocked her. Was that how she had been, on guard always? It was, of course. She had almost forgotten. But she thought, I'm past all that now. She can't touch me anymore. She knew she must cling to a distant, objective view of her mother. She must not go back to being the little girl she used to be.

It was strange seeing Mom in this new house with a proper back kitchen – water and a sink, Ajax on the draining board, Ascot heater, the lot, instead of the old wrecks of houses they had always lived in.

Rita moved round the kitchen making more toast and spaghetti, smoking. Mom dispensed orders. 'Pass me that...' 'Don't put that in there, Reet...' Rita pressed a hand to her back every now and then as if to remind them all that she was pregnant. Motherhood had given her a bossy kind of confidence. But she's still here hanging round Mom, Evie thought.

She saw the freckly boys all eyeing her, this strange auntie, nudging each other. She smiled at their mischievous faces and patted Tracy reassuringly. Andrew, sitting across from her, stared, fascinated by his cousins. They started vying to make him laugh. Soon Evie heard giggles coming from her little boy, he creasing up at the face pulling and general antics. She was warmed by this.

As they ate she asked after Dad and Conn and Shirley.

'Yer father's still driving for Docker's,' was all Mom said. ''E's all right.' Conn was working for a mechanic in Northfield. Shirley ... well, Shirley... Rita looked pitying. Shirl was living back here with Mom. She'd had a little girl called Ann, but her husband Howard had left her for another woman a couple of years ago. So she was back working – Rita said this with snooty disdain – for a doctor again, also in Northfield.

'Oh,' Evie said. 'Poor Shirl.' Her and me both, she thought. She was looking forward to seeing Shirley.

'His Mom helps out still, though,' Rita said pityingly. 'Ann's with her today – it's half-term, see.'

'Oh,' Evie said. 'Yes, I s'pose.' So Shirley had still not got away from Mom either. A feeling of oppression passed through her. Their mother was like a planet that they circled round and couldn't seem to break away from.

'But she'll be in after work,' Rita was saying. ''Er's on a half day today.'

They didn't ask her much, not about Canada. It was too far beyond anything they knew. Rita asked how old Tracy and Andrew were. Mom kept looking at them and Evie could see her children found their grandmother rather alarming. She kept leaning round and smiling and saying things like, 'Ooh, look at you two. Fancy – two more grandkids. I dunno what your grandfather'll say.' And just, 'Look at you two,' seeming to want their attention.

After they'd finished she said to Rita, 'Give 'em all some sweet stuff – that'll keep 'em quiet.'

Rita reached into a cupboard and brought out a bag of broken biscuits and a handful of tubes – sherbet dips and fruit pastilles. Tracy and Andrew, wide-eyed, were allowed to take what they wanted. Tracy kept looking back at Evie, as if for approval. Evie nodded to say it was all right.

'Go on, take 'em!' Mom said. 'Have what you

like. And you can go in the other room and give us some peace.'

Uncertain, but seeming to want to go, Tracy and Andrew followed their cousins next door. Evie hoped they'd be all right, but thought she would soon hear if they weren't.

They drank cups of tea, the orange-smeared plates all still on the table. Mom and Rita smoked and ate fruit pastilles. Rita plonked her feet up on another chair. Her legs were a mottled white and very thin.

Evie waited for someone to ask her something about her life. Since no one did, she said, 'I've been in Canada – getting on for seven years.'

Her mother pulled the cigarette from her mouth, inhaling. 'Oh ar,' she said, breathing smoke. She sounded neither interested nor uninterested. With her other hand she patted her hair. But suddenly, to Evie's amazement, she added, 'Looks like you've done all right for yourself, bab.'

With her lifetime of sensitivity to trouble, Evie listened for sarcasm, for the sting in the tail which always came from Mom somewhere along the line. Since when did Mom call her 'bab'? But she couldn't hear it. She looked at her in confusion, almost forgetting to breathe. Could Mom actually be saying something nice?

'Couple of nice kiddies you've got there,' Mom said.

An astonished, joyous feeling stole through Evie. It was going to be all right. Mom was welcoming her home, was pleased with her! And she was the new person she had become in Canada – stronger, more grown-up. All the harsh words,

371

the pain of the last time she had seen her mother were forgotten. Tears filled her eyes.

'Thanks, Mom,' she said. 'I wanted them to meet their nanna and granddad.'

'Oh, yer father'll be pleased to see another wench,' her mother said. 'With all these lads about.'

Evie sat waiting, wanting more, more of Mom being nice to her. She felt herself open, like a flower that can at last bloom in its own soil. Say more, she thought. Talk to me!

'Is he all right?' she asked. 'Dad?'

'Oh ar, 'e's all right.'

A silence fell.

'It's a bit different here, isn't it?' Evie said, reaching for conversation as no one seemed to have anything more to say. 'Nice house.'

'Oh, it's all right, yeah.' Her mother leaned one elbow on the table, the cigarette burning in her hand. 'Least it would be if it weren't for the neighbours. Cowing awful lot they are... All kippers and curtains.'

Evie felt the breath sigh out of her. Here we go, she thought. Some things never change.

Shirley arrived later, with Ann, a little girl of seven with almost white-blonde hair and a pale, doll-like face. The child was not pretty exactly, Evie thought. She had a sour look about her.

'Look who's here,' Rita announced, before Shirley could take in the new company.

Shirley, though looking tired, was more beautiful than Evie remembered. Her combination of their mother's strong bone structure and their

372

father's swarthy looks had developed into appealing proportions now she had matured. She was dressed in work clothes – navy skirt, court shoes, blouse. Ann was a skinny little thing, in baggy mauve corduroy slacks and a pink ribbed jumper. She seemed shy and put out to see new children in the house.

Shirley stared at Evie for a moment, then her face broke into a grin. Her mouth was wide and sensuous.

'Eves! Oh my word! What're you doing here? Where've you *been?*'

She came over and hugged Evie, who felt tears rise in her eyes at this sign of affection.

'*And* she's got two kids,' Rita said.

During all the introductions Ann and Tracy eyed each other. Tracy was a little older and Ann looked uncertain to begin with. But soon the two of them were in a corner whispering and giggling.

'She all right now?' Rita asked, nodding towards Ann.

'I asked Doctor Holmes to have a look at her,' Shirley said, adding importantly to Evie, 'he's my boss – *ever* such a nice man. It was a bit of a favour, like. She's been poorly. He says she's on the mend – nothing to worry about. They pick up everything at school.'

They all sat drinking tea. Rita and Shirley talked about their lives, everyday things. Mom moaned about Mrs Butcher who lived across the road. None of them wanted to know much about Evie. But for now, Tracy and Ann were hand in hand and Andrew and Wayne seemed to be getting along all right, tittering together over something in the living room. And Mom had been nice to her.

Evie felt herself begin to breathe more easily. Could she tell herself she had come home and that she might fit in at last?

Forty-Five

December 1971

They waited at the school gates in the cold wind, the sky gun-metal grey. Evie had her collar up, scarf pulled tight, hands in her pockets.

'I'm surprised you feel it if it's so cold in Canada,' Shirley said in the snide tone she used now any time Canada was mentioned. She was jealous of her younger sister's experience, bitter that she had never got out and gone anywhere.

'It is,' Evie said. 'Much, *much* colder. But the wind's mean today.' It blew round the shabby brick buildings of the little school and seemed to worm its way in between seams and buttons, into the core of you.

'Huh,' Shirley said, not looking at her. She smiled at one of the other mothers, but it was a fake kind of smile, Evie thought.

It was so grey and dismal. The children kept asking when was it going to snow, like in Canada? And when was Dad going to get here? To the second question she gave vague answers, putting off the time she had to tell them the whole truth, which for all the upset and Jack's stony rejection of her in their final weeks, she still could not fully believe herself.

She had promised the children that she would be there with Shirley on the last day of term. Shirley went to the school every day, between morning and evening surgeries, but Evie had already missed the nativity play because she was at work. Today she had taken an afternoon off specially.

There was the usual chatter of mothers and crying of younger children who had been dragged out into the cold.

The doors opened and out into the winter light came the colourful stream of children. Evie soon saw Tracy, in her blue anorak and cream pompom hat, hurrying towards her as if she was bursting with information, carrying something importantly in front of her. Dawdling behind, with a sulky expression, was Ann. Somewhere at the back would be Andrew, with the little ones.

'Mom, Mom!' Tracy was excited. 'Look what the teacher gave me!'

She held out a flat parcel, wrapped in bright paper.

'It's a prize! She gave it me because she said I'd settled in so quickly!' Tracy beamed up at her. Most of Canada had, in three months, almost entirely disappeared from Tracy and Andrew's accents. Evie was so proud of them. They had become Brummies almost overnight once they were at school.

'Ooh, isn't that lovely!' Evie said, delighted for her. She had been so anxious, with all the changes they had had all at once, about sending them to this new school. But Tracy's teacher, a young woman called Miss Barnes, had been very good with her and Andrew was so young he had adapted quickly as well.

'I think it's a colouring book – and crayons,' Tracy said.

'I never got anything like that at school,' Evie told her. 'It was different in them days.'

'That's 'cause you never did anything,' Shirley muttered. 'Half asleep most of the time, you were.'

Ann came up then, tense with annoyance, her pale face sulky.

'*She* got a prize!' she stamped furiously.

'Hey!' Shirley snapped. 'Watch it – you nearly got my foot!'

'But why does *she* always get everything?' Ann snarled. She looked with loathing at Tracy.

Tracy's face clouded. Things with her cousin were not as easy as Evie had hoped. Tracy had made friends with a girl in her class called Sharon. Sharon was a sweet, plump girl, black, or sort of – her dad was black and her mom white. Evie had wondered about her at first but Sharon was a good-natured girl with an infectious giggle and she soon warmed to her. But Ann was jealous and the remarks made by the rest of the family about Sharon made Evie blush with embarrassment. 'That blackie friend of yours' and 'eat a lot of bananas, does she?' and Mom said much worse, crude things that made Evie curl up inside.

'You can use it as well,' Tracy said, to appease Ann. 'We can go and do some colouring together at Nanna's, can't we?'

Evie was often amazed by her daughter's sweetness, the way she chose, somehow, to believe the best of everyone. She put it down to all the kindness of the people they had known in Canada.

'I don't want to use your stupid things,' Ann said nastily, turning away with her nose in the air.

'Oh, shurrit, Ann,' Shirley said wearily. 'Let's get home – it's freezing out here.'

Andrew came up and slipped his hand into Evie's. 'You all right, babby?' she asked him. He nodded silently. She worried about him constantly, knew he was missing his father, that he found all the changes draining. But he was little and Canada now seemed like another life to them all. He was doing all right at school.

She took each of their hands and followed Shirley, who had Ann stumping sulkily beside her. But at least today, the kids didn't have to go to Mom's. Most days Shirley picked them up and they waited at her mother's house until Evie finished work for the day. At first Evie had been happy that they had offered to do this. It felt as if they were really making her and her children part of the family. But gradually she was coming to feel uneasy about it, seeing how spiteful Ann could be. And the house was chaos with all Rita's boys there so much of the time. When she asked Tracy and Andrew if it was all right, though, they never complained.

Evie had a strong sense of gratitude to her children, for their strength, for being nice kids. She clasped their hands tighter and bent down to whisper, 'I've bought some nice fat crumpets. Let's go home and toast them on the fire, shall we?'

It may have been a sputtering old gas fire in their lodgings, but with a knob of butter and them all cuddled up, it would feel like a feast. Today they could just be the three of them.

Her first weeks back in England had been a blur of busyness.

She applied for a job on comptometers again, at a firm out on the Bristol Road, called Kalamazoo, which made, she was told, a wide range of office equipment. The person who greeted her when she went to see about the job was a kindly, apple-cheeked lady called Maureen Benson. Evie admitted she had not done comptometer work for some time, but Maureen reassured her.

'If you could do it before, you can do it again – like riding a bike. They've updated them – they're electric ones now – but they're still the same really.' She assumed Evie had been at home with her children, which was most of the truth. 'Anyway,' she added with a wink as she saw Evie out after giving her a job, 'it's the blind leading the blind round here. They're a good crowd, though.'

Her search for lodgings was also soon rewarded. In this – what seemed to be – honeymoon period with the family, she wanted to be near, for her children to share their lives with her cousins. Her father had seemed quite pleased to see her, though she had been shocked by how much he had aged.

'So, you're back then, wench?' he said, when he first saw her. Evie was so busy trying to reconcile this almost toothless, tired-looking man with a scant fuzz of dirty grey hair, the bloated cheeks full of broken veins, with the father she remembered that it took her a moment to reply.

'Yeah ... Dad,' she said. 'Well, for the moment.'

She just couldn't tell them what had happened with Jack. She was full of shameful feelings that she had failed in her marriage. And despite everything, she still ached with missing him and all that they had together. Even though she was an ocean away, there was a part of her that could still not believe that it was all over. At night, once the children were asleep, she often had a cry. She found herself waiting to hear from him, for him to ask them all to come home and start again.

They were living not far from her mother and father in Weoley Park Road. It was a big house, owned by a kindly couple called Eric and Jean Grant. Their children were grown-up and had moved on, and now Mr and Mrs Grant had decided to rent out some of their rooms. Mr Grant worked at the colleges nearby in Selly Oak and they were keen Baptists, originally from Yorkshire.

Mrs Grant was a faded, gentle lady with wispy grey hair in a bun.

'We thought it wrong to have all this empty space,' she told Evie. 'With so many young people needing homes.'

She reminded Evie a little bit of Mary Bracebridge, with her dutiful Christian kindness. Looking them all up and down, she said, 'Hello, children. I'm sure we'll all get on famously, so long as there's no running about upstairs late at night.'

Evie assured them there would not be and she and Tracy and Andrew took two bedrooms upstairs. They shared the bathroom and had another room at the back as a sitting room. All the rooms were of a good size. Mrs Grant told Evie that she could use the kitchen but that she was just as happy to cook for all of them in the evening for a modest payment.

'I must admit, I miss cooking for my own family,' she said. 'I always like to see everyone gathered round the table of a night.'

Evie was very pleased to agree to this. The house looked as if it had not been touched in any way since the 1940s, with its Bakelite switches, coffee-coloured walls and brown linoleum, covered in places with rugs, trodden wafer thin. Their rooms upstairs were all in the same drab colours.

'Everything's rather old,' Mrs Grant said as she showed them round. 'But it's all perfectly serviceable.'

But there had been a nice smell of baking apple pies in the house all through the autumn.

'There's a tree out the back that produces in great profusion,' Mrs Grant told her. 'I don't like to see them go to waste. There'll be plenty of pies so I hope you like them?'

They did – and ate them most evenings, with Mrs Grant's thin custard.

The children slept in one room and Evie in another, both rooms a sea of brown shades, with yellowed card lampshades clinging to the central bulb in each room. But for the money, it was luxury. And the Grants were kind and did their best to make them welcome.

At first it seemed a good idea to have the children at the same school as Ann, the only other girl in the family. Rita's tribe went to the Catholic school, St Rose of Lima. Her in-laws, the Hennesseys, had also moved out to Weoley Castle and she and Conn had come out to live next door to them, even though Rita seemed to spend most of her days over here with her mother. Rita talked about 'going to Mass' and other things about the church in a dramatic way, as if she had stepped into a superior realm.

'Joseph and Sean have made their First Holy Communion,' she told Evie proudly. 'It'll be Jimmy's turn soon.'

Evie could see that one of the reasons Rita was so desperate to have a girl was so that she could have a frilly white First Communion dress.

Motherhood had made Rita feel very important and in the Catholic Church, motherhood was made much of. Rita thought she knew best about everything, especially when backed up by Conn's mom or one of the fathers at the church. And she was doing the right thing, breeding lots of new little Catholics into the estate, so she received approval all round. Rita, now awaiting the birth of her fifth child after Christmas, seemed to be having the time of her life.

This was not so true of Shirley, who had found herself living back home because, working part-time, she could not afford to do anything else. She was envious of Evie having a job which paid better but snapped anyone's head off who suggested that she might do the same.

Sometimes Shirley came round to the Grants' on a Saturday night, bringing Ann and staying so late that Evie had to ask her to leave. At first Evie had been pleased to see her, thinking Shirley wanted to spend time with her. What she really wanted was to get away from Mom and Dad's weekend drinking habits – at the pub, at home, almost non-stop. But having her there meant that it was hard for Evie to get her children to bed. And she worried that their moving about would disturb the Grants.

She and Shirley would sit with cups of tea by the gas fire. Shirley hardly ever asked Evie anything, so she didn't even have to lie about Jack. Shirley spent most of the time moaning about her own life – about Howard and how she had been left on her own and how none of it was fair. It didn't even seem to dawn on her that Evie was staying rather a long time now she was back, with no sign of a husband. Finally, just last week, she had told her.

'It's all right for you,' Shirley had started off, sitting on the sofa in Evie's rooms with her legs tucked under her. Being Shirley, she still looked striking even in the old jeans and shirt she had on. 'You've got a better job...' She was about to embark on one of her long moans.

In the end, fed up with all this, Evie blurted out, 'I don't know what makes you think that. In case you're wondering, Jack's left me – for someone else. That's why I've come back, all right? So you needn't think life's a bed of roses for me either.'

'He's *left* you?' Shirley looked stunned for a

moment. She pulled herself more upright and Evie saw a movement in her lips, an upward curve of triumph. 'Oh ho, that's rich, that is!' She burst out laughing. 'Takes you all the way over there and leaves you! No wonder you never said before!'

Evie saw the spite in Shirley's eyes. It was a horrible moment, a memory reviving fast. Why was it like this? Why was she not kind and sympathetic? It was possible, she knew now. Some people were kind. Hadn't she come back with some hope of finding kindness in her own family?

'So,' Shirley declared with relish, 'that means you're no better than me then, doesn't it?'

Forty-Six

They woke on Christmas Day to another grey, bitter morning.

Andrew had been up in the small hours, excited, and Evie managed to lull him back to sleep, saying Santa wouldn't come if he was awake. So it was Tracy who came first in the morning and sat on her bed. Evie felt the little girl's weight arrive near her feet and she rolled over and sat up.

'There's still no snow,' Tracy whispered. 'I looked out the window.' She had thought it must snow at Christmas, when in Canada the snow sometimes arrived as early as September and went on for months.

'Hello, lovey. Happy Christmas.' Evie sat up.

'Happy Christmas, Mom.' She was wearing soft red pyjamas with white edging round the cuffs and a pink cardi over the top. Her hair hung loose and Evie melted at how sweet she looked. But she saw that Tracy had not started to open the little stocking she had laid for her and she was frowning in a troubled way. She wouldn't meet her mother's eye.

'What's up, babby?' Evie asked.

Tracy looked at her then, her eyes filling with tears. 'When are we going back home?' she said. 'When's Dad coming?'

Evie felt a lurch of dread inside her, the dread of having to tell your children news they don't want to hear. She couldn't keep fending the two of them off, evading the questions, especially now Shirley must have told everyone. Most of the time they did not seem to miss their father, as he had spent very little time with them. But today... Jack had always been there on Christmas Day, the four of them on the bed in the morning, unwrapping presents. She leaned forward and took Tracy's hands in hers, looking deep into her eyes.

'You know, don't you, Trace, that we're not going back to Canada?'

Tracy's eyes overflowed, the tears running down her cheeks, silver drops on her cardigan. On a sob, she said, 'And Dad's not coming here, is he?'

Evie's own eyes filled at seeing the grown-up look on her little girl's face. She missed Jack at that moment, missed him as if they were still together, still happy, like at the beginning. If she had not had these beautiful children, would they

384

still be happy? She doubted it.

'I don't think so,' she said. 'I think Daddy wants to stay in Canada.' She released a hand to wipe her cheeks.

'But why don't you want to stay there too?'

This was hardest of all. Evie looked down at the pale pink coverlet.

'Thing is, Trace ... you know in the stories, when the girl meets the prince and they live happily ever after?' She glanced up.

'Sometimes they're a frog first,' Tracy pointed out.

Evie laughed through her tears. 'Yes, they are, aren't they? All I mean is, life's not always the same as that. Your dad ... he wanted to be with someone else.'

Tracy stared at her. Evie wondered what was going on in her mind. 'He does know where we live, though?'

Evie felt another pang. 'Yes, love, he does.'

Tracy did not ask the other question – did he send us a present? Jack had never written or sent a card to the kids. Not once, not even for Christmas. Jack had moved on, it seemed, the way Jack did, as if he was catching the next bus.

She saw Tracy taking this in solemnly. In the end, she said, 'It's quite nice here. I don't mind staying. I like Sharon and my other friends – and Ann,' she added, though this sounded a little bit forced.

'We'd better not tell Andrew, had we?' Evie said. 'Not yet.'

'I think he knows – sort of,' Tracy said. 'Mom? Are we going to Nanna's today?'

'Yes – I told you. Why?'

'No ... nothing,' Tracy said, looking away. 'I was just asking.'

Evie wondered what Tracy thought. For her own part, Evie paid short visits, always with the children, always pulling a protective inner screen round herself. So far, Mom had been all over Tracy and Andrew almost as if Evie herself barely existed. And she had avoided her parents at their worst, when the drink was in.

'Oh, here're some more of my grandchildren!' Mom would cry when they arrived. 'Come and give Nanna a love! Trace, Andrew, c'm'ere!'

She made a great fuss of them, giving them sweets and little presents, buying their affection and attention. Evie could see Mom was loving being the great big queen bee, in the middle of everything, everyone running round her, bossing Rita about day after day. More fool Rita, Evie thought. But if that was how it was going to be, she didn't really mind. She wanted her children to have grandparents, people to love them. And who else did she have? Jack's family were a dead loss... Pray God it would be all right.

'Aren't you going to see what Santa's brought for you?' Evie said, desperate to lift her daughter's sombre mood.

Tracy lit up immediately. 'Let's get Andrew up now, shall we?'

Soon the two of them were pulling paper off their presents as fast as they could.

Evie had saved every penny she could for Christmas. She had put some paper streamers and tinsel up in their little sitting room to make it festive. She wanted to lavish presents on her children, not wanting them to feel they were missing anything, however much she was feeling desperate herself.

There had been drinks down the pub after work on the twenty-third. Everyone had asked her to go along. Some of the others she worked with, sitting in rows, number crunching on the comptometers, were nice, friendly girls. To her surprise, a shy-looking man who she saw in the canteen sometimes asked her if she was going. Only then, she discovered his name was Alan. He was a quiet, gentle-looking man, a fair bit older than her, Evie realized, with a pale face and mousey hair. Nothing all that special to look at, except for his eyes, which were brown and smiling and seemed to radiate kindness and good nature. You couldn't help liking the look of him.

'I was hoping you'd be going along,' he said. 'Can I buy you a drink?' With a twinkle he added, 'Or even two?'

Evie was flattered, but also a bit panicky. She just couldn't cope with anything else at the moment. And anyway, she was still married – still *felt* married.

'Sorry, I can't,' she said quietly. She smiled at him, though. He looked nice. 'I can't stop out late – I've got to get back to my kids.' At the moment they were all that mattered.

'Oh.' He looked taken aback. He had obviously assumed she was single. 'That's a shame. Well, another time, maybe?'

'Yeah, maybe,' she said. But she didn't really

mean it.

She had bought little bits and pieces for their stockings – a pair of old brown wool ones of her own. Tracy was mad about writing and drawing, so she had put in felt tips and paper, some plastic stencils and a fat pen full of all different coloured biros you could choose in turn by pressing a button, along with sweets and a tangerine. For Andrew she chose jack stones and Dinky cars and marbles. She had bought each of them some striped socks as well and a main present: a View-Master for Andrew, into which you could put little slides and watch them almost like a film. They did not have a television – the Grants did not have one in the house at all – so she hoped that would make up for it a bit. For Tracy she bought a Sindy doll, with shiny black hair and a selection of clothes to dress her in.

'Oh!' Andrew yelled, the grey specs of the View-Master pressed to his face, clicking down the little lever at the side to turn the slides. 'It's Dr Who!'

She had to prise them off him to have breakfast. 'Come on, we've got to get to Nanna's and help!'

They exchanged Christmas greetings with the Grants who were hurrying off to church. Later they were to go to their son's in Bartley Green.

'Have a lovely day!' they said, in their neat hats and coats. 'So nice to have all your family to go to!'

As they approached along Alwold Road, they could hear raised voices. Immediately Evie's stomach knotted up. Not Mom... Please no... But she could already hear that it was.

They could see people outside the house, Mom in a red frock, someone else the other side of her, Shirley on the step, her hair hanging down, still in her nightie. Evie saw Ann lurking up by the wall of the house, as if trying to disappear into it.

She took her children's hands. Tracy looked up at her, seeming scared.

'What's happening, Mom? Is Nanna angry?'

Evie wanted to turn back and go home. She could see her mother had already got more than warmed up. One hand was on her waist, the other waving in the air at the other person. The old shame washed through her – Mom, always spoiling for a fight. The mom everyone looked down on, wanted to keep away from. But she couldn't just walk off – not now Tracy and Andrew were here. Not on Christmas Day.

'Don't you tell me what I can ******g well do in my own, ******g house!' she heard.

'Don't you shout at me, you dirty cow!' the neighbour shrieked back. 'This neighbourhood's gone right down since you and your tribe of yobs moved in 'ere. It was all right before.'

'Well, yow should teach yower brats to keep their mucky hands off other people's belongings!'

Evie could feel the silent shock of her children. She knew from experience that her mother had begun on the drink, that her aggression was already beyond reason. She was swaying slightly, slurring her words, and there was no way of talking any sense into her when she was like that. Weekends were the time of dedicated drinking. Evie always kept away at weekends and even

Shirley escaped if she could. She had not expected it yet – not at this time on Christmas morning.

'Why's she shouting?' Tracy said in a small voice.

'I don't know,' Evie said, despair washing through her. 'Something's upset her.'

So far as she could make out as they drew near, the neighbour's son had taken something he shouldn't have.

A man appeared out of the next-door house, dressed but barefoot as if disturbed by the racket.

'What's going on, Susan?' he yelled.

'Oh, it's just this' – his wife couldn't seem to find a word and flapped her hand in Irene Sutton's direction instead – 'carrying on!' She seemed bolder now she had back-up. 'Roddy borrowed a scooter or summat, that's all, and now she's acting as if it's a bank robbery.'

'Stole, more like!' Mom roared. 'Your lad's a thieving little–'

'Irene!' Now Dad came storming outside in his vest. 'Get in 'ere and shurrup!'

'Don't yow cowing well tell me to shurrup! It's 'er yer want to be talking to. Tell her to keep that little runt of 'ers off of things that don't belong to 'im!'

A four-way shouting match then kicked off between the two couples. Evie was just on the point of turning round and going away, sick at the sight, when Shirley looked across and saw her.

'Evie!' she called, beckoning. Evie felt as if she was being rescued. But she wondered afterwards, many times, whether if she had refused then and turned for home, things would have been different in the long run. But she knew, really, that they would not.

Forty-Seven

The house smelt, as ever, of stale fags and burnt toast and some unsavoury whiff whose origins Evie did not want to think about. On the kitchen table lay an enormous turkey, plucked and indecent-looking.

'It's too big to fit in the oven,' Shirley said. She seemed tired and jaded. 'I dunno how we're s'posed to cook the thing. Dad'll have to saw a bit off.'

'Started already, have they?' Evie did a drinking mime.

Shirley rolled her eyes. 'Jimmy came round, before they went off to church – with a scooter he'd had. He left it here for later and that lad fancied a go on it.' She rolled her eyes again.

'Why don't you go and find Ann?' Evie said to Tracy.

'Go on, Trace, she's upstairs,' Shirley put on a syrupy voice. 'Why don't you go with her, Andrew?'

Andrew hid his head in Evie's side. She knew he was unsettled by what he had seen.

'He's staying with me,' Evie said. 'He's not used to all this carry-on.'

'Ooh,' Shirley sneered. 'Listen to you, Lady Muck.'

'What? I just said—'

'Oh, shut it,' Shirley said, slamming out of the room.

Everyone was in the foulest of tempers. Mom and Dad finally gave up lambasting the neighbours and came in, slamming the front door so that the frame cracked.

'Look at that bleeding thing!' Dad erupted at the sight of the turkey on the table. 'Yer daft cow, Irene! Why in God's name did yer buy one that size?'

'It were a bargain, that's why.' She slumped down on a chair by the table, eyeing the oversized fowl.

Dad pressed a finger to his temple, twizzling it round. 'It were a bargain – *that's 'cause no one wanted it,*' he said, as if addressing a very stupid child. '"Cept you fell for it, dain't yer? You're barmy you are, Irene. Soft in the cowing 'ead.'

'Oh, shut yer cake'ole,' Mom said, looking round for a drink. Evie knew from lifelong practice that that was what was on her mind. 'Get yer saw out.' She gave a belly chuckle at this double meaning. 'Go on, get it out, if yer still can! You'll 'ave to cut it in half.'

While Ray was at the table, sleeves rolled up, sawing along the turkey's back, a ripe stream of curses falling from his lips, Rita, Conn and all their crew arrived, all spit and polish in Sunday best. The boys all had their hair slicked back and were now acting up after having to be unnaturally demure during Mass.

'Look at you lot!' Irene mocked them. 'Done up like fourpenny cowing rabbits! That soap in your hair, Jimmy? You look like the Brylcreem boy!'

Jimmy, who hated church with a passion, unlike Joseph who was an altar boy, blushed furiously and kicked a chair.

'What's that horrible stink?' Rita said, screwing up her nose. She was swamped by a huge flowery frock and walked about all the time pushing her hands into the small of her back as if to emphasize to everyone just how pregnant she was, which was very. The baby was due next month. She pulled out a chair and sat down. 'Sod off, kids. I've 'ad enough of you all this morning. And what're you gawping at?' she snapped at Evie.

'Nothing,' Evie said. 'Only ... you sure it's not twins?'

'No, it ain't sodding twins, all right?' Rita lashed out.

'Get that cowing bird in the oven,' Mom said, to no one in particular, though obviously not intending to lift a finger herself. 'And you can all get on and do the spuds. Pour me some of that ale, Ray.' She kicked her shoes off and sat back.

Evie decided she'd take herself upstairs to see how Tracy and Ann were getting on.

'And where d'yer think you're off to?' Rita bawled at her. 'You ain't leaving me to do everything as usual, Lady Muck. You can stay 'ere and do the veg – and get Shirl wherever she is. Thinks she can just sit on her backside an' all.'

One day... That was all. Just one day with her family. Was it so impossible to think they could get through that?

But Christmas Day crawled past with agonizing slowness and by the end of it, Evie knew her honeymoon with her family was truly over.

The boys roared in and out, overexcited and needing their dinner, which would not be ready until nearly five o'clock. They had fights, bawled, yelled, bled, even with Conn out there kicking a ball about with them and limply trying to keep order. Evie peeled potatoes and scraped carrots, Rita waddled around bossing everyone about while Mom bossed her about. She groaned that her back hurt. Shirley, like a vicious storm cloud, took on a pile of sprouts. With glowering slowness, she cut the stalk off each as if she was beheading someone. Tracy and Ann appeared every so often, looking hungry and miserable. And Irene and Ray drank. And drank.

Evie slipped out of the kitchen once her jobs were done, wanting to get away from them all. She felt more and more desperate. If it had just been her, she might have left – just slunk out of the front door and never gone back. Nothing ever changed. Nothing. But there were the kids...

In the front room, on the grey nylon carpet, were a couple of defeated-looking armchairs covered in threadbare grey velour, with dark circles worn by previous owners' heads. There was a small table with ring stains and an overflowing glass ashtray, but most of the surface was hidden by the television on which Bing Crosby was singing in a heartfelt way to the empty room.

Someone had stuck up a few half-hearted crepe streamers, draping the wall over the gas fire, but a large part of the room was now taken up with a huge Christmas tree, laden with tinsel and plastic shiny baubles. Among the branches Evie could see packages in red paper.

The tree was the best thing in the room. Evie looked into it with a sense of sinking desolation. Why were Mom and Dad so incapable of making a home that anyone would want to live in? Why was Mom so lazy and filthy? Why was she always the one who had to open her great big mouth and get into a fight?

Standing in the doorway, a sense of despair washed over her again. Why had she left Canada and the gentle life they had had there? Oh Jack, Jack... Tears filled her eyes. It happened like that, she found. Missing him suddenly, knowing all that she had lost, like being stabbed. It wasn't just that he had fallen for another woman. It was her fault. The children. She had forced him into having them. She had never been good enough.

And coming back here, she had thought things might have changed, that *she* had changed enough to face this family. Now, standing here, listening to Rita moaning in the kitchen, to a loud, wrenching belch from her father, to the wrangling of the boys outside, she felt five years old again. Stuck here, with them. And she had allowed it to happen. She had come running back – back to nought, right where she started. Less than nought.

'Eves!' She heard Rita's voice bawl for her. 'Where are yer? Get in 'ere and help, yer lazy cow!'

They all squeezed into the back kitchen for dinner. Even with the table at full stretch, some of the boys had to eat off their laps on stools away from the table. Andrew and Wayne, the smallest, sat perched side by side on the back doorstep.

By the time they were eating it was already dark outside and the gloom was offset by the bulb hanging over them, shrouded by a brown shade. Rita doled out the food at the cooker, like a dinner lady. By this time, Evie was desperate, her thoughts turning like a rusty old roundabout. How had she got herself into this again?

Mom and Dad were so tanked up that Evie could see her father's eyes drooping over his puffy cheeks. He never said much these days. The minute dinner was over he'd be snoring in the front room. Mom was in full fighting mood. She managed not to say anything about the Irish because Conn was there and she had to be careful. Conn, as usual, said not a word anyway, but ate huge piles of food. Everyone else except the Irish came in for a drunken tongue lashing.

''Ole of cowing Birminum's full of blackies and Pakis now...' She thought this rhyme very amusing and often repeated it. Her face was a deep pink, her voice slurred. 'Comin' 'ere, taking our cowin' jobs... That feller Enoch Powell was right, send 'em back to the cowing jungle... 'Ere, pass me the Bisto. Don't go and tip it all on yours, Ray! 'Ow can you 'ave a proper Christmas with all them blackies about, eh? The government ought to do summat, they oughta...'

On and on – they'd never shut her up now.

Same old thing. Then it was the Pakis and their stinking food and then the neighbours and that stuck-up cow across the street with her husband who thought he was too good for them all because he worked at the Austin.

For God's sake, change the record, Evie wanted to scream, as her mother rambled on. *All these people you're being so nasty about – I bet every one of them's better than you are!*

Everyone else ate, hungry, not daring to interrupt, except Dad, who now and again said halfheartedly, 'Oh, shurrit, Irene,' while knowing she wouldn't now she was off. The sun rose in the morning; Irene Sutton – wife, mother, dreaded neighbour – quarrelled with anything that moved. What was new?

But suddenly, as Evie finished up her last mouthfuls of potato and gravy, she realized Rita was staring across the table at her. Looking up, seeing her, she felt a cold stab of dread. The look was so familiar, like the old days...

'So...' Rita sat back with her nasty face on, the one that said she had spite to pour over someone and that someone was Evie. 'Looks like that husband of yours ain't coming back then, eh? Left you, 'as 'e? Miss High and bloody Mighty?'

Evie froze. Tracy and Andrew were both in the room. She could hear Andrew and Wayne tittering and shoving each other. But Tracy had gone pale and was staring at her, eyes wide, an anguished expression on her face. Evie felt as if her heart was going to slam out of her chest.

'Reet,' she tried to protest. 'Not with the kids here...'

'Oh!' Rita, who was next to Tracy, leaned towards her, put her arm round her niece's shoulders and squeezed her. 'Our Trace don't mind her Auntie Rita, do yer, babby?' She kissed Tracy's cheek.

Tracy turned awkwardly and gave her a forced smile.

'There,' Rita said. 'You're gorgeous, ain't yer, Trace? Ooh.' She stroked her bump. 'I 'ope this is going to be a little girl like you, Trace, eh?' She nudged Tracy again, laughing. 'Yer auntie dain't mean anything. She loves you, yer auntie does – and your little brother. 'Ere' – she chucked Tracy under the chin – 'I've got ever such a nice present for you, Trace – and you Ann, so you don't need to put that face on.'

Tracy, blushing, looked pleased and confused. Ann looked sulky at the attention her aunt was giving Tracy. She had been used to being the only girl.

After the dinner was over they all moved into the front room with the telly on, cups of tea and boxes of Maltesers and Quality Street. Soon there was a mess of bright-coloured wrappers all over the floor, mingling with the paper the boys had ripped off their presents. Evie had bought smellies for her mom and sisters. She'd had no clue what to get for her father, so had bought him some fags.

She handed out her packages. 'Here you are, Dad.' She passed him the cigarettes.

'Oh, ta, wench!' Had he even noticed she had not been there for seven years, she wondered?

'Here, Mom. Happy Christmas.'

'Oh ar,' Irene said. She ripped the paper off it, but as she did she was looking at Rita and Shirley, a mocking expression on her face, like a child trying to make trouble. Dread filled Evie again. She had a horrible feeling that Mom was biding her time, that trouble was brewing, of a kind she remembered so well.

Her mother barely looked at the Cussons talc Evie had given her. She glanced at it with a look of contempt and dropped it down by the side of her chair like a piece of litter. Evie felt it like a knife going through her. She hates me. She still hates me... A sense of desperate loneliness filled her for a moment, but she was distracted from it by Rita's voice, sweet as syrup.

''Ere you are, girls. These're from your Auntie Rita and Uncle Conn.' Rita was in a better mood now. Sitting on a chair she had brought in from the kitchen, she beckoned Tracy and Ann and gave each of them a long rectangular package. Evie saw Ann eye Tracy's to see if she had anything more than her. But they looked just the same.

'Barbie!' Ann cried, after ripping off the red paper with Santas on. 'Malibu Barbie! Look, Mom!' She went over to Shirley. 'She's wearing a bikini!'

She flew back then to see what Tracy had been given. Another Barbie, this time in a floaty costume in pink and purple trousers with flared legs. Round her waist was a wide suede belt with suede bits dangling from it and a suede band round her head, with its long, ash-blonde hair.

Ann stared at it and her face turned stony. 'I

want that one, Mom!' she shrieked. 'Hers is nicer than mine – it's got better clothes!'

'No, Ann,' Rita tried to appease her. 'Your Barbie's on her holidays, babby. She's going to the beach. And you can dress her and undress her, look.'

But Ann was heading into a full tantrum, throwing the doll in its box on the floor, stamping and howling, 'I want the other one! Hers is better!'

'Oh, shut up, Ann,' Shirley snapped. To Rita she said furiously, 'Well, that was a really good idea, wasn't it? Why didn't you get two the same so we dain't have all this?'

Tracy stood holding her doll, looking worried and embarrassed. In the end she went over to Ann holding out her own Barbie.

'You have this one,' she said. Evie had never been more proud of her. 'I don't mind. Mom gave me a nice Sindy doll as well so we can swap – you can have my Barbie.'

Ann stopped crying like a switch being snapped off. Without a second's hesitation she grabbed the Barbie in the pink and purple outfit and thrust Malibu Barbie at Tracy.

'Here, you have her. This one's mine now and she's *much* better.'

'How about saying thanks, Ann?' Evie said. 'Don't just snatch it like that.'

It was as if she had just done the worst thing ever. Everyone's eyes were on her – Mom's (not Dad's, who was snoring, head back), Rita's and Shirley's. The hostility almost fizzed on the air.

'What did you say?' Shirley said.

In those seconds, she was right back there – the

door slammed, her on the outside looking in. All the chill loneliness of it. She tried to get hold of herself, to fight it. Tracy was here, looking at her, trying to make sense of it all. She must say something. She was grown-up. She didn't have to be trodden down by them all.

'I just thought she might say thanks,' Evie said. 'Tracy didn't have to do that.'

Rita sat forward, with an air of menace. 'Who d'yer think you are, Eves?' She spoke quietly, the quiet of a playground bully before they get going. 'Think yer really someone, don't yer – coming back 'ere with your airs and graces and "oh, I've been to Canada ..."' Her voice was horrible, mocking, made worse by a round of applause from the telly.

'No,' Evie started to protest. But she was surrounded by the old female spite.

'Come 'ere, Trace,' Rita said, waving Tracy towards her. She put her arm round Tracy, holding her close. 'Don't you take no notice of us. You got your dolly? Nice, ain't she? You're a good girl, swapping with Ann like that. You gunna watch some telly now?'

Tracy nodded, wide-eyed, and crept across to sit in front of the television.

'Can't even keep a husband.' Mom was already joining in, always game for a fight. She was slurred, pugnacious. 'Soon got shot of you, dain't 'e? Crawling back 'ere. You always was cowing trouble – thinking you was better than the rest of us.'

Evie noticed Shirley was keeping quiet. Any comments about being deserted by husbands were a bit too close to home for her. But she sat watching with an intent, spiteful expression, as if enjoying seeing them beating Evie down. It was like a wave, knocking her over, leaving her dizzy.

Mom kept on then. 'Don't think you can come back 'ere pushing any of us about. Yower...' She hiccoughed, then belched. 'Scum, that's what you are – always was.' She looked blearily at Tracy. 'Yower kids are all right. You're all right, ain't yer, Trace?' Her fleshy face creased into an ingratiating grin. 'You glad to see yower nanna and aunties, ain't yer?'

Tracy turned for a second and nodded obediently. She cast an anxious glance at Evie before turning back to the refuge of the TV.

'Thing about yower mom is,' Evie heard her mother continue, talking loudly at Tracy's back. Evie had lowered her gaze to her lap, her cheeks burning. 'She ain't quite right in the head – never was. You don't want to take any notice of 'er. If you want any help, bab, you come to Nanna and your aunties.'

Evie forced herself to her feet, her legs unsteady. 'Right, we're going now,' she said. Her voice trembled. 'Come on, Trace, Andrew.'

Tracy got up, seeming relieved, and came to her side immediately, but Andrew started crying that he wanted to stay and play.

'Oh, let them stay!' Rita urged. 'You're spoiling Christmas for 'em. You can't just take them away. What you gunna do? Sit in that miserable bedsit all evening?'

Evie was gathering up her things, head down.

'Andrew,' she hissed at him, desperate, her

402

body tight with weeping that would soon escape, must not escape while she was here. 'Will you just *shut it?*'

'I hate you!' Andrew bawled. 'I don't wanna go home!'

'Go on then, yer silly little bitch,' were her mother's parting words. 'Good bloody riddance!'

Evie stepped out into the night with her distressed children, Andrew still gulping with sobs. She found she could barely swallow. It was as if a trapdoor had opened in the floor and she had fallen down it, right back into the past, into the lonely place of her childhood which she thought she had left far behind. A place where she was hated, where she was stupid and of no account. At that moment that was exactly how she felt.

'Oh dear, dear,' Mrs Grant said as they stepped into the house and she heard Andrew grizzling. 'Have we had a little bit too much excitement?'

This being one of those not especially helpful observations, Andrew cried more loudly. Evie did not meet Mrs Grant's eye. She felt too bad, too taut with hurt and sadness.

'I'll just get him up to bed,' she muttered.

'Happy Christmas, dear,' Mrs Grant called up the stairs after her.

Still close to tears which she did not want to shed, she undressed Andrew. He clung to her then, like a little monkey, sniffling and exhausted. Evie found comfort in his warm body, his damp cheek pressed to hers.

'Come on, little feller,' she said, laying him

down in his bed. 'What you need is some kip.'

Tracy was waiting for her in the other room, sitting at the edge of a chair, eyes wide with worry.

'Mom ... why were Nanna and Auntie being so nasty to you?'

Evie could see that she could not make sense of her own nice treatment from Mom and Rita set against what she had seen today. She could see the girl's confusion and she struggled to find something to say.

'Oh,' she said, trying to make light of it. 'It was just the booze talking. You don't want to take any notice.'

'But didn't you mind, Mom?' Tracy said.

She forced a smile. 'Oh no, not too much. They didn't really mean it.'

When Tracy was asleep, Evie lay in bed in the dark. She knew it was true – about the booze. But she felt flayed by what had happened. She had got used to being grown-up. To kind people who took her as she was and didn't attack her. But now she had driven her husband away and was back here – where she had chosen to be. And she could not see any way out.

Forty-Eight

It was not just the booze.

Over the next days and weeks, Evie felt as if everything had tilted in a downward direction and she could not seem to right it.

404

She woke on Boxing Day, feeling desperate. Andrew, who had been so upset the night before, woke fresh and happy. He was too young to have noticed what was happening. Tracy, though, Evie could see, was subdued. It made her feel terrible.

Why the hell didn't I stay in Canada? Her mind was in a turmoil of pain and regret. Why did I think things would be different?

She had come rushing home in search of this dream of a family she had never had and she thought she was strong. Canada had felt a safe, clean place, away from this hurt and shame. She would have had to live closer to a different hurt – the hard truth that Jack was with another woman. And Bea had left, who she had considered her best friend. But she could have made new friends. Looking back now, Rosette and the people there felt like a haven of innocence and kindness. It had lulled her into forgetting.

Now she felt as if she was beginning to crack all over under the force of her family. All the strength and confidence she had built up in Canada, the new Evie who belonged, who was not forever shut out, was beginning to drain away. She was letting herself slide back into being the numb, bruised child she had always been, shut out again on the cold step, and she couldn't seem to stop it.

They stayed away from the family that day, even though Andrew kept asking why he couldn't go and play with Wayne. Evie took them to the park, trying to keep up a cheerful atmosphere, forcing her laughter as she watched them by the pond, wrangling over a heel of stale bread for the ducks.

But she was close to tears all day. Once they got back to the flat they toasted crumpets on the gas fire and she made herself play games with them – Ludo and Snakes and Ladders. The afternoon seemed endless and only when the two of them were finally asleep and she lay in bed did she give way to her bitter sadness.

It would be a relief to get back to work and into the routine of things, even though it meant Tracy and Andrew going to Mom and Dad's after school.

They were all right with the kids, so far as she could see. More than all right. Mom, Rita and Shirley were all sugar sweetness to the children. Every time they clapped eyes on her kids they were as nice as anything. No one, she realized, likes to have children dislike them – not even her mother. With the grand exception of herself, she thought bitterly. Mom had never shown any signs of caring about that.

'*Nanna* lets us,' Andrew would say when she stopped him eating sweets before a meal or leaping about on Mrs Grant's furniture.

'Well, Nanna can do as she likes in her house, but this is my house,' she tried once.

Andrew stared at her with hostility. 'S'not your house – it's Mrs Grant's. Why ain't we got a house, like Nanna, and Auntie Reet?'

'It's not "ain't" Andrew,' she told him. 'It's "isn't". Try and speak properly, will you?'

'But Nanna says–'

'I don't care what Nanna says!' she erupted. 'You do as I tell you!'

Then, of course, she was furious with herself.

Tracy was more unsure, more torn. On work days, Evie fetched them from her mother's. These days she avoided going in if possible. She would call to Tracy and Andrew and wait until they came out – even if it was raining sometimes.

'Not good enough for you, are we?' Mom kept saying nastily, when she bothered to rouse herself to say anything.

On the walk home, Tracy had started saying things like, 'Mom, Auntie Rita said that when you were all little girls, you were always dirty – and you were spiteful to everyone.' She would look up at Evie in a troubled way, wanting and not wanting to believe her aunt, who was sweet and nice to her.

Evie burned with frustration and rage. How dare Rita tell all these lies to her kids? But she didn't want to get angry with Tracy. If only she could send them to someone else after school – but who? There was no one. And she would have to pay. It would take most of her money. She felt trapped.

'Oh,' she said dismissively. 'You don't want to believe everything Rita tells you.'

Tracy frowned from under her bobble hat. 'But why were you dirty, Mom?'

Because Nanna neglected me. Because she never bothered with me from the word go...

'Well, love, we were all quite grubby in those days.'

The frown deepened. 'Why?'

'Because we didn't live in a very nice house. You've never lived in the old back-to-back houses like we had in Ladywood.' She paused. Some of

407

their neighbours had kept themselves fastidiously clean even in those old rat-trap houses. She didn't really want to explain that her own mother just couldn't be bothered, except with titivating herself.

'There weren't any baths, you see. There wasn't even any water in the house. We had a wash in the scullery and brought the tin bath in by the fire once in a blue moon.' Thinking back, the times Mom had got round to giving them a bath were so few she could only remember two or three occasions.

Tracy was looking at her. 'She says I shouldn't be friends with Sharon – that she's dirty too.'

'Trace.' Evie stopped and took her daughter by the shoulders. 'Sharon's a nice girl, and she's your friend. You be friends with who you want, right?' She spotted a tube of fruit gums sticking out of Tracy's coat pocket.

'Who gave you those?' she asked.

'Auntie Shirley,' she said. 'Ann had some so she got me some as well.'

'Your teeth,' Evie said. Her heart was like lead but she spoke lightly. 'They'll be black as night soon.'

The second week in January Rita's baby arrived. She was taken to Selly Oak Hospital in the middle of the night.

When Evie went to pick up the kids after work the next day, Shirley came to the door. She had taken to looking at Evie with a sarky kind of expression all the time. Evie noticed that since Christmas there had been no talk of her coming round on Saturday nights. Shirley had joined the camp of mother and sister, the camp of the old days – three against one.

'So,' Shirley said, folding her arms and standing in the doorway. She was in her work clothes and Evie imagined her standing like that to guard the doctor from his patients, officious expression and all. 'She's had it.'

'What? Reet?'

Shirley nodded. 'It's another boy. Conn was round earlier. They're going to call him Dean.'

'Oh,' Evie said. 'Not a girl then.'

'He said she's not very pleased,' Shirley said with a smug expression which said, *Well, she may have a husband and a home of her own, but that's one thing she can't do.*

'She'll get used to the idea,' Evie said.

'You coming in?' Shirley seemed torn between wanting company and wanting to be nasty.

'Not today. Kids ready?'

Andrew ran past then, in some game with Wayne. 'Oh Mom!' he groaned. 'I don't wanna go home – *s'boring.*'

On the way home, Andrew sulked, dragging his feet. Evie asked Tracy about her day. She seemed subdued as well.

'It was OK – at school. But Ann broke my pen.' From her pocket she pulled the fat, orange plastic pen with all the different coloured inks inside. 'It doesn't work anymore.'

'Oh dear,' Evie said. 'I don't s'pose she meant to.'

Tracy looked up at her. 'She *did* mean to.' Tears came into her eyes. 'She's nice sometimes and then other times she's really horrible. I never did anything to her.'

I know the feeling, Evie thought. She looked up at the grey winter sky. Why had she come back here? Why didn't she escape – go somewhere else, away from everybody? But that all seemed far beyond her. Here she was. She had nowhere else. Her children were settled in the school, she had help – even if it came at a price to her. And she liked her job and earned a reasonable wage. How could they get away again now?

Work at Kalamazoo was a good part of her life. She found herself chatting and making friends with the other girls on the comptometers. They were work friends at least, even if she did not see anything much of them outside. She thought sometimes about getting in touch with Carol, her old friend. The two of them had dropped each other a note, just at Christmas, over the years. Carol was married now and had moved up to Walsall and Evie just couldn't seem to get round to contacting her.

For the moment she had enough to cope with. She had still heard not a word from Jack, although she had written to him a couple of times to tell him her address and how Tracy and Andrew were getting on. Not that he cares, she thought bitterly. We might just as well not exist. The Grants, though kind, were rather sober people and all Evie felt most of the time was the lonely weight of having to bring up her children on her own.

If it had not been for the others at work, she might have spent more time brooding. But usually, if her thoughts were sinking down, sitting in the rows of girls all number crunching, as often as not some joker came along and told a funny story and she found herself laughing along with them. And often – very often – in the canteen, she found Alan Dickson, that gentle, friendly man, at her side, chatting about his three-year-old nephew, asking how her day was going. She just seemed to be in too much of a daze to take much notice.

One afternoon at the end of January, she came out of the building into a louring, windy afternoon. The sky looked fit to burst itself upon them with either rain or snow and it did nothing to lift the spirits. She was just about to shut the door when she saw Alan coming along, also on his way out, so she waited a second.

'Ta,' he said, hurrying, then added, 'Thank you,' as if he had not been polite or grateful enough. He smiled at her and it lit his rather plain face.

'S'all right,' Evie said.

He had a black mac on over his brown suit. In the fading daylight she tried again to assess his age. About forty, she thought, though it was hard to tell.

'Looks as if it's going to come down any minute,' he said, eyeing the sky. Red tail lights glowed in the gloomy afternoon. 'You heading for the bus?'

'Yeah,' she said, as they turned onto the Bristol Road. She had her hands pushed down into her pockets and did not feel like talking. That was the thing about Alan, she realized. She didn't feel like she had to make a big effort. He seemed happy just to be beside her whatever she was like. He was never pushy. No wonder he's never married, she thought. He's probably too shy ever to ask a girl for anything. But she was glad. He just seemed like a nice man.

'I'm going the other way.' He nodded his head in an out-of-town direction, towards Longbridge. Hesitating for a moment, he looked as if he wanted to say more, but she was not being encouraging.

He gave a slight shrug and smiled. 'Better go – before we get drenched.'

They said their goodbyes. Evie walked up the Bristol Road, then waited to cross over to the bus stop. As she stood waiting, a figure appeared in the corner of her vision, hurrying towards her, heading out of town. Something about his gait immediately triggered her memory. Turning, she watched as the tall, lanky person hurried towards her, seeming to lead with the left side of his body, almost running, his arms bent at his sides. He wore a donkey jacket that looked far too big, a lime-green knitted hat pushed down over shaggy hair, specs...

'Gary!' The word left her mouth almost before she had time to think, she was so certain it was him. He had almost gone past.

A second later, as he turned back, she was less sure. She saw a lined, leathery face, the stooping body. He was staring at her through smeary specs, his eyes seeming bigger than she remembered, the skin sagging under them. Was it him, this broken-looking man?

'Who...? Are you...? Evie! Oh!' He hugged himself in excitement, grinning, suddenly the old Gary, except his gums only showed a sprinkling of brown teeth. 'Is that you? Well, well, fancy seeing you!'

He was laughing, a sound she could hear welling up from damaged lungs. A laugh that became almost instantly a cough and he doubled up for a moment. When he came closer and stood up, she made out that the specs had no side arms. They were black-rimmed and seemed to be tied onto his head with string which disappeared under the hat. He wore ragged black trousers and a pair of rancid-looking Green Flash plimsolls which must once have been white.

'Gary,' she said, feeling appalled and tender all at once.

When had she last seen him? Before ... before Julie, and all of it. After his beloved Pete had been found dead

He was so aged, so wrecked looking. She didn't know what to say, so she asked, 'Where're you off to?'

He seemed anxious, his feet moving on the spot. When he spoke it was fast, restless talk. 'Looking for Carl.' He nodded along the street. ''E got a job, like, at the Austin. Not on the cars I don't mean...' He spoke slowly, seeming to have to reach for the words. 'It's outside, like, in the grounds. It's his first day. 'E should be back by now – come to look for 'im...' For a second her presence penetrated his preoccupation again. He seemed unable to focus his mind. 'Nice to see you, Eves. You all right?'

413

'Yes, ta.' There was too much to say to begin on anything. He seemed about to rush onwards so she said quickly, 'Gary, where're you living?'

'On the cut.' He was starting to drift away. 'Gotta find Carl... Along a bit, from the Dingle. Come and see us, like, eh?'

'Yes,' she said. 'I'll try, Gary, when I can.' Did anyone live on the cut these days? She had heard that all trade down there had moved onto the roads by now.

'The boat's called *Pearl!*' he threw over his shoulder.

'Yeah, it'd be nice to see...' But he was already off along the road at top, shuffling speed, at once old man and boy.

Forty-Nine

Rita was sitting up in Mom's front room like a queen – albeit a very bad-tempered one – smoking and issuing orders. She wore one of her old pregnancy smocks, a pair of nylons and her sloppy pink slippers.

Their mother was in the other armchair, smoking, yelling half-heartedly at the boys to shut up. On the television, a man with heavy black specs was talking beside a blackboard, his chatter turned down low.

The room looked empty with no Christmas tree taking up half of it. Cold winter light seeped through the window facing over the scuffed grass at the front and filtered through the smoke in the room. It was grey and drizzling so the kids were all on the rampage inside. There was constant banging and crashing from the floor above as the older boys were letting rip, jumping on and off one of the beds. Wayne was downstairs with Andrew, both of them roaring from room to room. The girls were taken up with the baby. Shirley was out of the room somewhere and Evie stood about, propping up the wall near the door for want of a chair, keeping an eye on Andrew.

It was a month since little Dean, Rita's fifth son, was born and she was still in no better temper about it. Dean, like three of his brothers, was going to be a redhead like Conn.

''Ere, take 'im.' She handed the baby to Ann, who was eagerly waiting. Sitting back, lighting a cigarette, she added, 'I don't know why I flaming bother. Conn only makes boys and they all turn out looking like peas in a pod – 'cept Wayne and 'e's another cowing lad.'

She was very bitter at not having a daughter, none of which improved her temper with either Shirley or Evie, proud mothers of daughters. It was the one thing in which Evie and her next sister up were united. Shirley, caught as she had been all her life between her sisters, sometimes turned and rolled her eyes at Evie when Rita was keeping on, in her high, moany voice.

Ann was sitting perched on the edge of a chair cradling Dean in her arms, shoulders hunched as if she was never going to give him up again.

After a while, Rita said, 'That's it, Ann. You hand 'im over to Trace now, it's 'er turn.'

415

'She 'ad him before!' Ann was immediately scowling. 'And she had him longer!'

'No she dain't, Ann. Hand 'im to Trace,' Rita snapped. 'Don't be a mardy little cow.'

Tracy, looking apologetic, took Dean from Ann's reluctant arms and crouched on the chair with him. He was not a big baby – had been barely six pounds at birth – but Tracy, skinny and slight, had to curve her arms right round him to hold on. She released one hand carefully to stroke his nose, then looked up in delight.

'He smiled, Auntie, he did!'

'Oh, he likes you, Trace,' Rita said.

Ann scowled more deeply at this sign of favouritism. She slammed out of the room, rigid with resentment. Evie thought what a sour little girl she was becoming, compared with Tracy. She sighed. She didn't want to be here in this noisy, smoky room, being ignored by everyone. But Tracy had wanted to come and see the baby.

Tracy sat cuddling Dean and Evie watched her. How lovely she was! She felt a swell of pride. Even if she herself felt like a nothing in this family, like worse than nothing, at least they were all right to Tracy and Andrew, and her children needed a family.

The scientific-looking man on the television was replaced by a different one, with black, greasy-looking hair, standing in front of some glass jars. Evie yawned and shifted from foot to foot. The stuffy, smoke-filled room made her feel muzzy in the head.

A moment later, there came a series of bangs and crashes from upstairs, so loud that the house shuddered. Mom snapped into life and hurtled to her feet, striding out to the bottom of the stairs.

'You lot! Cowing well shurrup! Get down 'ere and get out!'

'It's raining out,' Rita protested feebly.

Her mother came back as they heard the boys' feet pounding down the stairs.

'A soaking never hurt anyone,' she said, whoomping back onto her chair again. 'Turn the telly up, Reet.' The front door slammed and the noise startled baby Dean who started to bawl.

'Auntie!' Tracy said in a panicky voice. 'He didn't like the noise – he's crying!'

'I can 'ear 'e's crying,' Rita said grumpily, though not moving to do anything about it. 'Just sort 'im out, will yer? I'll get fag ash on 'is 'ead if I take 'im.'

Evie moved forward, seeing that Tracy was not sure what to do. The child was only seven – how was she supposed to know how to sort a baby out?

'Here you are, I'll take him,' Evie said, going over to them. Dean's face was red with outrage, his little mouth issuing yells.

She was just trying to take him from Tracy when Mom said nastily, 'Don't *you* pick him up.' She spoke as if Evie was a vile, contaminating thing. 'You don't want 'er picking 'im up, do you, Reet? Move over.' Once again she wrestled her bulky body to its feet while Evie stood, stung and shamed.

''Ere y'are, bab, give 'im to Nanna.' She leaned over to Tracy and scooped Dean into her arms, ignoring Evie.

'That's it, you take 'im, Mom,' Rita said, with a

nasty look in Evie's direction.

She's mad, Evie thought, with a sense of despair. She had held Dean before. If it suited Mom, anything could happen. Kids could romp round the house, anyone could do anything if it went with her mood. But if it didn't, she would turn... And she had taught Rita so well to be spiteful. Being nasty to Evie was a lifelong habit.

'Come on, Trace,' she said softly to her daughter. 'Time to go.'

Tracy, who had had her hold of the baby, slid obediently off the chair and put her hand in her mother's. Evie almost cried at the warm feel of her child's skin. She could see in Tracy's eyes that she hated the others being nasty to her mother.

Mom and Rita were talking about some woman along the road, bitching again.

Evie left the room without saying goodbye. Wearily, she knew it was going to be a fight to get Andrew to come home. He and Wayne had escaped being sent into the rain and she could hear them upstairs in Shirley and Ann's room. When she went up, she found Shirley lying listlessly on her bed, one arm bent under head, staring at the ceiling. Ann was sitting on the edge of the bed looking bored and mutinous and the two boys were on the floor, bent over a mess of little cars and trucks.

'Andrew.' Evie stood at the door.

'Ever heard of knocking?' Shirley said nastily.

'Sorry,' Evie said. 'Need to get him home.'

'Go on, Andrew,' Shirley said indifferently. 'Go with yer mom.'

Andrew ignored them both and he and Wayne

put their heads together, tittering about something.

'Andrew!' Evie said, more sharply, though she was full of a dull sense of futility. She was dragging him out of here, back to the Grants' house – for what? It was pouring with rain now and the rest of Saturday spread out before them like a sea of nothingness.

She stepped over to Andrew and hoicked him to his feet. 'I *said* we're going home. *Now.*'

Andrew started fighting her and screaming like a pig being killed. 'Don't wanna go!' he roared. 'I wanna stay here!'

'Oh, for God's sake!' Shirley sat up furiously. Ann stared at the scene with a blank face. 'What d'you have to go and set him off for?'

'I'm just trying to get him to do as I ask, that's all,' Evie said, choking back her helpless rage. '*Stop it, Andrew. Right, that's enough.*' She lifted him into her arms and he was horribly strong, kicking at her and throwing himself about as she tried to go downstairs, so that she nearly lost her footing. Tracy watched from the bottom, hat on and anorak already zipped up.

'Listen to that,' she heard her mother say from the front room. 'Even 'er own cowing kids don't like 'er.'

She heard Rita's nasty laughter from the front room. It was like being kicked – far worse than Andrew's real blows.

They hate me, she thought, fighting Andrew into his coat as he tried to punch and kick her. They've always hated me and nothing's different.

She had always hoped, always tried. One day

419

she would please Mom, make Rita nicer, be close to Shirley...

She attempted to ignore Andrew's tantrum as they walked home along the wet street, he pulling on her hand, Tracy slightly ahead of them, hunched up in her blue anorak.

She felt wiped out, a terrible, dizzy feeling, like falling with no one to catch you.

Mrs Grant saved that afternoon. She took one look at Evie's face as they came in through the back door. The Grants had just had their dinner and the house smelt of stew and boiled carrots. Mr Grant, a newspaper in his hand, smiled vaguely at her and slipped away to the front room.

'Oh, hello, dear,' Mrs Grant said cautiously. 'What a wet day, isn't it? Have you all had your dinner?'

Evie was about to pretend, but Tracy and Andrew – who had finally wound down into silence – shook their heads. Evie saw that Mrs Grant now seemed to have at least an inkling of her problems.

'Well, I've got a nice little bit of meat and some potatoes over – and stewed apple and custard. How would you fancy that?'

Tears welled in Evie's eyes. Usually Mrs Grant supplied their evening meal, not the one at dinnertime.

'I can pay you,' she offered.

Mrs Grant moved past her with a bird-like movement, touching Evie's arm briefly as she did so.

'No, dear, no need. I made too much. Still in my old habits of cooking for a family, you see. I cook

420

potatoes for five instead of two! Come along, sit yourselves down. I don't suppose you're going to be able to go out this afternoon, are you? How about I see if I can find some of our old games, and you can come and sit by the fire.'

The children brightened considerably at this, and even more so when they had some food inside them. The dread inside Evie eased a little at not having to face an achingly empty afternoon. Another fairy godmother, she thought. Those people in her life who had kept her going, kept her believing kindness was possible. Like Rachel Booker and Mary Bracebridge – and Bea, in Canada. Where would she be now without them?

Fifty

March 1972

'Evie?'

The voice only just penetrated the fog of her thoughts. She was sitting in the coffee bar at Kalamazoo, over a cup of weak coffee, about to go back to work. The other comptometer girls had just gone, so Alan must have seen his chance.

She looked up into his kind face.

'Sorry, didn't mean to disturb you.'

'It's OK,' Evie said, trying to drag herself into the present moment. The room was emptying after the morning break, tinny music in the background, *I've got a brand-new pair of roller skates...*

She felt as if she needed to shake herself the way a dog does when getting up from sleep. It was so hard to concentrate – on anything.

'It's a while since I've seen you,' he said, holding on to the back of the chair opposite her, solid, somehow reassuring. He had told her he worked in the print department as a litho artist, which, other people said, made him a 'clever bugger'. He was close to his sister, his young nephew and niece. He seemed kindly. He was single. And he was so obviously interested in her. The other girls were always nudge-nudging, saying to Evie that he fancied her, it was obvious. She was flattered. She liked him. But she was exhausted, as if she just had no energy for it, no room in her life.

'I s'pose it is,' she said, getting up and pushing her chair in. She was dressed in her office clothes, straight skirt, blouse, little navy court shoes. People said she looked good in them.

'Oh, very nice,' Mrs Grant said sometimes when she left the house. 'Don't you look neat and businesslike?'

She had not been avoiding Alan. In fact, she had barely given him a thought. Since Christmas she had not felt herself. Things seemed to be sliding out of her grasp and she was not sleeping well. She felt distant from everything.

'I, er … I just wondered if you'd like to come out for a drink one night,' Alan said. She could hear the nervousness in his voice and she liked him for it. 'Friday, maybe?'

She looked at him, trying to take in what he was asking her. It took her time to reply.

'Sorry, I can't really,' she said.

'Oh.' He looked down at the floor, pushing his hands into the pockets of his brown suit trousers in an abashed way. 'Sorry. I just thought ... you know, maybe now and then there might be someone who you could get to look after them? I mean, my sister said she could...' He stopped. 'One of the other girls said...' He looked ever more awkward. 'That ... well, that you're not married anymore.'

'No,' she said, not wanting to reject him. He was a nice man. 'I'm not. At least ... I'm not divorced yet.' Now her own face was hot. It was a hard admission. She still felt married to Jack – *was* still married to him, in law. 'But he's in Canada. I'm on my own with the kids, so it's difficult.' She spoke fast, wanting to make things better because he seemed a nice person. 'I mean, maybe one day I could find a babysitter, but...'

She didn't feel she could ask Mrs Grant. And she was not sure she really wanted to go out with anyone. Looking at Alan, though, at that moment, seeing his amiable face, a longing filled her. Oh, to be looked after by someone like that – someone older and mild and solid. Their eyes met for a moment before he looked down.

'I see,' he said. Looking up again, he smiled. 'Well ... the offer's there, all right?'

She managed to smile back, but still as if she was distant, at the end of a long tunnel. 'All right. That might be nice. Thanks.'

After work she went, as usual, to pick up Tracy and Andrew. Even they, like the rest of her life, now seemed to her to be on the other side of a glass screen which she was forever trying to reach. It wasn't as if they were behaving any differently from before. Tracy was being a good girl, as ever. Mom, Rita and Shirley all sucked up to her; Ann was friends with her some of the time and bitterly envious and bad-tempered at others. Tracy tried to please everyone – Nanna, aunties, cousins and Mom – and at times she looked strained and confused.

It was Andrew who played up more, never wanting to go home when Evie came to fetch them, his favour being bought by the family with toys and sweets and lots of cousins to play with. She dreaded picking them up every day because it was almost always a fight and she ended up feeling exhausted and in the wrong.

'Oh *Mom*,' Andrew yelled rudely as she came to the door that afternoon. 'It's not time to go – I'm *playing*. Wayne and me are playing *football*.'

'Andrew,' she said sternly. She had never known him behave this aggressively before, rejecting her on sight. It pierced her already wounded heart.

'Come on, Andrew,' Tracy said. 'We've got to go.'

'Here y'are, you two!' Rita was there, as usual, baby Dean in her arms. 'Here's some sherbet dabs to take with yer.'

'Cor!' Andrew grabbed one.

Tracy took hers more politely. 'Thanks, Auntie.'

There was a sickly smell in the hall, as if every child in the family was breathing out sugar.

'Is that my other daughter who can't keep a man?' she heard her mother bawl from the living room. 'Got us doing all her dirty work, ain't 'er?'

Shirley passed through the hall in a slouchy jumper and jeans. She didn't say a word. She gave Evie a look which once she might have thought of as sympathetic, but now she wasn't so sure. The look seemed to contain malice. Evie blinked. You never knew with Shirley.

'Come on, Andrew,' she said wearily, as he started to kick off. She did not want to go inside. She just wanted her kids to follow her out, slowly and quietly so that they could slip away.

'I s'pose 'e don't want to go with 'er,' she heard Mom observe to Shirley. ''Er might just as well leave 'im 'ere for all the mothering she does.'

'Trace, get him, will you?' Evie whispered.

Tracy disappeared and came back dragging her yelling brother by the arm. Evie stepped in, twisted him round and picked him up from behind. Andrew started to kick back at her and she felt sharp pains in her thighs.

'Hark at that,' she heard Rita say. 'I don't s'pose we'll get no thanks, neither. She ought to be paying us, by rights.'

'Bring his coat,' she ordered Tracy.

Tracy, who had her own anorak on, grabbed Andrew's red one and Evie bundled them all out of the door. Further along the street she plonked Andrew down, grabbed his shoulders and found herself shrieking into his face.

'Stop it! Just stop that noise, Andrew, or I'll...'

Another, older lady was staring at her as she walked past.

'What're you bloody looking at?' she roared at her and the lady turned away, walking faster. Tracy stood next to her in mute misery.

'I hate you!' Andrew bawled, beside himself. He was writhing and stamping. 'I hate you! I want my dad!'

It was the first time in ages Andrew had mentioned Jack and the word 'dad' stabbed Evie again with guilt and hurt.

Well, he didn't bloody well want you – ever! she wanted to snap back. But she managed not to say it.

She knelt down and took her little boy, still fighting, in her arms.

'Come 'ere, babby.' Her own tears were flowing now. She felt more sobs swelling in her chest. 'Come on, it'll be all right. Mommy's sorry.'

He fought for a moment, then stilled and cried like the tiny boy he was. Tracy was crying too and Evie pulled her into her arms as they all wept there in the street.

'Why're they all so nasty to you, Mom?' she sobbed. 'I don't like them being so mean to you.'

'I don't know,' Evie said. 'I just don't know, babby. As long as they're not nasty to you, though?'

She pulled back and looked at the two of them. She couldn't have cared less if anyone in the street was witnessing this scene. Her children and their feelings were everything to her.

With tearstained faces the two of them agreed that no, Nanna and the aunties were not nasty to them.

'Auntie spoils us, really,' Tracy said, wiping her eyes with the backs of her hands. 'And Nanna. They're always giving us sweets and we can do anything we want.' Her face beneath the cream bobble hat looked pained and bewildered. 'Only I wish they'd be nicer to you. What did you do? You must have done something to make them be so nasty?'

'Is that what they told you?' Evie said. A chill feeling went through her of terrible aloneness. Were they trying to poison her own children against her?

'Well, no.' Tracy looked down. Andrew was gulping and sniffling. 'Not exactly.' She seemed to consider for a second what answer to give, then looked up again. There was a pained look in her eyes but she shook her head. 'No.'

Evie lay under the heavy brown blankets and thin eiderdown that night, turning from one position to another, desperate for sleep.

She could hear her children's breathing from across the room, usually reassuring, but now, on these fractured nights, any sound seemed to echo through her head, jarring her, sending her even further from the sweet oblivion of sleep that she wanted to enter.

The bedclothes weighed on her. She lay with her eyes stinging from exhaustion staring up into the darkness which seemed to pulse round her with a new malevolence.

She found herself thinking about Gary again. It didn't make her feel any better. She felt she had betrayed Gary back then when they were young. But then she had had her own problems. Seeing him just after Christmas she had been shocked. He looked a wreck. So much time had passed, so much had happened to each of them. That smile he had flashed at her, just for a second, brought back the old Gary, the funny boy she had loved. But now... She only had the vaguest idea of where he might be living and she knew she was not going to go and find him. There was no time to try.

Turning over yet again, she sighed in despair at the thought of struggling through the next working day.

If only I could get some sleep, she thought. I'm blowing things all out of proportion because I'm so tired. Her head was crowded with horrible, jarring things. Her blood seemed to race round her body and she could not stop it. She drew in some deep breaths but felt no calmer.

Alan's face, gentle and smiling, floated into her mind. But the thought of him only gave her more pain. He was keen on her, in his shy way. But what was the use of longing to have someone love her, of giving him hope? It only went wrong every time. And if Alan knew her, knew what she was really like, this hopeless, hateful thing, he would not want her anyway.

Fifty-One

Spring 1972

'Are you all right, dear?' Mrs Grant met her as she came in with the children that evening after work. 'Only Bill and I have been saying you're looking awfully pale.'

Evie heard her landlady's voice as if echoing from the bottom of a well. Gently she ushered Tracy and Andrew along the hall, which smelt of recent baking. *You go on up*, she nodded to the children and they crept away, Andrew in his usual overwrought state after being at his grandmother's house, from too much rushing about and too many sweets.

Mom and Rita were now firmly in charge of her children. That was how it felt. Evie had kept them to herself over the Easter holidays and taken time off to go about with them as much as she could – to Cannon Hill Park, even all the way to Dudley Zoo. But there were all the work days, when she could not be there after school.

'Thanks, Mrs Grant, I'm all right,' Evie said, trying to suppress her irritated exhaustion. Usually she was grateful to Mrs Grant for mothering her. But now all she could think was, just leave me alone! All she wanted was to sink down, down into the darkness and peace of a proper sleep, to lose the world for a time and all her worries in it.

'Probably just the end of the winter,' Mrs Grant said, her own pasty face examining Evie's. Evie felt her gaze like pins pricking into her. It was like being spied upon. She wondered for a second if Mom had been talking to Mrs Grant, was trying to get her on her side. She pushed the thought away. What was the matter with her?

'We all need some sun and we'll feel much better now spring's coming.' She was turning away, in her usual busy, practical fashion. 'They say it's going to brighten up again tomorrow. Would you like a cup of tea with us, dear?'

'That's kind of you. But no – I need to go and sort the kids out.' Evie could not bear the thought of sitting trying to make polite conversation with the Grants. She turned away, adding, 'Thanks. Thank you.' Words wouldn't seem to come out in the right order when they were needed.

'All right. Well, our high tea will be ready in about half an hour.'

Mrs Grant's high teas were bread and butter, with a scraping of jam, tinned fruit with custard or evaporated milk and a frugal cake.

When she went up the stairs, Andrew was waiting on the top step, his back to their door. Tracy seemed to have gone ahead. Andrew held the banister and was sliding his feet off the top step onto the one below, then stepping back up to begin again. Seeing her, he stilled and just stood on the last but one step, staring at her.

Evie stopped. She was about to say, 'Go on then, in you go,' when she felt the force of her little boy's stare. His expression was blank, sullen, his fringe long over his forehead, his eyes fixed on her. His gaze chilled her.

He looks like a devil, she thought, her breath shallow in her chest. He's a devil and he hates me! She was possessed, for that moment, by the conviction that her son had evil intent towards her. She blinked, trying to make his expression change, but he kept giving her that fixed, concentrated look. She froze, unable to move.

After a moment, Andrew started kicking one foot against the step.

'Come on, Mom,' he said, sounding like a normal, hungry boy. 'Has Mrs Grant done our tea?'

Evie felt her breath return again. Tracy came out of their door as if to check where they had got to.

'Mrs Grant says tea in half an hour,' she reported. 'High tea.'

'Oh goody!' Tracy said. High tea usually meant a break from stew, which was not her favourite. 'Cake!'

Evie swam through the days. Sometimes when she was sitting in front of the comptometer she felt like a machine herself, doing her job, trying to keep going. The click of the new machines – not like the metallic 'thunk' of the old ones – throbbed in her head. She felt foggy and far away from things.

'Oi, dream boat!' Her friends had started to tease her. 'Blimey, Evie must be in love!'

'It's that feller from the print department,' one of the others said. 'He's chatting her up every chance he gets.'

Evie smiled mildly in the laughter that followed this. Although Alan nearly always came and had a chat in the coffee break, he had not pressed her any further into going out with him. He was sweet, the way she imagined a nice older brother might be. He treated her with shy respect and she liked him. The only trouble was, she was never properly *there* these days.

Once or twice, when he had obviously already said something to her and she had not responded, Alan said, 'Penny for them.' And she stared at his brown sleeve, his cuff there on the table beside her cup of coffee, and tried to think what on earth it was he had just said.

'Sorry,' she mumbled, looking into his face. Often when she looked at him he was looking back with an amused expression. Today, though, he seemed concerned. 'I'm ... I'm not sleeping all that well at the moment. I don't feel very with it.'

'Never mind,' he said. 'That's all right. I have that trouble sometimes.' And he started giving her advice about ways to get to sleep, from counting sheep – or cats, what about cats? he said – to a nice warm bath. As if she had not tried those things a hundred times already.

Every day after work, she left the office, heading out into the lightening evenings and changeable spring weather, and the Bristol Road traffic. She had to concentrate hard to get across the road. She was so exhausted that she could scarcely judge how far away the cars were. Sometimes she stood dithering for some minutes and one day she found Alan beside her, taking her arm to lead her across.

On the other side, he stopped her and looked into her eyes. She found it difficult to meet his. She felt ashamed, as if he might see the dark horror that really waited inside her instead of the blonde, pretty little thing that faced the world.

'Is there something wrong?' he asked carefully.

Her throat tightened at his kindness, tears waiting to force into her eyes.

'I'm all right,' she said, managing to look at him. 'Ta, Alan. I am, really.'

His face wore a slight frown. He looked full of tenderness and he was standing close to her.

'You know...' he began. He looked as if he wanted to put his arms around her. For a second that was all she longed for, to be held, for someone to rescue her. But no. He was good. He was lovely. And he didn't know what she was really like. She looked down at his brown thin-laced shoes.

Alan felt her retreating from him and released her arm. 'You'll be all right, then?' he said. 'See you tomorrow, Evie.'

May arrived and the sun shone more warmly, but as the weeks passed, Evie was finding it increasingly difficult just to get through each day.

Getting up in the morning was one of the hardest things. She would wake, feeling as if her whole body was weighted to the mattress. If it wasn't for the kids – 'Mom, come on!' – she would not have managed it.

Other times, at her desk in the office, she found it almost intolerable having to stay there all day. Nothing felt right, as if she could not sit content in her own skin; she wanted to crawl out of it, get away from herself and hide away, somewhere dark, safe and peaceful – away from all her struggles.

Mom's nasty comments and Rita and Shirley joining in was something she could not protect herself against any longer. The words slashed through her and she was bleeding inside.

Before things grew this bad, she had gone over and over in her mind a conversation with Tracy and Andrew that she had imagined.

What if we move away from here? Let's just go somewhere else – start a new life.

She could imagine Andrew's fury. *I don't want to move. I want to stay here with Wayne, and Auntie!* Andrew was attached to Rita, who spoilt him

433

along with all her own lads.

And Tracy's puzzled expression floated before her. *But Mom, you said when we came here we were starting a new life. Where're we going to go?*

Where? Yes, where? She had no idea. And now she had no energy, no hope.

One sunny afternoon, after she had picked them up from Alwold Street, they were walking back along the road towards Weoley Avenue. For once Andrew was not making a fuss and seemed glad to be outside. It was so warm that Evie had taken off her mac and slung it over her arm along with the children's coats and a bag of their school things. The road ran alongside the cemetery and the green space beyond the railings made it a tranquil place to walk. The sound of birdsong came from the flowering trees between the gravestones.

Tracy and Andrew skipped along in the sun, friends for the time being. Evie watched from behind in a moment of calm at the sight of their happy movements in the warm afternoon. How beautiful they were, both of them. Despite everything, they seemed to be all right.

'Mom?' Tracy ran back to her. 'When we get home, can we play in Mrs Grant's garden?'

'Yes, I s'pect so,' Evie said, the trace of a smile on her lips. She knew Mrs Grant liked to see the children out there, amid the apple blossom. It was what gardens were for, she said.

Tracy hesitated, looking up at her. Her slender body had a solidity to it and her face a gravity which made her seem older than her seven years.

'Mom?'

'Yes?' Evie stopped.

Tracy looked down. 'I just... Nanna said she thought there was something wrong with you. And I... Only now you look all right...'

Evie felt her pulse race again, her breathing compress. It was as if a hand, her mother's fat, malignant hand, had reached out for her once more, pressing on her throat.

'Oh,' she said, trying to sound light-hearted. 'I'm all right. Go on, let's get home to the garden.'

Tracy looked doubtfully at her, but ran along again to catch up with Andrew.

As they reached the corner, where the grounds of the cemetery ended, the children stopped, as she had trained them to do, to wait for her to cross the road.

Evie had almost caught up with them when she saw something lying in the weeds, close up to the cemetery railings. What she first saw was something watching her which jerked her attention. An eye. Her already banging pulse slammed harder. It was a doll, she saw, a greyish rag doll thing amid the grass and dandelions. Leaning down, she saw that it had straggly brown wool hair, big blue eyes inked on, a dull red dress of some sort. It was slumped, head to one side. And it was watching her.

She knew for certain as soon as she saw it that it was there to watch her. That someone had left it there quite deliberately to spy on her – Rita and Shirley most likely. Even in her jangled state she could not imagine her mother bothering to walk all the way down here and plant this spy to report back on her movements.

A sense of fearful, helpless rage filled her. She bent over the doll, nervous in case it leapt up at her in some horrible way, snarling up into her face.

'You needn't think you can get me,' she hissed at it. 'I know why you're here and I know who sent you. You can just go away and leave me alone. All of you. I know you hate me but you shouldn't be spying on me.' She felt close to breaking down, sobbing and howling in the street. 'Just leave me be! What have I ever done to you?'

'Mom?' Tracy was running back towards her. Evie straightened up. Tracy must not, on any account, see the doll. She would creep out later, once the children were settled, and move the terrible thing. She could lob it right over into the graveyard.

'What're you doing?' Tracy said.

'Nothing. I just dropped something. It's all right.' Evie shoved her hands under the coats and bags in her arms so that Tracy could not see how much she was shaking. Her legs would hardly hold her and she was not sure whether her voice sounded normal.

'Come on. Let's get home.'

Thanks to Mrs Grant, she was able to get through the next few hours. She knew that if she had been alone up in the flat, her mind would have raced out of control. But Mrs Grant made tea and they sat in the garden on the Grants' rusty garden chairs. Mrs Grant, in a pale yellow frock, brought out tea and chatted about the church bazaar that she was knitting for. The children rolled and cartwheeled across the square of lawn and Mr

Grant came out and stood in his shirtsleeves, smiling at them.

Evie hardly took in a word of what Mrs Grant was saying, but the effort of trying to appear normal did make her pulse slow down, and the image of the doll fade, for the moment. Though now, carved into her as never before, was the knowledge that her family did not just hate her, they were out to get her.

She felt terrifyingly alone, as if she was standing at the top of an endlessly high pinnacle, just waiting to fall.

Three days later, at breakfast time, amid the smell of boiled eggs and toast, which Evie felt quite unable to stomach but urged the children to eat, Mr Grant came into the kitchen and said, 'One for you today,' pressing a pale blue envelope onto the table.

Evie had barely ever seen Jack's handwriting, but the envelope, edged with red and navy chevrons, came from Canada. She muttered a thank you, taking it from him. It was surprisingly stiff and would not fit in her skirt pocket so she slid it up under her jumper.

'Aren't you having anything again today?' Mrs Grant said as she got up from the table.

Evie knew that a lecture would follow about breakfast being the most important meal of the day.

'No thanks, Mrs Grant. Just tea's fine. I just need to...' Trailing off, she ran upstairs.

Sitting on her bed she tore open the envelope with trembling hands, unexpected hopes rushing into her mind. Jack was missing her! He realized he had made a terrible mistake and wanted them all back!

Inside were three postcards. They were all similar, all of the Rockies near Calgary. Two were for the children – 'For Tracy, with love from your pa.' Similar for Andrew. The only time in these seven months that he had bothered to send them anything.

Her card said, 'Evie, me and Linda want to get married and it seems the right thing to do. So I've started on getting us a divorce. You'll be hearing from a solicitor in England soon. Hope you're all getting along all right. Jack.'

It was a long time before she managed to get downstairs again. Her whole body was shaking so that she could barely stand and it was only hearing voices downstairs, knowing that soon Mrs Grant would call to her, that made her force herself to her feet.

Afterwards she could remember nothing about that last day at work: who had spoken to her, whether anything had been said. There was a vague memory of Maureen Benson's face, pink and concerned, her mouth moving. They must all have noticed something but she could not recall.

She could just about remember the greyness as she walked out of Kalamazoo to the Bristol Road. The spring sunshine had gone, the sky a pewter plate, red tail lights the only bright dots in the storm-lit afternoon.

As she left the building, she heard a voice call 'Evie!' after her. Later, she found out that it was

Alan, wanting to walk with her, but she was walled in, nothing from the outside reaching her, as if she actually had her face pressed up hard against cold brick and could no longer see out.

Usually she crossed the Bristol Road and walked a little way along to catch a bus. She had a hazy memory, later, of standing at the kerb, the rush of traffic, colours, lights, her feet in their court shoes at the edge, waiting; a feeling of knowing that somehow, this was the moment everything must end.

She stepped out into the road. And stopped.

Fifty-Two

'I'd say she's been very lucky, stupid bloody woman... Things some people will do for attention...'

It was a man's voice. She heard other voices, murmurings, the shuffling of feet. She realized she was lying down on something flat and hard but she could not seem to move or open her eyes.

'Get her up to a ward. We don't need her cluttering up the place down here.'

'Yes, doctor,' a woman's voice said, from somewhere near Evie's head. She could sense people close to her, that there was a light coverlet laid over her. She could feel the flicker of her eyes, the air slipping in and out of her lungs, the throb of pain all down her right side, especially her hip. And a sense that there was a weight pressing down on her, a massive dog of exhaustion and despair parked on her chest.

Someone's hand slipped into hers. 'You'll be all right, love,' a voice said softly, close to her ear. 'Don't you worry. You're safe now. We're just going to make you comfy upstairs.'

Evie heard herself make a small sound, a moan of acknowledgement, but she could not open her eyes.

Soon she felt herself moving, being wheeled along a corridor, and the motion lulled her back into unconsciousness.

Now she was aware of light pressing on her eyelids. There was movement, voices in the distance, the clink of cups on saucers.

A swish of curtains nearby, then whispers.

'Suicide attempt, they think. Walked out into the traffic.' The voice was stiff with disapproval.

Evie kept her eyes closed, pressed to the mattress by shame. Was that what she had done? Was this what they thought of her – stupid, a waste of time? This was true, she knew. All she could remember was leaving the office building yesterday in the gloom of the afternoon. Then nothing. A screech of tyres. Darkness.

And yet here she was, still pressed under the weight of life. Why was she still here?

'Poor soul,' another female voice replied.

Poor soul. Tears rose in her eyes at the kindness in the voice.

'Poor soul maybe,' the other voice said, 'but she's taking up a bed which someone who's really sick could be in.'

'You go, I'll see to her,' the kinder voice urged.

She sensed someone standing by the bed, leaning over her. It seemed safest to keep her eyes closed still, but in a few seconds she heard a gasp.

'Evie? Can you hear me? It *is* you, isn't it? Evie Sutton?'

She didn't know the voice. Very slowly she peeled back her lids. The woman looking down at her, her brown hair pulled back under a nurse's cap, had a kindly face and her eyes were full of sympathy and wonder.

'Evie, it's Melly. Melly Booker.'

Evie focussed. She knew her then, vaguely, now she had been told. Melly was a couple of years older than her.

'Remember the old end, over in Aston?' Melly said. 'God, d'you know, you've barely changed!'

Tears ran from Evie's eyes, down into her hair. It was as if someone was squeezing her inside, wringing grief from her like juice from an orange.

'I remember ... your mom,' Evie managed to say, as sobs broke from her. 'She ... was ... k-kind...'

'There, there,' Melly said. She cradled Evie's hand between both of her own, sounding upset. 'Oh Evie, we always remembered you and wondered what had happened to you. I think Gladys – Dad's auntie... D'you remember her? She saw you once, I think, years ago.'

Evie knew she had seen Gladys Poulter, that night she had come out of a pub near the markets with some bloke or other in tow. She had known exactly who she was – you couldn't miss Gladys Poulter. But she had pretended not to notice,

441

ashamed of herself.

'Evie.' Melly was looking at her soberly now. 'It's ever so nice to see you. They said you've got a couple of cracked ribs – just bruising otherwise. It knocked you out, though – you must've hit your head. The driver's all right too – no one got hurt badly. But...' She hesitated, her eyes wide with sympathy. 'He said it didn't look like an accident. If you meant to do it ... well, you must've been in a bad state.'

The tears just came and came. The feel of a warm hand in hers, Melly's kind, familiar eyes, opened a chasm of need and sadness in her.

'I... My kids...' she began. 'I can't ... just can't...' And then she was sobbing.

Melly rubbed the top of her arm, trying to be comforting.

'Oh Evie, I'm ever so sorry. I know things were difficult for you...' Evie could see all the sympathy in Melly's face, but she could sense that it was hard for her to know what to say.

'Where are they, Evie? Your children? Is someone looking after them?'

Evie nodded. They would have gone home with Shirley. She felt a sense of surrender. Mom and the rest of them were always trying to take over her kids. Now they'd won. She knew they'd keep them, when she didn't come back. Mom collected grandchildren like trophies.

'Good,' Melly said. 'As long as you know they're safe. All right. Look, you need a cup of tea and some breakfast. I'll go and get you a cup before they've finished serving.' She squeezed Evie's hand as she began to move away. 'You're going to be all right. Don't fret. I'll be back in a minute.'

Melly brought her a cup of tea and some cold toast and helped Evie sit up. Her body felt battered and her neck hurt once she was upright, propped against a pillow.

'I'm on an early today,' Melly said, stirring in sugar for her. 'After that I'm off for a few days.' She looked as if she was about to say more, but stopped herself. 'Look, you just have a go at this cup of tea. I'll come and see you later, all right?' She smiled, a sweet, sadness-tinged smile. 'It's really nice to see you again, Evie.'

Evie sipped a little of the tea, then slid back down under the bedclothes. She had been put right at the far end of the long Nightingale ward and felt as if she was in the dunce's corner, in disgrace. All she wanted to do was hide from everyone.

As it turned out, she did not see anything much of Melly until after dinner. All morning she lay still, turned away from everyone, and she was left alone. She dozed. For the first time in a long time she was able to sleep, woken off and on by the sounds of the ward, but sliding back gratefully into unconsciousness again. She could not think straight about anything. She could not think about what she had done.

Had she tried to kill herself? Yes, she thought. She had wanted only darkness and release. Still wanted it. But she was in disgrace. No one approved of a suicide. She felt guilty, a wicked fool. Her children! She kept the sheet pulled over her head and lay hurting in the dark warmth of the bed, longing not to be here.

Food appeared beside her but she didn't notice and it was not until Melly arrived again and pointed it out that she saw a plate with two sausages, some lumpy-looking mash and a few peas.

'D'you want some?' Melly asked.

Evie shook her head.

Melly drew the chair by the bed closer.

'Sorry, we've been rushed off our feet. I wanted to come and see you, but Sister kept finding me things to do. Why don't you try and sit up for a bit, Evie?'

Evie looked around fearfully. 'Everyone hates me,' she whispered.

'What?' Melly sounded disturbed. She spoke very quietly. 'No they don't. What're you talking about? Come on.' She got up and helped Evie sit against the pillows. Looking closely at her, she smiled. 'You're so pretty still – you always were.'

Tears rolled down Evie's cheeks again. Melly took her hand and sat down.

'D'you want to tell me about yourself – you said you had children?'

Evie shook her head, looking down at the strip of sheet, the miracle of a hand in hers.

'All right.' Melly was quiet for a moment. 'I'll tell you about me then.'

Evie listened as Melly told her that she had married Reggie, one of the Morrison boys. Did Evie remember them from Aston? Little blond buggers, she called them. Of course she remembered – a swarm of little fair-haired boys; their mother, with her dark hair and a laughing, pretty face.

'Dolly,' Evie said.

'Yes! Of course you'd remember Dolly. She's my mother-in-law! Reggie and I live upstairs. Years back, they won the pools – at least Mo did – and they bought this great big house in Moseley and then of course they wanted to fill it up. Dolly loves kids around her and now Donna's gone, she's... Little Donna, the babby? Oh, she's so beautiful. She's an actress, gone down to London to work. Anyway, Reggie and me've got two kids. Tina's nine and Christopher will be seven this year. And d'you remember my kid brother Tommy – same age as you? If you remember, he had problems, from birth. But he's done ever so well – lives over in Wolverhampton. He's got a job and he's married to a lovely girl, Jo-Ann. Then there's all the others – Mom had six in the end. Too many, I'd say.' She laughed.

There was a silence, then Melly leaned forward to look up at her.

'What about your kids? How old are they? What're their names? I'd love to hear.'

Evie didn't look at her. She couldn't seem to stop trembling suddenly, couldn't hold herself together.

'T-Tracy,' she managed to say. 'She's seven. And ... and Andrew...' The image of her little boy's face swam before her and it was her undoing. 'He's five – only five. He's a babby...'

She put her free hand to her face and shook with dry sobs, feeling herself fall apart and lose all control.

'Oh Evie,' Melly said. She came and sat on the bed beside her, pulling her into her arms as she

445

shook and began moaning with grief.

While Melly was holding her, stroking her back to try and comfort her, she became aware gradually that they were not alone. Someone was talking to Melly. She heard the words 'psychiatric assessment'.

And afterwards Melly rocked her like a child, saying, 'They'll help you, Evie. That's what we're all here for – to help you get better.'

Fifty-Three

'Evie. Evie! There's someone to see you. It's a lady – says she's called Melanie Morrison. Are you going to come and talk to her?'

'… … …'

Sandy Hoskins, one of the nurses, plump and reassuring, hair smoothed back into a bun, came and stood before her. Evie, on a plastic-covered chair in the day room, stared down at Sandy's feet, stolid in black lace-up shoes.

'Come on, Evie. Why don't you come down to the visitors' room with me and see her? She looks ever so nice. A little chat might make you feel better?'

'… … …'

There was a long pause as Sandy waited. Evie stared at the woman's feet, her black lace-up shoes. She felt muzzy and separate from everything. It was the pills, she knew, that made her mouth dry and her innards sluggish, sent her into

446

a sort of haze. But it wasn't just that. She had let go of everything outside. It felt like another life that had happened to someone else. Melanie Morrison? The name was like a faraway echo. How could she go and talk to anyone? She could not find words, had nothing to say.

'No? All right, I'll tell her. It's a shame, though. She looks such a nice lady.'

'Evie? Another visitor for you. A gentleman this time. Says he's from your work. Alan Dickson? No? All right then. I'll tell him you're not feeling up to it today.'

When she was admitted to Rubery Hill Hospital, Evie stopped crying.

Melly had set off her tears, perhaps because of her kindness and her familiar link with the past. But after that Evie moved into a blank lethargy. She shut down, could barely move. But she felt safe in there, as if within the ward, the long corridors, the high brick walls, she could just let all of it go. It was as if she had released herself from everything and everyone. Even amid some of the griefs and tragedies of the hospital, it was as though she felt held, cupped within huge hands that would stop her falling right to the bottom. People here seemed to know something she didn't. She couldn't understand what it was, but she knew there was something she needed.

She could not have put this into words.

There were the smells of gravy, cabbage, disinfectant; the confused, shuffling ladies reeking of wee. Other women in her ward gradually became known to her: Phyllis, the silent secretary who had had a breakdown; the exotic-looking middle-aged lady called Miranda, with long black hair, who seemed to have come from somewhere abroad. Old Alice who, if not distracted, sat rocking on the rim of her bed hour after hour, her head wrapped in a rough towelling turban and mewling like an animal in pain. There was Mavis, a young black woman, eyes filled with pain. 'My babies die,' Mavis told her later. They might have been friends, had either of them had the strength. There were the nurses who bossed and cajoled, were sometimes kind and sometimes sapped of energy themselves, spoke to people as if they were overgrown, deaf children. There were cries and moans and shouts.

There were the routines and pills, the attempts by Dr Rose in his office, sitting beside his desk covered with papers and phones, to penetrate her blankness. There was Sandy Hoskins, with her pink, rough hands, fleshy face and a soul, Evie thought later, deeper and more loving than you could ever guess from her farm-girl body.

Sandy, who quietly advised her, 'Dr Rose isn't keen on ECT – he thinks people need to talk. And you will need to, Eve – try and start opening up to him. Otherwise...'

She saw some of them, after the treatment, stunned and silent.

There were the polished linoleum corridors, like dimly lit intestines. Somehow, even while she felt incapable even of dressing herself or making a cup of tea, Evie learned where the female wards were in relation to the nurses' office, the dispensary, the chapel, the rooms for occupational therapy.

And there was the sky. She watched the sky in all its moods, through the long windows. She refused to talk, to think. She took the pills. Everything outside was gone from her, was beyond her. She would not think about anything, anyone. She had crawled in here, into this shut-away place, and here she would remain.

'Who do you have outside?' they asked her, wanting names, addresses. 'D'you have a job somewhere?'

'... ... ...'

'Is there anyone who might visit you?'

'... ... ...'

They knew her name, from Selly Oak Hospital, as Evie Harrison. She had not told them whether Miss or Mrs.

They must have got other information from Melly when she came, because they started saying, 'You've got relatives, haven't you? Why don't you tell us where they live?'

'... ... ...'

Eventually, when they kept on, she told them she had nothing, no one.

'I've just come back from Canada.'

'*Canada?*'

'Yes.'

Dr Rose sat beside, rather than behind his desk, his right arm resting on a pile of folders. She noticed he had a nice fountain pen, a gold signet ring. One of his legs was crossed over the other and they were very long. He had black, tufty hair, black-rimmed spectacles and his hands were huge with wide, oval nails.

'When you stepped out into the road, was it your intention to take your own life?'

'... ... ...'

'You are feeling depressed. Sad?'

'... ... ...'

'Can you look up at me, Miss Sutton. Miss? Mrs? That's better – well done. Have you ever tried to commit suicide before?'

Dr Rose kept running his finger under the bridge of his spectacles as if they were giving him discomfort. There were red marks each side of his nose. His face was saggy and long. She found she liked him.

'... ... ...'

Evie looked down into her lap again. She was wearing loose brown slacks that did not belong to her and a sour-yellow blouse. Her hands looked strange to her.

'No? I'll take that as no, shall I?'

'... ... ...'

'We'll give it some time, Miss Sutton. I do hope you know we are all here to help you. Perhaps after a bit of rest you'll feel able to talk to us.'

Evie raised her head again. Dr Rose had taken off his spectacles and was rubbing his face. He looked weary and his weak eyes were watery grey.

'Whatever's troubling you, my dear' – the corners of his mouth twitched at the ends, almost into a smile. She felt it was a kind look – 'there are people you can talk to. It's safe here and it's very often the best remedy.' He stood up. 'I'll see

450

you in a few days, all right?'

She managed a tiny nod, to her own surprise, before leaving the room. She felt beckoned into something that she was not yet ready to enter.

A letter arrived for her, the envelope addressed in blue ink, in careful looped writing.

Dear Evie,

I realize you don't want visitors at the moment and I'm sorry I didn't manage to get back to you again before you left the ward. It was really nice to see you. I'm sorry you're having a rough time of it at the moment, but I'm sure the hospital will help.

We're all thinking of you. When you're better – and you will be, Evie, I'm sure, even if things feel very dark now – it would be lovely to see you.

With love from Melly

Evie wondered who 'all' meant. It was peculiar and warming to feel that anyone was thinking of her.

Days later, another note arrived.

Dear Evie,

I'm sorry if coming to the hospital was the wrong thing to do. I suppose I'm quite good at putting my foot in it. In fact, it feels as if whatever I do will be the wrong thing. So this is just to say I'm thinking of you. The firm isn't the same without you around and I do hope you'll feel better and be back soon. I shan't bother you again but I hope to see you when you're back.

All best wishes, Alan

It all felt so far away, Kalamazoo, the world outside, the family – everything. It was kind of him to write, she thought, in an abstract way. Kind of this man she hardly knew. But she didn't dwell on it.

She watched the days rise to reach the bright, baking height of summer. The pills made her mouth dry, made her constipated. Her legs and waist felt fatter and there was a new little wad of flesh under her chin. She asked if she could stop taking them. Maybe soon, they said. We think you need them a bit longer.

The sky arced blue and there were light, drifting clouds. They were allowed to sit outside sometimes and the sun on her face startled her. It stroked her as if it cared about her. This was July – the first time she felt anything. It brought tears to her eyes, feeling a breeze and the fingering warmth on her cheeks.

'Evie?' Sandy Hoskins said to her. It was August. She had stayed blank and quiet for weeks, but she had started to notice flowers and bright leaves outside. 'How about coming to the OT room today. It's time you started doing something.'

They tried everything, these nurses. They asked if she wanted to go to the chapel. They put on music and got everyone to dance, slow and stiff as corpses trying to breathe life into themselves. You could do things and not do them at the same time, Evie discovered. You could comply – and she wanted to please them, to make them feel they were helping – but if your mind is not with your body, it's as if someone else is doing it. They were not drugging her heavily – what would the point have been? She was quiet enough as it was. She was awake; she was just in hiding. They put on shows, encouraged those who could find it in them to do basket-weaving or draw pictures. Evie could not – not then.

Sandy took her to Occupational Therapy that afternoon. They asked her what she would do – a basket, some sewing?

Evie looked round the room, at its tables of coloured offerings and a tangle of stuff for weaving. She saw some squares of coloured felt.

'I'll sew something,' she said.

'Good! That's a great idea!' Sandy said with jubilation in her voice. Evie could feel her looking at the OT lady over her head, their eyes saying *progress*. 'I'll leave you in their capable hands,' Sandy said, giving Evie's shoulder a squeeze.

Next to her Phyllis, who was a grey, sad-looking lady, was stitching two rectangles of cotton together. Evie looked at her long, plain face and felt sorry for her. She looked like someone who had worked hard and done as she was told all her life and been kicked in the ditch for it.

'What're you making?' she whispered, wanting to be kind.

Phyllis's gaze swivelled slowly in her direction. She looked back at the material in her hands and said, 'I don't know, exactly.' Her voice was deep and well spoken. She stopped sewing and, staring ahead of her, said, 'I suppose it's a bit silly stitching this when I don't know what I'm doing. Just silly.' Her eyes filled with tears and she bowed her head to hide it, wiping her eyes with her knuckles.

Evie felt sorry for her. This was new. She had looked at the others before and seen their pain, but it had not touched her. 'It could be something nice to go on a table?' she said.

Phyllis looked gratefully at her. 'Yes. I suppose so. What're you making?'

Evie shrugged. 'I don't know. Nothing yet.'

Some people talked, others just sat, mute and shut in on themselves. Evie, for the first time, found herself looking round. She liked the colours in the room. She had chosen some felt – scraps of red, green and yellow and coloured threads.

'You've got something in mind then, have you?' the OT lady said brightly. 'Some little toys perhaps? I've got some shapes you could cut around if you like.'

Evie shook her head, relieved when the woman had to hurry away to help someone else. She had never done much sewing but she had something in mind, something precious, which made her heart beat faster. Mary Bracebridge had taught her a little bit when she was very small and she had done some repairs on the children's clothes. The feel of a needle in her hand, the act of squinting to push the end of the thread through the hole, brought a rush of memories so overwhelming that she had to stop for a moment.

Sitting at the table in the house in Rosette, white glare from the snow outside, edging napkins for Tracy before she was born; sewing a button back on Jack's shirt; fixing a snag in the table cloth... She closed her eyes and breathed in and out, feeling the rise and fall of her chest. It was her turn to lower her head.

Who am I? Give me something to hold on to... Please...

She felt someone nudging her. Looking up, Phyllis was staring at her, then at the OT lady, as if to say, *She'll notice in a minute. She'll be back. Sew something,* her eyes instructed, *so she doesn't ask why you're sitting there with your eyes closed.*

Evie nodded back, grateful. She picked up a scrap of buttercup-yellow felt and with the blunt-ended scissors cut a square, about three inches by three. With the dark blue thread, she started stitching.

By the end of the session she had three creations, like tiny mats, two square, one round. Blue thread on yellow – she had sewed a T. It was rough and wobbly running stitch, but somehow she loved what she had done. Yellow thread on red – A. And on the bright, grass-coloured circle, in bottle green – J.

'Oh, those are lovely!' the OT lady said when she saw them. 'Aren't they colourful!'

Evie didn't like the woman holding them. She almost snatched them back off her and the lady noticed.

'So,' she said gently. 'Who are they, Evie?'

Head down, gripping the coloured squares in her lap, she said, 'These are my children.'

Sandy Hoskins came and sat beside her on her bed the next morning. They were facing away

455

from everyone else. She felt that having Sandy sitting there was like having a hillside or a big dog beside her.

After a pause, she said, 'D'you know what I do, at home? I've got kids – two boys. Not that they take any notice, not now, but I want them to remember it. I always get flowers and put them in the house. Cheap ones – anything. Daffs when they're in season. Bluebells from the Lickeys if we go out. Or off that lady in the Bullring if I'm in town. My husband sometimes says, what're you spending money on them for? They'll only die! But I always try and have them in the house. We can't manage a puppy or anything like that, although Kev and Danny would love one. But at least I can do flowers. Anything that brings life and makes you happy just looking at it, see?'

Evie sat listening. Tears waited behind her eyes, and her throat squeezed tight. All these things she had stopped herself thinking about. About how *they* had won. Mom, Rita, Shirley. She'd let them win. They had her children, the children she never deserved to have, who were better off without her.

She knew now, she wanted to be asked.

'Children, Evie?'

It was all pushing up, coming to the surface like a cork from underwater. Evie felt a sensation for a moment as if she was going to be sick. Instead, she began to cry. She felt Sandy Hoskins put an arm round her shoulder and pull her close.

'I've done a terrible thing, Dr Rose,' she wept. She was like a one-woman flood now, couldn't stop.

'I've abandoned them. They'll be with my mom because they would've been at hers after school, when I didn't come home. And it's the worst place they could be.'

'Do they know where you are?' Dr Rose said gently. 'No? I suppose not. Well, of course we can let them know and find out for you. But why would your mother's house be the worst place for them?'

She could stop neither talking nor crying. Everything poured out, over several meetings with Dr Rose, under the tired, tolerant watch of his eyes. How Mom had always hated her, shut her out, taunted and belittled her. About giving Julie up, about Jack and Canada. About how she was hopeless, not a fit mother to look after her own children.

'I don't know why Mom hates me so much,' she said one day in a pool of calm between bouts of tears. 'I mean, I do – it's because I wasn't a boy and our father was playing away with someone else. And she had a boy – his.'

'A tough situation for your mother,' Dr Rose observed.

'I know.' Evie looked at him. She wiped her eyes. 'It was our father's as fault as well – he never stood up for me. Never did anything 'cept please himself. Least line of resistance, that's the old man. Long as he could pour something down his neck and do as he liked he didn't give a monkey's. That was the two of them – all our lives, to be honest. Doesn't sound very nice, does it?' she said, filled with shame. 'But she turned my sisters against me – especially Rita. Shirley's never

457

known if she was coming or going really.'

'But you were the one who felt left out on the doorstep?'

'I *was* left out on the doorstep! At night time sometimes. She just shut me out and wouldn't open the door.' She was surprised at the rage which raised her voice. 'She's a horror, my mother is. Of all the families to be born into. There are nice people out there – why did I have to get them?'

Dr Rose watched her in silence for a moment.

'What do you know about your mother? Her own life?'

'Not much. She hardly ever told us anything.' Evie tried to remember. 'She came to Birmingham from over in the Black Country. Netherton, I think. She never talked about family and we never met any – not once. I never met my grandmothers – not on either side.'

'Why do you think that might have been?'

'I don't know.' She looked at him. 'Maybe it was bad? *I* don't like telling people about bad things.'

Dr Rose nodded, twizzling his nice pen between his fingers. His question came out haltingly.

'Would you say that your mother ... is capable of sympathy ... fellow feeling towards others, I mean ... in general?'

Evie thought. She struggled, tried to be fair. This was her family after all. How good it would feel to be proud of her family, for there to be hope of being embraced and loved. She had come home with hopes of something new. But in the end she shook her head.

'No, doctor. I don't think I would.'

VI

Fifty-Four

November 1972

'She looks ever so pale. She all right, d'yer think?'

Evie was gripping one of the railings near the school gates, clenching its cold roughness so hard that her hands ached. Her breath came fast and shallow, as if she had been running.

'Are you all right?' The woman ventured closer, kind, but wary.

'Yeah,' Evie managed, keeping her voice under tight control. She didn't turn to look at the woman. 'Ta. I'm fine.'

'Right then. Just asking.' The woman returned to her friends, sounding affronted.

Evie didn't meet anyone's eye. She was afraid they would recognize her, even though she had seldom been to the school, and it had been such a time since she was there. They didn't seem to. Do I look different? She felt like another person altogether. Her hair was lank, had not been cut in months. She let it fall forward to hide her face. On the way here she had felt the rub of her thighs, thick and white, against each other as she moved, in bobbly grey slacks. They had given them to her because she had put on weight. All that time indoors. She did not feel like the person they might have remembered. So far there seemed to be no sign of Shirley.

461

Six months, *six months* since she had seen Tracy and Andrew. The full impact of this was only now coming home to her. She was appalled at herself. Six months was a big slice of Andrew's whole life. Would he even remember her? She had missed both of their birthdays. Tracy was eight now and Andrew six. All this had happened without her. She had deserted them, disappeared...

The hospital had been in touch with the school in Weoley Castle and established that Tracy and Andrew were living with their grandparents. The school had passed on the information that their mother was in hospital. Not once had any of the family set foot through the door of Rubery Hill Hospital to see her.

A baby was crying in a pushchair. Smoke whorled out from cigarettes. The voices swirled on behind her.

Clutching the railings until her hands hurt, the fragile flames of hope which she had carried from the hospital began to gutter and bend in the cold wind. She had kept each lit – each a phrase from Dr Rose or Sandy Hoskins or some of the other patients, like Mavis: 'Go and be a mother to your children, Evie...' Or Sandy: 'You can have a life, Evie – just like anyone else... Your kids will forgive you, bab – in the end, anyway. They know you've been poorly. They'll just be glad to see you back.'

Dr Rose, towards the end of her time in there, had taken off his glasses once more and swung them by one arm between his long finger and thumb.

'I wouldn't say this to many people – though

I'm sometimes tempted. But in your case, Evie, I will. I would advise you, very strongly, to keep away from your mother if at all possible – for the sake of your health. Some things are redeemable. From what you've said about her attitude to you, your relationship is one of the most destructive I have ever seen. Save yourself, Evie – and your children. I'm sure you can.'

She had come away full of this hope and support. Some of the others who were there when she first came into the hospital were now gone, but she said goodbye to the women on her ward, all of them wishing her well.

The first thing she would do would be to go and find Tracy and Andrew, tell them she was back, that she had been unwell but she was better now, that she had thought about them all the time, that they were going to go away – she had no idea where at this moment; they would leave Birmingham, start a new life...

For now, the hospital had given her the address of a hostel in Edgbaston where she could stay as she had told them she had no address in Birmingham. She could not face Mr and Mrs Grant after vanishing for six months. Not yet, anyway.

She walked out of the hospital carrying a plastic bag containing her few belongings. Nestled inside were the three little coloured mats she had made and some other small toys she had sewn in the OT room, little offerings of her thoughts of them in her absence. She had poured love into every stitch.

The wind gusted along the Bristol Road as she stood waiting for the bus. Evie felt raw and

463

exposed. Everyone must surely know she had just come out of *that place*. The warmth of her departure cooled, as if she had stepped naked from a bath. The fragile inner flames in her already felt the force of the cold wind.

Already she felt so alone...

And now, at last, the door of the school opened. Evie stood back, away from the railings, then wished she had not let go because her legs and hands were shaking so much. She gulped in a breath, praying that no one was looking at her.

The children were a colourful, jostling surge of movement across the playground's tarmac. Evie crossed her arms tightly, peering to make out the beloved features of her daughter, her little son. Tracy Rachel Harrison, she found herself reciting inwardly; Andrew Jack Harrison...

Voices rose all around her, mothers greeting children, shouts and laughter, a kid bawling about something.

Oh my God, Evie thought, what about Shirl? Is she here somewhere? She twisted round, peering out from under her hair. There was no sign of her. Angrily, she thought, why hasn't she come to pick them up?

There – was that her? Tracy! She saw hair the right colour, a girl, taller than she remembered – six months! – a ponytail swinging. The child looked thinner, as if she had been stretched. She was waiting by the door of the school. Yes, it was her! There was the blue anorak. Tracy looked quiet, responsible as ever. Evie's heart hammered. Oh, my girl, there she is! She knew Tracy was waiting for Ann and Andrew.

464

The mothers were gathering up their children, ticking them off, moving away with pushchairs with kids clinging to them.

Tracy turned and looked back into the school. Another group of children was coming out and then Evie saw Andrew. Shock went through her. He too was taller, his dark hair in need of a cut. But his once chubby child's face had shrunk thin and had grown longer. Tracy went to him to take his hand and he threw her off, but she insisted and he gave in.

Ann did not seem to be there. Maybe she was poorly, Evie thought sourly. So her sister did not bother to turn out for her two.

They were coming to the gate, with another bunch of children. Evie did not want to stand right in the gateway. She was too scared, wanted this meeting of her children to be private, for them to catch sight of her, for their faces to light up and them run to her – but all this without anyone else seeing. The moment was coming.

Another couple of children stopped right in the gateway, blocking it. One of them seemed to have forgotten something, was going back, the mother saying, 'Go on then, and don't be all night about it...' All this came to Evie from a distance. My kids, was all she could think. Oh, my lovely, beautiful children...

They were coming nearer. Clasping her hands fiercely together, she stepped forward, waiting for them to look up and see her. She was so close now, only a few feet away.

Tracy led Andrew out onto the pavement. She looked up for a second, in Evie's direction.

Tracy's face was serious, preoccupied. Her eyes moved over her mother but her mind seemed to make no connection. Andrew did not even look. Tracy turned away, taking Andrew to the kerb where they waited to cross the road.

Trace! The cry never made it out of her throat. She watched them hurrying together along the street, Tracy being the big sister, leading Andrew home from school as she had no doubt been doing every day, along to Alwold Road. Tracy who had looked straight at her mother and not recognized her.

Evie stood, unable to move or call out to them. She didn't see me. She didn't recognize me. It was like being dead. She felt the rejection like a blow, taking her breath. She turned away, so full of pain that all she could do was stand there with her face to the railings until all the other children had gone. The gates of the school stood silent except for the wind whipping through the railings in the darkening afternoon.

Fifty-Five

Afterwards she could not remember getting to the hostel. She found herself standing outside a tall row of dingy Edwardian houses. A few were in good repair, but mostly they were shabby, with cracked paintwork and grimy windows, some shrouded with nets, others staring at her like dark, hostile eyes.

The one she had been sent to stood alone, behind a low front wall and a couple of scrubby bushes. A wooden sign jutting from the wall announced 'Lincoln House Hotel'. It was very large and imposing looking, but wore a mantle of drab sadness.

Evie stood outside with her plastic bag in the cold dark, sick with nerves. There was one light on in a downstairs room behind pale curtains and she thought she saw the shadow of someone moving inside. It looked bleak and grim.

It looked exactly what she deserved.

The landlady was thin and scraggy, not old exactly, but goodness knew what age, dyed black hair scraped up into a coiled nest. Narrow, calculating eyes peered out from a face tan-coloured with powder. She was wearing pale green overalls over her clothes and men's slippers, pushed out by bunions.

'You come from the hospital?' she asked, looking Evie up and down in the dimly lit hall. She had a loud, grating Birmingham voice. 'They said you was on your way.' As Evie nodded, she stood back. 'You're at the top with Ethel. I'll show you in here first, though.'

Evie could see that it was one of those places where the feeblest light bulbs were used at all times. She was hit by a variety of smells, the most pungent of which was burnt toast, but with strong undertones of unwashed human bodies and lavatories. She started to feel even queasier. Who else was living in this place? She thought it was supposed to be a hotel.

'The lounge is here.' The lady pushed on the

door to her left, from where Evie must have seen the light coming outside. A strange sight met her. Through the blue-tinged air she saw four men in a row in upright chairs with wooden arms, side by side and rigidly straight against the wall to her right. Despite the fact that they were a variety of ages: one grey-haired and bearded, one solid with mucky ginger hair, two younger men, one skeletally thin with shaven hair, the other wearing a black and orange woolly hat – a Wolves supporter, Evie thought – they all looked somehow the same. They were not doing anything, but sat side by side staring in a dazed way across the room as if waiting for a bus. It was like being in the hospital again. A telly in the far corner was blasting out *Crossroads* but no one was taking any notice of it.

In the hearth squatted two other people, a man and a woman, both middle-aged and plump. As Evie and the landlady came in they jumped back from the gas fire, bits of scorched toast impaled on blunt-ended knives. Flabby slices of bread lay scattered on the floor.

'You'll set fire to the whole house if you go on like that,' their landlady shouted over the boom of the telly. It seemed to be more of a statement of resignation than an attempt to stop them.

'Sorry, Mrs T.,' the man said, giggling. He was round-faced with a pudding basin haircut. The woman, with long brown hair hanging round her face and rabbity front teeth, sat frozen as if in terror, a piece of toast dangling from the knife in her hand.

Mrs T. shut the door on them and led Evie up

two flights of stairs, both clad in a thin pretence of carpet, its colour impossible to guess.

'Here we are, Ethel, I've brought some company for you.'

By the light of another dim bulb with a meagre paper shade, Evie saw a room in which two black metal-frame beds, two chairs and two small wonky chests of drawers, both licked over unevenly with white paint, had been crammed in onto the bare floorboards.

Someone, who had been lying flat out on the bed to her right as they came in, sat up very slowly, like a statue coming to life. Evie saw a sagging figure with grey hair in tufts about her head looking up at her with alarmed eyes. The room smelt of sweat, but the bottom of the sash window was open a good two inches, cold air pouring in, so it was fresher than it might have been and perishing cold.

'Hello,' the woman called Ethel said.

Evie was reassured. She looked odd – though God knew, she had seen enough odd sights in the past six months for nothing to be all that alarming – but she sounded friendly enough. Most people she had met in the hospital were not mad exactly, just very sad, or shut in on themselves as she had been. Ethel was wearing some sort of dress in dark wool which rode up over thick white knees. Below she had on blue football socks with the tops turned over.

'You settle in then,' Mrs T. said. 'Dinner in fifteen minutes.'

Her scuffing tread disappeared and Evie put her bag on the bed. There was a pale green

469

candlewick bedcover. The bed sagged badly in the middle.

'Dinner! Huh! That's one word for it,' Ethel chuckled grimly. Her accent sounded as if she came from somewhere up north. 'Welcome to Hotel Invalidity Benefit.'

With this Ethel sagged back and lay on her side, supporting her head on one hand, reaching to tug at the hem of her dress, in an attempt to cover her knees. Evie sat on the bed and looked at her. Now she was taking Ethel in more closely, Evie saw that chunks of her hair were missing. She guessed Ethel was in her fifties, but she could have been any age from forty to sixty.

'Where've you just come out of then?' Ethel said it as if it was what you asked, not because she really wanted to know.

'Rubery Hill.' Evie didn't feel like talking. She wanted to sink down onto the bed and go over what had happened today, the school, that moment when... But Ethel was watching her. She made an effort. 'You don't sound as if you come from round here.'

'Me? Oh ... I don't. From Hull once upon a time. I've been in and out of those places since I was twenty. Thirty years this year. Rampton was the first.' She sounded almost proud. Seeing Evie's blank expression, she went on. 'That one's near Nottingham. Eight year in there. I've just come out of Whalley. Where next? I thought. They said to come down here. Everyone's going to Birmingham – there's these hotels.' She gave a mirthless grin. 'Meks it sound like a seaside holiday, eh? Got all the pills in a cupboard, she has, in the kitchen

– dishes them out like sweeties.' Another grim laugh. 'This is one of the better ones, I believe.'

She sat up with a groan and belched softly several times.

'Time for some of her muck to eat. Soup – that's all she ever does. Out of a packet. Thin as yoo-rine at that.' She pushed her feet into her shoes and shuffled to the door, the smell of body odour wafting from her.

Evie was glad to be left alone. She could not bear to hear any more. At that moment, thinking of Dr Rose's tired, kind eyes, his fatherly manner, she wanted to run back to the hospital and beg them to take her in again.

She didn't go down to eat anything. She wasn't hungry and she didn't want to see anyone else. Once Ethel had taken herself off in her baggy frock and clumping shoes, Evie crept down to the floor below and followed the smell to a big, old-fashioned lavatory at the end of the corridor. The stink was awful. On a string hung the last scraps of a roll of Izal lavatory paper.

She rinsed her hands in cold water and ran up to bed, climbing in on the screeching springs without undressing. Now she was alone, her mind played the day's agony over and over. Again and again she saw her two children in her mind, hurrying along the street away from her. They didn't know me. Their own mother. They don't need me anymore.

The tiny flames of hope she had been nursing inside her, carried from the hospital, all blew out in this one savage moment.

Her mind hurled thoughts at her, poisoned

arrows. Tracy and Andrew were living with Mom and with Rita and Shirley. They had told them terrible things about her. *Your mother's in the loony bin.* They would have turned Tracy and Andrew against her. And it served her right, didn't it? Hadn't she just deserted them – disappeared without a word of warning? What kind of mother was she? What were the poor kids to think? Six months was an eternity. How had she let this happen?

When Ethel came up again later, she pretended to be asleep, even though she was as far from sleep as it was possible to be. She had to grip the metal edges of the bed to stop herself jumping up and smashing her arm through the window, if only to feel some other pain than that which raged inside her. She thought about cuts and blood, the release of it. But she did not do it. She imagined going back to her kids swathed in bandages, like something in a horror film. No... No. Because she had to go back – somehow.

She heard Ethel wander over and stand looking down at her for a moment and she felt a prickle of alarm, but soon Ethel was thumping her way to the door to switch off the light and then to her own bed.

Evie turned onto her back and lay with her eyes open. There were no curtains, but the windows faced over the back, so that very little light reached the room from the dark winter night. Once or twice a gust of wind laden with rain buffeted the window.

After a time, she heard Ethel say, 'You awake?' She didn't answer.

All night she lay with her heart thudding, her blood hammering through her. What was she doing, here in this horrible place, when she had dreamt that tonight she would be with her children? And over and again came the memory of Tracy's face looking through her, seeming to have no idea who she was...

She couldn't go back there. Not yet. She had to get better, had to find a place for them before she went and tried to see them. She must get a job. She could not go back to Kalamazoo, could she? That seemed like another life now. All she had left of it were the few things in her bag – her work skirt, blouse, shoes which she had been wearing that day. Her purse with a couple of quid.

She needed a place to go. She couldn't stay here. It was worse than the hospital, this 'hotel' packing in the sick and desperate. She thought about Ethel, lying there across the room. If she tapped Ethel, a great gout of suffering would come out – a life in and out of asylums, cruelty, punishment, imprisonment. She had heard it from other older women in the hospital and she could not face it again.

That's going to be me, she thought. If I stay here. In and out of the loony bin forever. No. Please God, *help me*.

Where could she go? The only person she could think of, because she had given her her address, was Melly Booker. For a moment, she longed to see Melly's friendly face. She might see her mom, the rest of the crowd from the old end in Aston. But no. Her mind shied away from that. How could she turn up like this? Shame washed through her. They had been nice but they had always been people to look up to, who were a proper family. Better than her and better than her shameful mom. But she didn't deserve them – not proper people like that, leading proper lives.

As the first hint of light began to seep through the windows, she eased herself out of bed, clenching her teeth in her desperation to be quiet. All she had to do was to pick up her bag, her anorak and shoes and feel her way out to the staircase... The upper stairs squeaked as she placed each of her feet at the far end of every tread. The second staircase was easier. She leaned on the greasy banister and half stepped, half slid to the bottom, expecting to hear Mrs T. – she didn't even know the woman's proper name – shout at any moment, in her grating voice.

She fumbled along the hall, and in the end found a light switch near the front door. There were bolts, a key to turn. Nothing to worry about. She was not trapped. Seconds later she was closing the door behind her and walking out onto the dark street, to find the only person she deserved or could dare to turn to – someone who had always been like her.

Fifty-Six

She walked through the gloom of the Dudley Road. It felt strange and nerve-wracking still, being out of the hospital, but at least there were not many people about. The half-darkness felt like a place to hide. After a while it dawned on her that the buses were running and she climbed on one into town and then another out along the Bristol Road. She got off near the railway station in Selly Oak.

The air was damp, though it was not actually raining. She turned off along the Dingle, a little path running down to the cut. Once on the canal bank it was darker, away from the street lights. A mist hung over the water, blurring everything in the seeping morning light. She pulled the zip of her thin coat up to the top and hugged her bag to her. Both the oily stink of the water and the shadowy path frightened her. Who knew what might be lurking down here? But apart from a dog barking somewhere and the early morning trains, it was quiet. And it would soon be properly light.

Pearl, Gary had said. There were hardly any boats down here in any case. The cut seemed deserted. She walked for what seemed ages without seeing anyone and a cold sense of hopelessness came over her. It was months since she had met Gary. He said they were at Selly Oak somewhere but he might have moved on weeks ago. She passed a couple of joey boats with no cabins, filthy with coal dust and half full of rubbish.

The sun was burning off the mist. The rain of the night before had blown away and it was turning into a fair day with only a haze of cloud. She started to feel the sun's warmth on her cheeks. The water in the cut was low, black and filthy with scum and bits floating in it, but the sunlight made even that look more cheerful.

She reached Cadbury's, the grand-looking factory on her right, and stopped. The sun was higher. She seemed to have been walking for ages, though she realized she must have come a couple of miles. She was starting to feel really hungry, but now she had come this far, she couldn't think of anything else to do except keep walking.

A few minutes later, in the distance, she made out the dark front end of a boat and a bulky-looking figure standing on the bank beside it. Walking on, she could make him out better – and she knew him. Although he was grown-up now he had not changed – this big bear-like man who was also a child, who had always looked the same. He wore a parka and was flapping his arms back and forth across his body to get warm, clouds of steam unfurling from his lips. Evie couldn't help smiling at the sight of him. Little Carly. And if Carl was there, Gary must be there too.

As she drew closer she saw someone else climb up out of the boat, but it wasn't Gary. A dog appeared on the tow path as well, a black, solid thing with pointed ears. Gary appeared a moment later, and she heard them talking, Gary raising his hand, 'T'ra then!' and the other man setting off towards her. The dog, seeming excited, tried to follow and Gary shouted, 'Oi! Rocket!' The dog turned back immediately, as if jerked by a string.

As the man walked past her, Evie saw a solid-looking bloke with a nice face, except for a wonky nose that must have once been broken, hands pushed down into the pockets of a black over-coat. He gave her a nod as he passed.

Gary and Carl weren't paying any attention to her coming along the path. They had both lit up cigarettes and were puffing away to the morning, looking out over the water. Gary had a red mug in his other hand. But the dog began to bark shrilly and started running towards her. The two men turned and stared.

Trying to keep her voice steady, she said, 'Gary?'

They were pleased to see her, pleased as pup-pies. Carl, a grin all over his big face, came up and flung his arms round her. 'Evie!' he said, half swamping her. Then she was caught in Gary's arms, shocked by how bony he was, how much he stank.

'Said I'd come, didn't I?' she said, trying to sound cheerful. 'Just took me a while, that's all.'

'I dain't think you were coming,' he said. 'I mean, when I saw yer... It were months ago now, weren't it?'

She noticed even more than before how haltingly he spoke. In her mind she had turned him back into the old Gary, the nippy lad of the Ladywood lanes and entries, the Gary of her childhood. Now, he seemed stranger than she remembered. Close up, Gary's face – his thirty-year-old-man face, surrounded by tousled, muddy-coloured hair, was lined and prematurely aged. His grin was as gappy as she remembered. His specs were now held on by a wonky combination of sellotape and a bit of elastic round the back of his head.

The dog was trying to jump at her and Carl grabbed it, a grin all across his face. 'No, Rocket, there's a good girl. Stay down.' Unlike Gary, he still seemed to have all his front teeth.

'I've been a bit...' Evie said. She stumbled, not knowing what to say.

'D'you like our butty boat then?' Gary nodded at it. It was a working narrowboat – or had been – with a small cabin and a long cargo area at the front, covered by a rotten-looking tarpaulin. On the side of the cabin, in paint so bleached and cracked it was all chipping off, she read, 'Fellows, Moreton & Clayton'. And below, *'Pearl'*.

'I know 'er's a bit of a wreck. I got 'er for a song,' he said. 'Well, it was Carl bought her, really.' He patted the cabin fondly. Evie wondered if he had been drinking, his speech was so slurred. She couldn't smell anything on his breath except rotten teeth. But she had a fearful sense that something was very wrong. She was surprised that Carl seemed to be the one earning the money. But what could she say? 'But she's our home, ain't 'er, Carl?'

'You always liked to have your own little place, didn't you, Gary?' Evie said. She thought of him in the old air-raid shelter, the safe nests he used to create for himself.

'Wanna cuppa tea now you're here?' he asked, seeming eager to give hospitality. 'Kettle's hot.' He stepped onto the boat.

'Oh yes,' Evie said. Her stomach ached with emptiness. She would gradually have to break it to Gary that she needed more of him than just a cup of tea.

'I can cut yer a piece an' all if yer like?' he offered, poking his head out of the cabin.

'Thanks,' she said. Her eyes filled with tears suddenly and she saw Carl watching her.

'Don't cry, Evie,' he said. He came to her, in his parka, the ragged ends of a grey jumper poking out of the sleeves, and wrapped his arms round her. That was the undoing of her. She broke down and sobbed, her head pressed against Carl's chest.

'But I can't live here – there's no room,' she said, half laughing as she looked round. The three of them were squeezed into the boat's cabin, the stove filling the place with warmth. But it was so small, with the tiny flap table pulled down, crowded with mugs, the remains of a packet of sugar, a milk bottle, a half-sawn-up loaf of bread. What with that and the stove, there was barely room to move. The place had not been decorated inside for many years. It was full of peeling paint and the floor was black with coal dust and dirt. She could already feel a desire to sweep and clean.

'Yeah, there is,' Gary said. 'Course there is.' He hesitated, as if having doubts, and glanced at Carl. 'For a bit, any road.' She watched him. What was up with him? He seemed aged and odd. Odder. Slowed down. But he smiled at her then, his old, crinkly smile. 'Carl and me can take turns – kip down on the floor. You can sleep here.' He patted the bench he was sitting on beside the wall. 'Whole families've lived in these – we'll manage!'

Evie thought, he wants a woman here – someone to look after them, to cook and clean. And because she was trying not to face things, wanted time, she was tempted to agree to it.

'Well, it's nice of you,' she said, even though this was why she had come, hoping. 'Just for a bit – 'til I get back on my feet?'

Gary took a sip of his tea and looked closely at her. 'What's up, Evie? What's happened to yer, eh?'

There was no point in hiding anything. She told the two of them, short and bitter, what had happened to her. Jack, Canada, Mom, the kids, the hospital.

Gary sat back and blew out through his lips. 'Blimey, Eves, that's ... that's bad, that is.' He shook his head, took a drag on his cigarette. His eyes rolled up into his head for a moment, disconcerting her. Then he was back with them. 'But you're going back to get yer kids, ain't yer?'

'I...'

'I mean...' Gary surged on with sudden force. 'If our mom, God rest her, had gone off ... instead of passing away like she did...' He stopped to cough, his chest rattling. 'I'd've done anything to see her and get her back. We would've – wouldn't we, Carl? We'd've gone to the ends of the earth.'

Seeing Carl nodding earnestly, Evie welled up again. Gary's words tore at her inside.

'I will... I want to – course I do. I just ... don't know if they want me...' Tears wet her cheeks and dropped into her mug of sugary, tan-coloured tea.

'Course they do,' Gary said. His sweetness made her cry all the more. 'All kids want their mom, don't they?'

'I just need to get myself together...' she sobbed.

'Eh, it's all right, wench.' Gary put his arm round her. She smelt a gust of his breath, the smell of rotten teeth and something else, an odd chemical smell. 'Course you can stay. We're mates, old mates, eh? Stay as long as you want.'

Fifty-Seven

To Evie's astonishment, Carl produced a pack of bacon out of a cupboard.

'Want a butty, Evie?'

'Ooh, yeah! I didn't think you'd have anything like that!' She had not expected any sort of organization here with these two; she had imagined she would have to do it all.

She realized she was ravenously hungry. The sun was higher now, brightening everything, and with that and the thought of breakfast, her spirits lifted. It was Gary who plonked a battered frying pan onto the stove. The dog lay beside him, attentive to the possibility of food.

'Gotta eat. Carl buys stuff on his way home – he's outside all day. Got to keep him going.'

Evie watched, surprised. She had assumed that Gary's care of Carl was a one-way street, but Carl was the one who was off to work. Soon the delicious smell of frying bacon filled the cabin.

She tried asking Carl a bit about his job, but did not get much out of him other than, 'Yeah, s'all right.' He ate two enormous sandwiches, bacon wadged between doorsteps of bread, drank another pint of tea and lumbered away to get the bus to his job at Longbridge.

'T'ra, Evie,' he said in his sweet way as he set off. 'See you later.'

Evie ate her butty, squeezed into the cabin with Gary. The bacon was crisp and fresh. Gary passed her the bottle of ketchup.

'God, Gary, this is the best thing I've tasted in ages.' Already she was feeling better.

Gary smiled, mouth too full to answer. The dog lay at their feet whimpering now and then to remind them not to forget her. Gary threw her scraps of gristle and bread.

She looked across at him. 'How long've you been living down here then?'

'Oh, you know...' His eyes wandered. He seemed distracted; he drifted, then returned to the conversation. 'A while. Since ... you know...' He trailed off.

'I ran into Ron.' Gary looked blank. 'You know, *Ron,* your brother. I'd just got back from Canada and I went to the old end. My God, I couldn't tell if I was coming or going – there's hardly anything left! Anyway, Ron was along there. Said he didn't know where you were.'

Gary shrugged. 'Carl sees Paul and Ron.'

She was about to ask after all the Knight brothers, but Gary didn't seem very keen to talk about them.

'I could help you clean up,' she said, full of sudden energy after the food and sweet tea. 'You could do with a woman's touch in here, Gary. It's a bit of a mess.'

Again, a shrug as he rolled a cigarette. His hands shook. They were rough and gnarled, the fingernails filthy.

'You not working then?'

'Me? Oh ... yeah,' he said. 'Off and on. The buildings – factories, sometimes. I don't like being stuck inside, though. Not after...'

'After what?'

Gary didn't answer. 'We get by,' he said. He seemed restless. With an upward jerk of his head he said sharply, 'I'm not a druggie, yer know.'

'I never said you were.' She had thought it, though, wondered what could have made him look such a wreck.

Lighting the cigarette, Gary nodded towards the steps. 'Let's go up, eh?'

It was a still, perfect winter morning, the murky ripples silvered by the sunlight. Though it was chilly, it felt good to be out. The cut, no longer the thoroughfare it had once been, was quiet and the towpath saw very few passers-by during the morning, except a couple of people with dogs and a middle-aged bloke in a shabby parka who wandered past, then back, as if looking for something, before disappearing.

For a few hours it was idyllic. Evie relished the feeling of being free, being back with her old friend, as if two ragged ends in her life had rejoined. It was like a dream world, away from everything. All she wanted was to stay here, fold her problems away. Just for a while.

They perched on the edge of the roof, shoulder to shoulder, and finished their mugs of tea. She looked at Gary's skinny legs drawn up onto the roof beside her in his ragged black trousers. She thought of the two of them, crouched in the shelter together, hearing the comforting little noises of Mr Waring's hens. She was warmed by the familiarity of him after all this time. She could smell him even out here – long-unwashed clothes, his breath, now laden with fag smoke. But then he always did stink as a kid, she thought. Poor little sod. And she'd not been much better herself.

She half wanted to talk about all of it – the past, Pete Rylance's death and how Gary had been afterwards. She wanted to say sorry for not sticking around. *Julie*... That's where she had been, while he was lost in his grief – sucked down into her own. Gary knew none of that and she said nothing. She had told Dr Rose, but she couldn't bring herself to talk about it now. Not that.

Behind them on the cabin roof was an old metal bucket, some logs, scraps of this and that, rough bits of wood and rags. At the far end nearest the hold, a rusty bike clung on somehow, half over the edge. In the bright light, the derelict state of *Pearl* was much clearer to see. The painted wood of the cabin was so cracked and dry that it looked as if you could just pull it apart. It seemed amazing that she was still afloat. The tarpaulin covering the hold was torn in places.

'What you got in there then, Gary?' she asked.

'Oh, nothing much,' he said. He twisted his neck, seeming edgy. 'This and that. Just junk.'

She could believe it. She flung the tea dregs into the cut and got up, suddenly full of energy. 'How about we clean up a bit then, if I'm going to stay here?' She frowned. 'Where d'you get your water from?'

Gary eyed the cut.

'I mean for drinking, you prat.'

'Oh, a way away. Carl'll get some later. There's a garage lets us fill up. There's still a bit left inside – in the blue container.'

'You could pull me up a bucketful for cleaning. It hasn't got a hole in, I hope? And've you got anything I can use – cloths?' Even as she asked, she could see this would be hopeless. She straightened up. 'D'you ever have a bath or anything?'

'Nah.' He shrugged and nodded towards the front of the boat. 'I can find yer an old rag.'

Evie grinned. She was desperate to be busy suddenly, to be in this lovely morning – just for a while – doing anything except think about what she, in her own life, had to do next.

With buckets of water from the cut and the old rag Gary had presented her with – the remains of an old shirt minus the sleeves – she did the best she could, sloshing water around in the cabin and wiping it down. It made her feel better even if it did not look very much cleaner than before she started. That would take a miracle. Oh well, one thing at a time. While she was working, Gary went off somewhere, the dog following him. It shadowed him everywhere. Later he came back with more bread, some margarine and a packet of sausages. He seemed very on edge.

485

'You didn't go in there, did yer?' he asked tetchily, looking towards the hold. 'You dain't touch anything?'

'No. I've had my work cut out back here without starting on that. Why? What you got in there?'

'Oh ... just junk. Here, bought you this,' he said, standing on the bank, holding up to her a bottle of the cheapest washing-up liquid.

'Oh, ta.' She was warm and sweaty from her exertions, even if they did feel a bit hopeless. 'Well, that's something. You didn't think to get any cloths or anything?'

Gary's eyes wandered. She looked down at him. What a pathetic figure he looked, bone thin in his sagging clothes, the elastic holding his glasses on pushing up his hair at the back. She felt a mixture of tenderness and impatience. However bad a state Gary used to be in, she remembered him being quicker off the mark than now. He seemed slurred, like someone trying to move with the brakes on. It reminded her of the way the women were after ECT, the shocks which, thank God, Dr Rose did not want to give to her.

'Well, I s'pose the soap's better than nothing. I've got some money. I'll give you a bit – for my keep.'

Later they ate bread and marg and a couple of sausages, poured water from the blue plastic container to boil for more tea, and sat out once more. It felt a happy thing, just thinking about nothing but the present – like being on holiday. She cut her mind loose from everything else. Just one more day and then she would face everything again... She still felt very strange being outside,

486

free from walls, from always being watched. She said so to Gary.

'I know,' he said, chewing. 'I still feel like that, after being in...' He jerked his head in a vague way.

'What d'you mean?'

'You know...' Another jerk of the head.

'The hospital?'

'Nah, the Green.' He swallowed. 'Her Majesty's cowing Pleasure.'

'Oh Gary! When? What for?'

He looked as if he wasn't going to say anything, and took refuge in his roll-ups, the slow ritual with his unsteady fingers. It took him so long that she almost offered to do it for him.

'I was nicked in the bogs, in town – over by the markets. Years back now. Been in twice.'

She stared at him. It took a minute to make sense of what he was saying.

She knew about him really – course she did. That he had never wanted her, or any other girl. He had wanted Peter Rylance, had been felled by grief when Peter died. But she had never said it to herself before, head on, in all these years. Homosexual. Queer. She had known and not known all at once. Only then she wondered about the man who had been leaving the boat when she first arrived.

'Oh Gary.'

He shook his head. 'I was more worried about Carl than anything while I was in. I couldn't pay the fines, see.'

'Is that when you came down here?'

'Well, in the end – I ain't been here that long. I was living in town. She's his really, see.' He patted the rotten wood of the boat. 'He was the one earning. And he wanted me to come with him. And being in a house sets me off. I like it out here.' He looked round at her, asking with a shamed expression, 'You got any ... you know ... stuff from the hospital? Pills, like?'

'No,' she lied. She was coming off them, she vowed. They slowed her right down. But she certainly wasn't going to give them to Gary. 'Any road, you said you never did anything?'

Gary nodded, as if to say he knew she was holding back from him. 'Well, not the hard stuff.' He flashed her his grin. 'Right cowing pair, ain't we?'

She looked out across the water. There were a few reeds, with some load of muck caught up in them – a tangle of filthy twine and litter. A moorhen paddled sadly round it.

'I hope there's another life after this one,' she said, eyes on the lone bird. 'I want everything different – different family, different mom. I want to know what it's like ... for things to be nice.'

For a moment Gary flung his arm round her shoulder and squeezed her. 'You're all right, wench. Whatever yer cowing family's like.'

Tears rose in her eyes. 'Not much of a mom, I'm not, Gary. Not now. Don't s'pose they remember who I am hardly.'

Gary released her and looked at her seriously. 'You don't want to stay here, Eves – take my word for it. It's nice to see yer, but you know, we're no good for yer. You need your kids. And ... thing is...' He looked away, suddenly shifty. 'I got a few things going on here.'

'What d'you mean?'

He didn't look at her. 'You're too good for us, Eves – you always was. Like a little princess, you are. You don't wanna be down 'ere. Just stay tonight and then you'd best be moving on, all right?'

She was startled, wounded. He'd been so welcoming at the start. She sensed that he was disconnected, could not remember what he'd said before.

Gary jumped down from the roof to the path. 'Oo, me knees,' he groaned as his feet hit the ground, his face creasing with pain. Then he frowned. 'Look, you don't want to stay here.' He stared up at her for a moment, but didn't say any more.

Fifty-Eight

She spent that night cramped on the bench bed in the tiny cabin, her coat over her, clothes folded under her head. Gary laid sheets of newspaper over her as well. It started off warm because of the stove, but by morning she was rigid with cold and stiff all over.

Carl, who managed to fold his body onto the cabin floor with a wad of newspapers under his head and others covering his body, seemed fresh and unconcerned when he got up. Carl was a confusing mixture of responsible and childlike. He had arrived back from work the night before carrying a bag of groceries and they had cooked up beans and eggs. He had remembered milk and more tea and some tins of soup. He had also gone off with the two blue containers and come back with fresh water.

This morning the weather had turned drizzly and Evie's spirits sank lower than they had been since she arrived.

Gary seemed dull and lifeless as well. They had spent the evening chatting about the old days and he had felt something like her friend, but now he was locked into a mood she could not enter or understand. He disappeared for a while, in his donkey jacket and woolly hat, not saying where he was going. She knew now that there were things he was keeping from her, that he wanted her gone.

Curious, she climbed out, shoulders hunched against the wet, and went to the hold of the boat, pulling back a corner of the tarpaulin. She wasn't sure what she expected to see, but all that was there were some more bits of junk and a mucky old mattress laid in the bottom. Somehow irritated, she let the tarpaulin drop and went back inside. So what the hell was the big secret? She just thought Gary was trying to make himself sound important, as though he was big business.

Inside again, she sat on the narrow bench, pulling her knees up, hugging them to her chest. She sat there for she didn't know how long, blanked out, keeping memories pushed away. Julie, Tracy, Andrew... Mustn't think, not about how bad I am, a bad mom, a bad wife, a bad person...

She had to move in the end because it was so uncomfortable.

I've got to get myself together, she thought, as the morning dribbled by and she had done nothing except look out at the rain falling into the cut. The glamour of the boat was quickly wearing off. But the effort she would need felt almost beyond her. How could she go out and get a job, or do anything, if she couldn't even have a wash?

Eventually she saw Gary coming back through the wet, hunched up, carrying a plastic water carrier in each hand – both white this time, not the blue ones. He must have decided to get the water instead of Carl doing it, she thought. She heard some thumping noises as he moved about in the hold of the boat. Then he appeared with a smaller plastic container and set the kettle on to boil. Evie felt impatience rising in her. All this, just to make a cup of tea! Her impatience drove her. What the hell was she doing sitting in this dump? She had to get her kids back.

'I'm going to the baths,' she told him. 'And then I'm going to look for a job.'

'All right,' he said. He looked down. 'Eves?'

'What?'

'Thing is ... I've got some mates coming round tonight. Later, like.'

She felt annoyance rise in her. Mates? Where was Gary going to fit them in? And where was she supposed to go? Why the hell had he said she could stay there?

She shrugged huffily. 'It's your boat.'

'We'll keep out yer way – in the front.'

'What – the hold? You'll freeze?'

'Nah, we'll just have a few drinks like. Got a mate who makes the stuff for us.' He grinned, showing his terrible, gappy teeth. 'Keeps yer warm, that stuff does.'

'All right then.' She knew she had to leave. This was like a cold shower, waking her up. She knew she should be grateful, that she needed to be pushed out and sent on her way. 'Look, take this.' She still owed Mrs Grant rent money which she had in her purse. She handed Gary a couple of pounds for food. 'I'm going to look for a job.'

She set off, tramping all the way back into Selly Oak with her bag of clothes. It was even further than she remembered. There were baths, in Tiverton Road. On the way she went into a chemist and bought a comb and some soap and she paid to go and wash. She rinsed out the undies she was wearing, which had been given to her by the hospital, and put on the spare ones from the bag which were actually hers. After this she did feel marginally better.

But dressing in her work clothes after all this time felt very strange and frightening. They meant responsibility, having to find the strength to get out and get something done. She wasn't sure she could. The clothes felt as if they belonged to someone else. Her skirt was tight on her and the black court shoes felt narrow and cramping after months of slopping about in slippers and old plimsolls. She dressed very slowly. Looking in the mirror, she saw her round, white, pimply face looking back at her.

God, I look terrible, she thought. For the first time she saw why Tracy had not recognized her. Her hair was hanging long and limp. She looked fat, pale, sad... Just not how she had been before. Maybe that was all. She had seen it as a darker, awful rejection. But perhaps her daughter had simply not recognized her.

Right, she thought. Wandering the shops in Bournbrook, she found a hairdresser's and came out after a good trim, feeling already better, and hanging on to her thread of hope.

She caught a bus along the road to Northfield on a wave of optimism. Maybe she should try and get her old job back after all. She at least knew people there. She could find somewhere to live – somewhere well away from Mom. And then they could all go back to normal...

'I'm so sorry, Evie,' Maureen at Kalamazoo told her. She spoke to Evie kindly but with an air of caution. They must know where she'd been. Alan had known. Despite the haircut and the way she was holding on tight to herself inside, she felt as if she was walking about with 'Mental Patient' tattooed across her forehead. And as soon as Maureen started speaking her hope quickly disappeared.

'I don't have a free position at the moment. I had to give your job to someone else – we didn't know when you were coming back, you see.' Evie did see, but still it felt like a personal rejection. She had got the job so easily before.

'It's not that we don't want you back. Look, give me your address – a phone number? I'll let you know as soon as there's a vacancy.'

'I can't,' Evie said. 'I don't... I mean, I'm moving and I don't know where I'm going to be yet.'

'I see.' Maureen looked even warier, but forced a smile. 'Well, look, love ... pop in again in a while, all right? And we'll see where we are then.

Or if you want a reference...'

She didn't specify what 'a while' meant. A reference. It felt as if they wanted rid of her.

She told herself that it was completely reasonable to find that her old job had been taken, but she was cast right down. Even though it was not the reason Maureen had given her, it felt as if every door was closed to her because she had been in that hospital. The life she had had before seemed shut away from her. Gone forever.

It felt terrible walking out of the offices at what was now almost the end of the working day. She wished to God she had never come back or felt that bright streak of hope.

'Evie? Is that you?' Feet hurried behind her and her heart seemed to buck with dread. She recognized his voice. The kindly man who had written to her in hospital.

Turning, she saw him, and was surprised in that moment by how familiar he seemed after all. Nice, reassuring Alan Dickson. She smiled faintly. Inside she felt lost, empty.

'It's nice to see you,' he said. She could hear genuine pleasure through the shyness. He was not the sort to pretend and she liked him for that.

She could not think of anything to say.

'So ... are you coming back to work?' he said. He put his hands in the pockets of his brown suit jacket as if he was not sure what else to do with them. He must have just had a haircut as the mousey hair was shaved close at the sides of his neck. 'I mean ... you're feeling better?'

'I'm all right,' she said. Her voice seemed to lack force. She wondered if he could even hear it.

'But they don't have a place for me at the moment.'

'What?' he said. 'Well, that's bad, that is. That's a shame.' He seemed really put out on her behalf. Maybe on his own as well. 'I'm sure they will soon. Where will you go?'

Evie shrugged. 'I'll try somewhere else,' she said, with no idea. 'In town maybe.'

'I...' He blushed then. His hands scrabbled in his pockets. 'I hope you didn't mind me writing ... when you were ... you know. I'd like to keep in touch – be friends, like... D'you... I mean, where are you living? Would you let me have your address?'

'I haven't got one,' she said. 'Not yet.'

He looked frankly into her eyes then. 'I don't want you to think I'm trying to push anything, Evie. Only, I really like you – care about you, see? That's all. I'd hate not ever to see you again.'

She wanted to be touched, grateful. In a distant way she was, but she could not seem to summon emotion.

'Thanks.' She tried to smile again. 'Only I really don't have an address.'

'Look, you know I work here.' He was patting all his pockets now, brought out a bus ticket, a biro. 'Here's my address. And phone.' He wrote hastily and handed her the ticket. 'If you ever fancy a drink ... a bit of company...'

He was so genuine, seemed to care so much about her, that she hardly knew what to say.

'Thanks.' She tucked the ticket in her coat pocket. 'Thanks, Alan.'

It wasn't until she was on the bus on the way back to Selly Oak that she realized there must be places where she could get down onto the cut much nearer to where *Pearl* was tied up. But she didn't know where they were. She was in no rush to get back there. She had a seat in the fuggy warmth of the bus and she sat back as they swept along the Bristol Road, looking out of the window, trying to fight the despair which rose in her like floodwater.

If Kalamazoo wouldn't take her back, it meant that no one would. She would never get a job. And she didn't deserve to get a job. People had seen through her, through her good looks, her trying so hard to please and do well. They could see what she was really like – rotten inside. Alan Dickson didn't seem to see it. She remembered his gentle kindness. But what good would I ever be to him now? she thought. To a nice man like him. He's got no idea what I'm really like. She felt like a person who was contaminated, poisoning everything she touched.

And so the wheel turned, down and down.

By the time she got off the bus, near Oak Tree Lane, the late afternoon was full of steel-grey gloom. She crossed over, towards the Dingle and the dank towpath. It was quiet. A bike passed her, but no one else. She was glad to be out of sight of other people, as if even the eyes of strangers were boring into her, seeing her badness. She felt injured, as if she might crack apart. Maybe she should start taking the pills again.

She had to find something, to get away from here. She knew Gary was hiding things from her, that he had only shown her a small part of his life.

A couple of trains passed not far away. As she drew closer to Cadbury's she heard the distant sound of a dog. It was letting out long, anguished howls which seemed to express how she felt herself.

It took her until she had almost reached *Pearl* to realize it was Gary's dog, Rocket. As Evie drew near, she could see the animal's low, solid outline on the bank next to the boat, her head back, howling to the sky.

What's up with her? Evie thought. Maybe Gary's forgotten to feed her. She was not too worried. Not until she saw Carl emerge from the front end of the boat. He jumped down to the bank and in that moment glimpsed her coming towards him.

'Evie!' He started to run, lumbering towards her, but not just running. His body flailed about in some desperate state. 'Evie, quick! C'm'ere! Gary won't wake up! There's summat...' He was sobbing as he reached her and seized her arm, yanking at her. 'C'mon!'

'All right, all right, Carly, calm down!' She reached for his hand but he was in too much of a state to be quieted. 'I'm coming. What's happened?'

Like a crazed bear, Carl hauled her along, not to the cabin but to the front part of the boat. He lifted the loose flap of the tarp by the cabin and, through his sobs, yelled, 'Gary! Gary! Evie's here. You got to wake up!'

In the dark of the hold Evie could make out the edges of the mattress and, nearby, ghostly white shapes – the plastic water carriers which Gary had brought back. On the mattress she could see a long, dark shape. Evie felt her heartbeat harden to a doomy thump.

'Gary?' There was no response. 'Come on, Carl, we've got to get in.'

They clambered over the side. Once under the tarpaulin, she was hit by it – a horrible pungent stink that made her wrinkle her nose.

'Gary?' Kneeling on the old mattress, she could tell as soon as she touched him, nudged him, that he was deeply unconscious. 'Oh God, Gary, what've you done?'

The sound of the dog howling and Carl sobbing behind her made her take command.

'Carl. You've got to get help. You run back – go the garage or wherever it is you get the water and get them to ring an ambulance. All right? Tell them we're on the cut and they've got to ring 999.'

She heard his mewling breaths as he hurried away. The dog stayed behind, still howling.

'Gary!' She spoke sharply now. Being alone with him felt frightening. 'Come on, you've got to wake up! What the hell've you been drinking?'

She shook and shook him, screamed at him.

But there was no response.

Fifty-Nine

She knew Gary was gone. She had not done anything like check his pulse or listen for his heart. But as she waited with him in the boat, with Rocket yowling in the dusk outside, as she rubbed his hands, his chest, wept over him, begging him to say something, just please, for God's sake, wake up and say something, she knew he had already left them. The dog knew it and she felt it too.

'Whatever he's been drinking...' the doctor said, his anger unmistakeable. He had drawn them to one side in the busy Casualty department, a few feet from Gary's prone body covered now by a sheet. 'Whoever made it should be prosecuted. Must be anti-freeze or some such. We're doing blood tests. This is manslaughter – if not worse. I'm calling in the police. I need you to stay here.'

He eyed Carl doubtfully. His body was jerking with sobs.

'Just give us a minute,' Evie said. 'He's not quite ... you know... I'll talk to him, calm him down.'

'What is it, Carl?' They stood out in the outer corridor, having calmed him enough to have a fierce, whispered conversation. 'What is the stuff? Who did he get it from?'

Carl's eyes were puffy and now stretched with fear. He couldn't keep still, kept beating his arms about as if warding off swarming insects.

''E got stuff from his mate – Wally. 'E makes it – sells it to people, like ... to 'is mates. Wally don't mean no harm. 'E's all right, Wally is.'

'Well, he may be,' Evie said. The doctor's expression had set light to a rage inside her. 'But whatever the hell he's put in that stuff he's brewing, he's killed your brother. What about whoever else drinks the stuff, Carl? You've got to tell them where he is.'

Carl's face stretched as if the thoughts he was

having were putting pressure on his whole head.

'Oh!' he moaned. He took his head in his hands and bent over. 'I can't... Oh, I dunno... Dunno what to do...'

She grabbed his arm, her body taut with the need to lash out and hurt someone, anyone, as an outlet for her own feelings.

'Sodding well tell them where this prat Wally lives – that's what you have to do, Carl! For God's sake, he's killed your brother with his ... hooch concoction or bloody anti-freeze or whatever it was in there! D'you understand, Carl?' She was up close to him, gripping his upper arms, shaking him. 'Gary's dead, thanks to him! He's not all right – he's a *murderer!'*

Carl began trembling and sobbing again so much that she relented and took a step back. It was no good, she could see. And she didn't want any of this – none of it. She needed to get away, to find her kids... For the moment, no one was around.

'Look,' she hissed to Carl, eyeing the long corridor which reached to the back doors of the hospital. 'We're just going to go, all right. Take my hand, Carly.' He was nodding, still sobbing. 'When I say run, you run, fast as you can, and we'll go home.'

She heard a door open somewhere and her heart lurched.

'Quick!' She hauled on his arm. 'Run!'

It was only when they were away, after hurtling along Oak Tree Lane and round onto the road towards the Dingle, that they slowed and she realized how much she was shaking.

They walked holding hands, both of them crying. It was a cold, clear night, a three-quarter moon reflecting in the black water. They heard Rocket, who they had had to lock in the cabin, howling from along the riverbank. The sound made both of them sob harder.

It felt terrible climbing down into the cold, damp-smelling cabin of *Pearl*. Evie lit the tilly lamp and the shadows flickered round them. They were full of Gary – his few possessions, the atmosphere of him, his whimpering dog. Carl got the stove going and she put water on for tea as the place gradually warmed up. Even in her shocked state, Carl's knowing so surely what to do surprised her.

Neither of them thought of eating. She sat by the warming kettle while Carl took Rocket outside, trying to keep warm, and worrying. They had just run off – would the police be looking for them right this minute? Chasing them? They should have stayed, she knew. This dangerous idiot, Wally, what he had done? Her breath steadied. The ambulance men knew where they had come from. Would they send somebody after them? For a moment she felt frightened. But then, she told herself, it was not her fault, none of it. It was not as if she knew where Wally lived and she didn't think Carl did either. That's all they would be able to say anyway.

She could hear Carl outside, talking to the dog through his tears. His voice reminded her of Gary. Her mind started flashing memories – almost all of them sad ones. Gary and Carl as kids, ragged, grubby, uncared for. Gary and Pete – Gary's wild happiness, his plunge into grief when Pete was found dead. Meeting him on the Bristol Road – the wrecked look of him, sweet still in the way of a boy who could barely look after himself but was always trying to look out for Carl.

'Poor little bugger,' she muttered. 'You didn't stand a chance, mate.'

She wept again, sobbing to the core of her; wept for Gary who seemed to show her at one remove all the hurt and neglect of both their childhoods, an everlasting pain which howled inside each of them, just as Rocket, outside, was howling her grief to the moon.

For a while she kept expecting to hear footsteps outside – the police coming to ask questions. But no one came. She settled Carl to sleep like a baby, which comforted her as much as him. He twitched and sobbed and she patted and talked gently to him, kneeling on the floor beside him as he curled on one of the little benches. The dog jumped up and managed to squeeze into the V of his bent knees.

As quietly as she could, Evie got up stiffly and put a little more coal into the stove to keep them warm into the night. She had still not even taken her coat off. She pulled her feet up, hugging her knees into her chest, and sat in the dim light of the lamp, trying to comfort her own raw feelings. Sleep would not come yet – not for a long time.

Now the first rush of shock and grief over Gary had passed, she felt wrung out and exhausted. She found sober thoughts arriving, found herself talking to him in her mind. *We were the same, you and me – sad little things, weren't we, as kids? Back in Ladywood? They'd call us 'underprivileged' now, wouldn't they – those of us without much.* She smiled for a second, thinking what Gary would say to this. *Underprivileged? Yeah, we were underprivileged all right. Yes, we were,* she agreed. *But it wasn't fancy houses and clothes we did without, was it? No one round our end had much. But we never had...* Her tears rose again at this thought. *We never had moms to love us, that was what.* At least, she thought, Gary's mom was dead. Dead and remembered with love and longing.

Her most bitter thought came then. Mine was alive and she couldn't even manage to love me.

Thoughts began to pound at her, the full force of what had happened reaching her. Gary's dead. Actually dead. Never coming back.

And worst of all, aren't I dead to my own children? I could be dead – I tried to walk under that car.

Dead. Gone forever. Forever.

She played the scene outside the school over in her mind again. Tracy and Andrew coming out, holding hands like lost waifs; Tracy glancing at a stranger who happened to be positioned by the school gates. Tracy who hadn't seen her mother in months, hadn't heard from her, had no idea where she was. Tracy who was a little girl, looking after her little brother like a little mom.

The pain and shame that filled her almost overwhelmed her. She had taken their not seeing her as a judgement, as if they didn't care, didn't want her. Taut with pain, she pressed her fists against the side of her head.

503

They were just little children, blown about by the force of all the adults round them. Adults who made their decisions for them. And the one adult they needed most...

I could be dead, she kept thinking. Like Gary. Dead. Not here anymore. But I'm not. I'm *here*.

I'm here. She relaxed her hands and sat up straight, gulping in deep breaths. She had a life. She had a chance. And whatever it took, however much pain and difficulty it might cause her, she was going to go back to her children and fight for them. She was going to grab hold of that life and live it.

Sixty

'Come on, Carl, wake up.'

He was like a giant baby, curled up on the narrow bench. Evie already had her few things bundled together. She was jittery with urgent energy. Every fibre of her wanted to get away from here now, to do the thing she knew she had to do.

The dog had been quiet in the night, but woke her before it was light, whimpering to be let out. She had got up and relit the stove.

'Carl.' She prodded him awake, holding out a mug of tea.

Carl opened his eyes and sat up. He looked around him, even more like a child, and started crying again, with great shuddering sobs.

'Oh Carly.' She sat down beside him, stroking

his wide back, her own tears welling. He was so big, so unprotected. 'Look.' She reached out and turned his head to face her. 'You can't just stay here on your own, bab. And I've got to go and... Well, never mind. You need to go and find your brothers – get them to help you. You know where Paul lives, don't you? And Ron?'

Carl rattled off an address in Quinton.

'That's Paul's house, is it?' She repeated it. 'And d'you know what bus to get?'

Carl recited bus numbers.

'All right. Well, you go and find Paul and tell him what's happened, Carl, all right?' They were family. They would have to sort things out. 'It's Saturday today so he shouldn't be at work. And you'll have to take her with you.' She eyed the dog who lay at their feet.

He nodded, quietening, as if glad to have an action to hold on to. 'Rocket,' he said fondly. 'You're coming with me, girl.'

The dog got up and pushed her muzzle into his outstretched hand. Thank God he's got her, Evie thought.

She fried them up some bacon and sliced hunks of bread, trying to slow herself for his sake. There was no point in her setting off too early anyhow, even if she was burning to be gone. She felt as if she had snapped, abruptly, into a different state where she could see everything in a new way, was acutely aware of being alive. She was suddenly full of energy. All she wanted now was to change, to make up for everything and begin again.

When it was time to go, they locked up the cabin. It was raining steadily, the drops stippling the surface of the cut. Carl stood on the path with Rocket at his side, his big parka on. Evie jumped down to join him.

'Go and find Paul then, all right?' she said, looking up at him, rain falling on her face.

'I will,' Carl said earnestly. 'I'll go now.'

He went to set off there and then.

'Hey, hang on, what about saying goodbye!' Evie pulled him back by the arm and wrapped him in a hug, his wet parka against her cheek. 'I'll see yer, kid. I will. Just got a few things I've got to do, all right?'

'All right,' Carl said.

She watched as he walked away through the thin curtain of rain, a lumbering bear with the dog beside him, at the edge of the dark thread of water, until he reached a curve in the path and she could not see him anymore.

She barely gave a thought to how wet she was getting, walking the towpath, waiting first for one bus into town, then another out. With no hood, no hat or umbrella, her hair was soon soaked. She rubbed the tickling drops of water from her face, felt it trickle down her neck. The cotton anorak was not much help and she sat in the steamy buses, legs encased in her wet trousers.

But none of this mattered. Nothing mattered now except for one thing.

When she reached the place, it was grander than she had imagined – one of a number of very sizeable, ornate houses along the street. Although Melly had told her that the family had come into money, she had still not been quite prepared for the size of it. The front garden was obviously lovingly tended. The windows looked huge to her, clean panes of glass, giving back the grey folds of sky.

Evie did not allow herself to be nervous. She went to the front door and, in the absence of a knocker, pulled on a metal handle beside the door. A mellow clanging noise came from within.

Would she be there now? Would she?

A moment later she heard noises and what sounded like the cry of a baby. Footsteps approached the door. The person behind it had to tug hard to open it.

'Oh! Er... Hello?'

The woman was holding a child of about nine months old on her hip. It looked like a little boy, with a cap of fair hair. The woman was slender, with thick, iron-grey hair caught up into a soft bun and liquid brown eyes. It was a beautiful face – one of a woman who had been lovely at every age. Evie knew well who she was.

''Scuse me ... Mrs Morrison?'

'Ye-es...' She seemed caught between caution and kindness. Evie heard other voices in the background somewhere. 'Sorry, love, I don't know you, do I? You look terribly wet.'

'I'm...' A lump rose in her throat and she swallowed it down, impatient that her emotions should not get in the way. 'I'm Evie, Evie Sutton, and ... well, Melly told me she lived here. I was looking to speak to her.'

Dolly Morrison's mouth actually dropped open. 'Evie?' she breathed. 'Little Evie! Well I never. Yes – I can see you now, bab, now you've told me. Course, she said she'd seen you...' She took a moment to collect her thoughts. 'Look at me! What's my trouble, leaving you out there in the wet? Come in, darlin'. Melly's not here at the moment – she had an early shift today. She works at the hospital, see. Well, of course, you know that.' She stepped back to let Evie in, closed the door, then led her to the back of the house.

'Come and have a cuppa tea – you looked half starved. Mo, look who's come to see us!'

Warmed by the way Dolly made it sound like a pleasurable social visit, Evie took in the enormous, homely kitchen with a big table at the heart of it, on which was a flowery cloth scattered with plates and mugs, marg on a plate, a pot of jam, a big brown teapot and a lot of crumbs. At one end of the table sat Mo Morrison, a burly figure with short, grizzled hair, in shirtsleeves, his thick forearms furred with grey hairs. Evie remembered him vividly, fondly, as one of the adults she had known in the yard in Aston, where her family had lived before they flitted off to Ladywood to dodge the rent. With Mo were two young lads with blond hair, aged about seven and nine, tucking into wedges of bread. They stared curiously at her. They were very like the blond boys – little blond buggers, Melly had said – who had careered round the yard in Aston.

'These are some of my grandchildren,' Dolly said, waving her hand vaguely over the three boys. 'Now, Mo, d'you know who this is then?'

Mo Morrison tore himself away from the paper he was reading and his fleshy face turned to Evie. He had pale eyes in a still boyish face. Evie felt such a mess, her clothes all clinging and damp. She was sure she must smell bad. But she felt both amused and foolish at Mo's obvious bewilderment.

'No.' He looked back and forth between Evie and his wife, awaiting enlightenment.

'It's young Evie. You know, the Suttons – Irene and Ray.' Dolly filled the kettle and set it on the big cooker, doing everything left-handed, the baby still stuck to her hip.

The light dawned. 'Irene and Ray... Oh my giddy uncle,' Mo said unguardedly, before realizing he was talking to the daughter of this much disliked couple. 'Evie – you was the little'un, right? Little blonde thing?'

Evie nodded, blushing, aware that her hair hung in rat's tails, stuck to her head, and worried that she was leaving a trail of wet across the floor. Mo peered at her. 'For heaven's sake, Dolly, the wench is soaked to the skin. You can't sit about like that, girl – you'll catch yer death! Get the wench a cuppa tea, Doll!'

'I *am*, Mo,' Dolly said. 'I'm making tea. What d'you think I'm doing?'

'What about a nice hot bath? D'you want a bath?' Mo asked, to Evie's astonishment. 'A bowl of soup? We got soup, Dolly?'

'Course you can have a bath,' Dolly said. 'Mo, go and run the girl a bath. You can have a cup of tea – I'll find you summat to put on while we dry out your things. Go on, you can take a cuppa with you. Soup later.'

'But...' Evie said, deeply touched and amused by this kindly fussing. They had not even asked her why she was here. Mo was already on his way out of the room.

'Not in a rush, are you, bab?' Dolly asked.

'No...'

'Well, Melly won't be back for a good while – her shift finishes at four – so you might as well make yourself comfortable. I'll do you some toast, shall I?'

Some minutes later, she found herself sitting in a huge, claw-footed bath full of warm water and pine-smelling bubble bath, with a cup of tea and a plate of toast, hardly able to believe that this was happening.

Dolly had even left her a hairdryer and laid out some pyjamas and a dressing down and slippers for her to put on. The dressing gown and the slippers were both pink and fluffy. Evie felt as if she was living in a luxury hotel all of a sudden.

'Oh yes, I can see you now!' Dolly said when she went back downstairs. 'You haven't changed all that much really. Still the same baby face! Want another cuppa? Mo's taken the lads down to the park – there's a little place with a lake down behind here. You have to get lads out, whatever the weather, or they drive you barmy.'

Evie thought of Andrew and nearly said she knew this. But she kept quiet, and anyway, Dolly was in full flow.

'My lad Reggie – he's Melly's husband; they live here, see, up at the top – he's taken their two out, to the Science Museum or some such. It's quite peaceful for once!' She swirled the teapot round, eyeing Evie. 'Those things belong to our Donna. Look, this is her. She's on the London stage, you know.' Evie heard the glow of pride in Dolly's voice as she reached for a picture on the sideboard. Evie saw a chorus line of girls dancing, the dark-eyed one Dolly pointed to glowing with pleasure and prettiness.

'She looks just like you used to, Mrs Morrison,' Evie said. It was true – how she remembered her. But she could also recall Donna as a tiny, black-haired tot already gorgeous to look at.

Dolly laughed. 'It'd be nice to think, but our Donna's a lot better-looking than I ever was. She comes home whenever she can, see her old mom and dad, though.' She sounded happy, surrounded by her family. 'Come on, sit down,' she added as Evie hovered by the table. 'And tell me how you've been.'

Evie had never imagined talking to Dolly. Since that day in the hospital it was Melly she had clung to the idea of. Melly, a person who seemed to live on the bright side of the world, not the dark side of the damned where she had been and felt she belonged. And it had taken until now to find the courage to come and ask.

But now she was sitting in this warm kitchen with all Dolly's pots and pans hanging from hooks near the range, the big table, the warm eyes of this woman opposite her, who she felt knew her, knew where she had come from, it all came tumbling out: everything, even Julie, because she knew Mrs Morrison would understand, and Jack and her children, the hospital, her own failure to care for them, Gary and Carl – everything. It was like emptying herself. Dolly's face ran with tears as she spoke. She went on for a long time, but Dolly

511

didn't interrupt.

When Evie finally ran out of words, she sat back, wiping the tears from her own cheeks.

'So I came to ask Melly for help. I know she tried to come and see me ... in there. I just couldn't... Not then. I can't go back there on my own. Dr Rose said I shouldn't tangle with Mom. But she's got my kids... I don't know what to do, Mrs Morrison.'

Dolly sat forward, clearly very affected by what she had heard. She reached for Evie's hand. She paused for a moment. At last, she said, 'You know, Evie, your mother was not like any other mother I've ever met, I have to be honest with you. There were plenty who were rough and ready, or hardly holding their heads above water – but not like her, the way she was over you. We all tried to look out for you, when you were small. I know Rachel – Melly's mom, d'you remember her?' She saw Evie nod. Tracy Rachel. She must tell them about her daughter's name. 'She found you locked out in the cold one night.'

'It wasn't the only time she did that,' Evie said.

'I've never known a mother turn on a small child the way she did you. She wasn't all that nice to your sisters, but even then I could see her turning them against you as well. And you...' She shook her head. 'She's the one not right in the head, Evie. She never was. Your mother seemed to have no fellow feeling for anyone. Not that your father helped the situation.'

She didn't go on, but they both knew what she meant. 'Your children need you, Evie.'

'I know.' She looked down into the pink softness of her lap, her tears coming again.

'Don't think they don't. Don't ever tell yourself that. They want you more than anything, I'm sure. And they don't need to be with *her*, however much she's making up to them. She always wanted the whole world to dance around her. Evie...'

Evie looked up at her and Dolly tightened her hold on Evie's hand for a moment, looking very seriously at her.

'Melly told me she'd seen you, darlin' ... when you were first in hospital. She's been fretting about you. When she gets home I know she'll feel the same as me.' Fiercely, she added, 'What you need is someone on your side. We'll help you. We *will*.'

Sixty-One

The afternoon was darkening by the time Melly came back. Her husband, Reggie, a tall, gentle-faced man, had arrived earlier, and with him a boy and a girl, introduced as Tina and Chris. Evie remembered Reggie when she saw him. He nodded and said hello and the children were sweet, friendly kids, though shy. Evie looked at them – they were a little older than her two. For a moment she longed to fling her arms round them and pull them close and a terrible pang went through her as Reggie took them off upstairs to watch TV. When would she be able to hold her own children? Would they ever be able to forgive her?

Mo had driven the other grandchildren back to

their respective families after their time in the fresh air. He returned claiming he was 'wrecked' and went off for a snooze, leaving the women to it.

Evie felt apprehensive when she heard Melly come into the house while she and Dolly were still in the kitchen. She had refused to see Melly when she was in the hospital and wondered if she would hold it against her. Even though Melly was only a couple of years older, Evie still thought of her as a 'big girl' – older and more knowing.

'Hello!' Melly called from the hall, evidently taking her coat off. 'Is Reg back with the kids? Oh, I could murder a cup of tea, I can tell you.' She stopped at the door and took in the sight of the two of them at the table.

'Evie!' Her hands went to her face and her manner changed from weariness to glad astonishment. 'Oh my God, am I pleased to see you!' She hurried over and wrapped her arms round Evie's shoulders.

Evie, fragile as she was, felt the tears rise in her again at this welcome.

Melly looked down at her, a hand still on her back. 'Oh Evie, you look better. I'm so glad. I went over to Rubery to see you – I don't know if they told you. A couple of times. There was ever such a nice man there the second time, said he'd come to visit you.'

Evie blushed, looking down. Alan Dickson.

'Alan he said his name was. Anyway, I meant to come again, when you were up to it, but... And then when I asked later they said they'd discharged you and I felt so bad because I don't know where you live or anything.'

'Here, love.' Dolly brought over a cup of tea, stirring sugar in, and handed it to her. Melly sank down at the table.

'Ta.' She took an ecstatic mouthful of tea. 'Ah, that's better!' She still had her uniform on and looked very trim and workmanlike, Evie thought, her hair smoothed back and fastened up. 'Aah, that's better. So, Evie, *tell me*. Everything! How are you? And where're your kids?'

'Tell her, Evie,' Dolly urged her, putting a cup of tea down in front of her as well and sitting at the table with them.

As soon as Melly mentioned the children, it all came out in a blurt. 'I don't even know if they'll want to be with me now,' she wept. 'I've been away such a long time – maybe they don't even remember who I am.'

Melly stared at her. 'You mean, the two of them are with your mom and dad?'

Evie nodded. 'And Rita. She's got five lads – she's round there half the time. And Shirl lives there – she's got a daughter, Tracy's age nearly. All one big happy family,' she finished bitterly.

'Evie.' She felt Melly's warm hand press down on hers and she spoke with great force. 'I'm sorry to say this but from what I remember about your mom, I wouldn't trust her with a pet rat, never mind my own kids. Would you, Dolly?'

'Well...' Dolly looked pained. 'Sorry, Evie, it's a harsh thing to say about your mother in front of you. But Melly's right. Course your little ones will want you. The sooner you get them away from there the better, I'd say. We need to go with her, Melly – go and get them.'

'But I've got nowhere to go,' Evie said. 'No job and, and...' She broke down. 'I'm such a mess! I don't even know if I trust myself...'

'Oh Evie.' Melly put an arm round her shoulders. 'Look, you're strong as anything – you always were. I remember Mom saying that. You've been through the mill, love. Stronger people would have broken down a lot sooner than you. But all I can say is, if my kids were with that vile cow...' Her expression was grim.

'Melly!' Dolly protested.

'No.' Evie felt a grin creeping through her tears. 'Thanks, Melly. She is. She really is. The doctor in the hospital said he thought I shouldn't have anything to do with her. But there's the kids... And I just don't know if I can face it – face them – not on my own.'

'There's no need to be on your own,' Dolly said. 'Look, Evie, why don't we go over tomorrow? We'll get all ready, and I'll do your hair...'

'My hair?' Evie said, bewildered.

'Her hair looks fine as it is,' Melly said impatiently. She stood up. 'No. Why not now? We have to get those kids away from that place now. Come on. I'll come with you.' As Dolly made noises of protest, Melly clamped her hands to her hips and went on heatedly, 'I'm not scared of Irene Sutton, Dolly. Or those sisters of yours, Evie. My God, some of the things I saw when they were living next to us... Come on, Evie.'

'But...' Dolly tried to interrupt. 'Reggie...'

'Reggie'll survive. He knows how to lift a kettle. I'll run up and tell him what we're doing.'

Melly was already on her way to the stairs.

'But...' Evie said. 'Melly, I've only got pyjamas on!'

This paused Melly's crusading fervour for a moment. 'Oh ... well, look ... you can borrow something of mine. Let's go up and find something. Come on.'

'Your hair looks quite nice anyway,' Dolly said, slightly doubtfully. 'Well.' She got up. 'I'd better rouse Mo to drive you over. Tell you what' – she took off her apron with decisive energy – 'I'll come, an' all.'

Before she even had time to think, Evie had dressed in a stretchy blue crimplene skirt, a blouse and a black polo neck. She was plumper than Melly so there was not a lot of choice, but by luck they had the same size feet, so she'd been able to borrow some high-wedged sandals with rope-covered heels.

'Make sure you look after those,' Melly teased as she quickly changed out of her uniform into slacks and a thick red jumper. 'They're my favourites. I know it's cold, but they look all right with tights – and you want to look your best, don't you?'

Soon the four of them were in the family's big comfortable Rover, driven by Mo, who, having been woken up, was bewildered at first, until the women explained emphatically why he needed to get himself together and get the car going.

'Irene Sutton?' he murmured as he looked for his keys. 'Dear oh dear oh dear. Oh yes, you want to get them away from her. Oh yes.'

Evie loved him for it. It felt astonishing to know how much these people were all on her side, to remember that, long ago now, they had been on her side then as well.

The car smoothed its way through the darkness.

'So ... which road?' Mo said as they crossed the south side of town.

'Alwold,' Evie said. 'The easiest way's down past the cemetery.' She was so tense that it was good to have the directions to think about so that she was not overcome by terror. She felt a deep pang of shame as the car passed the Grants' house.

As they turned into Alwold Road, the blood began to surge so fast round her body that her breathing struggled to keep up. Her children were just along this road... She wanted to cry out, *Stop! Not now – I'm not ready!* But after these astonishing, kind people had brought her this far, she knew she could not back out.

Mo pulled up just along from the house, the engine still running. Evie drank in the sight of it. There were lights on inside. Out at the front, there were lads moving back and forth playing something. She strained her eyes to see if one of them was Andrew, but it seemed to be Rita's older lads.

'What're we gunna do then?' Mo said, sounding apprehensive now.

'I'll go with her,' Melly said. Evie was impressed by how fearless she seemed. Evie found her own mother terrifying. But Melly must be used to dealing with all sorts by now. 'You two stay here – if we need you we'll let you know. Just move a little bit closer, eh, Mo?'

He slid several yards along the street, braked and cut off the engine. The boys gave a curious glance for a second, then turned away and moved further down the street into the gloom as if they were up to something that they did not want anyone to see.

'Right, Evie,' Melly said. 'Come on.'

Once they had climbed out, Evie felt Melly take her arm and tuck it firmly into her own.

'Don't want you falling off those shoes, do we?' She smiled. If she was nervous, it didn't show and Evie was full of admiration for her.

'Oh God,' she said.

'Evie.' Melly paused and spoke firmly to her. 'They're your kids. Not hers, or Rita's, even if they do want to take over everything. They're yours – and they need you. All right?'

Evie nodded, her whole body seeming weak and boneless.

There was no bell or knocker, so Melly banged her hand on the chipped front door. They could hear the sound of the telly, an endless chatter inside. Evie wondered if they were all there. Saturday night – booze night. Dad might be in the pub – they both might. She prayed for her mother and father not to be there.

At the second attempt, the door flung open, letting out the sound of the telly and the smells of fags and, Evie realized, fish and chips. A tall, skinny figure stood there with a baby on her hip and a cigarette in the other hand, rocking from one foot to the other to placate the child. Her mousey hair lay in feathery layers round her gaunt face. It looked freshly done. She wore trousers and a smock top in hectic black and white patterns.

'Yeah?' she said unenthusiastically.

'Rita?' Melly said, before Rita had clocked Evie

behind her. 'Long time no see.' She spoke with chilly but firm politeness. 'Evie's come to fetch her children.'

Rita pushed most of her weight onto one leg so that her hip jutted out and took a long drag, giving herself time to take in this information.

On a billowing mouthful of smoke, she said, 'Who the f*** are you?'

'Melly, Rita. Remember me? The good old days down the old end in Aston when we were kids together?'

Evie wasn't sure whether the sarcasm would be lost on Rita. Most likely. She was distracted in this thought by a movement behind her sister. A skinny figure with honey-brown hair hanging over her shoulder leaned out of the front room. Tracy was peering out, curious to know what was going on.

Evie's heart was ready to explode. If she could only get to her, get Andrew, and just run for it! She moved her hand to attract Tracy's attention and saw her notice. Tracy froze, as if she couldn't believe her eyes.

'Reet, shut the cowing door, will yer!' the voice boomed out. Her mother's unmistakeable tones. Oh no, oh no... 'We'm freezing our arses off in 'ere!'

But in that second, as Rita turned to give her away, to shout that she was here, she saw Tracy recognize her properly. She could see it in the child's eyes, the dawning, the straightening up of her body, her moving closer, in her little pink corduroy trousers, short on her now, her pink jumper, clothes that she, Evie, had bought for her. She came ducking round Rita.

'Mom?' Her voice was faint, her eyes stricken and hungry and still not quite believing. 'Is that—'

'Tracy!' Evie burst towards her. 'Oh Trace! Come here.' She knelt down on the step, holding out her arms as Tracy stumbled to her, like someone falling into an oasis, and clung to her. Evie's tears wet her daughter's hair as she sobbed, her eyes closed, not caring what else was happening, only about this moment, this little beloved body in her arms.

'Mom...' she heard Tracy saying, over and over. 'Mom... Mom... You're here...' And her body quivered with sobs as if they had been waiting there all this time.

There was a moment when everyone was stunned, before Rita shouted over her shoulder, 'Well, guess who's come swanning back after all this time!'

'What yow on about?' Evie heard her mother bawl from the living room. True to form she could not be bothered to get up. She wondered if her father was in the house: Saturday night. Ten to one he was down the pub.

Evie opened her eyes. She drew back from Tracy a little. The girl's wet face looked hurt and heartbroken and still only half believing. She raised her hand and touched Evie's face.

'I knew you'd come back one day,' she said. 'But where've you *been*, Mom?' And she was crying again.

'Trace, where's Andrew?' Evie stood up.

'Upstairs, I think.' She shrugged, hauling her sleeves across her eyes.

Rita had moved to the door of the living room. 'Madam's just turned up after all this time,' she informed her mother. 'You've got a cowing cheek, you have.' She spoke to Evie with a new, nagging pecking motion with her head, like a self-righteous hen. 'Coming back here after dumping your kids on us all this time? Who d'yer think's been paying for their keep, eh? And I s'pose you think you can just–'

'That's enough,' Melly said, stepping into the house.

'Who the...' Evie could hear her mother making moves at last. She appeared round the door, in the baggy red dress, shoes wide as barges, her hair hanging down. She was pink in the face and obviously well into the evening's drinking. She screwed up her eyes to peer at Melly. 'Who's this?'

'I'm Melanie. Rachel Booker's daughter – remember? The one who used to take Evie in when you left her out on the step at night. Evie's been ill, which is why she hasn't been around. Now she wants to see her children and take them home. So if you wouldn't mind telling us where her little boy is, we can be on our way and they won't have to be your responsibility anymore.'

Evie saw her mother gape in astonishment at Melly. She took the chance to bend down and whisper to Tracy, 'Go up and get him, will you, love?'

Tracy slipped past and was about to go upstairs.

'Where you going?' Rita grabbed Tracy by the arm.

'To get Andrew,' she said. Evie's heart contorted at the sight of her daughter's anxious face.

'Oh no you don't,' Rita said.

'Rita,' a voice said from the door. 'Let her get her brother. Let go of her.'

Evie turned to see Dolly and Mo in the doorway. Dolly came inside and stood in front of Irene. They looked so fine, the Morrisons, Evie thought, almost with awe. So kind and solid, distinguished almost. So not like her mother.

'Let her take her children and go, Irene,' Dolly said.

Evie saw her mother take one look at Dolly and Mo. There was instant recognition and Irene knew she was defeated.

'Oh, look who's 'ere, eh – Dolly Morrison. You always was a bossy cow,' Irene said, petulant as a child who has been found out.

'And I could say what you were,' Dolly retorted.

'She abandoned those kids. If it weren't for us, they'd be in a home by now.'

'I'm sure Evie will repay you anything you're owed when she's back on her feet,' Dolly said. 'But by God, Irene, there's not a farthing that kid will ever owe you. Not even mothering. You never did a thing for her if you could help it. All you did was make her life a misery. You were cruel and unnatural then and you're cruel now, heaven help you.' She looked Rita up and down sternly. 'Let go of her,' she ordered. She smiled encouragingly at Tracy. 'You go and get your brother, will you, bab?'

'Where's Ray then?' Dolly said, as Tracy ran upstairs. 'The usual place?'

'Oh, shut yer cake'ole,' Irene said, slouching back against the door frame and folding her arms. Once more she reminded Evie of a big, unformed child. 'Take the bloody kids then, I don't care. Got enough brats round 'ere as it is.'

Tracy appeared at the top of the stairs holding the hand of the long, thin boy Evie had seen her with at the school. How her little boy had grown! He had obviously had a haircut again recently – he had a very short back and sides. The almost military haircut made his cheekbones stand out even more. He was only five, but he looked like a hard little man. A moment later, Wayne appeared behind him.

'Andrew,' Evie breathed. 'Come 'ere, babby.'

'Babby,' Rita muttered scornfully, still jiggling Dean on her hip. 'Who're you babbying? Some mother you are.'

Andrew came down with halting steps. His face did not look glad. His expression was solemn, mutinous.

'S'all right, Andy, you don't have to go with her – you can stay 'ere with yer Auntie Reet if you want.'

He glanced at Rita and came to Evie, looking up at her. There was no smile, no word, nothing. Something about him made her feel afraid.

'Andrew.' She knelt down again in front of him. He wouldn't look at her, and stared past her, at the floor. 'Love?' She stroked his bristly hair, his cheek. She didn't like having to talk to him in front of all of them. 'It's Mom, babby. Are you coming home with me?'

He looked at her then, a hard, detached look and, to her horror, shook his head.

'See!' Rita came to life, triumphant. ''E don't

wanna go with you. He doesn't even know who you are!' She laughed then, blowing smoke into baby Dean's face, and he sneezed. 'That's it, Andy, you stay here with your family!'

Adding to Evie's distress, she saw Melly begin to look uncertain. None of them had expected this reaction. Evie felt desperate, as if it was all spinning away from her. It was such a long time since Andrew had seen his mother. No wonder he had got used to Rita as the person always in his life.

'Rita,' Dolly said, with such gravity and firmness that even Evie's hard-faced sister looked taken aback. 'Stop playing games with this child's feelings, for heaven's sake! You're not his mother – Evie is. Haven't you got enough children of your own? Just stop it, right now. It's wicked.' She turned to Andrew.

'Look, love, I'm a friend of your mother's and she's staying with us tonight. How about you come and see your mom tonight – you and Tracy? Just come and see where she's living. You can spend a bit of time together. We've got a nice garden, and–'

'That's right – bribe 'im!' Irene put in.

'No!' Andrew broke into screams. 'Don't want to! I don't want to come with you!' He began to throw himself about, distraught, lashing out at Evie. He landed a punch in her stomach and she doubled over, hurt, but much more by the force of the rejection than the blow itself. 'No!' he kept yelling. 'No! No! No!'

Evie straightened up, desperate. She seized hold of him, taking him tightly in her arms.

'Andrew. *Andrew!*' She found herself shouting

as he flailed and wriggled against her. 'Listen. Just *listen* to me, son. I've done you wrong, I know.' She was having to shout but she didn't care now who heard. 'I left you and I shouldn't have done. It's my fault – your mom's been poorly, see? I've been in the hospital. But I'm back now – and I want you. I want you more than anything in the world, and I'll never go away again. I won't. I promise.' He went limp at last. Not giving in fully, but still at least.

Carefully, Evie went on, close to his ear: 'Andrew. I know I've been away a long time. And it's all wrong. But let's try and start from now, my love. Just come and see – for the night, eh?'

'We ought to call the social, Mom,' Rita said officiously. 'Evie's a mental case. She ain't no good as a mother. They ought to know.'

'What a good idea,' Dolly said, staring at Irene. 'Shall we get a social worker to come in and talk about the whole situation – the background to it all? What a marvellous mother you've been, the way you treated your child? They take a proper case history, you know.'

Evie saw her mother's face crease into a snarl. If there was one thing on earth Irene loathed, it was any thought of interference by 'them' – the social, the bossy do-gooders.

'Just take the little bleeders,' she said, flouncing away into the front room. 'I never wanted yow 'ere! Who said yow could just come and dump yower brats on me anyhow? Yow can go and get out of my sight – the whole lot of yow – and don't cowing well come back!'

VII

Sixty-Two

April 1973

The train rushed across the countryside, weak sunshine brightening and fading as the wind hurried a procession of clouds across the sun.

Evie sat beside Andrew, whose nose was pressed to the window. It had been a long time since she had seen him so excited at the idea of a day out, of going on a train. Tracy, opposite them, also by the window, gazed out dreamily. Evie looked at her with bottomless fondness and gratitude. She didn't know what she had done to deserve a daughter like Tracy, but whatever it was, she was thankful to her very bones.

Opposite her sat Carl, hunched up in his parka, who smiled when Andrew kept turning and exclaiming loudly, 'Look, a bridge!' 'Look, a tractor!' Carl was nearly as excited as he was.

Even if the reason they had come today was such a poignant one, Evie still felt bubbles of excitement and happiness inside. On the luggage rack sat their sad little burden in a box. They would do what they had to do. But she wasn't going to lay this heavily on her children. They had had quite enough. This was a day out – they were going to the seaside. She longed to see colour in her children's cheeks.

'Want a butty?' Carl asked, delving in his bag

and looking round at them.

'No ta, Carl,' Evie said, laughing. 'It's not even elevenses time yet.'

Carl looked surprised. 'I'm starving, I am.'

'You're always eating,' Andrew said, glancing round. 'You're a great big piggy-wig.'

Carl grinned, chomping into a ham sandwich. 'Piggy-wig,' he echoed, seeming pleased by this title. 'Want one, Trace?'

Tracy turned and smiled dreamily at him. 'No thanks.'

Carl beamed back at them both. He adored Tracy and Andrew and the feeling was entirely mutual.

'We're gunna 'ave a nice time!' he announced, indistinctly. 'By the sea!'

The elderly couple in the seats close to them glanced at him and smiled.

Evie looked out at the hurrying green of the spring countryside with a sense of amazement. Six months ago... Just six months ago she was still in the hospital, still crawling along in the very dregs of her life...

The night they brought Tracy and Andrew back to Moseley in Mo's car, Andrew sat stiffly beside her, still an angry, tough, lost little man. He looked out into the darkness without a word. In the flash of light from other cars, Evie could see his clenched jaw. The sight of him filled her with grief and remorse.

Tracy, the other side of her, beside Melly, was quiet, strained looking. She had given a wan smile when Melly said a proper hello to her and told her that she had known Tracy's mom since they were young. It was all too much to take in. Then she sat back quietly, gripping Evie's hand throughout the journey.

It felt very late, as if they had been out for hours and hours. Evie was amazed to find that it was only eight o'clock when they got back to Moseley. Evie was completely in Dolly and Mo's hands. And what kind hands they were. She had nowhere to go, but they had already made it clear that she would be staying with them that night.

'Course you can stay,' Dolly said. 'Melly and Reggie live on the top floor, but this house still has more rooms than we need.'

The evening was a blur in her memory. Dolly made them all cocoa. Evie and the children were silent, overwhelmed by the strangeness of it all. But Dolly's kindness radiated over them as ever. She took Evie aside.

'Look, bab, Melly'll help you make up the bed upstairs. I'd say what you need is to sleep with them – keep 'em close. They're like little babbies after all that's happened – losing you and everything. And they need holding, like babbies. Least,' she finished, 'if they were mine, that's what I'd do. They need to know you're solid for 'em.'

Evie looked gratefully at her. She knew Dolly, who looked after everyone, was now setting out to mother her and if there was one thing she needed, it was a decent mother. And she sensed that Dolly was right. Whether she felt solid at all was another matter. She had to be – *had* to. From now on, whatever happened, she had to be the most solid mother there ever was. It was a daunting thought.

Andrew was still silent and mutinous as she put him to bed. They had brought nothing with them, but Melly found the two of them some clothes they could wear in bed, and Evie as well.

'You're so kind,' Evie said to her tearfully, as all this was done for them.

'Oh, it's all right,' Melly said cheerfully. 'We're glad to help. Mom'll be ever so pleased to hear you're here, you know. We used to wonder sometimes where you were and how you were getting on.' She squeezed Evie's arm, looking into her eyes, and Evie could see a hint of her mother, Rachel, in her face. 'That doctor's right, you know. Your mother's no good for you. I know it sounds hard, but she never was, was she?' Her face was full of sympathy. 'Your poor kids.' Evie was warmed by what a nice person she was. 'Anyway ... look, you get into bed with them. We can talk more tomorrow.'

She slipped into the double bed with its lovely fresh sheets and thick blankets. The room smelled slightly of polish and lavender. Tracy and Andrew were both already in bed, and she felt nervous as they watched her silently.

'Shall I get in between you both?' she asked, afraid of them rejecting her.

Tracy sat up and moved her legs to let her mother move into the middle. After a minute, all lying down, Tracy said, 'Oh Mom!' and flung herself towards her, wrapping her arms round her, and burst into tears. Evie stroked her skinny back which was heaving with sobs. With her other hand she reached for her little boy.

'Andrew?' she said softly.

Silently he turned to her and with a force that came close to snapping her heart in two, grasped hold of her round the waist with desperate strength, clinging on. She cuddled him to her.

'I'm sorry,' she wept with them both. 'I'm so, so sorry kids. I was poorly and they had to take me to the hospital to make me better. I couldn't help it – I never meant to just leave you. I just wasn't up to doing anything. But I'm here now...'

'Are you better?' Tracy asked. Evie could hear all the tension of uncertainty in her voice.

'Yes. Yes, babby,' she said, hoping to goodness. 'I'm here and I'm going to be here always. I promise.'

When she woke the next morning, Andrew was still clinging to her arm, his head pressed against her ribs.

For the rest of her life, Evie would feel grateful to the Morrison family for all they did for her during those weeks. They all talked and talked things over with her. For the first time ever in her life, Evie felt she had people round her who cared about her, who could help her think things through.

With their help, she started to make some firm decisions. Andrew kept going on about Wayne to begin with, and it seemed to Evie so hard – wrong – to deny him his cousins, especially as she felt all this was her fault.

'Evie,' Melly said to her several times. 'I know it's tough, but what'll happen if you go back there? Andrew's too young to go by himself and you've got to keep away from her for your own sake.'

Above all, Evie was grateful that the Morrisons knew her mother of old. She recognized, really, that they were right.

'It seems unnatural,' she said to Dolly once when they were discussing it.

'It may do,' Dolly retorted, 'but she's not natural herself, that one. I'm sorry to say it, Evie, but regardless of what made her the way she is, she's no good for you. Sometimes to make a tree grow you have to cut off some of the branches.'

Evie stared at her. 'I've never thought about it like that before.'

By Christmas, also with their help, she had found a new job in the offices of a brass foundry in Balsall Heath. She found a little terrace to rent in Kings Heath and a lodger to share it with. Melly insisted on being with her when a couple of prospective lodgers came to see her.

'Don't you trust me?' she asked Melly, gratefully.

'Let's just say another set of ears and eyes is always a good thing,' Melly said.

Of the two women who came, one was very young, evasive in her answers and, they had the impression, in some sort of trouble. The other, June, was a plump, reassuring person in her late thirties who worked at WHSmith in Kings Heath. She was single and the couple she had been renting from before had just had a baby and wanted the room.

'What d'you think?' Evie said, truly wondering whether she could put any faith in her feeling that June seemed a very nice, trustworthy woman. Was she capable of judging anything? she wondered.

'Perfect,' Melly said. 'She's very nice.'

This was the reassurance she needed. June even offered to drop Tracy and Andrew off at school on her walk to work. One blessing seemed to fall after another. She didn't like the fact that they had to walk back on their own each afternoon – latchkey kids, she thought. But it was only round the corner and Tracy assured her that they had been doing it for months already as Shirley had given up collecting them.

'She's quite a girl you've got there,' Melly said. 'So strong. It must be because she has a strong mother.' This brought Evie to tears. She felt anything but strong, but it was wonderful that Melly thought this of her.

'You need to make your own life,' Melly said, when they moved in. She gave Evie a hug. 'But we're always here, you know that, don't you?'

'I do,' Evie said. She was starting to believe it too, day by day. Believe that things could settle.

She found time eventually to go back and apologize to Mr and Mrs Grant, who, once hearing what had happened, were forgiving and asked after the children, saying they had missed them all.

'We've got your things. Oh, and there are letters for you, Evie,' Mrs Grant said, handing her a couple of envelopes. From the official look of one, Evie realized this was something to do with her divorce. She felt it as a blow for a second, but the feeling passed. She and Jack had to cut each other off – it was the only way. She thanked the Grants and promised to bring the children over to see them – while steering well away from

Alwold Road.

If her own survival lay in the loss of her mother and sisters ... well, so be it. She could see that she must cut off some branches to allow herself to grow in freedom, gathering around her the people who cared about her.

While she was packing up to move to Kings Heath, Evie found the bus ticket on which Alan Dickson had written his address and number.

'What's that?' Melly asked, seeing her hesitating over it.

'It's just someone I used to work with – sort of. Gave me his number.'

'Not that man I met when I came to the hospital?' Melly held out her hand and looked at the number. 'He was trying to visit you as well.' Melly sat on the edge of the bed and eyed her. 'He seemed nice,' she said carefully.

'He is ... I think,' Evie said.

Melly smiled. 'Look, you've got enough on your plate...'

'What, without another bloke as well, you mean?' Evie smiled.

'Yes ... well ... I suppose what I mean is...' She stopped and thought for a second, choosing her words. 'You've had a lot to cope with. Maybe you just need to be on your own for a bit. Not just rush from one man to another. But...' Their eyes met. 'He's ever so nice, Evie. He really seemed to care about you.' She passed the ticket back with the number on. 'Just don't throw it away, eh?'

'Oh, I won't be rushing into anything,' Evie said. 'My kids come first. But...' She had a warm feeling suddenly, warm and confident. She remembered

Alan's kindly ways, his eyes smiling down at her. She knew she liked Alan and could trust him. He had already shown her that. And given time, maybe there could be more. 'I could just meet him for a drink – say thank you?'

Melly's lovely face smiled up at her. 'Well, I can't see how that could do any harm, can you?'

The children tore up and down the long sandy beach at Weston, shrieking in the wind. Sunshine came and went and the wind buffeted them all, but it did not actually rain. The tide was coming in and when the sun came out, the waves glittered with light. All of them soon had pink cheeks and were screaming with delight.

Walking from the station, Evie had bought a bucket and plastic spades for Tracy and Andrew and she and Carl watched the other sandcastle diggers along the beach to see how you did it. They started on a huge excavation, drawing a circle and digging out sand all the way round it to make a moat. Carl was as enthusiastic as they were.

Evie watched him with a lump in her throat. Even while trying get her own life in place, she had been worrying about him. She went over to Paul's house. He, skinny like most of the Knights and with tiny children peeping out behind his legs, just said, 'He ain't 'ere no more.'

Evie was horrified. She asked if he had gone to any of his other brothers, some of whom had families, but Paul just shrugged, seeming neither to know or care.

There was only one other place she could look.

One Sunday morning, she and the children went over to Selly Oak.

'We'll have a bit of a walk by the cut, shall we?' she said. She hoped they wouldn't find anything terrible, but she couldn't go in the week and if Carl was back at work he wouldn't have been there anyway.

The boat was in exactly the same place.

'Oh look,' she said as they approached. 'Look at this boat.' Though decrepit, *Pearl* looked beautiful. The mist was taking a long time to clear that morning, the sun trying to burn it off, and the boat's dark shape was shrouded in a golden haze.

As they came up close, she eyed it carefully. Someone was in. Smoke was drifting out of the chimney and she could see that things had been moved since the last time she saw it.

'I wonder who lives here,' she said. 'Shall we see?' She jumped down onto the stern by the tiller and rapped on the cabin door. A moment later, Carl poked his head out.

'Evie!' he beamed. His delight at seeing her and his creased-up, smiling face, reassured the children. Rocket ran out barking in greeting.

'Oh Carly,' she said. 'What're you doing back here all on your own?'

'I'm all right,' he said, nodding vigorously. 'I am.'

'But are you?' she said. 'Are you coping all right?'

'Yeah,' he said. 'Didn't like Paul's. I'm all right. She's my boat – I know what to do.'

He did, she thought now, watching him shovel up the sand and pile it in the middle of the sandcastle. If you showed Carl things he could do, he just kept doing them. He had been looking after Gary even more than she had realized and he knew how to run his life on the boat.

'I like it here,' he'd said that day. 'I'm all right.'

Her kids had loved the boat and loved Carl and Rocket. She had promised to come down when she could and keep an eye on him. To her shame, she realized that whatever had happened to Gary's body, it had happened without any of his family being there. She and Carl had been so bothered by all the talk of police and everything else that had happened that no one had been near to give him a send-off. Carl looked blank when she asked if Gary had had a funeral. Apart from Paul, she had no idea where the others were, or whether Old Man Knight was still alive. Still, she thought, they never cared about him when he was here. There was no use in going looking now.

She found out from the cemetery at Lodge Hill that the council had paid for Gary's funeral and that his ashes were there for a member of the family to collect if anyone was forthcoming.

She and Carl went together. She thought Carl would be upset, but he didn't really seem to make a connection between the brother who had looked out for him and this little urn of his remains. Gently, she explained to him.

'Thing is, Carl, now we can scatter them somewhere. A place Gary would've liked.'

Carl looked blank.

She thought about the cut, down near the boat. Then she remembered Gary's little face that day, that ghostly, skinny little boy who had been her pal, in the gloom of the air-raid shelter.

One day, I'm gunna go and live at the seaside!

She doubted Gary had ever set foot at the seaside, never mind living there. Well, that's where he's going now, she thought.

She had set the bag containing the things they would need down near where they were digging.

'Kids, you carry on for a minute, all right? See how big you can make it. Carl?' She nodded towards the bag. 'We'll be back in a tick and when you've finished your castle we'll go and get some fish and chips, all right?'

Tracy and Andrew were digging frantically. She smiled. They had a fragile peace after everything they had all lived through so far. A peace she hoped would keep on growing and growing, even if it meant losing some of the branches as Dolly said.

She and Carl went to the water's edge, away from the other few people walking their dogs along the sand. In the bag she had the urn and two little bunches of flowers.

'Here, Carl, you do it. He was your brother. He'd've liked it here, wouldn't he? Watch the wind – throw it sideways, like this.'

She showed him. His face very serious, Carl dispatched the grey slew of ash in one sweep of his arm.

'T'ra, Gary,' she whispered. 'Rest in peace, mate.'

She took the bigger of the two bunches of flowers – a mix of yellow and white chrysanths – and scattered them on the waves. The blooms lay in the shallows, washing peacefully back and forth.

'There,' she said.

'There,' Carl said.

'We've done it. D'you want to go and help them dig now, bab?'

Carl hurried along the beach to join the children, seeming glad to be released.

Evie stood by the water's edge with her other bouquet of tight pink rosebuds. With the waves lapping at her feet she allowed the distant ache to rise in her again at the thought of her little girl's face, her curled fists now grown into the hands of a twelve-year-old girl who she would never know. All she could do was pray that those hands, that little body and spirit, were treated with kindness and love.

'Goodbye, Julie. Bless you. Bless your sweet life.' She didn't know what else to say. She wanted the sea to take all her wounds, all her sadness, leaving her unburdened.

The flowers curved in the wind and fell, as Gary's had done, quite close to her, into the froth of waves washing up on the sand. People would wonder what they were doing there, she thought. Never mind. She had done all she could do.

Her heart lifting, she walked back towards the stooped, busy figures on the beach and the new castle growing in the sand.

Acknowledgements

For some information about Canada I am indebted to *Invisible Immigrants* by Marilyn Barber and Murray Watson, as well as to Peter Sherrington.

A number of websites have been useful for all sorts of small details in this story. The Birmingham History Forum is always a fund of information and pictures, as were sites about the Tower Ballroom, Rubery Hill Hospital and www.motherandbabyhomes.com. Also thank you to Debbie Carter for filling me in on various details.

The publishers hope that this book has given you enjoyable reading. Large Print Books are especially designed to be as easy to see and hold as possible. If you wish a complete list of our books please ask at your local library or write directly to:

Magna Large Print Books
Magna House, Long Preston,
Skipton, North Yorkshire.
BD23 4ND

This Large Print Book for the partially sighted, who cannot read normal print, is published under the auspices of

THE ULVERSCROFT FOUNDATION